BONDS

OF

BEAUTY

AND

BLOOD

First Published by M.Everitt 2024

First edition

2024

ISBN Print: 978-1-0670296-0-9

For the Brats

PREFACE

Trigger warnings:

This novel contains scenes depicting or discussing abuse of all kinds, violence, explicit content and BDSM Kinks, including brat play, discipline, and restraint. In the primary relationships, consent is always present.

ONE

Fuck. Millionaire. CEO's.

Not literally.

Well ...

No. Definitely not.

Glaring through the unreasonably tinted window of her boss's hundred-story high-rise office, Sylvie Hart mulled over her decision to take the executive assistant position. Necessity. Vanity. *Poverty.* How she still had a job was beyond her. *Too slow, Hart. Too messy, and too many questions.*

She gnawed on the inside of her cheek, her thumb rhythmically circling her cuticle, searching for a piece of skin to pick.

Elias-fucking-Ambrose.

Brooding, dark-haired god, but still a rich, entitled, asshat. How anyone needed that level of wealth would never make sense to her. Especially when she lived in a rat-infested apartment with a mild case of black mould. If you could even call it mild.

"Hart. What the hell are you doing in here?" She flinched at his throaty tone and spun, hiding the tremor of her hands by clasping them at her front. The glass doors to his office swung shut with a heavy crack.

"Sorry I—"

"Have you already forgotten our conversation from this morning?"

The performance management meeting. Not really a conversation but a lecture, one that took her right back to her school days getting dressed down by the headmaster for fighting.

"I hadn't, sir, but yesterday you told me to bring you the Jurin contracts," she replied, gesturing to the stack piled on his obnoxious orewood desk. "They arrived ten minutes ago." She tried to keep her voice even, but his powerful aura had it straining. He was too beautiful. It was sick. Even a glance at his glacial blue eyes had her insides twisting into knots.

She swallowed, scanning his office again as he regarded her. The room, which resembled a small house aesthetically, was neatly adorned with a three-seater charcoal couch, perfectly dressed in cushions and a sage throw, a copper-accented coffee table, and a tidy kitchenette. She hadn't snooped but was certain the closed door in the back corner hid an en suite bathroom, considering he often passed her office with damp hair and the mouthwatering scent of expensive cologne on clean skin.

He could live there if he wanted to. *She* wanted to.

Ambrose strode past her with a grunt and picked up the top file on the freshly printed stack. She faced him as he flicked through the pages with a tight jaw.

"I didn't hire you to stand there and watch me read, Hart."

Sylvie ground her teeth so hard they squeaked. Why had he hired her? Dozens of viable candidates with better clothes and better references had waited outside his office, but he'd chosen her. Worse, he'd picked her on the spot, even making her fetch him coffee. Black, no sugar. Boring.

She wove her shaking hands behind her back until the fastenings at her breasts pulled, her lacy white bra peeking between the buttons. *Shit.*

His gaze flickered towards her a fraction before she released her hands and clenched them at her sides. She shouldn't have stolen her roommate's clothes. While Fern had the superior wardrobe, her tiny chest always caused issues for Sylvie around the bust.

"Why are you still here?" he demanded, dropping the papers and placing his palms flat on the desk. His pale forearms sported thick veins popping out from the pressure of his rolled sleeves.

Dear gods. Don't look.

"Sorry, sir. I'll go now," she said, dropping her gaze to the floor and gliding to his glass doors, praying her ankles didn't buckle in her heels as she sensed his gaze drilling into her back.

With rounded shoulders, she gripped the metal door handle, wincing at its coldness before glancing back one last time. Even after four weeks under his scrutinising gaze, she still wanted him to do dirty things to her. She always got over her work crushes after a few conversations and harmless flirtations, but this felt different.

He was different.

Don't get sucked in. He's just hot.

His dark curls brushed his forehead as he stared her down. Even at their distance, she still shrank under his shrewd gaze.

"Speak, Hart."

She swallowed and cleared her throat. "Just—just let me know if you need anything else." Then she added, "Sir."

He blinked and turned around, using his hand to wave her away. If she didn't know any better, she could've sworn an unfamiliar bulge pressed at the front of his tailored suit pants. No, it was just her imagination. An imagination she needed to get out of the fucking gutter. Two smut-filled books a week really wasn't helping her case, but it didn't take a sexual deviant to acknowledge that he looked damn good in black.

Not wanting to tempt fate and risk a scolding, she wrenched the door open and hurried from his office, passing more rooms resembling aquariums until she reached the last one. She slowed her steps, letting her heart calm.

Positioned right by reception and the elevators, the room offered little privacy, but it was hers. Clutter and files on both walls surrounded her second-hand desk and computer setup. Wires wove like vipers from her monitor to the sockets, often curling into her rolling chair wheels and stalling them. She'd likely look a complete mess to any passerby, with papers strewn about and coffee stains all over her workspace. The remnants of a rubber band ball she'd broken, and a pile of unwound paperclips found their home there too. She sighed. No wonder Mr. Ambrose hated her. They didn't have many visitors, but when they did, she was always on display. The clueless assistant, just trying to stay ahead in an industry that wanted to burn her.

"Sylvie! Over here," Natalie called from the front desk, where the transparent panels lay covered in various magazine covers. Gold media exclusives with Sterling city's most eligible bachelors posed on the front in impeccable suits, hands clasped to show off their pure gold rings, watches, and perfect tans, which were impossible in this city. Even her naturally golden skin had become washed out from the perpetual drizzle.

"What's all this?" she asked, fingering the glossy papers. *Where was he?*

"Don't touch anything! I'm making an inspiration board," Natalie whispered, snatching a picture of some silver lingerie and gluing it to a cream piece of paper.

"Okay, I'm gonna go then." She had so much to do. Cleaning up her desk was first on the list.

She was already half turned when Natalie waved her hand, beckoning her closer again. "I was gonna ask you if you received any emails from a sh—a man named Rowan Hex."

Natalie's whisper invoked a shiver.

Sylvie flipped through her mental log of work emails from that morning and the day prior and shook her head. "Doesn't ring a bell, sorry."

Natalie pulled a face and stuffed her inspiration board into a manila folder before sliding it between a black concertina file at her feet.

"Who is that anyway?" Sylvie asked, crossing her arms to hide the adrenaline-fuelled tremor still present from her Ambrose encounter.

Natalie scrunched her nose. "Just someone wanting to reach out. Offer some investment opportunities to the business."

"This business?"

"Yup." Natalie popped the *p* and smiled. "He's gonna get me a better position. I could ask him to help you too."

"Oh." Sylvie glanced at Ambrose's office with a frown. She was lucky to even have a job, and this paid far better than her previous retail position. After another six months of frugality, she could even afford a new apartment sans the rats.

She backed up a step. "I'm good, thanks." Best not to be caught discussing her boss's business lest she get fired on the spot. It wouldn't be the first time.

"Don't worry," Natalie said, grinning again, "he'll like the change. Believe me." She used her pointed acrylic nail to pick between her teeth, then ran her long tongue across them.

Dubious. But Sylvie smiled with pressed lips. "Okay, well, I should get back to work. I'll let you know if I get an email from anyone with that name."

Natalie's wolfish grin followed her as she turned and scampered back to her office, trying to ignore the tingling down her spine.

* * *

"Delete. Delete. No. Delete all." Sylvie's emails never stopped coming. Providing Elias Ambrose with club and hotel sales reports, contractors' requests, and planning meetings with ridiculously influential people were only a few of her responsibilities, and she barely understood any of them. A few of her messages even appeared written in code—or at least she hoped—as the contents were gibberish to her untrained eye.

"Artefact signature traced: 54.16199, 70.04486. Wolf retrieval equipment located and destroyed."

She searched the numbers on Gold's search engine and found the location in the middle of the Western Ocean. When she asked Natalie about it, she seemed just as clueless.

The mention of artefacts, though, made her wonder if Ambrose was doing some shady, secret antique dealings. She watched far too many crime shows, but the thought of him being a thief helped ebb her desire for him each time they spoke.

Sighing, she sent another hotel sales report to the printer, hoping it was the one Ambrose wanted. Oasis Hotels. He said he needed the sales numbers and nothing else, so she triple-checked that the select page to print was sixteen and closed her eyes as the copy darted from her printer.

Her nose scrunched at the scent of the burning ink. Airdropping would be so much faster and less wasteful, but Natalie had already warned her not to bother Ambrose about trivial conveniences. That time, it was about ordering a coffee machine instead of forcing her to take a stomach-twisting trip eighty floors down to the communal staff room. Apparently he preferred traditional methods. It wasn't worth the scolding.

From her window, the company's name reflected at her mockingly from the twin building opposite. Another one of his. *Ambrose Horizons*. She rolled her eyes. *Grumpy millionaire playboy names every building he buys after himself and lives in his office.* "And I'm obsessed with him," she whispered, burying her head in her hands.

Grow up. Sylvie rolled back in her chair, swiped up the paper, and marched to the door. After this, she could clock out and head home. No more emails, no more grumpy asshat bossing her around.

The clack of ferocious typing echoed through the corridor, and Sylvie stilled. What the hell could Natalie be writing? She was the most leisurely—correction—lazy person Sylvie had ever met. Fern would correct her again and call the behaviour "efficient." However, Fern was also lazy, so Sylvie didn't consider her words often.

Before returning to the dungeon Elias called an office, Sylvie wandered to Natalie's desk. Even as she neared, the touch-typing on Natalie's baby pink keyboard picked up speed. Her fingers moved so quickly they blurred, and Sylvie scoffed, startling Natalie right out of her writing.

"Shit! You scared the hell out of me. I thought you were Ambrose."

Sylvie laughed. "With that insane typing, I'm surprised the entire building hasn't come up here to see what you're doing."

"Really?" At Natalie's wide eyes and quivering lip, Sylvie's grin fell.

"Are you okay? What's going on?"

Natalie pressed the escape key a dozen times and pulled her inspiration board out again, tucking her white-blond hair behind her dainty ears. She fingered the images on her lap and jiggled her leg. "Nothing, nothing. Just take your papers and go before he—"

Her words died in her throat, eyes widening as her head lifted, staring over Sylvie's shoulder.

Without turning, Sylvie knew the motherfucker was behind her. The hairs on her nape stood, and she spun too fast, losing her balance on Fern's favourite stilettos, the force throwing her nose-first into his rigid torso.

"Son of a—"

TWO

"Bitch!"

Sylvie bounced off the stupidly hard chest of her boss and clutched her nose. Her eyes watered as her hands filled with blood. *Oh shit.*

Natalie gasped, shoving her inspiration board papers into a folder and hurling them into the bin. "Mr. Ambrose!"

"Not right now, Miss Edwards," he said, grabbing Sylvie's shoulder as she swayed on her feet.

She wrenched herself backwards, shocked by the sudden touch, and bumped into Natalie's desk.

"Stop moving." Ambrose gripped her chin, tilting it with surprising gentleness. He turned her head left to right.

Sylvie batted her lashes, clearing the tears with a few blinks, and met his icy stare.

"Come here," he said, pulling her down the hall towards his office.

She protested with a few muffled groans but followed him, her hands curling into a cup to catch the deluge of crimson.

"Mr. Ambrose!" She peered over her shoulder, staring at the red trail dotting the grey carpets in their wake, and swallowed a lump in her throat. "I'm sorry. I didn't mean to."

He continued guiding her to his office, his giant hand pressing against her mid-back. "Just stop flailing before you spray more blood all over my floors."

It was already too late for that, but her mouth snapped shut, the taste of copper saturating her tongue. She shuddered and winced as another drop sloshed across the threshold of his office. He said nothing. Instead, he sat her in his plush office chair and grabbed a small white cloth from his bottom drawer, the Ambrose Enterprise logo embroidered on its middle in a cursive *"AE."* Even in pain, she huffed at the pretentiousness of it.

She was certain Ambrose's lips quirked as he walked to the fridge, pulling out an unopened water bottle and wetting the fabric. He returned quickly, kneeling at her feet and guiding her hands away from her face. So gentle. So *not* like him. Her heart quickened at the sight of him beneath her. Kneeling. Her mind dived headfirst into filth as he stroked the damp cloth across her cheeks and around her throbbing nose. He paused, not meeting her eyes, and murmured, "It's stopped."

His attention dropped to her bloodied hands next. Without giving her a chance to get up and wash them, he wiped each finger slowly and assuredly, taking care not to jostle her irritated cuticles before moving to her palms with firm, measured strokes until only a pink tinge remained.

Her skin tingled as his warm breath fanned across her lap. "Mr. Ambrose?"

"Elias," he corrected, lifting his narrowed gaze to hers. His blue eyes appeared bottomless in the office lighting, and without thought or reason, Sylvie leaned towards his full lips.

"Elias," she breathed. Her focus felt magnetised to him, the urge to touch his fair skin making her fingers twitch. "I have to finish printing the copies of …" Her voice trailed off as his irises flickered a deep shade of red. She blinked. "What's happening to your eyes?"

As her husky whisper ruffled his dark curls, he pulled back. The moment passed. Thank the gods, because she was about to tell him to stroke her firmly somewhere else.

Elias stood, brushing a stray curl from his forehead before looking at his bloodstained hands. *Yikes.* He probably should've worn gloves or something. First aid 101. He froze then, holding his long fingers up to the light, and Sylvie stared up at him in horror as he brought them to his lips.

"What are you doing? Mr. Amb—"

His eyes shot to hers, a thunderous scowl across his brow as his hands dropped to his sides, curling into loose fists.

"Elias," she corrected herself, growing hot as a smirk formed on his lips. "You should wash your hands or something," Sylvie continued, standing and looking pitifully at the stained blouse. Fern was gonna kill her.

"How is it I find you not doing your job every time I look for you?"

Sylvie stuttered, edging the opposite way around the desk, keeping her eyes glued to her boss. His broad shoulders and muscular frame swayed somewhat, as if he were about to pounce any second.

"I was on my way, but Natalie was—"

Elias shook his head, his brow rising along with a disdainful smirk. "You want to blame Miss Edwards? That's rich, considering she gets her work done when I ask, and you don't."

Sylvie's emotions flared, and she clenched her jaw. What was his problem? Elias's eyes twinkled, and she frowned in response, letting her voice rise higher. "Are you baiting me?" *Stay professional.*

His smile and prowling made her back up, and she tripped on his lounge suite, her ass catching the arm of the couch and her stomach lurching as her life flashed before her, all twenty-something tedious years of it. She fell backwards, legs flying into the air as her spine smacked into the couch cushion. It wasn't graceful, but at least her head didn't hit the ground.

"Ambrose," an unfamiliar voice said, accompanied by a few clicks of tongue on teeth. "Didn't I teach you not to play with your food?"

Food? Sylvie swallowed her rage, swinging her legs off the couch's arm and planting her shaking heels on the floor. If a person could die from embarrassment, she would be long dead. Next she'd be falling at his feet. *Clumsy idiot.*

"Fucking hell." After smoothing her clothes, Sylvie realised she had lost a very important button off her blouse. Fern was really going to kill her now. She held the sides of her shirt together as a gorgeous man sauntered into the room, his deep-brown skin glowing under the cold office lighting. His perfect smile and russet eyes hypnotised her until she was sure she wasn't breathing any more. Who was this guy? Her knees inched apart as she imagined his hands sliding up her legs.

"Get out of here, Kian. It's not happening," Elias growled.

The sensation along her thigh stopped, and she gasped faintly.

"Ah, what a shame. I thought we were friends."

Elias rolled his eyes, standing between Sylvie and the strange visitor, Kian.

Ki-an. Pretty.

"Yes, but that doesn't mean I need to share everything with you," he said.

Sylvie's heart raced as she listened to their words. They made her sound like a meal. Then, without thinking of the consequences, she stood and pushed against Elias's back. He didn't even sway, but the shove felt good as she snapped, "What the fuck do you think you're talking about?"

Kian's smile grew wider as he stared at Sylvie and approached her, hands raised. "Forgive me; I truly, desperately apologise. Will you give me your name so I can make amends properly?"

Elias stepped between them again, his broad back bumping Sylvie back onto the couch. He stared down at her over his shoulder, a warning in his gaze. *Lie.*

She swallowed, scoffing, before coming up with, "Jade."

Elias's approving nod and Kian's falling smile made her stomach swirl with conflicting emotions.

"Good girl." Elias tilted his head to the door. "Head home."

She stood, clutching her top together and ignoring the praise before rushing past and praying he couldn't tell how much she liked it.

* * *

That night, Sylvie pulled out her favourite toys to ease the rising need in her body. However, after her third orgasm, she realised nothing would put out the fire those two men had set ablaze.

Sylvie dreamt of them every night for a week, each taking turns using her body in ways she had only read about. Then, after clocking in for work every morning, she prayed she wouldn't cross paths with either of them.

And as if blessed by fate, for that week, she didn't.

Besides serving coffee, printing contracts, and answering emails, her days remained as mundane as ever, and her nights unsatisfying.

At the end of that week, Natalie appeared in her doorway and Cheshire-grinned, playing with her sharp acrylic nails. "Are you gonna tell me what happened in his office last week?" she asked, wiggling her brows.

Sylvie sighed, pressing her fingertips to her nasal bridge. "Natalie, please stop asking me. Nothing happened."

"Your shirt would beg to differ. You were clutching it pretty tight on your way out."

That damn button. She had sewn it back on before Fern noticed, but she wouldn't risk wearing it again. The blazer she had taken from Fern's closet instead was doing its job for once and hid her cleavage.

Sylvie sniffed, riffling through the bag by her feet and pulling out an apple and the switch-knife she always carried. Painstakingly slow, she carved off the rind and left it in a full spiral on her desk before slicing the white flesh and taking a bite. Natalie squirmed, as if the wait for gossip physically pained her.

After swallowing, Sylvie asked, "What do you know about a man named Kian Rengevere?" Her searches for him in her work emails came up with nothing exciting besides a few offshore business deals—big bucks.

Natalie smirked; her arms crossed. "Information for information?"

"Yes. Just hurry before someone comes in here."

"Mr. Rengevere owns half of this company, but he's like the secret benefactor, and Ambrose is the face. They're friends too. If you want any more, you have to tell me what happened."

Sylvie pretended to mull it over, relishing Natalie's frown. Finally, she raised her hands in surrender and blew air from her lips. "He cleaned me up, and I fell on his stupid couch, which is what popped my button off, by the way. Then Kian came in, and they started saying weird shit, and I left." Sylvie rolled her eyes, remembering how they looked at her. Like a four-course meal served at the highest-rated bars in upper Sterling, not the downtown area she was slumming in. Her lips would be the appetizer, and they would feast on her all the way to her painted toes. She cleared her throat and straightened, praying Natalie couldn't read her expression. Her imagination was getting way out of hand. *No more smut.*

Natalie sniffed lightly. "That's interesting."

Sylvie glanced at her, expecting a sarcastic expression, but the pure confusion on Natalie's face gave her pause. "What is it?"

Nothing. I've just not heard of anyone resisting—"

Sylvie interrupted Natalie with a groan. "Natalie, I've got work to do. I'm not interested in your innuendos. Please." *Resisting?* Was it that obvious how much they made her unravel? She needed to get laid, and soon.

Natalie flicked her platinum ponytail over her shoulder and backed off. "Alright then, talk later," she purred, strutting from the room on her red stilettos.

Finally. Sylvie returned her focus to the screen, scrolling through dozens of mind-numbing emails until her eyes turned hazy. She was supposed to be organising a meeting between Elias and a competitor, Warren and Co, but the fucking email thread had vanished.

"Where is it?" She was so engrossed in the task she didn't hear anyone coming until the throat clearing of an intruder startled her.

She bolted upright on her chair, knocking her empty mug onto the ground and gasped as Kian Rengevere filled the doorway of her office. In two long strides, he was there scooping up her stray cup, promptly placing it back on the old coffee stain circle on her desk.

His dark skin seemed to give off a warm glow in the confined space. "Did I frighten you?" he asked with a mischievous grin.

Rolling her chair back a fraction to create space between them, Sylvie bit the inside of her lip and tucked her dark waves behind her ears. "I'm fine."

He chuckled and crossed to the opposite side of the room, flopping onto a spare chair. People in the office used her space like a storage closet, so she wasn't even sure where it came from. The wall farthest from Kian was overflowing with files and paperwork, which execs in the lower levels had stacked from floor to ceiling. A total quake hazard. But then again, it wasn't worth fretting over files crushing her when her office breached the smog. She'd be dead either way.

Kian's warm voice pulled her from her morbid thoughts. "When you look at me, what do you see?" Kian said, smiling again and swivelling as if displaying himself.

The urge to speak the truth swirled in her throat, but she pressed her lips together and shook her head. "Aren't you my boss?"

"I didn't ask you to say anything inappropriate." His dark eyes sparkled, and her heart raced under his gaze. Something about him reeled her in. Well hook, line and—

"You're perfect," she said, realising too late that the words had left her mouth.

He smiled and pressed his lips together as if holding in a laugh. He was toying with her, and she liked it.

Clearing her throat and clasping her hands in her lap, she tried again, "I mean, you're *too* perfect," she said, hoping her light foundation covered the burning heat across her cheeks. "You don't even seem real."

At that, Kian's brows lifted, and he stood abruptly. Sylvie leaned back in her chair as he crossed to her desk and peered into her eyes from an inch away. "What are you?"

"Back up, Kian," Elias boomed from her doorway.

Why everyone seemed drawn to her tiny office was beyond her.

"She's—"

"Back up. She's mine—she's my assistant." Elias's strange claim affected everyone in the room. A muscle in Kian's jaw jumped as if gritting his teeth as he backed off, turning to face Elias with a glint in his dark eyes. Sylvie's heart raced, and her core throbbed; she hadn't been so turned on in ages. The urge

23

to trail her fingers down her front to her waistband hit her intensely as she perused Kian's body.

Taut muscles rippled through his cotton shirt and dark jeans. Unlike Elias's massive form, Kian's musculature appeared more defined and symmetrical. He really was perfect. If he were carved in marble, Sylvie would lust over the stone.

"Well, perhaps she would like to be my 'assistant' too," Kian challenged.

Sylvie looked between them in confusion before standing and grabbing her bag. Then, pushing past them both, she kept her head down and jogged to the elevator, slamming the button to the ground floor while ignoring Natalie's gaping mouth. When it finally opened, she darted inside. *Crazy alpha male bullshit!* Her heavy breathing echoed in the steel box as the blinking red light in the corner mocked her. She scowled at it before crossing her arms and waiting for the doors to open.

Once outside, Sylvie could breathe again, the thick sexual chemistry no longer affecting her brain. She ran to a nearby shop and bought some lunch before returning to the office. To her relief, both men were gone, and she ate in a somewhat peaceful silence.

"What the hell was that?" the blond bombshell finally called from her desk.

"Not now, Natalie!" Sylvie growled right back. She didn't have an answer for her, anyway. She opened a new document and began formatting her resignation.

THREE

In her office, days later, Sylvie let out a groan when she opened her email and found a summons from Elias at the top of her unread messages. *"To examine a new artefact in my office,"* it read.

"So you are a thief then," she said, typing back a quick, *"I'm busy."*

After her weird interaction with Kian and Elias, she no longer cared about being tactful. Her resignation was sitting in her drafts, but she was waiting for the right moment. Maybe after a few companies responded to her recent applications.

The only reason she took the job with Elias was to get out of the retail industry—and destitution—but they almost seemed preferable to having two insanely attractive men act like psychos around her. *Almost.*

Elias responded immediately with a non-negotiable, *"Now,"* and she groaned louder into her hands. She gulped the last dregs of her cold coffee and stormed from her office.

The satisfaction she got from stomping down the hall was nearly enough to steel her nerves as she arrived outside his office. The doors were closed, obscured by drawn curtains, and muffled voices sounded from behind them. Kian and Elias. Maybe she should just turn around. *Don't be a little bitch.*

She took a calming breath and knocked, and Kian's brilliant smile appeared from behind the curtain a second later.

Sylvie swallowed and clasped her hands in front of her. She didn't miss the casual flicker of his eyes at the movement. "You called?"

"Come on in." Kian beamed. "I've brought something to show you."

Elias sat behind his desk, hands steepled under his chin. His dark curls were messy on his head, as if he had run a hand through them a few times.

Her eyes locked with Elias as she stepped inside and Kian brushed past her, the wind from his movements caressing her body like a gentle touch. He reclined on Elias' sofa, ankle over knee, his long arms draping across the back of the couch. It should've been illegal to look that good.

"I need you to look at something and tell me what you see," Elias said as he stood, picking up a flat object and holding it tenderly before carrying it to her. She tried not to focus on his gentleness, the energy reminding her of the way he tended to her after her nosebleed.

Conflict swirled through her as she accepted the artefact as he held it out, his fingers brushing hers. She shivered from his icy contact and focused her attention on the object. This was so ridiculous. She refrained from shoving the object, which was a mirror, back in his hands and storming from the office by exhaling slowly through her nose as she scanned it. This wasn't in her job description. Maybe instead of quitting, she should ask for a raise.

It looked like a regular hand mirror with intricate golden carvings on its border. None of the symbols resembled anything she had seen before, and an uneasy energy wended up her arms. The reflective surface shimmered and moved, like a cell phone screensaver was embedded in it.

"What is this?" she said.

"An artefact. Now, what do you see?" Kian asked, mirth clear in his voice.

Sylvie sighed, turning it in her hands again and began describing the piece, "It's a hand mirror of some kind, but the glass isn't reflective. The border is gold—"

"Can you see yourself in the reflection?" Elias asked, leaning over her shoulder. His arm brushed against her and she shuddered at his soft, frigid skin. Couldn't the man afford a jacket?

"No."

She tilted the mirror at different angles and squinted. She thought she could see a castle structure overrun with vines in the mirror, but it shimmered away before she could get a solid look. Then a flash of thick trees zipped past as a distinct cityscape with twisted silver spires emerged over a dark horizon. The buildings were a mix of glass and silver, each window a beacon filled with thick honeyed light that had violet traces.

It was nothing like she'd ever seen on the continent she lived on, Erus, before. The central continent of Maeheim, Erus, was far more derelict than the city in the mirror, with ramshackle buildings of steel and rust spots in every city with a few eclectic towns spattered between Sterling and the Iron Peaks in the north. Maybe the eastern cities had such things. She spun the mirror, looking for a charging port, or even a false back where a battery might be hiding.

"I saw a castle, though, I think? But, seriously, Mr. Ambrose, what is this? Is this a joke? Is something gonna jump out at me if I stare too hard? Because I'm not in the mood."

Elias took back the artefact, hiding his face from her as he shuffled to his desk. Kian's smile had returned, and she blinked. What was he so happy about, and what had made Elias's posture stoop?

"You saw the palace?" he said.

She nodded. "Yeah, and a glass city thing."

Kian's mouth dropped open, and Elias spun, returning to her side in a single stride and gripping her wrist lightly. She pulled away, but his searching gaze made her pause.

"Say that again," Elias said.

She looked between the men and swallowed. "After the castle disappeared, there were trees, then a city that looked all glass and silver appeared. But, seriously, what is happening?"

"Has this ever happened before?" Kian said. The effort he seemed to use dragging his eyes from her had her heating all over again.

Elias's eyes narrowed as he dropped her hand and began pacing the open floor. "Not in my lifetime."

A knock at the door drew each of their gazes and she darted for it, glad for the interruption, but she stalled, a pair of warm arms encircling her waist. She almost screamed, but the tenderness of the touch eased her panic.

As she peered down, umber-toned forearms came into view, smooth and unmarred. *Warm.* Kian turned her in his arms and put a finger to his lips. Despite her frown, she complied, and he pulled her back into his chest. Elias nodded their way, and she mirrored his movements until she realised what she was doing. She did *not* need his approval.

Elias rubbed his eyes and mussed his hair before pulling the curtain back a few inches, squinting. He tugged the door open less than an inch, just enough for Natalie's voice to chirp through. "Hi—"

He grumbled, interrupting, "I've told you before not to wake me, Miss Edwards."

"Sorry, sir, I was looking for Sylvie. I saw her walking this way, but she never came back."

"What could you possibly want with her? She isn't your assistant; she's mine."

Tingles exploded in Sylvie's body upon hearing him claiming her once again.

"Of course, sir. I wasn't suggesting—I was just … sorry. But is she here?"

Elias scowled. "No. Is there anything else?"

"Uh-uh."

The clacking of her heels faded, and Elias shut the door. Nobody moved until the faint clacking of Natalie's keyboard resumed and Elias closed the curtains, pressing a finger and thumb to his nasal bridge.

Sylvie untangled herself from Kian and wandered over to Elias. "Can I go now?"

His throat bobbed slightly, and he peered at Kian with a slight frown before facing her. She prepared for bad news, her index finger finding her thumb cuticle and digging until blood beaded around her nail.

"I'm afraid that's not possible," Elias said.

All sound diminished from the room and Sylvie's stomach lurched in what felt like a free-fall to the ground floor of the high-rise. "What do you mean? Are you saying I can't leave?"

It wasn't the first time in her life her internal alarm bells had screeched for her to escape, and finally, her body came back online. In a rush, she retreated from both men, her attention flicking from one to the other. If they even leaned in her direction, fate fucking help them. Both held puzzling expressions filled with frustration, displeasure, and even fear. They should be fucking afraid. She wasn't someone they could just corner and control. *Hell no.*

"Do you have any family, Ms. Hart?" Elias finally asked, taking a seat on his couch's arm.

Sylvie shivered under his attentive gaze before shaking her head. She should lie. She really should lie, but it just came out. "No." *Dammit.*

"None?" Kian asked, sadness crossing his face.

Sylvie sighed, crossing her arms with a scowl forming. "No, okay, I grew up in foster care. I have no family."

Elias and Kian shared a look before staring back at her yet again, watching her movements like predators.

"Friends?" Kian said. "People that would miss you if you were absent?"

She backed up and shuddered. "Are you planning on murdering me or something?"

Kian jumped to his feet, hands placating. "Of course not, Princess. But we might need to take you somewhere to keep you safe, and we want to know if anyone will panic if you disappear for a while."

Kian's words did little to ease her alarm as she distanced herself from the males, her back bumping into the fridge. Her legs shook as she leaned her burning body against its cool metal.

"Why would you need to keep me safe?" *Alright, just hear the crazy people out.* If she acted compliant, they might let her go. She had watched plenty of true crime documentaries. *No secondary locations.*

Elias strode closer. She tried to shrink away, heeled feet scuffing the carpet, but his frown stopped her.

"Because once others know what you are to us, you will become a target," he said, offering his palm to her.

Sylvie looked at it warily before placing her trembling hand on top of it. His huge fingers enclosed hers, and he turned her hand in his, examining it with a trace of his other finger, from the veins to the little mole atop it. She expected him to let go, but he didn't.

He just kept tracing from her hand to her wrist, up her forearm. A blush erupted across her chest as she realised the compromising position she was in with her boss.

Her bosses.

She tried to pull her hand free, but he held her steady.

"I'm your assistant. Why would anyone care about that?"

Kian approached and propped an arm against the top of the fridge, his forearm resting against her shoulder. She jerked away, but not before she noted how their touching skin was a stark contrast to the humming fridge's freezing exterior. They surrounded her now. How had she let herself get into this position? Why was her brain so fucking foggy?

"You're much more to us than that," he said.

31

"I don't understand. Will one of you just tell me what is going on? This doesn't feel like appropriate workplace behaviour," she added the last part with a scoff. It definitely wasn't, but that had never stopped her before. Something about the risk made it sexier. But that was with colleagues, or at her most risky, a store manager. These men were in a league of their own. Powerful.

Dangerous.

Kian exhaled and Sylvie could hear the humour in it as Elias hummed lowly. "You're ours. Take that how you want, Hart. But you won't be going anywhere without one of us to escort you until we know you can protect yourself."

As the words sank into her jumbled brain, she scowled and snatched her hand back. Elias let her go, and she shuffled towards the room's outer windows so neither could touch her again. Instantly, some of the fog lifted, and she looked for an escape.

"If you don't let me out of here, I will scream," she threatened. "Don't fuck with me, okay? I have a knife in my pocket." She pulled the tiny iron-plated switch-knife from her blazer pocket and held it in her sweaty fist. It had been hers since she turned fourteen. She could protect herself plenty.

Kian hmphed and stood, crossing the room and looking at Elias expectantly. The latter sighed and held his hand out, palm open. His eyes captured hers, and he clicked his tongue. "Give it to me now."

The urge to comply rose, but Sylvie only tightened her grip. "No. Now move back," she said, waving the weapon in front of her. She didn't want to point it at either of them, but she had to get out. "I want to go home. I do have someone that

32

will notice if I'm gone. My roommate, Fern. She'll call the cops if I don't get home tonight."

It was a lie. Fern didn't give two shits about Sylvie. Half the time, she didn't even return home, but they didn't know that.

Elias's jaw clenched as he stood and backed up, holding his hands open non-threateningly. *Too late, I'm already threatened.*

Walking the perimeter of the room, Sylvie kept her eyes on both men before grabbing the icy door handle again. She pulled. It didn't move. "No." She yanked again, tears burning her eyes as her throat constricted. "No!"

Kian's arm snaked between her and the door and she yelped, nicking him with the knife. He hissed, continuing to unlock Elias's door before withdrawing his arm, a look of betrayal on his face.

Sylvie glanced at the golden fluid leaking from his wrist with an open mouth. *Is that blood?* Her brain refused to process what it was seeing; instead, she breathed a quick apology before running to the elevators.

Natalie was surprisingly absent from her desk, and Sylvie prayed she wouldn't run into her on her way out. She would make assumptions, and Sylvie didn't have the energy to deal with it.

Punching the garage button, she rode in the elevator in silence, clutching the tiny knife in her violently shaking hands.

The farther she ran from Elias and Kian, the more her fear grew, which made zero sense. She should have felt better, getting away from those psychos, not worse.

Finally, pushing the thoughts away, she bolted to her ancient burgundy shitbox, climbing in and locking the doors.

Sylvie threw the weapon into the passenger seat, turned the car on, and sped away, surprised to find her journey home uneventful besides the growing pool of dread in her belly. At least her resignation was ready to send. She'd do it the second she got home. Not that it mattered. After assaulting one of her bosses and cursing at the other, she was totally fucking fired.

Goodbye, new apartment.

FOUR

As expected, Sylvie's second-floor apartment was empty, except for a lone rat who scampered past as she opened the door. She was too tired to jump, and instead hung her bag on the hook by her entryway and dragged her feet to the kitchen. Despite the patches of mould, the space was tidy enough. Mainly because she and her roommate weren't there often enough to make a mess.

Since moving in, she only used the apartment to sleep, shit, and shower. Sylvie threw her phone on the table and took a few dozen calming breaths. Then, heading to the fridge, she frowned at the lack of food. Nothing but rotten fruit and expired juice boxes.

"What the hell?"

The freezer wasn't much better, but Sylvie salvaged an expired ready-made meal, throwing it into the microwave to nuke it to death.

"Hey, dummy!" Fern's laughter filled the lounge space.

"Hey," Sylvie muttered, pulling her piping meal out of the microwave and onto the table. "How was work?" she asked, forking the molten pasta into her mouth, crying out as it burned her tongue.

Fern leaned against the kitchen counter with a pout. "Lame. You?" Her pink pixie cut swished in front of her eyes as she tilted her head in fake interest.

"Fine," Sylvie lied, blowing on her food. "If I disappeared for days, how long would it take for you to notice?" Her shaky voice and dry swallowing made Fern pause, but her confusion quickly turned into obnoxious laughter.

"I'll be honest, Syl. You could be dead for weeks in your room, and I wouldn't notice."

Sylvie squinted at her roommate, noticing the red veins covering the whites of her eyes, and sighed. "Did you drive home high?"

Fern laughed again, waving her hand as if shooing a bug. "No. I got a taxi. I think." The laughter grated Sylvie's brain, so she scarfed the last bits of her meal and retired to her room. It was sparse. Nothing but a bed, side table, and small desk to call her own. And a half dozen outfits in her closet she cycled through.

She slipped out of her work clothes, kicking them into a corner, and rifled through the laundry pile on her desk chair, throwing on a pair of loose pyjama bottoms and a singlet that barely contained her breasts. She must have grabbed Fern's top by mistake. Oh well. If Fern didn't want Sylvie to steal her shit she shouldn't have kept sneaking it into her washing load.

Sylvie's emails pinged from her phone the second she turned it on and sat on her single bed. The room echoed the irritating alert as she searched for the mute function with growing fury.

Natalie had set her phone up to boost work emails so she would never miss an important message, but Sylvie contemplated dropping her device in the toilet bowl right then. "Stupid freaking junk."

The temperature in her room dropped a few degrees as she fiddled with her phone and absently dragged her comforter across her lap.

"Sylvie," a voice hissed in her ears. She jolted sideways, glancing around for the voice's owner, but her room was empty.

A shudder trailed across her back, and she hurried beneath the covers, pulling the duvet to her chin.

"Sylvie!" Straight into her right ear, the whisper called again. A rank breath hit her cheek and she screamed, pulling the blanket over her head and curling into a ball.

"Fern? Fern!"

She could only hope her voice would penetrate the fabric and the closed bedroom door.

"Sylvie …"

This time the name came out in a singsong tone, the voice taking on a masculine rasp.

"Fern!"

Her blankets came alive, clinging to her as if the air between them and the mattress was getting sucked out. Sylvie kicked and screamed, pressing the duvet away from her mouth. Horror doused her limbs in ice as the fabric smothered her.

"No!" Her lungs burned as the cotton stuffed her mouth and her vision dulled. The future news headlines flashed across her mind. *Twenty-six-year-old assistant, Sylvie Hart, suffocated by a blanket."*

Gods dammit.

* * *

Sylvie blinked against the shift in lighting, trying to make sense of her surroundings. The stippled ceiling above her shimmered, and a small, barred window panel near the roof let in a dull orange glow.

Her back cracked and groaned as she sat upright on a rigid stretcher, her rapid heartbeat matching her growing terror. The space was about the size of the bathroom in her apartment, and the walls leaked a copper-coloured substance.

Sylvie's mouth dried as she remembered her near-death experience with her rogue duvet and kicked the stretcher bedding to the floor. Then, standing with a groan, she walked to the wall, swiping her finger across the fluid.

It burned her skin and she yelped, wiping it on her pyjama pants before burying her face in her hands. "What is happening?"

She sniffled, pressing her palms into her eye sockets to stop the building pressure. "Don't cry, don't cry—"

"Well, well. The human is awake," a snide feminine voice cooed. Sylvie's head lifted, and she shot back as a pair of purple eyes stared at her through a slot in the wall. The whole wall panel slid across, and Sylvie backed away more, careful not to bump into anything.

The woman regarded her for a second, her ebony skin sparkling from the room's orange hue, a contrast to the purple armour she wore. An intricate bronze satchel was slung across one shoulder, tinkling lightly as she adjusted her posture. Besides her eye colour, she looked like a regular person, but when she smiled—sneered— her razor-sharp teeth had Sylvie's heart pounding. She could tear flesh off bone with those if she wanted to. *Who would do that to themselves? Plastic surgery these days …*

"Who are you?"

"None of your business, *human*."

A frown furrowed Sylvie's brow, and she crossed her arms. *Why does she keep saying that?* "Where am I then?"

"The dungeons," the woman responded.

"Kerensa, stop playing with it. Give it the clothing," another voice shouted from a distance.

The woman, Kerensa, growled, then pulled a rucksack from behind her and kicked it towards Sylvie's feet.

"You have five minutes. Then you will see the queen."

"Queen?"

The wall-door slid back in place with a loud thunk, and she let her questions die in her throat. *Fine. Piss off then.* Annoyance laced through her as she eyed the rucksack, gnawing her lower lip as she prodded it with her toe. It didn't move or make a sound, so she squatted to peer inside it.

It took about two minutes to loosen the knotted drawstring, but once she opened it, her mouth dropped open.

"No way," she breathed. The attire inside looked straight from her favourite fantasy films. A navy velvet gown with pearls, dried flora, and lace embroidery flowed like a liquid in her hands.

The bag contained other items she didn't recognise, so she tossed them aside. They probably had a purpose, but she didn't have time to guess. Instead, she stripped off her pyjama bottoms and pulled the gown over her head. Its inner texture was as soft as the outside.

As she smoothed her hands along the skirt, the wall slid open with a resounding bang.

Kerensa appeared again with a twisted scowl. "Where are the ruff and bodice?"

Sylvie eyed the bag briefly before retorting, "Where are the shoes?"

Kerensa growled and snatched the rucksack. "There is no time. Hurry." She turned and marched away, leaving Sylvie to trot behind her to catch up. The stone floors froze her feet, and she hastened to limit their contact with the frigid concrete.

Kerensa led her up a winding stone staircase for agonising minutes. She moved so quickly that Sylvie had broken out in a sweat by the time they breached the last doors.

The sudden shift in lighting turned her vision white. As she raised her arm to shield her eyes, a rough grip yanked her wrist and pulled her further into the bright room.

Sylvie took in the space and tried not to squeak. Stone pillars with vines of ivy framed the area, and dozens of intricate sculptures in varying poses stood before them. The glass-domed ceiling above them was laden with flowers and spiralling leaves.

She walked farther inside, and the ground beneath her feet smoothed into polished stone, warm to the touch. Her numb toes appreciated the change as she followed Kerensa. The room appeared empty until Sylvie let her gaze soften. Then dozens of colourful eyes appeared, blinking from the outskirts. Behind every pillar. Watching.

Sylvie straightened her spine, scampering closer to her purple-eyed companion and focusing her attention ahead. Her heart thumped harder, sweat beading on her brow as more creatures moved in her peripheral vision.

She had to be hallucinating.

Or dreaming.

Her feet grew heavy as a throne of gold and climbing hydrangeas shimmered before her, a serene figure materialising into view.

"Mother," Kerensa said, bowing. "The human."

Sylvie frowned as Kerensa dragged her by the bicep in front of the woman she presumed was the unnamed queen and forced her down. Her head bowed automatically, and when she lifted it, the queen's mouth pressed into a firm line.

"Stand up."

Sylvie stood, lifting her gaze only to be swatted on the back of the head. "Keep your eyes down," Kerensa hissed.

Breath shaking, Sylvie fixed her gaze on the floor as soft footsteps pattered around her. A gentle touch to her hair made her shrink away, but after another slap on her back, she stood numbly.

"You are a pretty wee thing. But you will never be suitable for a fae prince."

A what prince? Sylvie squeezed her eyes shut, imagining she was anywhere else in the world because she refused to believe the current events were happening. This couldn't be real.

Sharp fingernails bit into her chin, and her head tilted upwards. The ethereal woman, who had skin the colour of rich sienna and warm ochre undertones, bore her violet eyes into Sylvie's.

"Now you listen to me, child, and you listen well. You are in a very precarious situation presently, and the only reason your organs have not been pulled from your belly button and woven into a necklace for a demon is me. You remember that."

"I don't think I'll ever forget," Sylvie replied with a downturned mouth, the vivid description stirring her stomach. She expected another hit to her body, but to her surprise, the woman smiled.

"My son will get here once word of your location reaches him. You see, the walls have ears, child. And eyes." She fanned her hands around, but Sylvie didn't look. She already knew what was hiding there.

"You are to choose the vampire and reject my son. Do you understand?"

Sylvie's mouth opened and closed, and before she could shake her head no, a furious shout echoed through the room.

"Mother! What have you done?"

The queen swished past her with silent grace, whispering a chilling command, "Break his heart," before booming, "My son! Welcome home."

"Mother, I am not playing games. Where is she?" Kian's anger crashed from his body in violent waves. Sylvie swore she could feel his emotions lapping at her bare feet.

Kerensa rolled her eyes and pulled Sylvie backwards, spinning her to face Kian. They were siblings. How did she not notice it earlier? Probably the razor teeth and purple eyes.

Kian raced over in a blink, his regal attire changing his entire look, the rich plum fabrics dripping across his rippling muscles like liquid silk. Sylvie gasped as his hand took hers, and he searched her face. "Are you hurt?"

Casting a quick look at Kerensa, she exhaled through her nose and shook her head. "I'm okay."

He traced her arm, snagging the delicate cloth between his forefinger and thumb.

"Why did you bring her here?"

The queen appeared beside him, her eyes flashing a warning at Sylvie before softening on her son. "You're lucky we found her when we did. She was about to be smothered to death by a lesser demon when Kerensa portalled her here."

So that's what that was. Sylvie blinked. The queen's words made logical sense. She must be going insane.

"Am I dead?" she asked, looking into Kian's dark brown eyes. *Huh, not just brown.* Mulberry stripes lined the iris.

He smiled softly. "No, you are alive. This is my home, the palace you saw in the looking glass."

"The artefact?"

"Yes."

Sylvie's breathing quickened. "Are you saying this is—this place is—" She brought her free hand to her neck and tugged the fabric away as she overheated. "Where are we, Kian?"

He pulled her trembling body into his chest, and she relaxed in his tender grip as he rubbed her back with soothing circles. After a moment, her breathing evened out.

"This is a dream, right?" she said, letting her eyelids flutter shut.

Her legs liquefied, and she fell before a firm grip curled beneath her knees and hoisted her into a bridal-style carry.

She blinked slowly, watching Kian's jaw twitch as he walked from the room to a different doorway from where she had entered.

"Nobody will harm or kill her while she is here, do you understand?" he boomed, his head swivelling to each corner of the room.

A collective hissed, "Yes," filled her ears, and she shivered harder in his arms.

"This is a dream, right Kian?" she repeated, gripping his silken shirt as if it were the only thing grounding her to reality.

"Shh." He planted a soft kiss on her hairline, and her body grew heavier. "No, Princess. It is not."

FIVE

A cramp in Sylvie's gut roused her from sleep, but the bed she lay in urged her to ignore it. She listened for a while, but soon the pain became unbearable, and she groaned, pushing her face into the plush pillows before another gurgle attacked.

"Ow."

With a steady kneading of her fist into her abdomen, she rolled on her back and gasped. Kian stood a few feet away by the window with a faraway look. Hopefully, he was too distracted to hear her growling belly.

She shuffled into a sitting position and gazed around the room.

Much like the queen's hall, live plants and flowers coiled around the bed frames, up the walls, and across the ceiling in intricate designs. Small pollen particles danced in the dappled sunlight and settled on the emerald bedspread.

She rubbed her eyes and noted the lack of coverage on her skin. Instantly, her attention dropped to her body, and she scowled. He'd changed her into a sheer cream slip dress. Her annoyance faded as quickly as it began, and instead of shouting at him, she pulled the blanket up to cover herself until a sudden, choking memory of her attempted murder flashed, the claustrophobic weight of the bedding crushing her chest until her breathing stalled.

Not again.

She thrust the fabric across the bed and stared, panting as it spilt over the ornately carved top rail of the footboard.

"If you didn't like the blankets, you could have just told me," Kian said, his white, very human-looking teeth on display as he smirked. Sylvie flushed and pulled her hair over her shoulders, covering her exposed flesh.

"I didn't dress you either. It was a fae maid."

Her annoyance dripped away to resignation. A maid. At least that was something.

His eyes followed her fingers as they combed through her wavy brown strands, the longest hairs brushing the base of her spine, and she smiled, trying to smother the embarrassment. She was a confident woman. He wouldn't ruffle her. The expression was closer to a grimace, though. "Sorry, um, I'm just a bit traumatised, I think."

He walked over and sat on the edge of the bed, observing but not touching her. She almost rued the distance between them. Maybe it was because of their last meeting at Elias's office.

"Because of the demon?" he said.

"I guess." She cringed. "I'm still lost about everything."

He nodded, shuffling closer and placing his palm near her knee, a thread's breadth away. "I know, it wasn't supposed to happen this way, but when Elias and I realised who you were to us, we got too caught up in it all."

"Not your assistant, then."

His raining laughter eclipsed her, and she could have melted away from the heat her body radiated.

"I think Elias only hired you because he recognised your bond without realising it." He laughed again. "I read your application. You had no prior experience, and for Elias, that's an automatic rejection."

"Our bond? Mr. Ambrose hated me. Until a few days ago, he treated me like any other shitty boss would."

Kian winced, a shadow of anger crossing his eyes before letting it drift away again. "I won't speak for him; he can explain himself when we meet with him soon."

"How soon?" She caught herself straightening from unexpected excitement and forcibly simmered down. Why was she so fucking eager to see the asshat that had stressed her out for weeks now? *Stop it, Sylvie.*

Kian's throat bobbed as he swallowed, and she homed in on the movement like a predator.

Her flare of desire filled her with anger, and she bit her inner cheek. These mixed emotions were going to drive her insane.

"As soon as you're strong enough to travel," he said, interrupting her thoughts. "It takes a lot out of humans to cross realms, especially into fae territory," he grumbled, rolling his eyes. "Kerensa shouldn't have brought you here. Elias will probably skin me for having time with you first."

Her brows furrowed, but she dismissed his strange musings with a shrug. "Well, thanks, I guess." He hadn't explained much. In fact, she only had more questions. Before asking any, her stomach gurgled, startling them both. She blanched, palming her abdomen.

"Is there anything here I can eat?"

Fear flitted across Kian's face, and he scratched his cheek. "Uh, it's not safe for humans to eat fae food," he said, turning away.

But they couldn't leave yet. So, she was going to starve. *Great.*

"So the stories humans write about your kind are true?" Sylvie had read plenty about faeries in a few particularly sexy books, but she wasn't ready to divulge that with a real prince of the fae.

Her heart sped up again as waves of realisation hit, her eyes flooding with tears, which she hid behind her trembling hands.

"What's wrong?" Kian asked, tucking a hair behind her ears as she choked on a whimper.

"I'm losing my mind, aren't I? This is all real, and I'm not even questioning anything. There has to be something wrong with me. Why am I not freaking out?" She lifted her head and searched Kian's eyes wildly. If it were a dream, now would be the time to wake up. *Why am I not waking up?*

He smiled and hooked a finger under her chin. "Take a deep breath."

She inhaled long and shakily before exhaling through pursed lips.

"That's it." His eyes crinkled as he watched her. He was beautiful. "The reason this isn't turning you mad, although now I'm not so convinced that is true …" He paused as borderline hysterical laughter burst from her lips, and she swiped her wet cheeks.

He continued, smiling, "Is that I have been priming your brain the second I recognised you as mine."

The last word came out as a whisper, but the effect on Sylvie was scorching. Her core throbbed as her brain replayed that word again and again.

Mine.

Elias had said the same thing, and the effect was mind-altering. Never did she think she'd be one of those women who liked the possessive alpha shit.

She tried to fight for the confident, independent woman she thought she was. "Priming? Like mind control?"

He winced. "In a sense, but you already believed; I just made it easier to accept." His searching look, like he saw deeper than she liked, warmed her, and her mental walls trembled.

Hell no. There were things better left caged. Shaking her head, she scampered across the bed and wrapped her arms around herself, willing the swirling desire to ebb.

"It's natural to feel this way," Kian said, walking around to meet her before she bolted for the door.

She blew out a breath and stared up at him. There was no running, not that she even wanted to, but she asked with as much sass as she could muster, "Can I get changed now?"

His eyes flickered over her sheer sleep-wear and he spun, walking to a dark wood cupboard against the wall and pulling the doors open wide. Sylvie couldn't see inside, but Kian reached in and plucked an item off a hanger before draping it across her lap. The elegant fawn-coloured dress with delicate white lace made her gasp.

"This is—"

"Yours," he finished for her, turning and heading for the door. "Call me when you're dressed, and I will take you for a walk through the gardens."

She nodded, pulling the dress to her chest, her cheeks reddening. It was stunning. And it wasn't Fern's. She could get used to this, even if he was just trying to distract her.

"Oh, and don't give anyone your name while you're here, Princess." He offered a half-smile and left the room, closing the door behind him.

A few moments passed and when he didn't return, she threw her head back and flopped onto the bed, hugging the dress to her chest with a tentative smile.

"This is insane. These people are insane." Her new mantra continued in her head as she gulped huge lungful's of air and sat back up. She looked for a zipper of some kind but found nothing. She frowned, staring at the tiny neck hole. *How the—*

"Uh. Kian? How does this thing open?"

Warm laughter sounded from behind the door, and she blushed and rolled her eyes. *Stupid heart.* Her belly growled. "Stupid stomach."

"Just put it over your head, and it will slip on. It's enchanted to fit your body."

She scoffed before tentatively lifting it above her head, stabbing her hands through the armholes and hovering it above her. In a blink, the fabric slid down her body and hugged her around her torso, arms, and collar. She laughed, half shocked, half delighted, as she stared at herself.

"Why don't we have this kind of thing in Erus?" she muttered. She'd read plenty of books with magic and spells, powers and heroes, but it wasn't real. Humans didn't have real magic, despite what some pious followers of the old gods believed. Kian's soft chuckle echoed again.

She palmed her cheeks as he said, "Are you decent?"

"Yes, but do you have any shoes I can wear?"

The door cracked open, and his smiling face greeted her. "It's better to be barefoot in the fae realm," he said. "The soil heals, and we need you back to your full strength before we portal back to Erus."

She grumbled, looking at her feet and wiggling her polished toes. They would not stay pretty for much longer.

"Why are you wearing shoes, then?" she argued, walking to the door, the swish of her dress like music to her ears.

He turned away and walked along the hall towards a pair of double doors without answering. She frowned. Had she upset him? "Are you okay?"

"I'm fine, Princess. Stay close to me." He reached out his hand, and she took it like she'd done so for years, noting the small smile from his side profile. *Why does this feel so natural?*

Hopefully, her palm wouldn't grow sweaty, though it didn't seem he would care. With a sigh of resignation, she interlaced her fingers with his. She was supposed to be breaking his heart, not holding his hand. They merged perfectly too. *Oh, hell.*

"So," she said, trying to regain common sense. "Why can't I tell anyone my name again?" She vaguely remembered the reason from her old, racy faerie books—something about power and manipulation.

"A name is a source of energy," he said, pushing the door open and waiting for her to come through. "Giving another being the knowledge of one of your energy sources gives them ways to control you. It's as simple as that."

It didn't sound that simple.

"So, I shouldn't give you my name, then?"

Kian looked down at her with a slight smirk. "I already know your name, little one," he jested before turning serious, "but no, you shouldn't *give* it to me until I gain your trust."

She scoffed before letting her gaze wander around them. The stone halls were windowless, but the roof had consistent holes where sunlight poured in. Rain too, as Sylvie couldn't make out any glass between them and the sky above.

"We're really in the fae realm right now?"

"Ilfaem, yes. Though the court we are currently in is my birthplace—Evergreen. It's the heart of Ilfaem and the surrounding courts. Ice, Moon, Sun, and Stone."

"Pretty basic names."

Kian smirked. "Translated from Ancient High Fae. Ctirac, Alunr, Rolas, and Leubodr."

Sylvie's brows scrunched. She didn't think her mouth could even make those sounds.

"Will I get to see them?"

"Not if I can help it. My mother may be queen, but the lords and ladies of the four outer courts are not overly welcoming to my family."

"Why?"

She realised too late how intrusive the question was and waited for him to admonish her, but he didn't.

"Let's just say there wasn't always one queen for all five courts, but when the Fates give you a role, you take it." *Well, that isn't cryptic or anything.* She sensed that was all Kian was going to offer her, though, and kept quiet. He squeezed her hand and guided her to a set of stairs. A gentle breeze ruffled her skirts, and she peered at the open doorway below where a small statue held the door ajar in the shape of a pixie. When she focused, it appeared to move, its mouth pulling into a mischievous grin. She smiled back warily, and Kian ushered her forward. Outside. When her gaze lifted from the shimmering stone, she gasped.

Rows of manicured flowers bordered the stone passage before them, with dozens of bumbling flying creatures pollinating and eating from them. The sea of colours faded in ombre blends, and she could have fainted from the garden's elegance and faultless design.

Tall swaying trees with dangling vines stole her attention from the end of the path, a giant swing suspended from one of their limbs.

She looked at Kian with eyes full of wonder.

Growing up in Sterling her entire life, she had never seen so much greenery in one place, and her body buzzed.

"Can I?" She didn't elaborate, but somehow he knew. Maybe he read her mind. Gods, she hoped not.

He nodded, though, releasing her hand, and she darted ahead of him. She let her fingers brush along the velvet petals and gasped as small humming creatures with humanoid bodies flitted out, buzzing and shaking their tiny fists at her. A soft laugh escaped before she could stop it. This place was beyond her wildest dreams. She flitted along, her bare feet enjoying the soft rolling friction of the stones underfoot.

When Sylvie reached the tree, she pressed her palms against it and breathed in the woodsy scent. It was so rich. Real. When her head rested between her hands on the bark, the smallest zap of electricity tickled her forehead. She pulled back, staring at the tree accusingly.

"What was that for?" she huffed. It wasn't painful, but she wasn't in the mood for abrupt sensations. She turned and noted Kian staring at her with a quizzical frown.

"What happened?" he said.

She shrugged with a growing frown of her own. "It zapped me."

Kian blinked, staring from Sylvie to the tree, and sighed. "You're quite the mystery, aren't you, Princess?"

He didn't make it sound like a good thing. Her attention dropped to Kian's hand, his wrist, where she had sliced him only a day before, the raised scar a permanent reminder of what she'd done.

"So … You have gold blood."

Kian exhaled through his nose a faint smile on his lips. "Yes. All pure-blooded fae do."

When he didn't continue, she nodded, gesturing to the mark on his wrist. "I'm sorry for that, by the way. I didn't think."

He pinched his sleeve and tugged it down, covering the scar. "No, it's good. I'm glad you know how to protect yourself."

She looked back at his face. "I do, kind of." Her last encounter with the blanket demon disproved that, but everyone had an off day. "But it's still not okay, Kian. I never wanted to hurt you. I mean, I did, at the time, a little, but I don't anymore."

He paused, lips parted, something flashing across his face, something painful, before he nodded. "Then I am grateful for your apology, Princess."

He looked over his shoulder at something past the zappy tree and smiled. "Here," he said, taking her hand again. "I have something to show you."

SIX

Kian tugged Sylvie past the two-seater tree swing and into a deep thicket, the earnestness from him palpable. She bit her lip to stop the smile. The pointed leaves of the underbrush, though, scratched her bare forearms as she pushed through after him. "What are these?" A branch smacked her across the face. "Ow! Are you trying to gouge out my eyes?"

Kian placed his hand in front of her to catch the brunt of the sharp leaves. "They're a healing plant."

She plucked a prickle from her hand and crossed her arms in front of her face, eyebrows rising in disbelief before she scoffed. Plants that hurt before they healed. That had to be some profound message.

She trudged on for a few more seconds and narrowly avoided another slice to her eye before she tumbled out into a clearing. Kian scooped her up, placing her back on her feet and she gripped his hand in hers as she took in the scene of a giant rolling paddock of calf-high grass and ferns.

"Wow." The swaying fronds tickled her legs. She smiled, bending to pull a strand from the ground and lifting it to her nose. The scent of fresh pasture and something sweeter was like nothing she had experienced. She almost wanted to eat it, but that was the hunger pangs talking. Ancient trees with trunks thicker than her office flanked the field, peering curiously down at her.

"This is beautiful, Kian. Thank you." She spun, wrapping her arms around his taut waist and squeezing before turning and running to the centre of the field. Her thoughts snagged briefly on how good it had felt to be pressed against him as she slowed. Her head spun, but it felt good. Weird, but good. *Maybe I have lost my mind after all.*

Beneath her bare feet, the soil softened and the grass danced around her. She flopped down with a sigh and starfished on her back, staring at the cloudless sky. The sun snuggled behind the trees, settling in for the night and turning the sky violet and azure. Sylvie hummed. It was later than she thought. How long had she slept for? The giant trees swayed in and out of her vision as if waving hello.

She waved back. A few moments later, the grass crunched and swished as Kian approached. With a smile, he lay beside her, tucking the long strands of green under his head to look at her unobstructed.

"Is this where you take all your conquests?" she asked, a flash of something ugly twisting in her heart before she pushed it down.

His expression flickered. "No. Only you."

She pursed her lips, trying not to let herself get too happy. Too eager.

"You have had other partners before, right?" she said.

She'd had plenty. Plenty didn't even cover it. It was a shock she was even single. Her last partner had broken up with her right before she got the job at Ambrose Enterprise. Talk about divine timing.

When he didn't answer her, she focused on him again, the dulling tone to his skin and glazed eyes triggering alarm bells in her head.

"Just one," he said. "A long time ago."

"Are you okay?"

He took a deep breath and gave her a tired grin, sprinkling a clump of grass shoots in her hair. "With you? Always."

Sylvie smiled despite herself, grabbing the grass and throwing it at him, her fingers halting as they touched his face, the glowing brown skin heating under her caress.

"You really are so perfect," she said, as if the words had forced themselves from her mouth.

He swallowed and turned his gaze upwards. "I'm really not." His jaw ticked a few times before she rolled to her belly and peered down at him, her side flush against his.

"Why do you say that? You've been nothing but kind to me since I met you." She'd tried her hardest to avoid his tempting beauty, but she couldn't. She wanted to kiss him. Badly. Was she being desperate? It had been a long time, though. Even her vibrator had started malfunctioning from overuse. And she knew he'd be a fucking good lay. He'd get her off so fast.

Kian blinked up at her, brushing her hair behind her ears, his touch making her tremble.

An easy smile played across his lips. "You look beautiful when you disappear in your mind."

Sylvie's mouth twisted, fighting a smile, and she tapped him lightly on the shoulder in playful reprimand. But he flinched. She paused, fingers poised above him. "Sorry. Did I hurt you?"

"No," he said, averting his gaze for a second before reclaiming her eyes. "You're just not what I expected." He stroked her cheek with his thumb and let it trail to the corner of her mouth.

Sylvie felt a sizzling heat bloom in her core, and she turned her face, letting the finger caress her lower lip. She kissed it softly and closed her eyes at Kian's intake of breath.

Fuck it.

She pushed herself up and threw her thigh across his lap, straddling him and lowering her lips to his. At first, panic gripped her when he tensed, but his hungry mouth latched on to hers, his hands clasping her hips tightly. She moaned into his mouth, her underwear dampening as their tongues danced.

She was wrong. He'd be the best lay she'd ever had.

Kian hardened beneath his clothes, the stiffening rod pressing between Sylvie's legs as she ran her hands along his arms and down his sides, desperate to touch his body. Her fingers were walking along his waistband, aching to trail upwards, when Kian clasped her wrists in a tight squeeze and tugged them between their chests. Their lips detached, swollen and wanting, but Sylvie sat up, pulling Kian with her, and climbed off him with heavy breaths.

"Sorry."

"Don't apologise."

They spoke simultaneously, and Sylvie swallowed, a flush branding her cheeks.

"We should go back," Kian said, standing and holding his hand out to her. She noticed the slight tremor before clasping his wrist and pulling herself up.

As she wandered back through the scratching plants, a trail of ice travelled down her back. She shuddered as they headed towards the pebbled path and cast her eyes towards the thicket. Nothing. She sighed, facing Kian as he walked slightly in front, his gaze scanning ahead, unaware of her discomfort.

Another jolt shot down her spine, and she spun, pebbles flying everywhere as she spotted the violet eyes of Kerensa spying from the giant tree. She was perched on a low-lying branch as thick as her thigh, looking completely otherworldly. Sylvie stared for a moment too long, surprised by the curious furrow on Kerensa's brow as she inspected the pair.

Before Sylvie could decipher the expression, she bumped into Kian's back, and he spun her to face him. "What is it?"

She thought about telling him about his spying sister but decided against it. "I was just admiring the tree one last time."

He bought it.

"I could bring you back here tomorrow if you'd like?"

She bit her lower lip and let the image of Kerensa drift from her mind. "I would like that."

Despite the abrupt end to their kiss in the meadow, a soft smile settled on her downturned face as he escorted her back to his room.

He showed her the en suite bathroom and found an excuse to leave the room with a genuine, understanding smile. She could've kissed him. Instead, she pictured doing so vividly over and over as she stared at the closed bedroom door.

Finally, listening to her distressed stomach and swollen bladder, Sylvie ran into the bathroom and locked the door. Hoisting her dress up, she did her business while staring dumbfounded at the decor.

More fucking plants, of course, but the skylight above her head radiated soft, warm sunlight on her face. As she stared upwards, she realised she hadn't seen a single light switch or electrical fitting for her stay.

No electricity.

Why they wouldn't utilise electricity intrigued her, but she was envious. No light pollution, no mindless scrolling on Goldtech devices, and no more emails! Sylvie didn't miss her job one bit. If they found a solution for her lack of food options, she could consider staying. There was nothing back on Erus for her anyway.

Her rat shit apartment hardly held any appeal, and neither did her belongings inside it. She was simple, and disposable income wasn't on the cards for foster system age out like her.

Finishing up, she undressed and climbed into the shower.

She used every soap his shower rack offered, and it made her smell like a walking meadow. When she climbed out, she borrowed a fluffy white towel.

"Shit." She stared at her dirty clothes on the floor. Those wouldn't do, even if they weren't that dirty. Then, after one last second of indecision, she peeked her head from the bathroom door. The main room appeared empty, so she drifted towards the wardrobe.

Her hand brushed against the strange handle right as the bedroom door flew open, and she recoiled, the fright causing her to lose her grip on her towel for a split-second—the exact split-second Kian walked in and looked directly at her.

Sylvie yelped, yanking the towel back to cover herself while Kian spun away, hands across his eyes. She panted, cheeks blooming the same colour as the flower garden as she buried her face in her hand.

The rushing blood in her ears covered the sound of Kian's approach, and she jumped as a soft graze of fingers trailed across her forehead. Her flushed face tilted to peek at him, and his dark eyes regarded her. "If you'd told me you wanted a shower, I would have brought you some clothes."

She wordlessly gestured to the wardrobe, and he smiled.

"I'll get some," he said. "But not from there." He left the room for a few minutes as she rocked on her feet, then returned with underwear and a flowing nightgown.

"Thank you," she said, taking the items while clutching her towel extra tight over her breasts.

He smirked and shook his head. "You shouldn't thank me, but since it's your first day here, I suppose I will overlook it and not consider you indebted to me."

Sylvie blushed harder and spun, hiding her smile and scrunching her eyes shut. Something about being indebted to him turned her on. There was nothing like getting on your knees and repaying—

"Princess?"

She spun back towards Kian's mischievous grin. "It will be night soon. Get some rest. I'll be just across the hall." With that, he turned and left the room while she dressed and tucked herself into bed, trying to ignore the returning gnawing hunger in her gut.

SEVEN

The next morning, heinously early from a gurgling belly waking her and halting any attempts to sleep in, Sylvie perched on the wooden tree swing, patting the spot beside her, beckoning Kian.

He smiled and sat, leaving a small space between them. Sylvie suppressed a frown as she scooted sideways until their thighs touched, and even through two layers of fabric, his warmth caressed her.

He cleared his throat and murmured, "I'm not sure that's a good idea."

"Why not?"

He didn't seem to have a problem with it the day before.

"The more we touch, the faster the bond will grow, and Elias will be displeased if I make it harder for him to …" he trailed off, wringing his hands.

Kian had never used such vulnerable mannerisms with her before. The lip drawn between his teeth made her want to reach up and pull it free, perhaps with her fingers, or with her mouth. Her mind conjured images of their lips meeting again, a flurry of tongue and teeth, stroking and suckling, and she slid her thigh away from his.

"To what?" she asked, swallowing her lust.

"Nothing. I shouldn't be filling your head with these things."

She huffed and let her gaze linger on the flowered path. "What do you think he's doing right now?"

Her mind conjured an image of her brooding, always frowning boss, yet her underwear dampened slightly. She squeezed her thighs together and folded her hands in her lap.

"It's only been a few hours for him since we found out about your disappearance. Time works differently here."

"I see." She pushed her feet into the grass beneath the swing. They swayed back and forth, Kian's legs mimicking hers.

She could see more of the palace from their seat, along with a small glass house. Inside, people tended to tiny saplings and plucked ripe fruits. Along the ground around it sprouted dozens of what looked like strawberry plants, their vibrant red fruit drawing her gaze.

Her stomach rumbled, and she licked her lips when a loud crunching assaulted her ears. She panned her eyes to the door the sound had come from, and they widened, spotting the queen's glower and the subtle warning flashing across her face. Sylvie swallowed, but before she could avert her gaze, the queen spun and disappeared back into the palace.

Sylvie looked to see if Kian noticed, but his eyes were closed, and his chest rose and fell in slow breaths; how he was sleeping sitting upright baffled her. He must have been exhausted. Only in this state could she see the sallow colour of his cheeks and the soft hollowing around his eyes he hid beneath dazzling smiles.

Her face softened, her mouth turning into a small frown as she turned her body towards him. She resisted the urge to touch his face, trail her fingers along his muscled chest, rub his shoulders, or kiss his—

"Stop staring," Kian's tired voice grumbled, causing her to jump.

She turned and stared at her lap before muttering, "Your mother." She stated it as if the words were a complete sentence. Kian exhaled and shifted in his seat as Sylvie continued, unperturbed, "She's pretty intimidating."

"That's an understatement," he said with a smile. He leaned back farther, as if getting comfortable, and closed his eyes again.

Sylvie nodded and chuckled softly, unsure how to continue her line of thinking. "Yeah. Well, theoretically, if she demanded something of someone, and they didn't do it, what would happen?"

His eyes snapped open in an instant, and he turned towards her. "What did she ask of you?"

Sylvie tried to backtrack, but Kian's firm gaze pinned her to the spot, her cheeks flushing a soft pink.

"I didn't really understand everything she asked of me. But I'm pretty sure she doesn't want me to be with you. Not that we would, right? Be together, I mean."

All his talk of bonding made it seem like they were destined to be together, but that was ridiculous. There was no such thing as destiny.

He clenched his teeth and forced air through his lips. "Would that be so bad?"

Sylvie jerked back and flushed more. "No, I mean, I didn't mean it like that. I just thought, I—" she stuttered and touched her throat, willing saliva to coat her drying mouth as she swallowed painfully. "I just don't understand any of this."

"And you don't need to," he said, tracing his finger across her cheek, causing a drop in her stomach and a flutter to tickle her rib cage.

"Soon, we'll be back with Elias, and he can explain anything you don't know."

She frowned. "Why can he tell me, but you can't?"

He stared at the brown waves framing her face, letting them loop around his index finger. "That's the way we decided it should be. He—he's older," Kian said as if answering everything.

"Older?"

"Yes, Princess. Why do you insist on asking so many questions? Perhaps I should have let you be a panicked catatonic mess for this entire stay." He huffed, pulling away and crossing his arms.

She huffed back and walked towards the palace, her brows knitting together. "You are ... you are ... argh!" Groaning, she spun and nearly fell backwards upon seeing him directly behind her.

"I'm what?" he taunted, taking a dangerous step closer. She tried to hold steady, but her feet betrayed her, as did the rising heat between her legs.

"You speak in riddles."

"Yes, I'm fae. It's common knowledge."

"Why? Why can't you just answer me?" Her voice rose higher, and she was sure the queen would hear her wherever she was—probably spying on them. "Why can't you just take me home now? I feel fine!"

Despite the rising tone between them, anger wasn't fuelling the conversation. And anyone watching close enough would see the trembling anticipation from her. She ached. One touch and she would undo her resolve completely.

Her stomach rumbled again, and she crossed her arms. "And I'm also fucking starving, Kian."

Perhaps it was the hunger clouding her mind or the rush to dissipate the undeniable sexual energy fizzing between them. Still, she stomped over to the strawberry patch, plucked the fattest berry, and shoved it into her mouth, biting the supple flesh.

Immediately, the sweet, juicy tang coated her tongue, and she swallowed, ignoring the shocked shout from the male behind her. He instantly swatted the rest of the fruit from her hand and squeezed her cheeks, making her mouth open painfully.

"Ow!" she yelled, the precious berry flesh tumbling to the dirt.

"Spit it out!" he demanded, shaking her shoulder with the other hand. She stared at the fallen fruit, and her frown tripled until her forehead hurt. Grabbing Kian's wrists, she pulled herself free and swallowed the small piece still in her mouth, then poked her tongue out like a defiant child.

Kian's face quivered in shock and rage. "What have you done?"

"What?" she slurred. "I feel fine!"

She did feel fine; more than fine. She actually felt a little drunk.

"You aren't in pain?" Kian asked, gripping her chin in his hands as he peered into her eyes.

She shook her head and gasped as another Kian appeared in distorted waves. When her head stilled, the second Kian disappeared.

"It's just a stupid strawberry!" she said, reaching for another and falling to her knees. The ground swayed under her hands, mocking her.

"No, it isn't." Kian groaned, scooping her up. "It's a hallucinogen."

She looked at his morphing face, his eyes turning black and horns sprouting from his short waves of hair. Terror filled her mind, and she kicked and screamed in his arms, pushing his face away with her shaking hands.

"Stop!" he growled, pausing as he followed her eye line. Then, with a tongue click, Kian lifted her higher, hoisting her over his shoulder.

Unable to see his face, she relaxed, burying her head into the soft fabric in front of her. The colour and the scent hypnotised her.

"How much for this?" she asked, giggling. The rippling fabric didn't respond, and she pouted. "Can I have it for free?" She wrapped her arms around it.

It stiffened slightly.

"Yes? Okay good. I like this colour." Sighing contentedly, Sylvie let her body swing from side to side. "Where am I, again?"

A strange voice chirped in her ear. "What happened to it, Prince?"

A rumble vibrated under Sylvie's chest. "She swallowed some verferum. Get me the antidote, Cedar, please."

"Yes, of course."

The scent of the body beneath her made her mouth water; it was like the soil after a cleansing rain storm. Burying her face deeper, she moaned, twisting her body closer, needing to climb inside it.

Her hands tugged at the bottom of the fabric, and she pulled it upwards, seeing a line of brown skin.

She touched it and gasped as raised parallel scars appeared along the visible section. Blinking, Sylvie went to pull the material higher when she abruptly flew away from the pretty fabric and abused flesh and onto a soft cloud.

Sylvie writhed, trying to orient herself, and spotted the seething demon from earlier. This time, she wasn't afraid. He was hurt. Someone hurt her little beastie.

"Who hurt you?" Her eyes shut despite her fighting to keep them open. She pried them apart with her fingers. "I'll kill them. I could. I—" She bit her tongue. "Can I see? Maybe I can heal you." She rolled on her belly and slid backwards until her knees hit the floor. Pressure under her arms hoisted her up and sat her back on the cloud.

"Stop moving," the demon said.

"I bet I could heal you if I tried hard enough," she retorted. "I never get sick. Or scarred." Maybe she was magical. She stared hard at her fingers, waiting for them to do something. A sparkle? A fizz? They wiggled lightly as she oohed and ahhed.

A strange little rock troll disturbed her musings and came in with a cup in his hand filled with blue liquid.

"Thank you," the demon addressed him before turning his black eyes on Sylvie. "Drink this, now."

"I thought you said no food here. Food is bad. No, no, no!" She smacked her hands along the cloud before sliding to the floor with the white mist all around her.

The demon stared. "I just made that bed."

Bed. A bed? No, it was her cloud, her fluffy misty cloud.

"Shhh …" She put her finger to her lips, giggling again until a firm grip on her chin made her squeak.

"Ow, stop it, demon! I don't like you." Then, as she opened her mouth to chastise him, a hot liquid swirled down her throat, and she gagged, swallowing some and choking on the rest.

Her coughing sprayed the blue dye across the demon's pretty fabric, and he sighed, scooping her into his arms again. "You are going to feel silly once you're better," he said. "Go to sleep, and I'll find you some food. You're high, which means you aren't all human."

He sighed again, rubbing his hands across his horned head. "Wait here."

She would wait there, but only because she couldn't move. He left her on the floor in his cloud-bed, still covered in hot blue ink. She sighed, letting her body fall to the side. The second her head hit the floor, she was out.

EIGHT

Loud voices from the hall roused Sylvie from the worst hangover she'd ever had in her whole fucking life.

Her eyeballs felt ready to pop from her head, and the arguing outside the door only made it so much worse. She pressed her hands into her eyelids to ease the throbbing as she processed the words being spoken.

"—she will be here by sunset, and you will accept her." The queen. She sounded pissed.

"I will not! She is not my fated." Kian.

"She has been your betrothed since you were children. Not so long ago, you were thanking me. Now, this!"

Sylvie's waterline burned as she imagined the queen gesturing to the door.

To the messy, hungover woman behind it.

"Stop, Mother."

"No. She is not fit to rule. Just come and greet her and see how you feel." The queen's voice took on a pleading quality, and Sylvie's stomach sank.

The elusive *she* was Kian's betrothed, and they had known each other since childhood. Sylvie didn't stand a chance.

She sniffed, surprised by the disappointment and pain cramping her insides. It was more than hunger this time.

"You don't understand. You've never experienced this before."

Even before the queen shrieked, Sylvie winced. That was not the right thing to say.

"How dare you? Do you think I never loved your father? We may not have been fated, but my duty was to protect this realm, whatever the cost. Have I failed to teach you this? Tell me before I trust the safety of my people in the hands of a love-drunk fool."

Sylvie lay utterly still, praying they would leave. She was hearing far too much, and every sentence stabbed into her body and brain like a hot iron.

What was worse were all the memories of her post-berry-eating hallucination returning to her in bursts. She suddenly remembered her ramblings of being magical, and she groaned loudly, forgetting to suppress it.

The voices outside abruptly stopped, and the doorknob turned. "I need to check on her." A pause. "I'll be there."

The three words burrowed into Sylvie's heart like a knife. Why did she care so much? He was supposed to be with the other female, so why did it feel like the worst betrayal of her life? She hadn't even felt this way when she found her first boyfriend of three years in bed with her old roommate.

The door opened, and Kian closed it quickly behind him before walking over and crouching beside her. "Are you okay?"

She lowered her hand and blinked up at him with a half-smile. There was no point in letting him know her pain. Kian had to do what was right for his people and his mother. He'd only met her days ago, so he had no obligations to care for her, stay with her, love her …

"Dammit," she said, blinking back tears.

"What is it?" Kian asked, brushing a fat drop off her cheek.

"My head hurts." She hoped the half-truth would do.

He offered his hand, and she took it, slowly wobbling to her feet. She sat back on the edge of the bed and took a deep breath. "I'm sorry about earlier."

Kian just smiled and waved her off, pulling a small platter from the bedside and placing it on her lap. An assortment of fruits, crackers, a thick soup, and slices of bread lay before her. She looked at Kian warily.

"So I *can* eat the food?"

He nodded, sitting beside her. "We weren't sure how much fae blood you possessed, but it has to be substantial. If it weren't, the verferum would have killed you."

"We?"

"Elias and I. He thought it best we didn't overwhelm you with too many bombshells."

"Oh." She picked a fat pink grape off the platter, eager to move on from the thought of dying from her impulsive choices. And the news that she wasn't completely human. That fact had her fingers trembling. "But these are fine?"

"Yes."

She bit into it tentatively and sighed at the bursting juice across her tongue. The relief from the easing pain in her belly and head almost made her eyes roll back. "This is magic."

"Yes. Need I remind you where we are right now?"

"No," Sylvie responded wryly, popping another grape between her teeth. Once the plate was all but licked clean, she took a deep breath and faced Kian.

His warm smile replaced the sullen look. "About one more day, and I'll take you home."

She nodded and swallowed, glad for some good news as she eyed him warily. "And what about you? Will you return here?"

His eyes flashed with darkness before turning away from her. Touchy subject. *Good.* She shouldn't be the only one feeling this pain. The weight of his emotions, though, had her placing a hand on his knee and squeezing. It wasn't really his fault.

He sighed. "You heard?"

She pulled back her hand, tucking it in her lap. "Yeah. I don't know who she is, but I'm sure she's wonderful, and I don't want to get in the way of that or your responsibilities."

His head whipped to her, hurt dripping from his furrowed brow to the quiver of his lips that pulled down in a contemptuous frown. She jerked back at the sudden movement, the platter clattering onto the floor as he said, "Never think that. Ever." His face twisted as if fighting an internal battle. "You don't know what you're saying."

She stammered, blinking back embarrassment. "I-I'm sorry."

Realisation appeared in his eyes, and he sighed, shaking his head. "No. Don't apologise. I shouldn't have said anything." He stood, running his hands across his head and bent to pick up the forgotten platter.

"I'll see you soon," he finally said, leaving the room without another word.

Fuck. *Fuck!*

Hours passed, and Sylvie lay staring at the ceiling, silent tears occasionally running into her ears as microscopic pollen particles irritated her ducts. That's what it was. Allergies. With a bang, the door to her room whipped open and slammed against the wall. Her head snapped to the side, unsure of what to expect when Kerensa stomped in. "Get dressed."

She stared back at the roof. Maybe Kerensa could take her home.

"In what?" she said. Her current attire was still stained a vibrant blue, and she didn't exactly have spare clothes.

Kerensa hissed, storming towards her, and she had no time to move as the female plucked a strand of hair from Sylvie's head and stomped to the wardrobe, yanking the doors open hard enough to make the hinges scream. Throwing the hair inside, she looked back at Sylvie for a moment before pulling a deep emerald gown out and tossing it. Sylvie caught it and stammered as Kerensa walked out and slammed the bedroom door shut again. "What the fuck?"

"Get dressed!"

Goosebumps ran down Sylvie's back as she hurriedly removed her soiled gown and replaced it with the velvety dress that hugged her curves, highlighting her bust in the plunging neckline.

Kerensa pushed the door open again and jerked her head. "Hurry. She's here."

"Who?"

Kerensa gave her a long, hard stare and bared her teeth. "Do you want him or not? Because *she's* about to take him."

Sylvie cast her a withering look before running her hands through her brown waves, trying to untangle any rogue knots.

"You look fine," Kerensa hissed before peering back along the hallway. "So? Are you coming?"

Sylvie rolled her shoulders back and nodded.

"Good, now move."

Kerensa ushered Sylvie quickly to the throne room. Too focused on suppressing the despair building in her chest, there was no time to absorb the beauty.

Kerensa's statement about the female taking Kian made her seem like an unconquerable foe about to steal his heart.

Of course, his heart didn't belong to her, and it wasn't her place to claim it, so why did the thought make her want to drop to her knees and scream?

"Keep your guard up, and don't talk," Kerensa said, wrapping her hand around Sylvie's upper arm. The grip was surprisingly gentle as she guided her through the throne room's doors and into the vast space.

The queen stood regally at the base of the throne, with Kian in his royal purple at her side. The light behind his eyes was gone. Sylvie's lips parted. He didn't want this.

When she spotted the object of his gaze, her shoulders stooped.

She was both Kian and Sylvie's opposite in so many ways. Her skin, the colour of milk, shone starkly, and her grey eyes floated across the room as she smiled. Her soft champagne gown fanned out behind her as she strolled arm-in-arm with a plainer-looking but still beautiful female.

"My Queen," she called.

Fuck. Even her voice was elegant.

"And Kian, it has been so long! You have become a man," she gushed.

Sylvie wanted to be sick as Kerensa escorted her towards the small group. When the echo of their footsteps reached them, the female spun in a gentle motion, making her light-blond hair flow over her shoulder like water.

The queen's mouth puckered, and she exclaimed. "It is wonderful to see you again, dear Lady Lazuli and Handmaid Zephrinah. I'm so glad you responded so quickly to my summons."

Zephrinah bowed, keeping her back stiff, while Lazuli turned back with a beaming smile and nodded. "Of course! My father was glad to hear of your wishes to honour your agreement. After not hearing anything for so long, we had almost lost hope."

Kian remained silent, offering a tight-lipped smile as his mother smiled too widely.

"Of course. I had only withheld my response as Kian has been spending much time in the human realm, and I was unsure of his return."

"Yes," Lazuli said, swaying on her feet. "What brought you back here?"

The queen moved aside and grabbed Lazuli's hand, avoiding the razor-sharp nails at the end. "Oh, come closer, dear. He is your future husband, after all. No need to be coy. I know you are already well acquainted."

Bile rose in Sylvie's throat as the queen's eyes lingered on her.

Lazuli stepped forwards and slid her hands into his, turning to face Kerensa and Sylvie hovering to the side. Zephrinah slowly disappeared into the fringes of the space until Sylvie couldn't make out her position at all.

Neat trick.

Sylvie wanted to disappear right then, too. But her eyes glued to a tiny bead of gold liquid trailing down Kian's wrist from where Lazuli's nails must have sliced. Her smug smile sent a fiery rage through Sylvie's body. Careless bitch.

Lazuli turned her soft gaze from Sylvie to Kian and back again with a smile, her eyes crinkling in the corners. "I'm sorry, but who might you be?"

Before she spoke her name, which she was absolutely about to, Kerensa stepped forward. "She's Kian's fated."

Surprise crossed Lazuli's face before she replaced it with hurt. "Oh, how terribly unfortunate."

Kian's eyes remained glued to the floor as Lazuli squeezed his hand a few times, the pearl of golden blood dripping on the floor.

Nobody noticed besides Sylvie as Lazuli continued, "I haven't heard of such a thing since the Division. How can you be so sure?"

Kian's jaw tightened as his mother spoke up. "We aren't certain, of course. Only the fated pair can feel the connection. But you know this," she said with a slight smirk.

"Mm, yes, Kian, after years of fated being practically extinct, how could you know she means that much to you?" Lazuli looked Sylvie up and down again, her brows furrowing softly. "She is a beautiful wee thing, but obviously not suited for the role of queen."

Kerensa's grip tightened on Sylvie's bicep, and she growled, "So, this is how it will be?"

"How it must be," the queen replied.

Without another word, Kerensa spun and dragged Sylvie from the room faster than she had time to look back.

NINE

"You won't be safe here anymore." Kerensa stalked across her room as Sylvie stood in the doorway shaking. "I need to take you back."

The fae growled and balled her hands into fists before punching the wall. Concrete and vines crumbled and dropped to the floor.

"Why do you even care?" Sylvie asked, her heart squeezing. "You didn't even want me here to start with."

Kerensa spun, her eyes flashing red before she ground her teeth and breathed harshly. "I saw you two, alright. Fated pairs are rare. I've never met a pair, but after seeing the connection between you, I know it is real. And it is sacred. My mother refuses to see what is in front of her."

Sylvie stared at her hands and lifted a shoulder. "I don't know what you want me to say." Her mind wandered to the golden blood trailing from Kian's wrist, and she shuddered. "Surely Lazuli would make a better partner for Kian if he's supposed to be king or whatever. Plus, your mother hates me, so there's that." She'd been with people whose parents loathed her. It never ended well.

Kerensa hissed and shook her head violently. "My mother is callous and blinded by duty. Now it is too late. Plus, I fucking hate that little witch. She used to tear pages from the oracles' tomes and blame me when my mother found them strewn about the palace." Kerensa stomped towards her and wrenched the door handle to the room at her back.

Sylvie quickly slid out of the way. "She what? And your mother still wants her to be with Kian?"

Kerensa pulled the door open. "She never believed me. Said I was jealous my father chose Kian to be betrothed and not me." She shook her head, disgust marring her features. "Stay here. I need to get some things for our travel."

With that, she disappeared, leaving Sylvie alone with her thoughts. Maybe it would be fine. Maybe Kian would be able to break the betrothal. He could return to Erus with her—a runaway groom. What did that make her, though? The other female? No thanks.

After a few moments of silence, a soft, husky giggle echoed from under the door. Whispers followed.

Nosiness taking over, she pulled the door open and immediately spotted Lazuli backing into the opposite wall with Kian's head buried in her neck, his back to her. Jealousy spiked in Sylvie's chest.

Lazuli's cheeks were flushed, and her eyelids fluttered at half-mast.

Bedroom eyes.

Sylvie knew those well. "What the fuck?"

Kian turned to her, but his face was slack, expression empty. She shook her head, furious when her eyes flooded with tears. What was he doing? She wouldn't let the tears fall, not in front of them. She stepped back and slammed the door shut. "Fuck you both." Her heart hammered in her chest as the soft giggles continued, and she stormed towards the nearest window opening.

The pleasant evening breeze ruffled around her, and she tried to shut her mind off from the sounds of betrayal. But Kian's low voice, followed by a lusty moan, felt like knives in her ears. That's it. She was gone. Without thinking it through, she swung her legs over the window ledge. How could he? If she hadn't seen him with her own fucking eyes, she wouldn't have believed it. What a fool.

She looked down, relief filling her as she spotted the familiar flower path and jumped to the grass below. She landed softly despite the drop and stormed towards the tree swing. The moment she reached it, though, memories of her and Kian filled her mind, only to be replaced by that fucking *perfect* bitch, Lazuli.

"What a stupid name!" she spat, racing into the spiky brush. Nothing cleared her mind, even as plant spines sliced and cut at her exposed skin, teasing her with the pain that ultimately felt good as the healing properties swirled in her bloodstream.

After reaching the grass, she ran across the clearing, letting the dew-coated strands drench her dress, and found the closest tree. With the sun, long curled up below the horizon, she relied on the light of the moon—no, moons—and stars to light her path.

Sylvie had only seen the night sky with a purple-orange hue from the street light pollution her entire adult life. She couldn't remember the last time she saw a star. They were brighter here.

Pressing her back into the tree, she let herself sob. Nobody was near to hear her awful wails, so she refused to feel ashamed. She'd never once cried over a man. Though, he wasn't really a man. A fae prince. And she was just an uneducated, poor assistant. "What a joke."

Sniffling, Sylvie slid down until she was cradled by the ancient trunk in the darkness, her face pressed into its side.

Kerensa was probably looking for her, but the thought of hearing a single mewling, pleasure-filled moan from Lazuli made her stomach lurch.

"Fuck that bitch." She sniffled again.

The trees rustled in response, and she smiled through her snotty tears before wiping her velvet sleeve across her nose. The forest's silence lulled her into a calmer state until her eyes grew heavy, and her lids took a much-needed rest.

"Princess—"

"Let me wake her, move back."

Voices roused Sylvie from sleep, and she blinked at Kerensa's glowing purple eyes. *Terrifying.* Sylvie's heart rate sped up as they locked gazes, but she was too tired to move.

"Sorry I ran away," she mumbled, turning her face back into the tree.

A shuffle and growl sounded in her ears as Kerensa knelt before her. "We must go now. Hold on to me."

"Kerensa!" Kian's sharp tone startled Sylvie and she gasped, crawling backwards, away from them both.

"She doesn't want to see you, Ki. Go back to the palace."

"I need to speak with her."

The desperation in his voice tugged at Sylvie's heart, and she paused. "What do you want?" she asked, her voice thick with emotion.

Kerensa moved back with a hiss as Kian's form took her place at Sylvie's feet. "I don't have much time—"

"I don't care." She wasn't interested in excuses. She detested how much she cared, and pushing him away was the only method she could come up with to protect her already aching heart.

He sighed, placing a tentative hand on her thigh. Sylvie hated the tingles radiating from his touch.

"This is real," he said, his fingers lightly curling in the fabric of her dress. "And I'm not giving it up; I just can't fix things right now until I figure out a way to break the betrothal."

Sylvie scoffed, scooting until his hands fell from her leg. "You didn't seem to mind her throwing herself all over you in the hall. She looked eager to fuck you, but you've already done that, right?" The bitterness in her voice surprised her, and she sighed. "Forget it, Kian. Don't worry about me. I'll get over it."

He looked between Kerensa's stern expression and Sylvie's resigned one, and gnawed his inner cheek. "There are things I cannot say, and not for lack of wanting—"

"More riddles?"

Kerensa groaned. "Just let him finish so we can go. I can feel the bitch closing in on us."

Sylvie sniffed and pulled herself up against the tree.

"Please trust me," Kian tried again. "I'm not giving up, even if it looks like I am. I promise." Kerensa's sharp inhale barely entered Sylvie's awareness. "Don't give up on me. Don't forget me." His stricken, wide eyes reflected the moonlight back at her.

She hugged herself and studied his hunched posture before closing the small distance between them, pressing herself into his torso. His arms wrapped around her, and she melted into him, but stopped her arms from encircling his waist. She was still pissed, but leaving on bad terms felt like a crime. "I won't forget," she said, pulling away and brushing past him.

"Don't come back here, Princess. No matter what happens. I'll come back to you when I can."

She swallowed a painful lump as Kerensa grabbed her outstretched hands, and they locked gazes. Her eyes swam as she replayed his plea in her mind. Fae and their tricky words. *When he could?*

When might that be?

Kerensa clenched her jaw before exhaling. "Ready?"

"As I'll ever be." Sylvie looked over her shoulder to offer a last goodbye, but Kian's gaze had already locked on the edge of the spiky brush. He was walking across the grass towards the location when Sylvie spun to see what or who captured his attention.

Lazuli stood all in white like an ethereal bride, with a soft tilt to her head. Her hair framed her bare breasts as her white satin bathrobe hung open, barely covering her waist. She trailed a hand down her chest, swirling her fingers around her nipple before dipping to the robes slit below her hip. The sharp nails of her other hand tapped lightly on her bare thigh.

A burning agony clenched around Sylvie's throat, but she withheld her pain and focused ahead. Kerensa's glowing eyes centred her as her vision grew hazy and the world around them tilted.

In the last moment before they slipped across words, Lazuli's faint, alluring voice echoed. "Come back to bed, my love. I'm not quite finished with you yet."

Sylvie's body expelled a few different liquids as her feet planted in her bedroom. Tears, snot, and vomit hit the floor in a splat, just missing Kerensa's feet.

Blinking, she spun around and ran to the bathroom, emptying the last remnants of acid from her stomach before sobbing again.

From the doorway, Kerensa groaned. "You need to pull yourself together."

Sylvie paused, pressing her hands to her eyes before letting her face crumple again. "I can't. I don't know why, but I feel so, so …"

"Heartbroken?"

Sylvie's blotchy face lifted from her hands, and she stared at Kerensa leaning against the doorframe. Her expression remained neutral with a smidgen of pity.

The idea of heartbreak seemed ridiculous. She'd never felt it that strongly before. And she'd only known him a few days, for shit's sake. She scoffed and looked down at the toilet bowl before flushing. "No. No way. It's not that."

"Whatever you say." Kerensa looked behind her as cautious footsteps approached.

Fern.

"Who are you—" A loud thud echoed, and Sylvie jumped up. Too fast. She swayed and bent over, hands on her knees as she took slow, steady breaths.

"What did you do to her?" she asked between inhales.

"Just a sleeping ward; she's fine. But hurry. This place reeks of demons, and I need to get you to the vamp."

"What?"

Kerensa groaned again, slapping the doorframe. "Why are you so useless? I'm talking about Ambrose."

"Elias?" Sylvie stood up slowly, keeping a fist balled into her stomach. Then, when she could step without seeing two of everything, she limped over.

"Yes, him."

Sylvie nodded and walked past, looking around for a change of clothes, when Kerensa grabbed her bicep. "No time."

She dragged her from the room and passed Fern's unconscious body in the hallway, giving Sylvie only a second to slide on some slippers.

They bumbled down the flight of stairs to the small car park and clambered into her car, Kerensa sliding into the driver's seat. Sylvie rolled down her window and stuck her head out as the nausea grew. She hoped Kerensa knew the way to her work and how to drive, because realm travel and heart sickness had ruined Sylvie. One word and she'd puke her guts up. Again. The car made smooth turns and stops, so her concerns ebbed as stared listlessly at the brightly lit roads of Sterling. Home, shit home.

TEN

Weightless and swaying as if in a hammock, Sylvie snuggled deeper into a cool fabric. The scent of crisp mornings and copper pennies swirled beneath her nose, but she didn't mind. Instead, she breathed deeper and slower, hoping the smell would fill her up.

Her stomach growled, and she wriggled until a soft rumble against her cheek made her freeze. She held her breath, and it sounded again. *No way.* Blinking bleariness away, she stared up at the icy eyes of her boss and gasped.

"What are you doing? Put me down!"

"As you wish," he replied, dropping her onto a plush surface. The distance made her heart plunge into her throat, but she relaxed when she recognised the grey couch from his office. She scooched into a sitting position, curling her legs up and wrapping her arms around them. He could've put her down nicely. *Asshat.*

Kerensa stood stoically in the doorway, looking between them with a raised brow. "Are you certain you are fated?"

Elias scowled, and her hands raised up by her shoulders. Even the badass Kerensa didn't want to anger Elias Ambrose. Interesting.

"My apologies," Kerensa said then, clenching her teeth a few times as if the words hurt to speak. "I've seen her with Kian for days, and it's different."

Yeah. It was different, but Kian ruined it, and she didn't want to see him ever again.

Sylvie sniffed and crossed her arms tight. "Let's not talk about him, please, Kerensa. He's made his choice."

Kerensa tried to protest, but Sylvie shook her head. "Nope. If he felt the way said he did, he wouldn't have gone and fucked her the second she arrived." Even the words brought pain to her chest and a nauseated feeling to her belly. Nothing made sense. He said what they had was real, but by the looks of Lazuli, he'd already moved on. She pinched herself to stop the thoughts. Thinking about him would not help her forget him.

Kerensa toyed with the straps on her satchel but didn't respond, instead staring at Elias's impassive face.

"Keep her close. Now that the demons and the fae know of her relationship with Kian, she will be a target to get to him." Her face scrunched. "And you, I suppose, Blood Prince."

"I know." His eyes cast towards Sylvie again, which she immediately ignored, and Kerensa scoffed.

"Whatever."

With that, she disappeared from the office, and the remaining pair stayed silent.

Sylvie was plucking at a surprising number of prickles in her hem when Elias sighed and walked to his desk, Kerensa's departing words swirling in her mind. *A target to get at Kian and Elias.* Like she was little better than their possession, not her own person with thoughts and desires. Anger settled in her stomach.

The steady, monotonous clicking of fingers on a keyboard drew Sylvie's gaze, and she stared holes into his beautifully sculpted face.

The typing paused.

"Are you going to speak to me, or just stare?"

She clenched her hem and narrowed her eyes. "I haven't decided yet."

His fingers resumed their fast pace, and Sylvie sighed before standing and stretching her arms above her head. The icy air conditioning breeze stiffened her nipples, and she dropped her arms, instantly worried that she'd flashed him. She peeked at him as she strolled the length of the room, but again averted her gaze once his eyes began following her.

He saw. He totally saw.

She crossed her arms and swayed, watching her emerald gown swish at her feet. The fabric was thick with mud and water from the clearing.

"What size are you?"

Elias's deep voice sent a thrill through her, yet she plastered a frown on her face as she turned to him. What kind of question was that? "I'm not gonna tell you that."

"Shall I guess then?"

"No!"

Elias's brow raised as he leaned back in his chair and crossed his arms, mirroring her. She let her hands fall by her sides in retaliation, but when he didn't say another word, curiosity got the better of her.

"Why do you need to know, anyway?"

Elias stood, cracking his knuckles one by one, and prowled from behind his desk, keeping his piercing eyes on her face. "I thought you might like something else to wear while you stay here with me."

Sylvie looked around, frowning. "You mean we'll be staying here now? The whole time? You don't have a house?"

His jaw clenched, and his upper lip twitched. "Work and responsibilities do not cease because I found my kindred—"

"What the fuck is a kindred?"

He laughed humourlessly before heading towards his fridge and pulling out a ...

What the hell is that? No. *It can't be.*

A blood bag—a literal blood bag. Sylvie's mouth hung open as he pinched the top cap off with his teeth and brought the opening to his lips.

"Please tell me that's fake."

He took a long sip before holding it out to her. "Care to taste?"

Her head shook as she backed across the room. Suddenly, Kerensa's words about "returning her to the vamp" made sense. And the queen. Choose the vampire and reject my son. *Oh, my fucking—*

Vampire.

Why? Seriously, what was with her luck? She didn't want to believe it, but it was right in front of her. His eyes had even flickered red. Contacts couldn't do that. Could they?

Her hands started sweating. To control her rising nerves, she stated, "So ... Kian is a fae prince."

Elias smirked and took another sip, nodding.

"Which means fae are real."

91

Another nod.

"And before I ended up in the fae realm, a demon attempted to murder me, so they're real, too."

Elias growled and dropped the empty blood bag in the trash. "It what?"

"You heard me."

Elias moved closer and scanned her body without touching her. "Fucking pests."

The anger meant very little to her besides providing a small rush from his random attentiveness.

"Right … but you're neither of those creatures."

"No."

"You drink blood and don't like the sun."

"Correct."

"So, are all supernatural creatures real, then? Werewolf, jinn, succubus?"

"Vampire," he added, a glint in his eye.

She swallowed and nodded. "Vampire."

Elias hooked one thumb into his belt loop and scratched his light stubble with the other.

"There are umbrella terms for each genus. Shifters include wolves, bears, and big cats, while vampire falls within night dwellers. Fae has a variety of subspecies. The rest you mentioned fall under demons."

She nodded, nibbling her lower lip. That was a lot of creatures roaming around that weren't human. How she had never met one in her life to that point was the most far-fetched thing. Maybe she had and didn't know.

Fucking hell, she was about to get a migraine. She frowned as her heart rate returned to its normal rhythm, clearly accepting the facts of the supernatural before her mind did.

"I think I'm taking this too well. Am I actually an insane person right now? Are you a figment of my imagination? Tell me the truth, because I'm about to admit myself to a psych ward."

Elias clicked his tongue. "Kian's been dosing your subconscious with acceptance of our kind. Didn't he tell you that?"

She shrugged. "He mostly said bullshit, to be honest." Her heart panged at her cruelty. *Stupid heart.* "I don't want to talk about him." She rubbed her face and pressed her fingers into her tear ducts—no more crying. It was done. Over. Finished. She was a grown woman, for fuck's sake, with dozens of shitty relationships under her belt. She barely even knew the man. Or fae.

They stood in silence for a few beats before Sylvie relented on an earlier question, trying to distract herself. "I'm a medium to large size," she murmured. "My chest, ass, and hip dips don't fit in medium, but large is too loose around the waist."

Elias blinked before returning to his desk and writing something on a pen pad.

"I'll get my seamstress to measure you and make some outfits."

Before Sylvie could protest, he cut his gaze to her. "You need clothes. And I'd rather not take you back to your unwarded apartment when you already experienced a demon attack."

She pressed her lips together and nodded. "Thank you," she said. "Will you take it from my wages?"

His scoff made her blush red hot. *Not again.* And he smirked. "No. It's on me."

"No, you can't do that! That's too much!"

"I'll tell you when it's too much, Sylvie Hart. Now, go rest," he said, jerking his chin to the couch. Sylvie felt compelled to follow his direction but sat cross-legged on the floor instead. After all the craziness of the past few days, he probably wasn't her boss, so he wasn't the boss of her anymore. She wouldn't follow like some slave. If it weren't for the threat of death, she wouldn't even be there. She clenched her jaw. What had her life become?

"Your defiance is only acceptable because you just realm jumped, but don't expect me to continue putting up with your brattiness once you fully recover."

Her core throbbed at hearing his husky words, and she forced a slight pout. "And if I continue to defy you?" she shot back, brow raised. He moved in a blur across the room until his glowing red eyes stared down into hers, his hand wrapped around her back to stop her from smacking into the carpet.

"Don't tempt me. You aren't ready for that yet, pet."

She swallowed, tilting her chin up defiantly when his hand suddenly gripped her jaw and exposed her neck. His cool breath had shivers erupting across her flesh.

"I can't sleep in this," she whispered, hoping the change in topic would distract her enough to stop her panties from dampening.

"I'll send someone to get you sleepwear then," he said into her ear, his lower lip brushing her lobe.

Her body shivered, and she let him lower her completely onto the carpet before moving away. She sat up again, flushed and damp, as he made a call.

Ten minutes later, a new night dress arrived in the hands of a small older woman, and she swallowed.

"I'm sorry, sir, it was the only size I could find at this hour. It may run small around the bust."

Elias barely lifted his gaze, simply waving his hand in her direction and then to Sylvie. "It's fine; you may go."

"Thank you, sir," she bowed and scampered away as Sylvie stared at the fabric.

"Sweatpants and a T-shirt would have been fine."

Elias ignored her as she fingered the fabric, noting the silky shin-length dress and lace over the chest area. Even in her hands, she knew it would "run small around the bust." Just what she needed, her boss getting an eyeful as she crashed on his couch six feet away.

With a grumble, she dragged her feet to the bathroom, washing and changing with a frown still plastered on her face. This was not the day or week she had been expecting to have, and gods dammit, the nightdress was way too small.

It was going to be a long, embarrassing night.

ELEVEN

It felt like days of sleeping, eating takeout, and repeating before Elias finally acknowledged Sylvie's withering demeanour.

"What is it? You've barely spoken in forty-eight hours."

"What, now I'm too obedient?" Her voice croaked from being so unused. "You told me to stop asking so many questions."

After confirming for the tenth time, he was, in fact, an ancient vampire who didn't sleep, didn't like the sun but could go in it briefly, and drank copious amounts of blood, he informed her that her questioning was getting on his nerves.

Asshat.

"Your outfits arrived an hour ago and are in your office. Go try them on."

She sat up and stretched, glad for the oversized tracksuit she'd convinced Elias to get her instead of the skimpy nightgowns. *Men.* She rolled her eyes.

"Fine, but only because I'm bored, not because you told me to."

His chuckle made her cheeks warm, and she darted from the room to hide her flickering arousal. After discovering he could tell when she became aroused through pheromones, she was determined to avoid the sensation at all costs, especially in his presence.

That fact also led to the most sexual frustration she'd experienced since her stays in the girls' houses between foster homes. No privacy to masturbate there. Not that it stopped some of them.

By the time she reached her office, tiredness had settled in her bones. The constant exhaustion was new, and she hated it. She prayed it would wear off soon, because she was about to lose her mind. Just inside the office, against the wall, stood two rows of clothing hanging on a dual clothes rack: pantsuits, dresses, jeans, and elegant blouses, all in her colour palette.

"Holy shit."

Sylvie nearly buried her face into the softness, opting to run her hands along the fabric instead. "This is insane."

She peered out the door, and when she didn't see Elias, she stripped and tried on the first suit. The navy-blue pants and blazer hugged her curves perfectly. A surge of gratitude towards Elias made her smile, then frown slightly as Kian's face invaded her head.

Why did she have to feel this way for them both? It didn't help her conviction not to be an adulterer. No. Not an adulterer. He was with Lazuli. *Move on, idiot.*

Shaking her head, Sylvie stared at her reflection in the window. "Wow," she breathed. Every angle looked phenomenal. A soft chuckle escaped her as she realised her wardrobe might finally be better than Fern's.

She went to unbutton the blazer when a compulsion hit her. Fern had occasionally done it to her, just like in her books. Surely he wouldn't mind.

Adjusting the clothes one last time, she padded down the hallway to the office and pulled the door open. Elias's head lifted from his computer, and his eyes ran down her body. "Turn around."

This time she did as he asked, peeking over her shoulder and revelling in his sexy smirk. She strolled back down the hall, darting into her office at the last second and changing into the next outfit, continuing until she'd displayed the last dress on the rack, and Elias sat back, a satisfied look on his face. He placed his clasped hands on his desk.

"Are they all to your liking?"

She finished her twirl and beamed at him. "Yes." She cleared her throat, adding, "Thank you for indulging me." She looked back down the hall at her impromptu runway. "I've always wanted to do that."

"I will always indulge you, Hart."

Her muscles tensed, and she quickly imagined anything and everything to smother her desire as he feasted on her body with his eyes.

"If that's true, and I must stay here for the foreseeable future, I need a bed."

His brows shot up, and he bared his teeth in a surprised smile. "A bed?"

"Yes. I want to have some normalcy. I feel like a burden, crashing on your couch all day while you work."

"You are not—"

"I know! I just feel like that, okay?"

Elias's jaw twitched, and Sylvie knew he didn't like her tone, so she looked at her feet. He seemed to like it when she did that. He didn't speak, and when she lifted her gaze to check on him, he had returned to his work. *Asshat.*

With an eye-roll, she spun on her heel, pattering down the hall to her office. Her computer stared at her accusingly while the sweatsuit on the floor called her. Then, with a sigh, she stared back at the computer and grumbled, "Fine. I'll do some work."

Tapping the space bar, her monitor fired up, and she logged in, heading straight to emails. 620 unread emails. "Are you fucking kidding me?"

Scrolling through miles of spam, meeting requests, and adverts, an email titled *"Business Opportunity"* from R. Hex sent shivers down her spine.

She clicked on it, remembering Natalie's remarks about "business investments" and read the email.

> Elias Ambrose,
>
> I believe an in-person discussion is long overdue about the whereabouts of the artefact of *Animae dimidium meae.* I know you have your creatures after it, and I do not doubt we will come to certain agreements about its uses.
>
> I look forward to our meeting.
>
> Hex.

She re-read the email a few times, quickly throwing the unknown words into Gold's search engine. "The other half of my soul" appeared to be the direct translation.

"Soulmate, maybe?" She looked further but found nothing of note. Even her private Ghost search engine had few results besides some racy cartoon fan art.

Her fingers hovered above the keyboard as she prepared to respond. She briefly considered forwarding the email to Elias, but thought better of it. He had told her all emails that came to her were for her alone to organise. She sighed and looked through Elias's calendar. His next available meeting slot was Thursday that coming week. That'd do.

> Good morning,
>
> My next available time to meet is 11 a.m., Thursday the 28th. We can further discuss your expectations of the artefact and its uses.
>
> Regards,
> Ambrose.

She proofread the template response Natalie had made for her and scheduled the email to send at eight a.m. the following morning before swivelling in her chair. The dark sky outside made another yawn rip from her mouth, and she glanced at her tracksuit.

"That's enough work for today."

She changed into lounge wear and dragged her feet back to Elias's office, but when she got there, the room was empty. "That's weird." He hadn't left her unattended since she returned with Kerensa, and she wrapped her hands around herself as a chill tickled her nape.

"Hello?"

After walking to her temporary couch bed, she sat and curled up, watching the open door. "Elias?" She didn't even hear him leave. With a sigh, she grabbed the phone from the coffee table he had given her days earlier. She could just wait. "Ugh." She pulled up her contacts and stared at his name.

Asshat.

If he knew she nicknamed him that, she'd probably get spanked. She swallowed, even the mere thought of that sending heat between her thighs.

Pressing call and speaker, Sylvie lay down, waiting for the ring. Instead, the device clicked, and an automated voice told her to leave a message. Elias Ambrose, millionaire vampire forgets to charge his phone. How human of him. Hanging up, she closed her eyes for a second as another wave of tiredness hit her. When she opened them to redial Elias, a pair of yellow eyes stared at her from an inch away.

The scream that tore from her lips made her ears ring, and she bolted upright, jumping and falling over the back of the couch. The creature peered over the furniture and sneered down at her. Its sharp, stained teeth dripped a brown goo that hit her bare skin and sizzled. She screamed again, swiping the liquid on her pants before crawling behind the couch and away.

"Fuck off, fuck off, fuck off," she chanted as if her words could compel the thing to listen. Then, popping out the other side, she spun to see the creature staring at her with a wide smile. The dirt and wet gunk coating its naked, wiry body now covered her couch. "Ew."

Its head tilted to the side. The metre-long curled hairs swished around it as it stalked closer on all fours.

Sylvie's eyes shot down to the phone crushed beneath its clawed feet, and her body trembled as she rose to stand. Lifting her hands, she shifted sideways towards the main doors. "Stay there." There was nothing in the office to fight it off with. As it crept closer, the smile stretching wider than humanly possible, Sylvie shouted, "Stay back! Elias?"

The creature stood to its full height, its head almost brushing the roof, and she lost all resolve. "Fuck no!" She screamed and sprinted for the door, her whole body shaking violently as giant footsteps thumped behind her.

Her pitiful life flashed before her eyes as she screeched louder than ever. "Elias!"

Sylvie raced down the hall with the humanoid creature skittering behind her. With the length of its legs, it could have easily caught up.

It was toying with her.

Where was he? "Elias, gods dammit, where the fuck are you!" Glancing wildly towards her office and the elevators, nothing stood out as a decent weapon. It was all pens, folders, and paper clips. Tears sprang to her eyes as she realised she might die.

Running full pelt into the elevator button, she spun and raised her hands at the creature. It towered above her, blocking the lights with its floating mop of black curls.

"What the fuck do you want?" Her spine pressed into the elevator as she slammed the open button repeatedly.

"I thought you'd never ask," it hissed, lowering onto all fours, letting its acrid breath line up with Sylvie's nose. Its voice had a dual quality, both masculine and feminine at the same time.

She had nowhere to go. She tucked her chin, trying to shrink away as it leaned in, its yellow eyes piercing her soul.

"I came to see how you taste," the creature elongated the *s* on taste, and Sylvie shuddered, pulling a face.

"What?"

It lowered further than she thought possible, sniffing her bare feet, and she squealed, jumping to the side as it straightened.

"You are not human."

She shook her head. "I don't know."

"I do. You are magically imbued—tethered to the one who leaves cracks in the veil. I almost couldn't find you with the scent of decay here. Death lingers, doesn't it, pretty?"

Death lingers. Sylvie shuddered as its mouth stretched open. Far too wide. The jaw detached and the top fell backwards, leaving a gaping hole.

Its claws reached for her just as the elevator dinged, and she tumbled straight into a tight grip.

The hands spun her body, forcing her into the back corner of the elevator, and she looked up through petrified eyes to see Elias. The fury in his blood-red irises as he took in the monster made her heart race.

"Stay here," he said as he slammed the close doors and ground floor buttons then stormed out, his fists clenched at his sides.

The creature hissed and recoiled, snapping its maw into place as Elias's fist flew and the doors slid shut.

Soft eclectic elevator music mocked her as she curled into the corner, letting herself sob. Its face flashed behind her lids. Yellow eyes. Brown teeth. Monster.

She wished she had asked Elias to stay with her. What if he got hurt because of that thing? Because of her.

Her body shivered so hard her teeth clacked as the floor numbers flashed. Sixty-seven, sixty-six, sixty-five, sixty-four, and beyond.

Wiping her dripping nose with her sleeve, she jolted in the elevator as it suddenly stopped its descent. Eyes wide with terror, she froze as the floor numbers started ascending.

"No! No, no, no …" She crawled over and smashed the emergency stop button, but nothing happened. "No! What the fuck?"

Slamming her flat palm across every floor button, she waited for the doors to open on seventy-eight, but to her horror, it didn't. She just kept climbing.

Succumbing to her fears, she dropped back to the floor, curling in the fetal position, her face buried in her tear-snot-drenched sleeves.

Her dry mouth quivered as the floor shuddered to a stop. "Please don't eat me."

TWELVE

At first, when the doors opened on the top floor, silence engulfed Sylvie and a painful certainty sank into her subconscious that Elias was dead. That thing ate him. Firm pressure around her waist jolted her, and she screamed until her voice went hoarse. She still had some fight left. Kicking and punching her arms, she barely heard the deep, calming voice in her ear.

"Sylvie, breathe. Open your eyes, love. It's gone."

Recognition pierced the horror in her mind, and she went limp, tears streaming as Elias scooped her into his arms.

"It's gone. It's gone."

Ashamed of her snotty, rashy face, she buried her head against his neck and used one hand to hide. As he walked, she peeked beneath her sleeve to see where the monster went, but couldn't spot a trace of it. Not one. She relaxed as the steady steps of his feet brought them closer to his office, but instead of putting her down, he sat with her on his lap at his desk.

She was far too tired to argue, question, or feel awkward about his tender embrace. The adrenaline draining from her body drew her eyes closed, even though her mind felt far too frantic to sleep. She jerked when Elias moved slightly, but he silenced her and stroked her hair.

"It's okay. You're safe. I'm just adjusting the chair."

She nodded, lifting one of her arms to drape across his shoulder, letting her shuddering breaths even out. Slowly, the fear faded. Or maybe it slunk into the chest she built for all bad things. The monster perched on the lid of that box and watched her, stroking its finger through the tiny slat where she deposited the memories like silver marks in a penny bank. She turned away, building up the iron wall around it, and she let her mind wander as if she were outside of everything. Beyond the self. All-seeing.

Sterling woke and stretched its limbs, the shops opening with light bursts and electricity surges. Not a patch of grass to be found. Instead, parks of plastic lawn surged with the squeals of children, the squeals of rusty swings. Used needles. Streetlights faded, replaced by the shine of a million phone screens, and Sterling yawned, dragging its feet through the cracked pavement and potholes to find a decent hit. Caffeine, nicotine, coke.

She was there too, weaving through crowds of bloodshot eyes and asthma. Something lurked behind her, though, its dark maw a vacuum widening until it consumed everything.

But then, slipping through an opalescent sheen, she was in back in the Evergreen Court again. The trees waved at her return. Home.

She jolted, coming back into herself and awkwardly unpeeled her hand from beneath Elias's buttoned shirt, despite the enjoyable softness of his skin and sparse tufts of chest hair. How long had she been dissociating? Did he notice?

She leaned back, tilting her head up at him, and sighed. "What the fuck was that thing earlier?" Her voice was gone, and she was unsure how he even understood what her squeaking rasps meant.

"You shouldn't try to speak yet." When she scowled, he answered, "A fae and lesser demon hybrid. Kian warded most greater demons from this place, but some of the lower born can slip in and out of Hel through the openings he leaves behind when he travels."

"It's dead?"

He nodded.

"Where were you?" She shuddered as its image scratched a nail down her mental walls. He had left her alone with that *thing*.

"Natalie came in to collect a few contracts. I had to take them down to her."

Sylvie's brow raised.

"I don't want her to know you're staying here."

"Is she like you?" *Does she want to kill me too?*

Elias shook his head. "No, she's human, but that means nothing these days."

Sylvie didn't feel like questioning him and rubbed her eyes. "Don't leave me again," she said at last, not ashamed of the warming in her chest as she said the words.

His finger curled under her chin and tilted her head up. Their eyes met, and he nodded. "Never."

Her eyes fluttered shut as his lips dipped and brushed across her mouth. Their soft, buttery texture made her melt deeper into his touch, but Elias pulled away instead of extending the kiss, tucking her head back beneath his chin. He seemed like an entirely different person, and she was never one to look a gift horse in the mouth.

Picking up his phone, he called someone and brought the phone to his ear.

"It's me. I need the room next to my office furnished immediately. A bed, wardrobes, curtains—"

"A potted plant," Sylvie whispered, letting a small smile creep across her lips as he repeated her raspy words with complete seriousness.

"Fully furnished and dressed." A pause. "It is to be used."

Sylvie sensed his growing frustration with the tension tightening his muscled chest. He was fairly restrained, and she hid a smile. Good. She didn't want to like a guy who was rude to service people.

"Twelve hours. Thank you."

He hung up and set the phone down before placing his lips on her hair, kissing softly. The tension in her flowed away like water, and Sylvie pulled back, staring at his handsome, serious face.

"What time is it?" she croaked, covering her mouth when a cough spasmed from her lungs.

Elias rolled his eyes, apparently giving up his attempts to stop her ceaseless questioning.

"Six a.m."

"Shit. People will get here soon."

"I'm sure there are already people here, Hart."

"I need to get changed." She started to stretch her legs down to the floor when Elias scooped her back into his arms and stood, walking her to the bathroom. The modern setup was tidy and clinical.

"Shower first," he said. "Then I'm going to take you out."

She eyed the shower and trembled. She couldn't go in there alone, no fucking way. What if another one of those things got in and snatched her? Or ate her?

"Where?" she said, avoiding the task at hand. Maybe she didn't need a shower after all.

"I have a cabin in the Silverwood Grove out west. About a three-hour drive."

The thrill of leaving the glass prison and seeing nature almost made her anxiety ease about showering alone. Almost. Not quite.

"Can you—will you …"

He lowered her feet to the ground, and she stood still, gripping his forearm as she stared at the shower stall. The clear glass door faced the mirror, but the wall nearest them obscured the inside of the shower. No way.

"I can't." She leaned into his body as if to push him back out into the main room, but he didn't budge. The thought of the monster hiding in the shower stall, its clawed limbs suspending its wiry body between the tiled walls—

"Do you want me to stay?"

She blushed at the idea of him seeing her naked, but it eased when she saw his neutral face. He knew it wasn't an invitation.

She tugged off her jumper in one motion and dumped it on the floor, reclaiming his hand. It was steady. She needed steady or else she'd crumble. She was bare beneath the jumper, but if he was surprised about her nudity, he didn't show it. Instead, he walked past and turned the shower on, still holding her trembling fingers.

"I can wait behind the wall—"

109

"No." That was still too far.

"You want me to come in?"

She nodded, tugging down her sweatpants but keeping on her cotton underwear. He didn't need to see all of her. Yet.

Following her to the door, Elias unbuttoned his shirt with one hand, eyes glued to her face. She was grateful for his resolve. Any ordinary man would have gazed down at her chest, but he didn't. Not once. A low standard, but she often scraped the bottom of the proverbial barrel.

Her resolve was far weaker, and she let her gaze rake up and down his rippling torso. While Kian had a leaner symmetry, Elias's muscles were bulkier and gave him a more substantial appearance. Basically, he was big. Everything was. Sylvie resisted the urge to trail her fingers through the troughs in his abdomen. *Dear gods.*

He kicked off his shoes and went to follow her into the steamy shower stall, pants still on, when she paused. "You'll ruin them."

He went to walk under the spray when she pressed her hand to his taut abdomen and lowered her fingers to his belt, slowly unlooping the leather. She pulled it free and unbuttoned him, letting the trousers fall to the floor, revealing his black briefs. She lifted her eyes to his and smiled, respectfully ignoring the semi pressing against the soft fabric.

She pulled him into the stall, keeping a soft grip on his wrist as she washed with his expensive cleansers and soaps. Finally, after watching her struggle and drop the soap bar twice, he pulled his hands free from hers.

"Sylvie, stop. I will not disappear. I'm here now." As her eyes turned glassy, he sighed, taking the shampoo from the shelf. "I'll wash your hair so we are still touching."

She conceded, half turned, and crossed her arms. In other circumstances, this would have led to slippery, hot shower sex. What a shame.

His finger pads massaging her scalp almost drew a moan from her. A damn shame. After forming a lather, she rinsed, and he did the same thing with the conditioner. Once they were all clean, he wrapped her in a large towel, and she slipped off her underwear. He did the same and pulled some clothes from a tall cupboard, turning to dress. She stared at his rippling back as he changed and walked to his side, burying her face in his freshly pressed shirt.

"You're getting me wet," he stated, but he did not move her away.

"I'm sorry for being so-"

"Don't be. I should have never left you alone, and I'll do whatever it takes to make you feel safe again. Kian's influence is wearing off."

He wrapped his arm around her body and guided her to his chair. "That being said, I need to grab you a change of clothes from your office. Natalie's here now, so unless you want her to see you in a compromising position, I suggest you wait here." After noticing her wide eyes, he knelt and brushed his thumb across her cheek. "Do you trust me?"

She thought about it and lifted a shoulder in a half shrug before nodding, the action drawing a sheepish laugh from her. He pressed his lips as if hiding a grin and left the room. Deep breaths. It was dead. Surely there wasn't another hybrid thing waiting in the wings to eat her. She pulled her towel about her tighter.

From her position, she heard a chirpy, "Good morning, sir."

"Morning. Would you mind heading to IT and informing them about a virus in Miss Hart's computer?"

"How did she manage that?"

"Natalie." The warning in his voice was clear, and Natalie's heels clacked as she walked towards the elevator. Elias's broad back blocked Natalie's view of his office and her until the elevator doors closed.

He glanced at her before ducking into her office and returning to her side in less than a second. The fresh whoosh of air hit her face as she processed his movements.

"You're fast," she said with a small smile, taking the clothes from his hands. He turned his back to her, a tug at the corner of his mouth visible, and she changed quickly before sitting back in his chair. He took her damp towel and tucked it away in the bathroom, disappearing for a few seconds.

Despite the increase in her heart rate, she calmed swiftly as she grew desensitised to his brief absences. When he returned to her side again, she let herself smile.

"So, about that road trip?"

THIRTEEN

"We're almost there." Elias turned down a long gravel path, the matte-black hybrid sports car gripping the road as they wound through lush woodland. They'd been driving for hours. His hand lay draped over the centre console, his fingers close enough to touch Sylvie's jean-clad thigh if she just opened her legs a fraction. She contemplated it for a long time before distracting herself with a long swig from her water flask. The liquid dried her aching throat and cooled her heating body.

"Does it snow here in winter?" she asked, staring into the dense rows of forty-foot evergreens.

"Yes. There's a ski field on the other side of this mountain. I'll take you there sometime."

"I'd like that," Sylvie whispered. She bit the inside of her cheek as she fought the smile threatening to grow across her face. He was the perfect gentleman. All attentive and touchy, nothing like the snarky asshole she was used to.

"What are you thinking about?" he asked, flicking his eyes over at her. "You're flushed." Then, placing a cool hand on her forehead, he pulled away with a smirk. "No fever. You must be experiencing something else then."

"Oh, must I?" she retorted before laughing softly. So he was making jokes too? "If you must know, I was thinking about how I would love to go skiing with you, but I don't know how. I want to learn, if you'd be willing to teach me." *Liar, liar.*

He hummed. "It would be my pleasure."

The way he said pleasure did exciting things inside her body, and she carefully crossed her legs and rolled the window down.

Elias's laugh made her reach for the back window button too.

"Here, let me," he said, pressing all the buttons at once. "You realise you don't need to feel ashamed about how your body reacts to me."

After pressing her cool flask to her flaming cheeks, she cast him a withering look.

His responding smirk sent another jolt into her core. "Sylvie, it's mutual," he added, turning his red-tinged eyes to face her. "It's part of the bond. I realise Kian probably told you nothing, as I asked to explain, so we'll talk when we settle into the cabin. Would you like that?"

She nodded and turned her attention back out the window. The trees whooshed past in a blur, and for a split-second, a black silhouette appeared to be standing a few feet into the forest. Her heart spiked in her chest, and Elias's hand gripped her thigh.

"What is it?"

She squeezed his fingers. The moment they touched, her anxiety ebbed. "Do hikers come out here?"

"No, it's too remote. There are bears, though."

"Bears." She nodded and turned to look ahead. That would explain it. It was a bear.

In the distance, the sloping thatch roof of a large cabin rose over the light cleft in the road, and she bit her lip to stop the gasp. Pink and acid-green moss grew across its face, the windows barely peeking through where a vining plant with dainty gold flowers weaved around the frames and door like a wreath. She squirmed in her seat. If he let her, she would run the rest of the way. A slice of the Evergreen Court on Erus. She couldn't believe it. She barely allowed Elias time to turn off the car before she jumped out and darted up to the front porch.

Her sneakers slapped and pattered in satisfying rhythm as she walked the length of the porch, which wrapped around the entire house. The solid log walls, notched together at the ends, were smooth, the rings on the end drawing her eye. She traced them with her finger. A faint light emanated from the logs, and she blinked. Instantly, the light was gone, and only ancient dead trees remained. Maybe she imagined it. Her sleep had been poor for days, so it tracked. Soft footsteps sounded behind her, and she turned to Elias. "This is beautiful. Thank you for bringing me."

He inclined his head. "Of course."

Heat stirred in her belly, and she coughed lightly, gesturing to the wall beside them. "So … when did you get this place?"

He smiled, a tiny crinkle reaching his eyes. "I built this place."

Sylvie's mouth dropped open as she touched the smooth timber and the dried lichen stuffed between each log. "When?"

"That would reveal my age, Kitten. Come inside." He offered his hand and she took it, swallowing another wave of lust as she followed him.

The first thing that hit her was the smell. Fresh, untreated wood and smoke. Not the toxic kind that billowed from the factory near her apartment, either. Rich, woody smoke that enveloped her mind as if painting an image. A wish. People dancing around a living flame, a heavy lingering scent clinging to their skin and hair. Stains of soot on her bare skin. Ash flakes floating onto her lashes, painting the ground in shades of grey. She gasped, pulling herself from the vision. Since when had her imagination become so vivid?

Elias's grip on her hand grounded her as she walked farther into the house and took in the rest of the space.

The main living, kitchen, and dining space was open plan with a giant stone chimney as the focal point, thick cuts of wood piled astride the column. While almost everything, from cupboards to the tables to the rocking chair, was wood, the space didn't feel unbearably rustic.

That's it; she was in love. In love with the house, not him. Not Elias, who stared at her with the most charming expression. A soft smile tugged his lips, and his eyes glistened as she leaned in, wrapping her arms around him. He pulled her into him, his forearms caging her waist as they embraced. She expected a kiss, or perhaps a bit of fondling, but to her surprise and frustration, he didn't.

Pulling back, she breathed a ragged, "Thank you." She tried to ignore it, but everywhere they touched, her body prickled.

He nodded and cleared his throat before walking to the fireplace and stacking some kindling inside the firebox, tucking a bundle of dry twigs beneath it.

His veined forearms flexed, and Sylvie's gaze locked on the bare skin. Rolled sleeves were the greatest fashion accessory of all time.

The stone hearth spanned a metre beneath Elias's feet, and Sylvie walked over and sat on it. The pull to be close to him was no longer out of fear, but a burning desire.

Elias studied her, and his jaw clenched before he turned back and lit a match beneath the kindling stack. The wood caught flame, which swayed like a stalk bending in the western winds before he placed a metal grating in front of the spreading blaze.

He stood and headed for a black linen cushion-backed couch, keeping his back to her. What was he doing? Sylvie followed and sat on the furniture, her body sinking as she tugged an emerald throw over her lap. She waved her hand at him.

"Sit."

Elias narrowed his gaze a fraction before twisting his gold watch.

"Before I tell you anything, I need to know exactly what happened with Kian in Ilfaem."

A jolt of pain shot through her, followed by rolling waves of shame and guilt. She had hardly thought of Kian in days. After he chose Lazuli, it felt deserved, but she had doubts after hearing Elias speak his name.

She sighed and looked away.

"I haven't questioned you until now because of the circumstances of your return." He paused. "And to be truthful, I suppose I wanted you to myself."

Sylvie flushed and pressed her back into the sofa cushion as if trying to shrink.

"But it's time," he finished.

"Fine." She wanted to tell him, anyway. Maybe then she could get over it. "I woke up in Evergreen, and Kerensa took me to meet the queen."

Elias nodded when she paused. "She told me to break Kian's heart and choose you."

A scowl crossed his face. "Queen Katarina should never have asked that of you. Despite how much I may want you to myself, Kian is your fated, too. You are his as much as you're mine."

She knew the idea of being anyone's should infuriate her, but the image of her body snuggled between them both set her mind aflame. *Get a grip.* She stood abruptly, crossing the room to pick up a short log and threw it in the sparking flames.

"I don't belong to you. To either of you." She bit the words out from between her teeth as she spun back to glare at him.

"You misunderstand."

"Then explain. What is a fated?"

He beckoned her back to the couch, and she sat with a huff.

"Shifters have mates; fae have fated. Vampires, well, they used to be called kindred. Now, it's more interchangeable. The concept is similar to soulmates for humans—a perfect match. But true human soulmates are long extinct."

Sylvie crossed her arms and gave him a stern look. He sounded almost as cryptic as Kian.

He sighed. "Centuries ago, even before my time, everyone had kindred, but as wars broke out over power and resources, and creatures left their realms, the pairs dwindled. It's been decades since a bond has been recorded. Some say the Fates cursed us for our greed and cruelty. Especially the shifters, since they need mates to procreate. They can turn humans, but the survival rate is poor."

"Why did the shifters get such a shit deal?"

Elias lifted a shoulder. "Nobody knows for certain. Some say there was a war. I was too busy escaping my home to be thinking about them. We don't 'get on' as a species."

She wanted to pry, but his eyes seemed to say "another time." She gnawed on her lower lip before asking, "How many realms are there?"

After a pause, he offered his hand, palm up between them. "Give me your hand."

She did.

He pricked his finger and traced a circle of blood in the middle of her palm. Her brows shot up, but his words drew her attention back to the markings he made. "This is Erus." He then drew three circles surrounding it, each touching Erus, but not overlapping. "Argyncia is the Vampire realm, Ilfaem as you know is the fae realm, and the shifters come from Beihllua. And here …" He traced the places where the outer realms touched Erus. "Is the liminal realm. Hel." He let her go and she cradled her palm in her lap, staring at the world— or worlds—she never knew existed. It was insanity. It was incredible.

She curled her fingers, returning to the last topic before the vastness of the realms overwhelmed her. "And the others? The fae? Do they need fated to have children?"

Elias tilted his head a fraction, like a predator assessing their prey. "They can occasionally bear faelings without fated pairs, but supposedly those relationships are never truly fulfilling."

She bit the inside of her cheek before blurting her satisfaction at Kian's mistake. Elias's flickering gaze seemed to catch the thought anyway, though.

"Now," he said, "those bonds are effectively gone. Cross-species partnerships were always rare and generally frowned upon, but multiple bonds? I still can't find any evidence of it in my library."

A library? She needed a slice of that.

"I still don't understand what it means for me." Sylvie tucked her feet beneath her and placed an elbow on the couch back, leaning her cheek into her fist.

Elias didn't move, but somehow he seemed closer, his gaze penetrating her from above. "It means that you are ours in every way." His eyes darkened when Sylvie swallowed. "And we are yours."

Her mouth opened and closed, but nothing came out until she squeezed her eyes shut. "But how do you *know*?" Images of Kian and Elias, naked and pressed against her side in a bed of torn sheets and flower petals, bombarded her mind again. Her eyes sprang open.

"The looking glass I showed you. It's a fae artefact designed to show images connected to your mate. If you don't have one, you see your reflection."

Sylvie gnawed at her bottom lip, and Elias frowned, reaching to dislodge it. She huffed and asked, "What did you see when you looked into it?"

"The same as you. Ilfaem. A tree, actually, and my home realm. Argyncia. The Glass City."

FOURTEEN

Sylvie and Elias sat locked in each other's gazes on the couch as the fire crackled and spat at their side.

"So," Sylvie said, rubbing her sweating palms on her thigh, her heart faltering in her chest. "Does that make me a vampire, too?" God's, she hoped not. Maybe it was all a big mistake. She was human. She was raised human; she would die human.

"I won't know until I taste your blood." He smirked after a long inhale, and Sylvie burned, his expression stealing her fear and replacing it with need. She wanted him to close the gap between them. She wanted to be tasted *by* him.

"But you still need to tell me what else happened with Kian," he reminded her. The name of the fae prince quickly quenched some of the heat in her body, and she nodded, leaning back into the couch and pressing the back of her hand to her cheek.

"After the queen told me to reject him, Kian showed up and took me to his room. Then we went to the gardens." She trailed off, remembering his lips on hers. "We kissed." Her eyes flickered towards Elias, but his face remained impassive.

She retold her faux pas with the not-strawberry, and he exhaled sharply through his nose. Almost a laugh. Static

Mikayla Everitt

sparkled across her skin where his breath touched and she nearly lost all words before choking out, "What?"

He shook his head. "Nothing. Go on."

"Then …" She bit her tongue. This wasn't the conversation she wanted to be having sitting in her dream home opposite an insanely attractive male. She would normally be halfway to orgasm by this point. He tilted his head, brow raised, and she groaned. "Then a female came. The queen had invited her. Lazuli. She's Kian's betrothed." Her heart clenched. "They were obviously well acquainted and picked up right where they left off. He promised me he wouldn't give up on me, and Kerensa brought me home, right after the bitch showed up half-naked, saying something about unfinished business." Her voice hitched, and tears sprang to her eyes. She wiped them away. Pathetic tears. "That's it."

She sniffed and dropped her hands in her lap, gluing her gaze to her trembling fingers.

"You didn't find that strange?"

She blinked. "What?"

"His promise."

A scoff rose in her chest, but she subdued it with a cough. "No. Men make promises all the time they don't keep."

"Human men perhaps. Not fae males. The fae don't make promises lightly. They cannot lie, either."

She shrugged. "Well, he did."

Elias's fingers gripped her chin, and she tilted her head to look at him. "I won't make excuses for Kian, but I know there's something she must have over him if he sent you away. A regular betrothal would not stand between fated bonds."

123

He slid closer until their legs were touching and searched her face.

"How could you possibly know that?" she asked.

"I know him."

She glanced away, picking at her cuticle. He knew him, but she *saw* him. There was no distorting the facts. Elias recaptured her attention, turning her head back with a gentle grip of her jaw.

"And because the thought of leaving you is inconceivable."

Her breathing stopped in her chest as she stared into his eyes. Building pressure pulsed in her abdomen and below as she let her gaze flit down his face. The way his lips parted slightly sent a thrill between her legs, and she sighed.

In a movement fuelled by lust and longing and desperate need, Sylvie landed hard in Elias's lap, her legs automatically wrapping around his waist, the friction of her jeans and his pants button sending pleasure through her clit. She moaned at his darkening eyes and smashed her lips against his, finally taking what was hers. He growled, pulling her closer, squeezing her hips and kneading her ass.

Whining into his mouth, she pushed her chest against his, lowering his body with her on top.

"Sylvie," he warned, flipping her off him and onto the couch. His knee pressed between her legs, dangerously close to her sex, and she blinked at him innocently.

"You don't like to be on your back?"

His lips rejoined hers with impassioned hunger. Soon her head spun, and she pushed against his shoulders, laughing, and said, "Don't avoid the question."

His hand slipped beneath her ass and squeezed, eliciting a squeal. "Elias!"

"Don't mistake my gentleness with you as weakness," he said, pressing his lips into her neck and biting slightly.

Sylvie gasped, tilting her chin to give him better access, and he chuckled against her fluttering pulse. "Not yet, Kitten. You aren't ready for that."

"I am." She ground her hips against him, running her hands along his sides and wrapping around his waistband. When she tugged, Elias pulled back, eyes flashing. His hand slid up her chest and around her throat like a perfect new necklace. Her eyes rolled back as he kissed her, sucking her lower lip into his mouth.

"Elias," she whispered, gripping his shirt in her hands. "Fuck me."

He drew back, fire in his eyes, when a frantic pounding slammed against the front door. Stony dread doused Sylvie, her heart thundering from the sudden noise. There weren't supposed to be any people around there. Too remote. Yet someone was. She didn't notice how tightly she was holding onto Elias until he unpeeled her and stood, keeping her hand in his.

"Hey! Help me!" The panic-laced voice wheezed and coughed, the sound rattling as if their lungs were full of blood.

Elias pushed Sylvie behind him, placing himself in front of the door.

"What are you?" he said, lowly. Quiet enough that no human would hear. Sylvie's pulse exploded, her hands violently shaking, and Elias turned to stroke her cheek as the person paused their assault on the door.

"I … I'm a shifter," he said.

No way.

"I saw you drive in. I've been hiding in the woods since they turned me. Please help me. You're a vampire, right? I-I could smell you. Please."

Elias's tense posture set Sylvie on edge. "Should we open the door?" she asked, but Elias silenced her with a quick finger to his lips.

He lowered his mouth to her ear and whispered, "Go upstairs to the first bedroom on the left and lock yourself in. Don't open it for anyone but me."

The thought of being alone made her tremble, and a growing tightening in her chest made each breath hard to draw.

As another loud bang rattled the doorframe, she turned and dashed up the stairs opposite the kitchen. Taking two at a time, she gasped as her foot slipped and her hands slapped the splintering wood. Elias's large hands latched beneath her arms and lifted her as he growled out, "Be careful." She hadn't even heard him move.

"Sorry." She speed-walked the rest of the way and ducked into the nearest empty room, cradling her stinging hand. Blood slowly beaded on her palm, where a large splinter dug into her flesh. She picked it out before pushing the door shut and swallowed, spying the two large deadbolt locks and sliding them into place.

Muffled voices rebounded through the bare space and Sylvie tiptoed to the window, hoping to catch some of it. The old frame squeaked as she lifted the window and lowered her face to the opening.

"Who turned you?" Elias's flat voice questioned. From her position, she still couldn't see the other person.

"I don't know. They used fake names and said they'd only tell us who they were after we turned."

"And why would you agree to be turned knowing nothing?" Sylvie nodded at the question. She couldn't imagine trusting people while knowing nothing about them. She still didn't even trust the pair of men claiming to be her soulmates.

"Because one of them, she called herself June, showed me her cougar form, and I-I believed. I was homeless before then, and they helped me with my addiction. I thought they cared." The voice cracked, and Sylvie's heart panged at hearing them sniffle.

"Then why are you here?" Elias asked, his voice deeper and more menacing.

After more sniffling, the person cleared their throat. "There were twenty of us, and only five survived it. That's when I realised they lied. I had to get away. Actually, I … I made a mistake. I should go."

Sylvie's brows furrowed as the shifter backtracked, and she leaned out the window to see them as they backed off the porch. She held the window steady so it wouldn't shut on her head, and she hissed as a drop of her blood dripped off her palm and onto a bush below. She snatched it back and dug her thumb into the cut, ignoring the sharp sting. The bleeding would stop soon enough. It always did.

The shifter appeared in her vision as she fussed with her palm, walking backwards, his waist-length black hair tangled with twigs and debris.

Elias appeared, too, his giant form dwarfing the shifter. She shrank back, hoping he wouldn't see her spying, when the shifter gasped. His eyes shot the bush, and he sprinted over, sniffing around like an animal.

Sylvie stared in horror as the shifter's eyes shot up to the window and his face morphed, jaw elongating and brown fur sprouting across his body.

"What is that? It smells so good." His guttural voice made her skin prickle, and she backed away as a vibrating roar shook the floors beneath her feet.

"Shift back now, or these will be your last seconds on Erus." Elias's bitter voice dripped menace as loud lip-smacking and grumbles filtered through the walls.

"What is she?" the garbled voice asked, and Sylvie whimpered from its savage quality. She needed to get away. The creature stood right beneath her window, and she was certain it would scale the house and break in to eat her.

She crawled back to the door as Elias spoke again. "She is not your concern!"

"Mates," the shifter stated, letting out another growl. "I can smell her on you. You dare prevent our alpha from ensuring our survival when you have claimed your own mate? Give us the artefact!"

Sylvie shakily eyed the deadbolts as the shifter let out another much louder roar. If he got in, she'd need to move fast. She palmed the knob, waiting. Waiting.

"I don't have it. And I won't give you an excuse to harm more people," Elias said before pounding blows shook the cabin. A deafening screech and gurgle resounded, and then nothing but pure, empty silence.

Sylvie swallowed and tightened her shaking grip on the doorknob, sliding the bolts free before cracking the door open and stalling at the sight of a rigid torso.

"Elias?" Deep red blood drenched him from head to toe, matching the colour of his eyes.

"I told you to wait until I said you could come out." The words barely escaped past his elongated fangs, and she shuddered. The sharpened points gleamed with saliva.

"I-I waited," she stuttered, looking down at her bloody palm.

"You didn't. And you injured yourself in the brief time we were apart."

Sylvie shrank back from his scathing tone. The old Elias she hated was back. Great.

"It was a splinter." She tucked her hand behind her back and squeezed her eyes shut to hold in the tears burning along her waterline.

"Give me your hand." He barely waited for her to follow his instruction before gripping her wrist and squeezing until her fingers uncurled.

His eyes flashed a brighter red as he stared at the drying blood before raising her palm to his mouth.

"What are you doing?" she asked, pulling against him. It was no use; she hardly even budged in his firm grip.

"Finding out what the fuck you are."

FIFTEEN

As Elias's tongue pressed along Sylvie's palm and licked with a long stroke, her panties immediately dampened. Despite her previous fear, his warm, wet touch sent a rush of excitement through her, and she pulled against him again. She didn't need him smelling how turned on she was by his tongue on her skin.

She met his narrowed gaze, fighting a lump in her throat. "So?"

Elias pulled back, his irises flickering as if reining in the beast inside him before turning away from her.

Sylvie repressed the urge to clench her thighs as she stared at his rippling back muscles.

"What am I?"

His form tensed as he turned side-on to her, his icy blue eyes moving up and down her body. The gaze cut through her clothes and skin and walls of iron. She felt the urge to cover herself, as if he saw too much. He saw inside that little box she'd neatly smelted, shaped, and stored. The one that now housed monsters and demons. Kian had done the same thing. Like they knew her secrets. She couldn't afford them having that knowledge.

"It doesn't make sense," he finally said.

She swallowed and crossed her arms, hoping she looked irritated and not as uncomfortable as she felt. Her tongue had turned to cotton.

He looked down at his bloodstained clothes and grunted, ripping the shirt off in one tug. Then, throwing it to the floor, he spun, walking down the hall without a word.

Sylvie stared blankly for a second before trailing after him. *No.* He wasn't going to keep this from her. Her heart thudded an unsteady rhythm as she shuffled to the last door on the right, still ajar.

Through the crack, she watched Elias's godlike, bare-assed form disappeared into an adjacent room, the sound of roaring water pouring out. She scanned the rest of the room, admiring the simple features, before her eyes snagged on the mirror on the ceiling and several hooks screwed into a wood beam behind it. *What the hell were those for?* She had a few guesses.

Tearing her gaze from the setup, she steeled herself, pushing the door in and padding across a dark jute rug. He'd left the bathroom door wide open. She gnawed on her cheek. It had to be intentional.

Elias's back was facing her, and she watched, mesmerised, as the steamy water cascaded down around him, slinking through the divots of his every muscle. *Fuck.*

He turned to look at her, keeping his hips facing away, and she swallowed, mildly disappointed. The firm roundness of his exquisitely sculpted ass helped ebb away some of her curiosity, though.

His eyes raked across her, and his brow furrowed again before he turned, running his hands through his black curls.

She bit her lip, moving closer until some hot spray misted her face. "What happened to the shifter?"

Elias kept washing and kept his gaze averted.

"Did you kill him?"

His soft chuckle made her cheeks redden. The amount of blood on his body made it quite clear the other creature had to be dead; she didn't even know why she asked him.

"Forget it." She turned away, grumbling, when she froze, as if hitting a wall. No. She needed to know. She was sick and tired of fucking beating around the bush. Sighing, she collected herself and spun back, ready for answers ... and perhaps more. After stripping herself to her underthings, she climbed in the shower behind him.

With a familiarity she wasn't sure she should have, she placed her fingertips on Elias's hips, and instantly he spun and pinned her wrists against the wall above her head, his face glowering.

"Don't."

Sylvie panted, looking up at him, lashes fluttering as the water sprayed her face. "Talk to me." Her words cut off as his thigh pressed between her legs and ground against her clit.

"I have nothing to say," he growled.

"Don't lie to me."

His eyes narrowed as he wrapped his hand around her throat. Not firm enough to stall her movements. Just a tease. "Who are your parents?"

She squinted, blinking away the shower spray. What did they have to do with anything? "Don't know. I told you they died when I was a baby. I only know their names from my files."

"What were they?"

"Lianna and Zach Hart."

Elias shook his head, pressing his body closer to hers. "Those are not their names."

Sylvie held her breath as he turned her face side to side as if he could see the lies in her flesh.

"Your blood is divine. I assume that to be your fae side, and I haven't much experience with different kinds of fae blood, so I can't determine what type you are, but you have old vampire blood, too." He scowled, clenching his fingers around her neck again, drawing out a moan.

"You're part born vampire."

The phrase sent waves of confusion into her fuzzy mind, and he lessened the pressure on her as he continued, "I know each born vampire that escaped my home realm when the newest king ascended the throne, and none of them had either of those names."

"Okay," she said, shrugging, despite the rising unease in her chest. The names of her parents meant very little to her. She didn't have photos in her file, so they were faceless anyway. Now they were nameless, too. "What does it matter?" *Was she human at all?* The thought was disarming. Frightening. "Why are you so mad at me?"

He frowned and pressed his cock against her hip, its hardness drawing her eyes, but his hand on her chin stopped her. She whimpered. "I'm mad because you disobeyed me." *What?* Her brain fogged with lust as the pressure on her amplified. Every inch of her sizzled with anticipation.

She rocked imperceptibly on his leg and bit back a moan from the friction.

"I'm mad because you are too fragile right now to get the punishment you deserve."

He dropped his hands to her hips and squeezed, forcing her to grind against his thigh. *Hell yes.*

"I'm mad because I want to bend you over and fuck you until you clench around me, but I can't until we bring Kian back to us."

"Why?" she whined, wrapping her hands around his neck. He hoisted her up and braced himself on a small shelf in the shower before lowering her back on his muscled thigh.

"Because you are *ours*." He caught her face in his hand and pressed his thumb past her lower lip. Sylvie wrapped her mouth around the digit and sucked, swirling her tongue around it.

His groan destroyed her as he ran one hand down her side, cupping her white lace-clad breast in his free hand. It was a simple moment, one she'd experienced before plenty of times, but she'd never craved someone's touch so much. Her eyes fluttered shut as he pinched and rubbed the nipple hard against the dainty fabric between his fingers.

"Swear to me that you don't know anything about your parents' past."

He pulled his thumb free from her mouth, and she sighed. "I swear it."

"Good." He wrapped his hands around her thighs and forced them around his thick abdomen as he carried her from the shower to the bed in the main room.

"We're gonna get your bed wet," she said as he laid her atop the luxurious charcoal comforter.

"We won't be sleeping in it." He prowled up her body, lowering his mouth to her neck. Oh gods, was he actually going to bite her? Would it feel good?

His cool lips brushed her skin, and the responding tingles answered her. *Yes. Finally.*

The torturous trail of his fingers down her body, past her soaked bra, and along her ribs and belly made her thoughts eddy away until only the desire to draw him inside her remained. With an arch of her back, his fingers swirled lower around her navel and lower until they teased the waistband of her matching lace panties. In measured movements, he slid his finger along the band left and right, slowly edging closer to her sex. "Please."

She would beg him. On her fucking knees, if she had to. It had all amounted to this. If this was what she was made for, then so be it. Fated to be his. She could do a hell of a lot worse.

He hovered above her, his kisses dipping to her collarbones and strategically turning into light nips as his fingers dipped lower. She arched for him, tilting her head right into the duvet to give him nonverbal permission. He could if he wanted to. She wanted him to. Lower and inside her panties, his touch grazed her unshaven front. She hoped he wouldn't mind. But to her relief and rising desire, when he touched her there, his breathing grew noisy. Uncontrolled. Messy. *Like her.* So this was where he came undone. But instead of continuing, instead of addressing the aching need and letting her fall over the edge of oblivion, he pulled back, rising to his feet and staring down at her shivering form.

She almost yelled at him when he turned to pull on some clothes. Instead, she raised a trembling hand to her mouth and wiped the light, moist sheen of sweat from her face. She was fucking throbbing, and he just stopped? The ache between her legs grew as he waltzed from the room, not even making eye contact.

What the fuck? She propped herself on her elbows, staring at the open doorway. Well, if he wouldn't help her finish, then she would just finish herself. She trailed her fingers between her legs, only to yelp when a hand latched onto her wrist. Elias had moved so fast that the wind from his wake didn't hit her for a full second.

"That is your punishment," he said, his sneer making her muscles constrict. "You are too fragile for the spanking I'm itching to give you, so this is the next best thing." Then, pulling her fingers away from her dripping core, he said, "Don't fucking touch yourself unless you want this to be your punishment from now on."

Her heart thumped in her chest and she felt light clenches in her sex from the gruffness of his words. His assured confidence made her belly tingle.

"Fuck you." She clamped her fists around the blankets. Her fingers itched to touch herself, even more so under Elias's disapproving gaze, but the thought of being denied an orgasm from him, even one more time, made her want to scream. He was good. *Too good.*

"Not yet, pet," he said with a shit-eating smirk. This time he turned from Sylvie and walked to the dresser, pulling out a cotton t-shirt and sweatpants before laying them beside her. They smelled like him. She fought the urge to pounce.

"Don't forget, I'll know if you touch yourself."

Sylvie sat up and frowned, reaching behind her back to unclasp her bra. If he was going to deny her, the least she could do was make him regret it. She thought he might leave, but he stood, hand curled around the doorframe tight enough to leave crescent moon cuts in the wood as her breasts spilled from their binding. She heaved a few full breaths for good measure before reaching for her waistband.

He moved then, his grin lighting his face before he disappeared down the hallway, his words lingering in his wake. "Get dressed. We're leaving." His absence didn't stir nearly as much fear inside her as it had when the hybrid attacked. He had killed the shifter with such ease, keeping her safe like he swore he would. Something within her trusted him, even if her mind was yet to catch up.

She snatched up his clothes and buried her face in them, soaking up his scent. Rich. Heady. It wasn't enough to dampen her disappointment. They'd just bloody got to this cabin. Going back to the office again sounded like her idea of hell. Maybe she was getting too greedy, though. She could be back in her apartment. She shuddered before jumping up, drying herself off, and dressing before looking for the asshat himself. Useful, protective asshat.

Down the stairs, she spied him, filling a bucket at the sink before walking to the porch and dumping it in a loud gush. Sylvie rolled her eyes about something else, still gushing. *Fucking bastard.* She shuffled to the couch as he made another trip from sink to porch, the diluted pool of blood spreading across the dirt in front of the house still visible.

Her thumb cuticle bled from where she picked at it. "Where's the body?"

"In the woods."

She bristled at his curt response. "Won't you get in trouble?"

"It's a dead bear, Hart. By the time the animals pick it clean, nobody will notice that it was decapitated."

Sylvie's mouth dropped open. "You took its head off?"

He dumped the last bucket and dropped it by the door. "Anyone that's a threat to my kindred will die." He looked her up and down, a faint light in his eyes, before he sighed. "I'm sorry we can't stay longer. But if that shifter found us, then others will be on their way."

She sighed too and padded to the door, slipping on her shoes. Before she could walk to the car, Elias spun her to face him, his piercing gaze capturing her in its embrace.

"You are my kindred, and we are equals, but when your life is in danger, and I ask something of you, I expect trust," he said the words with a softness she adored, and she noted the glance he made from her eyes to her lips. "And when I say don't open the door until I say, don't open the fucking door. Do you understand?"

She nodded, restraining her smirk as her mind drifted to the steady, dull ache between her legs.

"Good. Now get in the car."

SIXTEEN

When they finally returned to the Ambrose building, the inky black sky had pitched the glass skyscraper into darkness.

Sylvie followed beside Elias, her hand itching to bridge the gap between them and take his hand in hers. Her fatigue had long eased, only to be replaced by jittery frustration. Being cooped in a car for three hours with an aching cunt would do that to a person.

After filing into the underground elevator, Elias pushed a card through the slot next to his penthouse office floor button. Sylvie watched in fascination as they ascended past the lit-up floors, not stopping once.

"So, you can skip floors?" she asked him. "Is that why I always ended up late?"

Elias shot a look at her, his brow rising. "How often were you late in the few weeks of working for me?"

Her cheeks warmed as his lip curled over his slightly sharp canines.

"Every day," she mumbled.

"What was that?"

"I said." She glared with what she hoped resembled defiance. "Every. Day."

He stared for a moment in stony silence before laughing. "I should fire you."

Sylvie pressed her lips together and wrinkled her nose. "I mean, I thought you were nuts for hiring me. I had none of the skills you were looking for. Was it my looks?" The teasing came so naturally it startled her. Only days ago, she was muted by his beauty, but now the banter was as easy as breathing.

His expression darkened as he visually grazed her body. "I couldn't take my eyes off you. I sent you to get me coffee so I wouldn't be tempted to take you right across my desk."

Sylvie's gulp nearly snagged in her throat.

"It was the bond, but I didn't realise it was a possibility until I scented your blood and couldn't compel you."

"Compel?"

"You defied me at every opportunity. That's impossible for others."

"Oh," she said, trailing off as the elevator doors opened to the dimly lit floor. Elias stepped out first, and Sylvie followed, giving in to her urge to touch him. Her fingers curled instinctively around his index and middle finger. He tensed at the movement before tracing light strokes on the back of her hand with his thumb. *Oh, man.* She was in trouble. As they crossed the threshold and passed Natalie's desk, she mulled over her daily coffee trips. Did Elias even drink it? She'd never seen him eat anything besides blood.

Her throat went dry as images of the demon eclipsed her vision. The sneaky little fucker had clawed free of her mental box, and she screwed her eyes shut, trying to shove it back in. She let Elias pull her to his side, practically carrying her, only peeking when he lowered her onto a soft surface. A gasp passed her lips as she twisted around and took in the fully furnished office-turned-bedroom.

Floor-to-ceiling curtains gave her privacy, and a tall carved wardrobe stood regally against the wall atop a plush oatmeal rug. In front of it was a bed, dressed in throw pillows and a luxury duvet the colour of expensive wine.

Tears threatened her waterline when she spotted the giant potted plant perched in the opposite corner nearest the exterior windows. People paid fifty silver marks for plants that vibrant, its emerald, tapered leaves variegated with stripes of gold and cream. She'd never dreamt of having one.

"Elias. This is—" She turned to him with a warm smile, which turned to a lower lip bite as she took in his appearance. A crossed-armed posture, sleeves rolled to the elbows, and casual recline against the doorframe.

"What are you doing?" *Stop it immediately before I become a puddle on the floor.*

She exhaled a quick laugh, letting her face scrunch as she waved him over.

He smirked as he shook his head. *No?*

The only sound that she could pick up was the gentle metronome of a clock on the bedside table as he uncrossed his arms and ran a hand through his hair.

What is he doing?

His next move had her inching back, towards the maroon comforter on the bed. In one fluid motion, he undid his belt buckle and pulled it free from his trousers, looping it in half and pulling it taut between his hands.

The crack of the leather snapping against itself sent a thrill through her.

"What are you doing?" she asked, trying to mask the rising desire. "I didn't do anything wrong."

"You just confessed you were late every day working for me, and you did nothing wrong?"

His smirk and twinkling eyes only made her sexual appetite surge. Not once was she fearful of him, but the urge to play, to tease, to rile up the part of him that wasn't human spread until it was all she could think of.

She'd let him spank her raw if it meant he'd touch her again. A shiver rippled down her back. She'd had worse beatings for a fraction of the sex appeal.

He walked around the bed until the mattress pressed against his thighs, and she was before him. Not letting him take her so easily, she crawled back until she hit the headboard. A soft, low hum sounded from his chest as he reached forward, quick as lightning, and pulled her by the ankle. She gasped, the sound flaring into a laugh as Elias flipped her onto her stomach and stood between her legs, spreading them wide. She wondered briefly if her borrowed sweats fabric would dull any of the incoming force she was anticipating.

It didn't.

The second a sharp snap hit her left buttock, she yelped, bunching the comforter into her fists. "Again."

Elias pulled her by the hips and ground his pelvis right over her sex, ignoring her desperate panting. The moan that escaped her mouth was debasing.

Deserved. His every touch gave her more pleasure than she had ever experienced with another man. Or woman. Or neither. Both.

Mikayla Everitt

Her mind stopped working as another hard thwack hit her right cheek, and she whined, burying her face into the mattress. The scent of fresh laundry swirled in her nose as Elias rubbed each spot, where she was sure there was a mark, and flipped her over onto her back.

She buried the growing smile beneath her shaking hands, and Elias tutted, pulling them away. "Don't hide from me."

"You're so demanding." Her face threatened to burst into the most smitten grin.

His nostrils flared. "You liked that, didn't you?"

"So? Isn't that the point?"

A smile pulled at his lips as he rubbed a hand across his jaw. "This is going to be fun."

Bubbling giddiness clenched Sylvie's stomach as she watched cogs tick behind his eyes, but she tamped that down and glared at him. "Why are you only trying to come up with punishments? Do you do rewards too?"

Elias snapped his eyes to hers. Wild elation brewed there, and it took everything not to prostrate herself before him. A sinner to a god.

"Oh yes," he said, stilling her mind. "But I can tell I'll be punishing you more."

"And why is that?"

With a sudden grip on her chin, Elias dipped his face to hers, offering a soft kiss to her lips before whispering against them, "Because you're a brat."

Brat? She was many things, but not that. "I am not!"

She pressed her hand into his chest, and he withdrew as she shuffled off the bed and walked to the wardrobe to grab a satin nightgown. She'd been saving this one for a special

143

occasion, but she wanted to give Elias a punishment of his own.

"Where do you think you're going?"

"Bathroom," she said, padding down the hall, through his office to his en suite. Her anxiety about being alone in the room drifted away as she spun around and spied Elias at his desk with a smug look on his face. She closed the door with a soft snick. He was right outside; she would be fine. *Just breathe.*

She did her business quickly, ready to be out of the tight space, and changed into the gown. In the mirror, she smiled at her reflection, running her hands along the cinched fabric around her bust and ass. The silver slip amplified her every asset, and she turned to leave the bathroom, taming the snarls of her long brown waves with her fingers.

Elias's eyes followed her as she sashayed past him, out of his office, and into her makeshift bedroom. As soon as she crossed the threshold, though, she paused, staring at the bed.

She couldn't do it. She couldn't sleep alone there. A warm breath caressed her shoulder, and she tilted her head against Elias's chest.

"Climb in," he said in a husky whisper against her hair. Her fingers intertwined with his as she walked over and climbed on the bed. He followed and pulled her duvet back and then up without a word, tucking her in gently.

"Will you stay?" she asked, pulling the blankets up to her chin.

He nodded and remained seated, placing his hand atop her covered leg.

Her breathing deepened as she stared at his dimly lit profile. The sharpness of his bone structure and the soft curls of his dark hair created the perfect juxtaposition.

"Are you a sadist?" she asked, blinking up at him. Questions for midnight. Questions she sometimes asked herself.

He turned towards her, his hair dropping in front of his eyes. "What do you know about dominance and submission?"

Sylvie shrugged, squeezing her thighs beneath the heavy blankets. "Besides porn and a few books, not much."

Elias hummed, trailing his hand up her calf to her thigh.

"What are the rules?" Sylvie asked then. "Do we have a safe word? Can it be strawberries?"

"Sylvie," Elias said, squeezing her thigh. "Go to sleep. We'll talk about it in the morning."

"No."

His eyes flashed red in the dark, and he leaned over her, lowering his lips to her ear. "This is why I called you a brat. It doesn't mean what you think, and you almost perfectly embody it. Go to sleep, or you'll wake up to my mouth on your clit, and this time I'll get you so close to the edge that you'll ache for days."

Her lips parted as she frowned in the dark. "Ugh, fine."

Broken sleep made the night drag. Each time she roused or shot up with a nightmare, Elias held her and guided her body back to the mattress. By the time she woke in the morning, though, he was gone. She jumped up, about to sprint from her bedroom, when a familiar voice trilled through the glass doors.

"Good morning, sir. I was looking for Sylvie. Is she here?"

Natalie.

Sylvie edged towards the door, and she brushed her finger against the drawn curtain.

"I sent her to get me breakfast." His voice sounded from behind her curtained wall, his silhouette visible through the fabric.

"What's in there?"

"A project."

Sylvie sensed their attention on the curtains before her. "Do not disturb the room. Are we clear?" A lingering pause dragged for a few seconds. Was that the compulsion he was talking about?

Natalie's chirpy response seemed to confirm her hypothesis. "Oh, okay. No problem."

"I need you to go down to the marketing team and ask them about their latest project for me. I want the ETA and any drafts they have made."

Natalie made a strange noise, a mix between a scoff and a cough. "Yes, sir, right away." As heels clacked away from her room, Elias opened the door and peeked his head in.

"Get changed and find me some breakfast before she gets back." He dipped down and kissed her lips. "Or would you like her to know you're fucking your boss?"

Sylvie rolled her eyes and placed her index finger against his lips. "Not yet, pet," she said, revelling in his smirk.

"You'll pay for that one."

"Can't wait."

He shook his head and grinned, as if planning all the ways he could punish her. Oh well, two could play at that game.

* * *

Ghost mode was Sylvie's best friend as she researched domination, submission, and "brats," desperate to know a little more about Elias's sexual pleasures.

She didn't think he'd care about work productivity, considering they were kindred, and her role at his business was bullshit. At that point, she was sure she could get away with murder.

He already had.

She scoffed when Natalie walked straight into her office like she owned the place, her navy skirt fluttering in her wake. Sylvie slammed the minimise button and scrutinised her with raised brows. "Hi?"

"Where have you been?" Natalie asked with a frown. "Are you sick?"

Sylvie pulled a face. "Uh, no. Are you?"

Natalie crossed her arms and tapped her glossy black pump on the carpet. "No. I'm just wondering what happened to you. Elias has been acting weird, and you've been MIA."

"Did you miss me?"

The shadows beneath her eyes and chapped lips drew Sylvie's attention as Natalie scoffed. "I'm just not wanting to do your work anymore. How the hell did you get a virus on your computer, anyway?" *Oh right, the virus.*

Sylvie shrugged and forced a bright laugh. "I don't know; some spy software in one of my spam emails. Sorry you had to deal with that."

Natalie gnawed her lip, regarding her for a few moments too long, and sighed. "Okay, well, I'm glad you're back. Now, do your job." The jab held little venom as Natalie disappeared, leaving Sylvie staring after her. There was something off about her, but Sylvie wasn't familiar enough to pry.

After waiting an extra few seconds, she reopened her browsing screen and continued reading the first article on brats. *"A brat is a submissive who loves playfully pushing buttons and 'breaking' rules. They deliberately behave in this way to provoke attention from their dominant."*

Her heart thumped as she realised she was very much a brat. "Shit …"

She skimmed the page, and heat rushed to her face and core when she read about the "brat tamer."

"The 'tamer' is the role the dominant takes on with their brat. A tamer's job is to bring the brat to submission."

That's what he had been doing. Trying to tame her. *Fun.* Her panties grew damp as she exited the site, and she adjusted her posture, preening as if he would walk in and catch her looking guilty. She returned to her emails but couldn't get her mind away from her potential sexual future. Before she screwed up an important meeting, she stood and headed for the shared bathroom, down a short corridor past the elevators. The sight of Natalie's empty desk brought both relief and surprise. Elias had likely sent her on yet another random errand.

She locked herself in the last stall from the door, pulling down her black pants, and finished her business before wiping herself and her panties. For a moment, she contemplated touching herself to get off. It had been so long, and even the thought of orgasm made her muscles clench.

The door outside the stall creaked open and closed, followed by the familiar sound of the lock turning. Sylvie froze, hand pressed against the stall door as footsteps tapped along the laminate floors. Her anxiety rose as the sound stopped outside her stall, and a light knock rapped on the door.

"Come out."

SEVENTEEN

Sylvie's mouth dropped open at the familiar feminine voice before she wrenched the toilet stall door inward. "Kerensa! What are you doing here?" She refrained from hugging her, pushing past to wash her hands. When she turned and threw her arms around her, Kerensa's face twisted into a grimace. "Why are you so happy to see me? It's only been a few days for you."

"I dunno." Sylvie released her and shrugged with a smile. "You're a welcome distraction." From touching herself in the toilets of her workplace … *Fucking hell, who have I become?*

"I have news."

Sylvie swallowed and nodded before walking to the locked door. "Come," she beckoned, but Kerensa shook her head.

"I need to take you back now."

"Where?"

Kerensa levelled her gaze at Sylvie and clenched her jaw. "Kian is about to make a mistake, and I need him to see it before it's too late for him and our court."

Sounded like a Kian problem. Sylvie turned the lock and went to twist the door handle when Kerensa hissed. "Let's go. Now!"

The insistence set her on edge, and Sylvie sputtered, thinking of Elias. "I can't go without him." She twisted the knob with slippery hands as Kerensa reached towards her. "Kerensa, wait!" Her cries stopped suddenly as the bathroom door flew open, and she was dragged off her feet and into Elias's arms.

"What do you think you're doing, Kerensa?"

Kerensa rolled her eyes and growled. "You know you can't come to Ilfaem. It's verboten."

"I'm sure Kian won't mind. He'll make an allowance as crown prince. Just this once," Elias countered.

Sylvie shook as she gripped Elias's shoulders tightly. The thought of being away from him made her whole body tremble. Even Kerensa noticed her shaking limbs. "You move fast." The judgement in her glare had a swirl of shame winding up Sylvie's guts.

"You know that isn't true, Kerensa. She is both of ours. It's the bond," Elias said.

Kerensa snorted, crossing her arms. "I know no such thing, but fine," she grated through clenched teeth. "I need her to come, and if that means I bring you, then so be it."

Oh, thank the gods. She was nowhere near ready to face Kian again, yet with Elias at her side, it would be manageable. Too bad they didn't have more time to get to know each other. They weren't even exclusive yet.

Sylvie relaxed, her white-knuckled grip on Elias's shirt loosening.

"Glad we came to such a smooth agreement," he purred.

Kerensa snatched up his forearm, then Sylvie's, and the world tilted unbearably. "Not again!" Sylvie squeezed her eyes shut, burying her face into Elias's warm shoulder, his grip on her body tightening as she jolted against solid ground.

This time her stomach contents stayed inside her body, but her brain exploded in a kaleidoscope of red, purple, and gold. Within the colours, shapes emerged. Intricate interlinking designs pulled her apart, then back together again. Broken to whole. Alone to encircled on all angles. She stood between the colours as they twisted by at hurricane speeds, her hair flying in all angles. *Hey.* She reached for them. *Stop.* Her vision slowly cleared, and above her, eyes with a familiar crimson hue hovered. The owner's shaking hands gently brushed the hair from her face.

Sylvie swallowed and tried to speak when Kerensa shushed her.

"Bring her this way," she said, walking down a long corridor. Even after her brief visit the last time, she knew the place was somewhere she'd never been before.

Elias scooped her up and followed along, kissing her hairline softly. "We won't be able to travel back again for a few weeks; otherwise, your portal sickness could become dangerous. It isn't advisable for anyone who isn't fully Fae to make so many jumps in such a short time."

She nodded weakly, closing her eyes as he carried her down the long, cold path.

"They're planning the engagement party," Kerensa whispered.

Elias's growl roused her, even as the words processed slowly. "What the fuck is he doing?" he said.

"He won't speak to me or Mother. She seems happier than ever, but I don't even recognise him. He doesn't know you two are here either, and I'd like to keep it that way. For now."

Sylvie's eyes fluttered open, and she looked up at Elias and Kerensa's tense figures. "What's happening?"

Elias set her gently in a foreign bed. Kerensa clenched her fists, not bothering to answer the question. They both knew what was happening. Sylvie just wasn't sure she cared.

"You've got three days to recover," Kerensa said. "I'll arrange food."

"Wait," Elias said. He leaned down and gathered some of Sylvie's hair in his hand, running the long strands between his fist. Finally, he pulled a single strand free and handed it to Kian's sister.

"Give it to your clothing enchantress personally. Tell her silver, champagne, and sheer. And tell her it's for me."

Kerensa clicked her tongue and slipped the long brown hair into her satchel. "She doesn't take requests anymore; that's why we have the enchanted wardrobes. She's retired from the damn court. Lazuli already tried."

"Trust me," Elias ground out. "We go way back."

As Kerensa left, grumbling and slamming the door, Sylvie attempted a frown.

"You go way back, huh?" She wasn't usually a jealous person. A previous boyfriend had convinced her to try an open relationship once, which inevitably turned sour, but she hadn't envied the other woman. With Elias, though, she could burn cities with the fire in her that craved him. He was hers alone. She straightened at the intensity of her thoughts. If he ever found out, he'd run a mile from her. Nobody wanted a clingy, insecure partner.

Elias sat at her side and stroked her face. "I'm five centuries old, pet. You don't see me getting mad about your past."

Sylvie scoffed. Five hundred years old? Surely an exaggeration, because he didn't act like an ancient monster. "Well, I haven't told you my sexual history yet," she said.

"Doesn't matter," he shot back. "No one will ever have fucked you the way I can. Kindred or not."

Sylvie lifted the pillow from her side and buried her reddening cheeks into the cool fabric. She was far too weak from portalling to let her heart race that fast.

"Now rest," Elias said with a low chuckle, pulling the pillow free and guiding her to her back. "The party will be upon us before we know it."

The vining plants around the bed frames dipped and shimmied in a phantom breeze. "Do you think he'll be happy to see me?" she asked. Hope flared like the light of a dying candle. *Unacceptable.* She squashed its wick between her burned fingers.

"We don't want him to be." Elias's jaw ticked at her raised brow, a why sitting on the tip of her tongue.

"I've known Kian a very long time, and I know when he falls into the darkness or takes too much from others. The only thing that burns through the emotions he's absorbed, despite his hatred of it, is anger."

She sighed. Elias sounded resolute and convinced of Kian's innocence. Sylvie wasn't so quick to forgive, but she would play Elias's game. If only because it drew him closer to her. Anger could be potent. She knew that fact well. It was the reason she kept hers bridled and replaced it with snark. Anger could kill.

She thought about another angry male in her life and shuddered from the pressure of his hand on her thigh. "I did some research this morning."

"Oh?" His question sounded like he very much knew about her extracurricular research.

"It made me realise I am a brat." Her voice trailed off as Elias's eyes darkened. "And I want you to tame me."

"I should punish you for bringing this up when you know damned well you're too fragile for me to act on it."

She bit her lip as he stood, pulling her hand and placing it on his crotch, the hard cock desperate to burst free. "Look what you're doing to me."

Sighing, Sylvie moved her hand up and down his length, squeezing softly. Her own sex dampened, and her other hand pulled off her bed covers to show him as she slid it between her thighs. She paused, hovering her fingers above her sensitive spot, looking at him for confirmation.

To her surprise and relief, he nodded. Her fingers descended and swirled in languid circles, immediately igniting a fire in her belly. Elias's lusting gaze only spurred her desire onward until she reached a glorious peak.

"Come, now."

She let herself clench over and over after his command and lay panting as the orgasm ebbed. It wasn't what she'd expected. She frowned. Elias's smile grew in response, and she only frowned harder.

"Didn't feel as good as you thought it would, did it?" he taunted.

Sylvie pulled her hand free from him and wrenched the sheets back over her. "What is happening to me?"

Elias sat, adjusting his trousers. "It's the first symptoms of a kindred heat. Your body wants to consummate the bond and will stop your self-pleasure until we do."

Rolling her eyes, Sylvie scowled at the roof. "And you still won't fuck me until Kian is back with us."

"Yes."

"We're about to go to his engagement party, so I doubt that'll ever fucking happen." With one last groan, she turned away from Elias and closed her eyes.

"Brat," Elias whispered with a chuckle as sleep stole her away.

* * *

"Put it on," Kerensa said, throwing the dress back over the screen between her and Sylvie.

"It looks like a fucking piece of lingerie! People are gonna see me." *See all of me, more like.* She wasn't a prude, but there were some parts of her anatomy that didn't need to be public.

"It's not a fae party without at least three orgies."

"Not helping!" Sylvie ogled the sheer, plunging gown behind the privacy screen, though you could barely call it a gown.

The champagne bodice had a corset in a leotard style that showed off her thighs and ass through sheer skirts. A plunging slit ran from her hip on each leg, and some extra straps wrapped around the tops of her thighs like dainty garters.

She stuck her arms in the lacy, off-the-shoulder sleeves and carefully tucked her breasts inside the bra.

Kerensa tapped her foot impatiently and peeked over the screen.

"Hey! I'm not ready yet!"

"Oh, grow up. They're just tits," Kerensa said with an eye-roll.

"Breasts. Who's the one who needs to grow up again?" Sylvie snapped back, smiling when Elias's low chuckle sounded from across the room.

"Well, does it feel good or not?" Kerensa said.

"It feels fine. The way it looks is where my problems start."

"What's wrong with it?" Elias asked from across the room. His rich midnight tailored suit dripped with wealth. She was never one to fawn over money—it was always too volatile to covet and often caused her to spiral when she lost it—but on him, it was everything. She would get on her knees in a second just for him to spank her and tell her she was a good little slut—

"Sylvie?" Elias's voice drew her back into the moment.

"Uh, yeah." She swallowed her thoughts and raked her fingers through her waves. The brown tresses tickled her waist, and she pulled some hair in front of her breasts to cover up. It didn't help that the entire castle was about to see her ass.

She stepped into a dainty pair of heels and walked out from behind the privacy screen. Kerensa nodded with approval, but Sylvie didn't care for her appreciation. Instead, her gaze shot straight to Elias, letting his darkening eyes and parted lips warm her scantily clad body.

He nodded and dipped his hand into his back pocket. "It's just missing one thing," he said, letting a silver string dangle from his finger. Not a string, Sylvie corrected. A choker?

"It's a collar," Elias said with a smirk.

Swallowing, Sylvie stepped forwards and spun, crossing her arms as Elias bunched her hair into a ponytail. He tugged slightly before asking her to hold it. She obliged, blushing profusely as Kerensa watched the exchange.

"Kian will hate that if he thinks it's real," she commented as the latch clicked. Sylvie probed the fabric around her throat and spun, still holding her hair.

Elias hummed. "Tie it up."

"No, I need it to cover me up a bit."

"That's exactly why I want it up."

Sylvie frowned but relented, not wanting him to say anything more risqué in Kerensa's presence. She knew he would, too.

Kerensa waved her hands in a hurry-up motion, and Elias slipped Sylvie's hand through his arm.

"Remember, our goal tonight is to rile Kian up. The quicker he burns the excess energy he's carrying the better. Even our presence here is going to ruffle many fae feathers. Vampires are not welcome in the fae realm. That's why portal sickness is especially bad for you. That and the volume of travelling you've been doing."

"Wasn't my fault," she murmured back.

"No," he conceded, following Kerensa out the door. "I might say or do things you won't expect, but know it's for show, understand? You can use your safe word if it gets too much at any point."

Sylvie swallowed but looked up at Elias's neutral face with a soft smile. "Strawberries?"

"Strawberries," he echoed.

She sensed from the severity of his tone that things were about to get insanely freaky, but the prospect thrilled her. Perhaps the heat he was referencing, or her desire to get back at Kian, was fuelling her, but she vowed that her safe word would go unused tonight.

The walk down the twisted corridors was quiet until the roaring rush of hundreds of voices carried from the throne room. Sylvie squeezed Elias's arm and slowed her pace as the path became familiar. So many eyes were about to see her half-naked.

"Sylvie," Elias said, "take a breath. When we go in the room, you will stay at my side, but you will keep your eyes on your feet and hands clasped behind your back."

She looked up at him with a quizzical brow but slowly unravelled her arm from his and clasped her hands behind her back.

"Like this?"

He smiled down at her and nodded. "Perfect."

Kerensa groaned from the double doors. "Would you two hurry? The greetings are almost finished."

Taking a deep breath, Sylvie locked her gaze on the floor and followed beside Elias, keeping his polished dress shoes in her peripheral as a guide. Tonight was going to be fun.

EIGHTEEN

Kerensa pushed the door open, charging through in her violet armour, the finer leather detailing around her limbs and velvety fabric making her look prepared for battle, not a party. That and the amount of clothes she wore. People could have classified Sylvie as a prude based on the fashions happening that night. Sylvie cast her eyes down, only catching the crowd of bare skin in her lowered vision as she and Elias crossed into the grand hall. The raucous voices ebbed to a soft stream of whispers, and she tuned into the sounds.

"What is that thing doing here?"

"Who is she?"

"I want that dress."

Sylvie gnawed on the inside of her lip to stop the laugh as Elias tugged her onward. Their clipped steps echoed around the room as they approached what she assumed to be the throne. She resisted the urge to look up even when she felt Kian's eyes on her.

Elias hummed low in his chest. "Good to see you again, Kian, and your beautiful fiancée. Though it surprised me to hear you weren't coming back with our fated."

Kian cleared his throat to respond, but Lazuli's ethereal voice echoed in the silent room. "Prince Kian has followed his duties, and the arrangements made by his mother, the queen."

"Ah, yes," Elias replied. "And where might she be on this fine occasion?"

"She had to make a last-minute trip to Lazuli's home to iron out the expectations of our union." Kian's gruff voice sent shivers down Sylvie's spine. She didn't recognise it. If it wasn't Elias who was talking to him, she would have thought Kian was an imposter.

The pain in his tone beckoned her gaze, but she fought off the impulse and stepped closer to Elias. His hand gripped her bicep roughly and pushed her back to where she was. He rubbed his thumb on the back of her arm, but growled harshly, "Stay put, pet. The grown-ups are talking."

She blinked and bit down her smile. "Yes, sir," she said in a fractured whisper. From her downward gaze, she swore she spotted his pants twitch.

"Well, we have no gifts for you besides holding your position in our company whenever you decide to visit Erus. We were in quite a rush to attend and didn't have time to stop on the way. Lady Lazuli, it was most informative making your acquaintance."

"I don't see how," she replied, her voice huskier than usual. "I hardly spoke a word."

Elias didn't respond, but Sylvie could picture the sexually charged smirk on his face as he gripped her shoulder.

"We'll take our leave now and enjoy the festivities. Congratulations again, my friend." He spun, dragging Sylvie across the floor. She barely kept her footing. As they moved, her eyes flitted over her shoulder to the pair on dual thrones, and she softened her gaze to one of innocence. She could play the part. Her childhood had beaten that dishonesty into her.

Lazuli, all dressed in white, pressed her lips together, taking in Sylvie's figure. The twinkle in Lazuli's gaze when she looked over at Elias, though, sent a flurry of anger through Sylvie.

Elias was hers. She wouldn't let Lazuli take another one of her males. At Lazuli's back stood Zephrinah, dressed in dark purple, as if attempting to blend into the room's dark corners. There was no hiding for Sylvie tonight, not when she embodied sex.

Kian appeared dull compared to Lazuli's shine. His brown skin held a grey hue, and his once beautiful dark eyes, lined with mulberry, sat sunken in his head and underlined by a worrying black shade. They met gazes for a second before Elias pulled her harder after him.

"Move your feet, pet."

In the last second before turning, Sylvie spotted Kian's fingers curling into the arm of his throne, clenching painfully, the bones visible beneath the taut skin. She turned away, a sense of unease wending through her belly as she locked eyes once more with the polished floors. This wasn't right. None of it. She ground her teeth as Elias pulled her away from the horror show. The throne room was larger than she remembered, and it was a few minutes of weaving through party goers before they paused in a darkened corner.

Elias dipped his head to her ear as the chatter of other creatures returned. "You did well."

She met his eyes and nodded before he tutted and gripped the back of her neck, making her look down again.

"I'm going to take you to one of the lounging beds, and you are to stay there."

"Yes, sir," she replied again, biting her lip, head down.

They headed to a busy corner, and Elias shooed two translucent, pointy-eared creatures off the daybed.

"I'll be back soon. Kerensa is watching you, so if you need her, she'll be there."

She nodded, strangely calm about being left alone, and crawled across the cushioned surface. The burning heat of lusting gazes caressed her ass, and she arched her back before turning and reclining on a few huge throw pillows. She battered her lashes up at Elias, noticing that she was in plain view of Kian and Lazuli, who were directly behind him.

Kian's eyes raked up her body, and she shivered before folding her legs delicately. She remembered being posed that way for modelling photos as a preteen when her fourth foster mother thought she was "too beautiful" to play sports. That was before she grew tits and an ass and became a distraction for the men in the family. She was sent back to the girl's home soon after that.

With a sigh, Sylvie waved over a tall server and stuck her hand out for a bundle of grapes. They placed the vine in her hands, careful not to touch her skin, and she picked the fruits one by one, placing each between her teeth and taking small bites as she watched the fae chattering and dancing near her. Dancing was a rather light description and not altogether accurate. Grinding was closer. She cast her gaze about the room. Hundreds of fae with skin in every shade of an oil slick, milled and dry humped. Some had wings, others horns, and a few had veins that glowed a vibrant sunset hue. Stunning. In her periphery, Kian's eyes remained glued to the lounge bed, and she hid a smile behind her hand.

Elias appeared in front of the throne once more, and Sylvie stilled as he offered his hand to Lazuli. She beamed down at him and accepted. Kian didn't seem to take notice; his eyes remained glued on Sylvie. *Don't react.*

A swell of lilting music drowned out the chatter of the fae, and they paired off, gliding elegantly across the room, their feet treading in perfect synchronicity. The ones that had been grinding slithered away into the darkened corners, their heavy breathing adding a layered effect to the melody.

Sylvie lost sight of Kian and Elias as the fae pairs spun and twirled, and she scooted to the edge of the lounger. Her pulse fluttered. *Lost lamb.* She stood and wrung her hands, searching for a familiar face when a presence warmed her back. A shiver took hold as a foreign wind fanned across her neck and a pair of lips pressed against the shell of her ear.

"Care to dance, Princess?"

Kian. Of course it was. She turned to Kian, reining in her emotions and noting his attention fixed on her face, and the hand offered between them. He was real. In front of her and asking for a dance. But he wasn't angry. Did Elias's plan fail? His dark eyes reflected her surprised expression as she processed his words.

"You want to dance with me?"

"Of course." He smiled, but his eyes didn't crinkle like she remembered.

Sylvie's brows knitted together as she lifted her hand into his and followed him through the throng of graceful fae. Placing one hand on her hip and keeping the other in his grasp, he stepped towards her, guiding her other hand to his shoulder.

Her cheeks grew hot as he stared like he was trying to absorb her image into his mind. The room melted away until only they remained, and the music.

She dropped her gaze. It was too much. She was supposed to hate him after what he did. But when his voice offered a pained, "No," she lifted her head, letting their moment extend. As if suspended in time, alone and yet united, her hope swelled with the music.

Kian guided her across the floor, and while she did not know the dance, he took control perfectly, as if he were a puppeteer of her feet.

"How long has it been for you?" she asked.

"How are you?" he said.

Their voices overlapped one another.

"You go."

"No, you go."

Kian smiled and spun Sylvie in a small arc, dipping her as he pulled her in.

"It's been a few years," Kian murmured into her hair. Sylvie's mouth dropped open, and she pulled her head back to look at him. The years had been unkind. Not on his physique, no, he was impeccable, but his soul.

"I-I'm sorry."

"How often have I told you not to apologise to me?"

She blushed and twirled again, enjoying the soft breeze beneath her skirts. Despite their transparent quality, they still held a ton of heat.

"Not enough, apparently. What have you been doing all this time?" She wasn't sure she wanted to hear the answer but asked, regardless.

"Meetings, treaty writing, fending off a horde of fae demons from the Stone Court, prolonging my betrothal as long as possible."

Sylvie blinked, taking it all in. "Fae demons?"

"Yes," Kian grumbled. "Hybrids. We think they're at the Stone Court because they have the largest portion of dryads in the realm. Their blood is addicting to the lesser mixed breeds."

The music changed and threw Sylvie off as she tried to match steps to the beat while being bombarded with images of the monster that almost ate her. Stumbling, she grabbed Kian's biceps to steady herself, pausing when he winced.

"I think I met one of those things at the Ambrose building," she whispered, returning her hand to Kian's, eyeing him warily. "Elias killed it."

Rolling his shoulders, Kian resumed his control of the dance and nodded. "Are you alright?"

She let the monster free of its cage to peer over her mental walls and let her fear bubble. "Yeah," she said, avoiding his gaze. Suddenly, lying to him felt all wrong. What if Elias was right? What if he wasn't to blame?

She spotted Elias spinning Lazuli in tight spirals, a tense look on his face. Bliss on hers, though. The witch.

Sighing, Sylvie lay her head on Kian's chest, letting her breathing synchronise with his. She needed the calm, and to hide her expression. Meek pet was the play for the night, not violent murderess. Her sight fell on the inner crease of his wrist where an old scar shone with puckered skin. That was her fault, though, it looked bigger. More jagged. She could've sworn she only nicked him. Her thumb went to trace across it when he tightened his hand over hers and tipped her back in a delicate arch, her ponytail almost brushing the floor. She couldn't stop the laugh as he drew her back in.

"I missed this."

She whispered the statement so quietly she thought he didn't hear her, but after a small sigh, Kian asked, "What?"

"The peace." The realisation hit her suddenly, mingling with shame. Despite her growing bond with Elias, true peace was something that she only felt when she was with Kian. His abilities had everything to do with it, but she found she didn't mind. The nagging anxieties that swirled in her mind days prior were gone. Even the monster that paced in her mental chest had shrunk into a pocket-sized creature. She tucked it back away.

"Are you manipulating my emotions again?" It wasn't asked with malice, but interest. If she could control her emotions, it would solve a lot of her issues.

Kian swallowed and dipped his head down, resting his forehead on hers. "Just easing your fears, Princess." He paused, his voice hitching as if the words he was about to say hurt him. "Is Elias hurting you?"

"I think my pet has had enough of your company now, Prince. It's my turn." Elias levelled his smug smile at Kian and pulled Sylvie away roughly. While she missed the tender touch of Kian, Elias's roughness filled another nagging part of her.

"She isn't your pet, Elias. She's our fated." Kian's tight jaw and narrowed eyes honed on Elias's strangling grip on her forearm.

"*My* kindred," Elias replied, hooking his arm around Sylvie's lower back and pressing her against him. "You gave up that right when you sent her back to me alone. I can do with her as I please, and I am."

His fangs glinted beneath the candlelit chandeliers, and Kian's body tensed. "You're lying," he hissed.

Lazuli appeared at his side then, laying her sharpened nails atop his suit jacket. "Darling, you're making a scene. Come dance with me." She stood with her upturned hand for a beat, then two, as Kian looked from Elias to Sylvie before grasping her hand and pulling her wordlessly into the crowd.

NINETEEN

Sylvie's chest twinged as Kian's face twitched when he sat back on the throne with Lazuli whispering something in his ear. Elias, though, hummed, a look of satisfaction on his face. He loosened his grip on her waist but continued to guide her back to the cushioned lounger. He pulled her onto his lap as he sat. "You have exceeded my every expectation tonight."

His hands wrapped around her hips and rocked her against the hardness in his pants. "I won't forget how good you've been, Sylvie." She shivered as he purred her name into her ear, but sat up straight instead of letting herself sink into his touch.

The guilt from her behaviour overrode most of the excitement she felt from Elias's praise. He pressed his lips against her lobe, murmuring, "I know it must hurt you to lie to him, but it's for his own good. Lazuli is hiding something dark. I could sense her probing my defences as we danced. Whatever it is, it's draining him."

She inhaled sharply as her gaze fixed on the princess-to-be, stroking Kian's arm with her talons and grinning from ear to ear. From their distance, the sharpened nails glistened as if dipped in silver. Kian could manipulate emotions. Could she?

Sylvie pressed her chin to her shoulder. "What did she say to you?"

"Not here," he responded, dropping his hand to her inner thigh and trailing his fingers in upwards strokes.

The surrounding lighting dimmed as if half the candles went out and a new sensual musical piece started. Sylvie's eyes darted around the room as all the fae's elegant moves became more intimate and erotic.

One couple to her right gripped each other's asses and ground their pelvises together as their mouths explored the other's neck. The other pairs, trios, and even groups of four all seemed to do the same thing, dipping hands into each other's clothes, groping and kneading.

Sylvie flushed hot, doused in lust by the sounds of music accompanied by heavy moans, sighs, and whimpers. The only ones not getting into the action were the engaged couple the party was for. Kian could've been mistaken for stone, a stoic poise about him as his fiancée draped herself over his lap. Closer and closer, the python wound about his neck. And she was that. A snake.

A wandering finger slipping beneath tulle and lace made Sylvie gasp, her attention returning to the male behind her. His long digit fingered the hem of her leotard, and she rocked her hips, earning a sharp hiss in her ear. "Careful, pet. He's watching. Don't want him to think you want me."

"But I do," she groaned, spreading her knees wider for him to better touch her core. The heat in her body rose as he rubbed a warm finger pad right above her clit, and she let her head fall back.

A rough grip around her thighs forced her to stand, and Elias spun her, pressing his face into her belly. He inhaled deeply before pulling her back into his lap, making her sit side-on. Her thigh pressed against his groin. It twitched against her. "I need you to be afraid," Elias murmured in her ear. "He needs to believe I'm not caring for you."

"Why?" she moaned, pressing her thighs together for some much-needed friction. She didn't know if it was the dry-humping orgies around her or a side effect of the mating heat, but she was feeling way more eager than usual to perform public sex acts.

"He's a nurturer, always has been. Far kinder and wiser than I'll ever be, but something is wrong with him, and it has something to do with *her*," he growled the last word and narrowed his gaze at Kian on the throne, with Lazuli on his lap. Kian's hand grazed absently up and down her thigh, rubbing dangerously close to her crotch before trailing down again.

"I know he wants you, Kitten. Now we need to make him believe he needs to protect you."

Elias grabbed her wrist and yanked it upward, letting his pointed fangs elongate. The gleam in his eye shot adrenaline through Sylvie's body, and she automatically wrenched away.

"Why do you think this will even work?" she asked in a rushed whisper, still trying to pull away from the fangs getting dangerously close to her wrist.

"Don't you remember?" he purred. "Kian hates it when I play with my food."

With that, he descended, and Sylvie squeezed her eyes shut, heart hammering as she waited for the sharp pain. Warm liquid dripped down her forearm, but the sting never came. Still terrified, she peeled her eyes open and saw Elias had torn his teeth into the flesh of his own hand and expertly hid it to look like he had bitten her.

Elias caught her eye and winked, standing abruptly and throwing her over his shoulder. A hard thump hit her ass cheek, and she gasped, wrapping her hand around her wrist as Kian's blazing eyes took in the scene. It was working. He stood, his fiancée sprawled on the stairs, like he'd dumped her there, and watched them leave the throne room, murder in his eyes.

* * *

"Go in and get changed. I need to clean myself up. I'm sure Kian will show up any second," Elias said, gesturing to the blood drenching his forearm and wrist. They stood outside their room and Sylvie nodded, wrapping her hand around the handle and letting herself into the dimly lit space. Based on Kian's expression, it surprised her he wasn't already barging through the door demanding Elias's head. *Good.* She needed to see Kian away from Lazuli's prying eyes and whatever influence she had.

Sylvie padded to the bed, brows furrowing. The room looked messier than when they'd left. Her nape tingled. *Shit.*

Before she could take two more steps, a cold, sharp object pierced into the front of her neck while a hot, sweaty body gripped her around the shoulders.

Her mouth opened to scream when a feminine voice hissed, "Make a noise, and I'll make it hurt more than you could ever imagine."

When she went to lift her hands, the voice growled, pulling the weapon across her neck an inch. Sylvie whimpered as blood squirted from her body. *Fuck, this is bad.*

172

The sharp pinch and burn made her eyes fill with tears, and her heart pounded faster, making the wound spurt more. "And keep your hands by your side."

Mouth closing, Sylvie pressed her head away from the weapon and into the attacker, getting a musty waft up her nose.

"Don't do this." She tried to lessen the pressure on her throat, but the blade kept burying deeper. Hot blood gushed down her front, pooling in her collarbones and between her breasts. The dress was ruined. They'd never get all the blood out. She'd often get nosebleeds as a child, and her foster family at the time would use cold water and a thick white paste to pull the stains. It took out most of the red, but Sylvie could always tell what had happened. They were never pristine again. She would refuse to wear them, despite her foster mother's chagrin. Eventually, they stopped trying. Everyone stopped trying.

She transported back to the present, the rasping voice cutting through her thoughts. "You will not jeopardise our new position, whore."

The weapon dug further into Sylvie's neck, only pausing its trail into her throat when aggravated voices echoed outside the door. Her eyes blurred completely from the unshed tears threatening to spill down her face.

"Release my arm," Kian's strained voice said from the hall.

"I am your fiancée. Not her. It's been four years. You love me. I know you do. She's nothing!" Lazuli snarled. The pinched statements sounded more like a spell than pleading from a jilted lover.

The door burst open, and four sets of eyes darted to one another.

Kian stilled, but his rage doused the room, swelling until Sylvie's breath caught in her throat. She tasted metal.

"Move away from her, now, Zephrinah." He edged closer, and Sylvie sobbed as the knife's pressure increased, her vision fading on the edges.

Lazuli's eyes widened comically as she trailed behind Kian. "Oh my. Zephrinah! What are you thinking? To kill a fated is treason."

Zephrinah's mouth clicked behind Sylvie's ear as if poised to speak when a wall of air struck them, and the slicing into her neck stopped. The arm around her body disappeared, and she whipped her hands up to stem the steady stream spurting from the wound.

Her vision grew spotty, and she spun, blinking as she saw Zephrinah's headless body crumpling to the floor, and her head, eyes still wide in shock, clutched in the hands of a quivering Elias. Sylvie swayed, reaching one arm for him.

He dropped Zephrinah's head with a wet thunk and tore his wrist open with his elongated fangs again while pulling her into his embrace. Her whole body shivered as he tipped his dripping arm above her face, wetting her chin and neck.

"Move your hands, love. This will help."

She shook, letting her hand fall away, the warm blood mingling with her own, and an immediate rush buzzed through her body. Her eyes grew laser-focused, and her body shook as adrenaline pumped Elias's blood through her veins.

As fear dissipated, an unbearable heat replaced it, burning between her thighs. Moaning, she gripped Elias' shirt and pulled her face into his chest. "What's happening to me?"

"I've got you," he whispered, wrapping his arms around her and burying his head in her hair.

Kerensa's voice barked from the doorway, "We left you alone for less than thirty seconds!"

"Not now, Kerensa," Kian hissed.

Elias's head lifted from Sylvie's, and she turned to look at Kian. His dark eyes flickered back at her, brows furrowed uncertainly.

"Where can I take her?" Elias asked.

"My room," Kian replied instantly. Then, when Lazuli gasped, poised to speak, he shouted, "Enough! You know killing a fated is treasonous, and I can't picture Zephrinah doing this without someone's guidance, so unless you want me to let Elias rip your head from your shoulders too, stop talking."

An ugly sneer marred Lazuli's face for a second before she buried it under a mask of innocence and understanding. "Of course."

"Kerensa," Kian cut her off. "Take Lady Lazuli to her quarters and ensure she stays there until the queen returns home."

With that, Elias stood holding Sylvie in a bridal carry while Kerensa escorted Lazuli away, not even deigning to touch the lady with a gloved hand.

Kian's expression remained unreadable as Elias carried her from the room.

"I need you to take her," Elias said then. Sylvie's head snapped to him. She wasn't a thing to be passed around. And besides, Kian still wasn't completely in her favour. He had plenty of explaining to do.

Kian rolled his eyes. "I thought you didn't share." The sardonic wit between them did something inside her.

"I'm willing to make an exception. Now hurry, I've started the marking process, and it's about to hurt like hell."

Sylvie frowned. "What do you mean?"

"Blood trading starts the consummation of the bond. Your body is about to …" he paused, searching for a word, "encourage you to complete it."

Her skin glistened, and she noticed a pulsing starting in her belly and rolling through her core to her toes. "I think I feel it."

"Take her," he said again, holding Sylvie out to Kian. She could bloody well walk. In fact, her feet itched desperately to tear through grass and stone and swamp. She needed to feel everything.

Outside the door, Kian reached for her as Elias wavered slightly.

"Elias?" Kian clamped a hand on his shoulder and searched his face. Sylvie quite enjoyed being sandwiched between them; the contrast of radiating heat and icy cold body temperatures both excited and soothed.

"I need to feed," he grumbled, readjusting Sylvie in his grip.

"How long has it been?"

"Two days."

Kian cursed, hooking his arms under Sylvie's knees and mid-back. "Go, I've got her. There are a few vials in the cellar."

Now in Kian's arms, Sylvie stared at Elias's rigid body. He peered down at her, thoughts ticking behind his eyes before turning on his heel.

"Wait!" she called as Kian walked them towards his room. "Put me down, Kian." When he didn't, she wrenched against him, throwing her body ramrod straight. "Alright, alright. Stop squirming." He let her down, and she darted to Elias's towering body, rounding his form and touching his chin lightly with her fingertips.

"Aren't you even going to say goodbye?"

"You can't imagine how much I want you right now, Sylvie. I can't."

She pulled at his collar until his lips were within reach and pushed onto her tiptoes, pressing her mouth against his. He parted them slightly, and she pulled away when her belly fluttered. "Don't be long, please. You should realise by now bad things happen when we're apart."

Elias rolled his eyes and scoffed. "I need to train you. You are part vampire. You shouldn't be so helpless."

"Shut up and come back to me."

Jaw clenching, he turned and disappeared faster than a blink. She sighed and trailed past Kian, not bothering to explain. Her gown was stained with sticky dark red all across the front, and her skin itched.

"Where are you headed? My room is this way."

She didn't turn around. "Outside," she said.

Kian scoffed, then appeared beside her. "Do you have a death wish? There are hundreds of fae here that would happily kill you simply for being associated with Elias."

"I don't care, Kian, and if you're so worried suddenly, then come with me."

She had plenty to say and a castle full of listening ears wasn't the place to say them.

Her shoes buckled under her new speed and she dipped to rip them off, the clasps snapping from her forceful tug. She thought nothing of it as she kicked them against the nearest wall and marched on with preternatural speed. The walls bent and pressed in on her as if attempting to claim her. Smother her. Even the realm wanted her dead. *Great.*

"Fine," Kian said. "Lead the way."

She didn't need the invitation. She knew exactly where she was going, and gods help anyone that got in her way.

TWENTY

Skin covered in scratches and feet buried ankle-deep in mud, Sylvie squelched past ferns and waist-length grasses to the wall of trees. The meadow hadn't changed too drastically over the years, besides a small stream that now wove from one end of the field to the next. They'd had unprecedented rain, Kian had told her. She didn't mind. She leapt over the stream with ease, revelling in the rush of wind, traces of mist in the air, the kiss of moonlight on her nose. Evergreen was beautiful, but this was where she felt most at ease.

"What will happen now?" she asked, running her bloodstained palm over the calloused bark of the central tree.

She didn't face Kian as he said, "We'll wait until the queen returns and hope Lazuli's attempt on your life is worthy of ending the betrothal."

The tree under her hand vibrated, as if growling. Sylvie patted it softly.

"It wasn't Lazuli, though, was it? It was Zephrinah, and now that she's dead, we don't have proof of anything."

Kian hummed, and she finally turned his way. "Elias clearly wasn't thinking of the consequences when he saved your life."

She lifted a shoulder, biting the inside of her cheek. She'd survived worse injuries. Not that she was ungrateful. Elias did what he thought was necessary, and his protectiveness filled her with need, but might've hurt them in the long run. Lazuli was clever, and a good actress. Plus, the queen had a history of favouring her lies, even over her own daughter. Sylvie was fucked.

"Your connection to him is strong."

She blinked. He wasn't wrong about that. In fact, she could almost feel a tether between her and Elias, a string of light emanating from her chest that overrode laws of reality and twined and looped, just outside her peripheral vision, before shooting towards the castle where he was. He wasn't as far as she thought, either. She mentally fingered the tether, and it pulsed. Her lust flared. So did something else. Annoyance.

"What's your point?" she said, turning and leaning her back against the trunk, arms crossed. "It could've been you if you hadn't tossed me to the side the second Lazuli arrived."

His face stilled, all expression stalling as she went on. She wasn't even sure he was breathing. "I saw her before Kerensa took me away. I saw the way you looked at her. You lied to me. You were never coming back to Erus."

"I didn't lie."

"Omitting truth is the same fucking thing, Kian." Her body burned as resentment bubbled up. "What? Is your engagement not treating you well?"

"This is just your heat talking."

She wouldn't hear him, couldn't accept it. If had told her the truth from the beginning, then maybe her trust wouldn't have shattered. The tree behind her warmed.

"You look like shit, by the way. Must be your punishment for abandoning me."

He flinched as if struck, and finally her awareness returned. She quickly wrenched her walls back up and breathed a few cleansing breaths. *Fuck.*

Instead of acknowledging her cruelty, he stepped forwards until they were only a few feet apart.

"I deserved that," he said, his voice soft. Broken.

Her lips quivered as she fought with her conscience. *Bitch. I am a bitch. Why do I care so much?*

"My father forged the marriage treaty when Lazuli and I were faelings. They cannot be broken unless either party commits treason."

Fine. She could accept that. But they made such a fuss about her being his fated. Like she was important. Sylvie sighed. The bonds were more hassle than they were worth, no matter how special Elias made them out to be. How rare. Her gut churned, seeing Lazuli's smug face. *How could you know she means that much to you?* The words echoed as a violent cramp like a sucker punch twisted her stomach until she doubled over, groaning. *Oh, my gods.* Warmth brushed her shoulders, and she leaned into it, riding the wave of agony as it beat her down to her knees.

"What the fuck is this?" She choked on the words, her muscles quivering and not responding to her will. *Stand up. Just get up.*

"It's the heat. It will pass. Breathe."

"I. Am."

The cramping ebbed and Sylvie pushed herself onto her ass, letting her back hit the tree trunk again as she heaved her breaths. Kian knelt in front of her, close but not quite touching.

Even with a duller appearance, there was no denying Kian's beauty. His full lips pulled into a frown as she regarded him. "Why can't you just tell me what happened?" she said.

He sighed before running a hand over his dark coils. "I need you to ask the right questions."

The right questions. She exhaled through her nose, barely able to muster a smile. *The right questions.*

"Do you love her?"

His throat bobbed, but he shook his head in a jerky motion. No.

"If the betrothal ended right now and Lazuli was out of the picture, would you miss her?"

"Not even a little." The words brought her some peace, only because of her trust in Elias. Fae couldn't lie. That's what he said. It seemed to pain Kian to say though, as if something weighed his tongue down. *Someone.*

"What is Lazuli's power?"

Kian straightened, his eyes widening a fraction. He swallowed again and again but didn't answer her.

"You can't tell me."

"No."

The right questions. Dammit, all she could think about was how desperate she was for contact. For Elias to touch her, to fuck her, to taste her or whatever the marking entailed. Even Kian was looking good enough to eat.

Her muscles quivered in anticipation, and she inhaled sharply. She could feel the wave of pain started once more. *Not again.*

"I can help you," he said, but a subtle fear rolled off him.

"How?"

"I would touch you."

The pain grew. "Okay."

"Between your legs."

Oh. *Oh.*

Needling pain exploded from her, moving in undulating waves to her limbs. Her fingers shook violently.

"Fine. Fine! Just do it."

"Are you—"

"Touch me, Kian!"

He nodded, pulling her onto his lap, her back pressed against his chest like she weighed nothing. She knew Elias was strong, his size showed that, but Kian held a hidden strength she hadn't expected. It was sexy. He clasped her upper thighs and spread them apart, sliding an adept finger into the seam of her leotard before circling it over her clit. He found it instantly. *Of course he did.* Her head fell backwards, hair plastered to her forehead as she panted through the pain. Some cramping eased instantly, and she ground her hips against his fingers, her body glistening with sweat.

"More," she moaned.

While one hand continued its circling, the other slid down to her pussy and curled in and out.

Whimpers poured from her as she reached down and grabbed his wrist, forcing his fingers to go deeper. He quickly changed his tempo, adding a second finger, and pushed all the way in before curling halfway out.

"Oh gods," the pain ebbed by the second, replaced by a burning desire to clench around his fingers. She imagined the thick digits were another part of him, and she brought her hands to her chest, pulling and kneading her breasts.

"I want you so bad," she groaned, rocking against his lap, loving the hardness of his cock pressing into her ass through his pants.

"Don't," he warned, dropping his lips to her ear. Warm wetness enclosed her lobe, and she tilted her head to give him more access.

He nibbled softly on her ear and peppered kisses behind it as her body shuddered harder. Her climax built to an unbearable peak, small faux spasms clenching his fingers until she felt the real finish. She stilled, her whole body a coiled spring, when finally, with a blush-inducing moan, she came. Hard.

Kian continued his ministrations until she went limp. Then he carefully pulled himself free of her and rested his hands on her thighs, palm up.

She stared at them, and the puckered scar on his wrist, gleaming in the moonlight. With a gentleness she hadn't been sure she still possessed, she slid her fingers along his palms until they interlinked with his.

The pain had dwindled to a dull ache, and exhaustion muddied her senses.

Elias's face appeared in her mind. Would he be mad? Would he class what they'd done as cheating? He told her she belonged to both of them, but would he get jealous if she acted on her feelings? Would he prefer to watch?

Kian's chin pressing into the top of her head drew her from her spiralling thoughts.

"What are you worried about?" he said.

She stilled, staring to the side. "Elias."

A soft hum left Kian's mouth, and he turned her hands as if studying them.

"This is what he wants."

Sylvie turned her head to peer back at him, her brow raised in silent question. She was fairly certain he wasn't a mind reader, so when had they discussed this?

"He doesn't want you to be with him first. He doesn't think he's good enough."

Her spine straightened. "How do you even know that?"

"My abilities. They reveal to me the emotions of others and allow me to influence them by taking their feelings into myself and projecting other emotions onto them. That, and he told me the night we realised who you were to us." She rolled her eyes at his attempt at a joke, but she barely managed the action. He took the feelings in himself. All her fear and anger. That's what Elias meant about burning it off. Taking too much was hurting him. She imagined a wall between her emotions and his influence. It was a long shot, but she didn't have a better idea.

"Well, that isn't his decision to make," she said. It was her choice who she wanted to sleep with, and despite the moment they were having, she still wouldn't choose him over Elias. The wall of muscle at her back tensed. *Shit.*

"Sorry."

Kian sighed. "The next time you say sorry, I'm going to make Elias punish you. It's a dangerous habit; anyone else would take advantage or see it as a debt to be paid."

"I'm—" She paused. Now was not the time to be a brat. Kian didn't know she'd pay for Elias to punish her, so after a few terse moments, she muttered, "I'll try."

Kian exhaled, the tepid air cooling her scalp. "Consider it my type of training. I teach you fae etiquette, and Elias teaches you to defend yourself."

"Sounds like fun."

She masked her thoughts and let her breathing settle. If she stayed still long enough, she'd probably pass out. But there was a reason she was here, wasn't there? A question. The *right* question.

"You're right, though. It is your decision, and I understand why I'm not first on your list," he said. "But the blood sharing is affecting him. He'd never let himself hurt you."

She frowned at the absurdity. "He wouldn't." At least not in the traditional sense. There were ways she wanted to be hurt by him.

Repeatedly.

Her aching grew, as if thinking about him ignited her heat, and she groaned, bending her knees and crossing their arms around her stomach. She needed a distraction. Kian would have to do.

"You should rest," he said then, scooting them forward and sliding his back down the tree to give her a steeper incline.

"I'm covered in blood, sweat, and mud."

"So?"

She huffed then, the slightest smile on her lips. She had missed his playful humour, without the constant insinuation of sex or imminent punishment. "Let's go back."

She untangled herself from Kian and stood, stretching her creaking limbs, a consistent throb still niggling in her abdomen. She could ignore it. Her monthly cramps were twice as bad, though she hadn't had any for a while, ever since getting her Goldtech fertility implant. It lasted for life unless she took it out. She didn't plan to.

He stood and matched her pace as she trudged by the light of the moon.

"Do you remember when you told me that what was between us was real?" she asked.

"I do."

She brushed her hands along the ferns, leaving a trail of her blood atop their heads. "Was it real with her?"

He sighed, and the sound almost pierced a piece of her heart. "I did what I had to do to make her believe it."

Not exactly what she asked, but it shared something else. Something sinister.

"She made you promise something, didn't she?" she whispered, blinking slowly.

Kian paused for so long Sylvie was sure he wouldn't answer, and when she splashed across the lazy stream, muddying her feet, she wasn't sure if the hushed, "Yes," was a figment of her imagination.

TWENTY-ONE

"Can you set it up here?" Sylvie blinked up at Elias's frowning face expectantly.

He held a giant sack filled with sand and rags over his shoulder, tied at the top with a thick rope. After following her through the spiky healing plants and gorse, he stared at the giant trees around the clearing where she'd first kissed Kian.

"Why do you have to be so difficult?"

She grinned, clasping her hands behind her back. "You said I could choose where we trained for being good the other night, and I love this place the most. And here, I don't have to see Lazuli's bitch face staring at me from her window." Lazuli's steel grey glare followed her even when they were on opposite sides of the palace. It was creepy.

Elias rolled his eyes and worked on stringing up the bag while Sylvie traipsed along the stream, stepping over the muddy patch she'd made two nights prior. With his blood finally out of her system, she no longer had to worry about deadly cramps spoiling their time together.

Kian sat on the edge of the clearing, reading a book, his back pressed against a smaller tree and his mouth occasionally quirking upwards at the pair's bickering. They hadn't entirely made up, as Sylvie's forgiveness was hard-earned, but she would accept his company. Between recovering from the heat and attempting to reconcile some of what they had lost, they hadn't talked about completing their bond. Not that she would want to with the betrothal still hanging over their heads. Unless treason was proven, the marriage would still go forward.

Elias watched her as she frolicked and spun in a circle before flopping on her ass and lying on her back. Thick blue clouds shielded her eyes from the sun, and she sighed to herself. After her attempted murder, the pair hadn't let her out of their sight beyond bathroom breaks, for which she vehemently upheld the need for privacy.

Kian hadn't brought up his past since their conversation, and she didn't ask. Figuring out the right questions gave her a headache.

"Don't get comfortable, Kitten. You're supposed to be training."

Sylvie exhaled a short laugh, gazing the length of her body and shaking her head at the ridiculous "training outfit." The full-body second-skin suit hugged every curve perfectly, and she *couldn't possibly* imagine why the two men wanted her to wear it. Elias had taped her knuckles too, and the inability to flex her hands irritated her.

"I know!" she yelled back, rolling onto her stomach. She was fingering the waving grass tendrils, then was suddenly flying over the grass.

"What the fuck?" Her brows shot up and a breathy laugh escaped as Elias carried her like a bag, his arm looped beneath her belly.

After placing her in front of the sack, he manoeuvred her body to stand with a firm stance and a guard by her face.

"All I want you to focus on is throwing a damn punch." Elias eyed her as she peered back at Kian. He hid a smile behind his book, and she chuckled, turning her gaze back to the bag.

"Okay. What about kicks? I did some defence classes when I was a teenager, and the instructor said I was pretty good."

"You know self defence?" Elias deadpanned.

She adjusted her stance, squaring her hips more and raising her hands. "Yeah, I did it for a year in my longest foster home stint but had to stop when they sent me back."

Elias remained silent, and she elaborated further, "I was seventeen, almost out of the system, and there were other children that needed them more. I understood."

Martine and Jared were the kindest foster family to her, and she always wished she could've thanked them for caring for her the way they did. They put her through therapy and helped her with schooling when she didn't think she'd survive into adulthood. They discussed her rage and abandonment issues a lot that year.

"Strike the bag."

She nodded and let out a tentative jab, jab, cross combo before looking back at him.

A glint appeared in his eye, and he nodded. "Again."

Running through some old combos, the muscle memory slowly returned.

She was going to be so sore the next day, and when she started practising her kicks, an uncomfortable twinge niggled her hamstring.

"Uh, I'm so rusty," she groaned, facing Elias. His eyes flicked between her and Kian, and he turned away, pressing his hand against her favourite tree.

He cleared his throat and turned back to her, raising his hands and mirroring her stance. "Use my hands like pads and don't stop until you can no longer continue."

His eyes flashed red as she scoffed. "Are you serious?"

"Deadly."

After suppressing the urge to roll her eyes, she repeated the same moves from the bag on his hands. Then, when one of them swiped towards her without warning, she ducked, watching it sail over her head.

"Keep going," he urged, catching her every move with his massive fists. Sylvie worried briefly she might hurt him, but he didn't even flinch when she kicked her hardest.

Maybe she wasn't that good after all.

Her muscles burned as she moved faster and faster, wanting to impress him before she gave out. Elias grinned down at her, noticing her vicious movements, and threw a punch of his own straight at her face.

Kian yelled something indecipherable from behind her, but she only smiled. She saw the jab coming from a mile off and ducked, letting it brush painlessly past her shoulder.

Practice finished with a push-kick. While Elias only shifted slightly backwards on the soft dirt, Sylvie's eyes widened with excitement. "Was that good?"

He worked his jaw as if finding the right words before stepping forwards and scooping her over his shoulder.

"Hey!" She squirmed as her belly pressed into him painfully and slapped her wrapped hands into his lower back.

Kian chuckled as they walked past. "I thought you were actually going to hit her."

"I was," Elias grunted, traipsing back through the gorse. Kian clenched his jaw, following behind and meeting her wide eyes from where she was pressed against Elias's back.

"You could've hurt her," he grumbled.

"Were you watching or too busy with your books, Kian? She moved faster than a normal human, and her strikes were *almost* more than a tickle."

Sylvie blushed, embarrassed by her earlier pride, and let herself hang listlessly behind Elias's back.

"You're saying her vampire blood is coming through when she fights?" Kian deduced.

"Perhaps," Elias replied, entering the palace and making a sharp right turn. "Or our bond enhances her abilities. Either way, I think our fated deserves a treat."

Just before Elias carried her through Kian's bedroom door, Kerensa appeared with a deep-violet glower.

"She's demanding an audience with you again, Kian. She saw you returning with the vampire and your fated through the gardens and is feigning distress."

With a sigh dripping in displeasure, Elias lowered Sylvie to the ground and flicked Kian's shoulder. When the men locked eyes, a silent conversation went on between them. *Rude.*

Sylvie met Kerensa's narrowed gaze, and she smiled awkwardly with a shrug, which Kerensa smirked at. "You can call me by my name by the way, Kerensa. I'm sure you know it by now."

Kian and Elias jolted from their conversation, and both tried slapping a hand across her mouth, which she promptly swiped away.

"What is your problem? You both are getting on my nerves," Sylvie hissed.

Kerensa chuckled and walked away, the faint tinkling of her satchel contents drawing Sylvie's gaze as the fae waved her off. When she was gone, her attention returned to the scowling men at her side.

Sylvie shrank slightly before rolling her shoulders back and placing her hands on her hips. "What? I trust her, and I'm sick of being referred to as your property."

Elias and Kian shared a look, and the latter reached for her, brushing a stray hair behind her ear. "There are eyes everywhere, Princess, and anyone could technically hear you give your name away and consider it being given to them."

Of course. How could I not realise? Sylvie started padding away from the room, eager to return to training, when a hard slap bit her ass cheek.

She yelped and jumped away, scowling at Elias's raised brow. "What the hell was that for?"

"I can see you're returning to your old self, Kitten, which means punishments resume. Don't be a brat."

"I wasn't."

A flash crossed Elias's eyes, and he prowled towards her as she scampered back.

He might've been right, but she would not bend at the waist and await his heavy hand.

Besides, if they weren't trapped in a different realm, filled with monsters and scorned lovers that wanted her dead, she wouldn't need to be so mindful of who she gave her name to and who she thanked or apologised to. She wasn't made to follow so many ridiculous rules.

"I want to keep training. If you two have shit to discuss, then so be it. I don't need to be there to hold your hands." Even if she had to be alone for a while. The fear was almost gone, and she was certain Kian had everything to do with it.

Elias's eyes sparkled as if the turning cogs for punishment were giving off sparks. Never the demure flower, she angled her head and crossed her arms, meeting his gaze levelly. "So?"

If they wanted to keep her in the dark, then she would live in it.

Elias broke eye contact first, which she took as a win, and faced Kian, who half shrugged.

"Let her go," he said. "I warded the clearing against intruders, and we'll know where to find her."

Elias faced her again. "Haven't we already discovered on multiple occasions what happens when I leave you alone?"

Sylvie fought a smile and closed the gap between them. His resistance was fading, and her confidence was growing. "That wouldn't be a problem if I practised more, now, would it?"

She snatched up his hands for added effect, placing them on her heart. "I don't want to be a weak, pathetic human anymore."

Little shit. She could almost see Elias thinking it as she batted her lashes.

He detached himself and gripped her chin. "You're anything but a weak and pathetic human. But fine," he grumbled. "Go. I'll be listening. Yell if you get into trouble."

She beamed and squeezed him in a bear hug, savouring the way his huge hands engulfed her, cradling her head to his chest. The inhumanly slow thud of his heart piqued her interest, but the weight of a stare on her back had her straightening and wiping her palms down the front of her bodysuit. She turned and walked to Kian. It wasn't as natural, but she wrapped her arms about him, regardless. His warmth contrasted with Elias, but it melted her icy walls a fraction, and as her hands brushed against his back, she faltered. Dozens of bumpy ridges pressed against the fabric of his shirt. She frowned into his chest and squeezed him tight before he gently detached her. Were those new? She tried to think back to a time when she had hugged him before and came up empty.

"Thank you," she whispered coyly, hoping concern wasn't etched across her face.

Kian went to scold her when he caught her expression and shook his head. "Insufferable," he groaned.

She forced a smile and spun on her heel, dashing to the nearest open door, weaving through the flower garden and back to her little piece of heaven, trying to push away the racing thoughts. *What happened to him?*

Hours passed as she worked the bag and mulled over different hypotheses for Kian's condition, finally settling on some kind of fae practice. Kerensa wasn't exactly the most human-looking fae, so it would make sense if her brother had unusual modifications of his own. Eventually her knuckles split, and the front of her shins and feet grew black with bruises. Surprisingly, Elias and Kian didn't check up on her. *Good. Trust has to work both ways.*

As the sun dipped behind the foliage, she slid down her favourite giant tree and closed her eyes, savouring its warmth through her damp bodysuit. The wind picked up, whistling tones through the grass, leaves, and twigs. Almost a melody. No. A voice. It swirled around her ears, weaving tales she couldn't quite understand.

Her body sank deeper into the tree bark until it cradled her in a soft embrace. The scent of dirt, sap, and chopped wood filled her nose until it became her. When she opened her eyes, the world glowed ultraviolet. Neon root systems stretched far beyond her and connected with every living thing. The tree's roots—no, *her* roots—weaved and danced deep into the soil near the small spring, lapping the liquid up to her trunk.

Everything was connected, and so beautiful. For the first time in her life, she belonged to something bigger.

She wasn't alone.

TWENTY-TWO

"Sylvie?"

"Sylvie, where are you?"

Elias's voice was close. Too close. Sylvie shuddered and stretched inside the tree, wanting to stop the noise. Too loud.

"Gods dammit. I can still smell your scent."

His hands pressed on her trunk, and she reached for him, his touch drawing her in like a magnet.

Liquid to solid, Sylvie seeped from the tree's bark and solidified between Elias's arms. Once her feet were planted firmly on the ground, she stared up at him, blinking rapidly.

For the first time in their entire situationship, Elias looked surprised. His mouth parted slightly, and his brows lifted in a comical arch. Dopey was a cute look on him.

"Sorry, I got tired," she said, swallowing a wave of unease. *What the fuck happened? Was I inside a tree?*

The moons were high, and a crisp chill burrowed through her training gear.

"What the hell did you do?" he asked, stepping back and clenching his teeth together.

She shrugged, but a rush of elation filled her until she was giggling behind her hands. The awareness surged back. She had seen the world through nature's eyes. It was *everything*. She chewed on a fingernail and rocked from foot to foot.

"Don't tell anyone about this yet," Elias said, easing the finger from her teeth. "It's better no one knows your bloodline affinities are manifesting."

"Why?" She was still shaking, the rush of connection she'd formed flooding her mind until she was certain she would burst.

"Then they would know you aren't human at all."

What? "What?"

"You're a halfling," he said. "You have to be."

She palmed her thundering heart, trying not to faint from the bombshell. Everything she knew about herself was a lie, and she had no idea how to feel about it. Instead of lingering in the shock, she tucked it away, compartmentalising the news for later. That was something she was good at. "I won't tell," she whispered, voice wavering.

"How did it feel?"

She blinked up at him, the genuine interest allowing a fraction of her breathless excitement to return. "Weird. But … amazing." More than amazing. It had felt as if she'd slipped on a cloak after wearing rags that were two sizes too small for her entire life. "It was like coming home," she whispered.

He regarded her for some time, before nodding, the corner of his mouth quirking. "The queen is back and requests our presence. Now."

Looking once at the tree, she pressed her lips in a smile and took his hand. "Lead the way."

Walking in silence, Sylvie ignored the occasional glances from Elias. After the tenth one, though, she was readying herself to snap when Kian appeared at her other side, the back of his hand brushing hers.

In one movement, she could lace her fingers with his. They could all be together that easily. It was their destiny, but she curled her hand into a fist instead. Not yet. Not until she wasn't the other female anymore.

Outside the throne room, Kerensa waited with a frown. "Hurry. She's tired and angry from the trip home. Let's get this over with."

"Yes," Lazuli said standing stoically at Kerensa's side, eyeing Kian's posture, which was enveloping Sylvie with everything but physical contact. Her misty eyes fluttered. "Let's."

Kian stepped passed, not glancing at either female, and pushed open the doors alongside Kerensa. The five all trailed in like they were about to be scolded by the principal for being unruly teens.

"Speak quickly and plainly. I have no interest in riddles today," Queen Katarina said with a sigh, pinching the bridge of her nose. It had obviously been a long trip back.

What decisions had she been making with Lazuli's father? Perhaps this conversation was about to fuck it all up. Sylvie glanced at Kian. Already a light had returned behind his eyes, the dullness of his skin replaced by rich umber.

He deserved better than what Lazuli had been giving him.

"There was an attempt on my fated on the night of my engagement party by my betrothed's handmaid, Zephrinah. I believe Lady Lazuli was behind it, and I am requesting an immediate end to this proposed marriage," Kian said, standing in the centre of the group.

Queen Katarina clicked her tongue. "Do you have any proof?" She looked across the group and settled on Lazuli with a raised brow. "Do you have a defence, dear?"

Lazuli swallowed and plastered a demure demeanour on. Sylvie pulled a face before Elias squeezed her hand in warning.

Letting out a slow, shaky breath, she watched as Lazuli walked in front of the queen, her footsteps tentative and unstable. "Please forgive me, my Queen. I've been stowed away in a room for days. I'm afraid I don't feel myself."

"That's quite alright," Katarina replied, waving her hand for the fae female to go on.

"I did not know Zephrinah had such tendencies, and I would never consider harming Kian's alleged fated. That would suggest I found her a threat."

Sylvie's whole body tensed, and her teeth clenched so hard she thought she heard them squeak. *Bitch.*

"The vampire tore her head from her body before she could say anything at all." One fat tear rolled down Lazuli's cheek, and Sylvie restrained her hands from giving a round of applause. What an act. Based on the queen's softening face, it looked like she was falling for it, too.

"Without proof, there is no reason this wedding cannot go forward. Send the girl back with the vampire and be done with it, Kian. I am finished with your constant excuses. Now get out, except for Lady Lazuli; I have a message for you."

Lazuli wiped her single tear and smiled softly. "Of course, my Queen."

Sylvie's heart beat so loudly in her ears that her mind felt like a giant metronome. Her whole body dampened with furious, stress-induced sweat, and she hardly noticed Kian and Elias guiding her from the room.

Kerensa cursed and muttered something about blowing off steam before disappearing. Sylvie should just disappear. It would simplify things. It was too much. The fantasy of it all. The power plays. The lies. Elias tried to say something, but Kian stopped him with a subtle head shake. They were clearly a package deal. If she were to choose one, it would hurt the other.

Enough. It was enough. Her eyes burned and itched from the lack of blinking. She'd had her fun. It was time to grow up and get back to work. To drag herself out of the gutter like she always had. She'd lived long enough without a kindred or fated. She wouldn't miss it.

Lie. Lie. Lie.

She didn't need them.

Elias gripped her shoulders, but she pushed him off. "I can't do this."

"What?" both men asked at the same time.

"I can't do this anymore. I can't." Her throat ached as she forced down her sobs and buried her fingers in her hair. She curled her hands into fists and focused on the sharp pain from her scalp.

"I can't do it."

"What can't you do, love?"

She didn't even know who asked; she just stared up at them, letting her face crumple.

"This! Us!" She faced Kian then. "As soon as I think that maybe this is real, that I might deserve happiness with someone like you, something gets in the way. Maybe this is a sign, Kian. You and I aren't meant to be."

Kian's lips parted, the shock in his eyes as potent as the hurt in hers. It was as if she held his perfect heart in her palm and had crushed it to dust before him.

"Please don't say that."

She barrelled on facing Elias. "You made it pretty clear that you're a package deal so I'm letting you both go. *It's fine.* I have been hurt before. Beaten. Abused. Everyone I thought that loved me abandoned me in the end. Every. Fucking. Time. I stopped caring. I move on, because that's all I have." Elias's expression held an unveiled fury. At what, she couldn't tell. "Survival."

The surrounding air buzzed. Pain and want and fury mingled in the dust. In the wind.

"Let me go. Before it's too late and your bond breaks me."

Her voice hitched at the last words, but she held firm, her nails digging into her sides to stop her composure from collapsing.

The silence between them stretched for a beat. Then two, before Elias moved.

So quick, she had to blink to process what was in front of her.

Her hands pulled to his chest, mirroring her earlier embrace, but this wasn't playful teasing.

"Only death would take me from you. Do you understand? I will never leave you, Sylvie. Ever." Her breathing quickened, but she forced her gaze to hold his, despite the honesty. Raw and pure. Unwavering. Undeserved. "I am yours for eternity, if you'll have me."

His thumbs ran small lines down her wrists, and she let her breathing steady. "Then take me home, Elias. Please."

She couldn't bear to look at Kian. Yet again, she was about to get stolen away, and he said nothing.

Elias shook his head and turned so Kian could see her. The cold, pale hands holding hers changed to warm brown ones before she could stop it. "Sylvie, I—" Kian's throat bobbed, and his eyes turned glassy. "I would only let you go to keep you safe."

She froze. The throne room doors at her back warped and groaned, the creaking agony mimicking the tearing of reality in her mind. From confusion to unbearable truth. That was it. The right question wasn't a question, after all. *It was a promise. He made a promise.* And fae promises would not be broken.

Her hands slipped free, and she spun, barging through the throne room doors, barely touching them as they blew inward, the frames shaking at the force. "What does her father have over you?"

Katarina's eyes narrowed, and she sneered at Sylvie with unbridled disgust as she crossed the distance to the throne. *Don't trip, don't trip, don't trip.*

"Tell me. Because any good queen, or good *mother*, would notice when their child is miserable and not force them to marry a monster threatening to kill the person who can make him happy."

Sylvie's heart pounded so loud she hardly heard her own words. She was certain her face was flushed, and the vein in her forehead protruded. "What is wrong with you?" she demanded of the queen. *What is wrong with me?* She was bold, but never this reckless. And over a male, no less.

Not just any male.

Her voice had come out in a vicious, breathy rasp, and she panted as Katarina flicked her gaze down to a red-faced Lazuli.

"Leave us." The queen's tone was sharp as a blade. How many years had she honed such a weapon? Hundreds? Thousands? Without a word, Lazuli stormed from the room, and the queen sighed low in her throat. "You too."

Sylvie tracked Katarina's gaze to Kian, staring at her wide-eyed from the doorway. Shock wasn't even the right word. Dread. Desperation. Elias hovered over his shoulder, rigid, an edge of steel shining in his stare. One that said he would kill anyone that touched her. She turned away. She needed answers, even if it meant mouthing off to a queen. And potentially getting beheaded.

Elias's voice let out a ghostly, "We'll be just outside," before their footsteps receded from the room.

"Speak your piece, child," Katarina muttered, letting her nails tap impatiently on the arm of her throne.

With a bitter inhale, Sylvie started, "Kian is my fated, and so is Elias, regardless of whether you like it or not." She didn't. "There can't be one without the other."

Katarina's indigo gaze shuddered. Too bad the floor was so hard and polished; perhaps if it were wood, she could sink into it and disappear for a while. Forget everything. Then she wouldn't care that the look her never-to-be mother-in-law was giving her made her feel like a fucking moron.

"How do you claim to know these things? Bonds have been absent for decades, and none ever boasted more than one fated in my lifetime." But then something shifted when she added, "Who do you think you are?"

The scathing remark did nothing but draw a smirk from Sylvie that would put Elias to shame. The dreaded existential question she never had—and never would have—an answer to.

"I'm a fucking nobody. A nothing. But that stupid little hand mirror showed me this place and Elias's home. That's how I know."

"Hand mirror? Kian took the Veltus Spect?"

"I don't know." But she did know, and Katarina's skin dulled a few shades. *Oh, boy.*

"What did you think? We were just making it up?"

The queen's usual pallor returned, along with a tinge of red rage. "Of course not, you insolent child. There are other ways to discover bonds." She exhaled. "The Veltus, however, offers no room for error."

That should have been a comfort, but instead, a wedge of fear slid into place. There was no mistake. Elias *and* Kian were her fate, and there was no going back.

She didn't know what else to say. Pleading had done nothing, and neither did tears. She settled on the facts. "He can't marry her. It will kill him."

The words erupted and blew through the room like a bomb, the wood doors rattling behind her as if sensing her rage.

Katarina glared over her shoulder before standing and looking down her nose at Sylvie. The look didn't hold the same disgust as before. She stepped down the two stairs until she was a foot from her and exhaled loudly from her nose.

"Are you quite finished?"

Sylvie met her stare and nodded, waiting for a painful strike or perhaps a clean slice across the throat.

"Despite your absolute lack of decorum and respect," Katarina started, "you're right about one thing."

A shudder ran from Sylvie's head to toes as she waited for the "one thing."

It wasn't surprising, though, in the end. The problems were annoyingly human.

"Lord Rheikar, Lazuli's father, has certain claims that must be upheld because of a life debt to my husband. He saved Kol's life, and my husband had nothing to offer but his son's hand."

A life for a life.

Her expression pinched briefly, as if a sour taste swirled in her mouth before she resumed her usual poise. "The only reason Kian is alive is that his father swore his hand in marriage to lady Lazuli."

She levelled a look at Sylvie before gently lifting the tiara from her braided scalp. Without the accessory, she looked like a normal human woman. Beautiful and ethereal, but not an intimidating dictator; a mother.

Sylvie picked at her cuticles and shook her head. "But doesn't a bond override that? There has to be something."

"There isn't. The promises between Rheikar and my late husband are forged in blood. If Kian leaves the Evergreen Court again without being wed, the contract gives Rheikar the right to take the kingdom himself," Katarina replied. "The only way to prevent that travesty is if Lazuli and Kian wed. Then at least my people are safe when the time comes for Kian to take over."

Sylvie narrowed her eyes. It seemed the apple didn't fall far from the tree in Lazuli's case.

"What's the worst that could happen if he doesn't marry her?"

"Pray you don't find out," Katarina said before walking towards a door hidden behind the stone pillars.

"Wait!" Sylvie jogged after her. "What if I talk to him? To Rheikar?" *Or get rid of him.*

Katarina just laughed and flicked her dark braids over her shoulder. "Be my guest. Either way, you'll solve one of my problems."

With that, Katarina slipped into a dark room, and Sylvie stared after her, wondering exactly what she meant.

TWENTY-THREE

Kian wouldn't look at Sylvie even as she paced across the ornate rug in his room. "If we claim it's an engagement tour, we could all go. No one would suspect a thing." She had argued the point for half an hour since wandering in a daze from the throne room. Elias had been a few shades paler, as if expecting her to be returned to him in pieces, while Kian was pale for another reason. Perhaps she'd done exactly what his mother asked in the end. She'd broken his heart.

"It's not safe there," Kian finally said, his back to her. The cool night air whipped around him as he stared into the darkness. Sylvie rubbed her arms.

From his position against the wall, Elias said, "She has a death wish. I think that's a moot point, Kian."

Sylvie threw Elias a wry look, but didn't miss the concern there. For both of them. Elias and Kian were close. Close enough to share a kindred and said kindred was hurting his friend.

She gnawed on the inside of her cheek and faced Kian again. She didn't know how to stop hurting him. Her relationships always turned into a tit for tat—a shit fight. She never backed down after being wronged, not until they cut their losses and left her for good.

But that wasn't what she wanted. Not really. She wanted him to fight for her. *Why wouldn't he fight?*

"What if we showed him the bond? Maybe he would—"

Kian rounded on her. "He won't care. You heard my mother. And I heard you, loud and clear. It's a sign."

She worked her jaw. "I shouldn't have said that, okay? I'm—"

"Don't say it."

She groaned and spun, lifting her hands in exasperation at Elias. He wouldn't help her. Despite his touching declaration earlier, he seemed distant. Wary. "Well, if you're both just gonna give up, then I don't know why I'm wasting my breath."

Elias pushed off the wall and took her chin in his hand. "We aren't giving up."

It sure as shit felt like it. She squinted at him, pressing her lips together as his eyebrow rose up. The first sign of his cocksure self returning. *Good.* She was done with sappy. She needed strength.

She detached herself from him and strode to Kian, rounding his statuesque form and sitting right on the window ledge, ignoring the drop in her belly at the height. She wasn't human, but the human fear was still there. Rightfully so. She'd had many near-death experiences, a few from falling from sickening heights—once from jumping—and hitting the ground still fucking hurt. A lot.

Finally, Kian's gaze settled on her, as if noting her spiralling thoughts, and she subdued them the best she could. *Back in the box, bitch.* She exhaled, nailing her eyes to his. "Do you want me or not?"

He went still with shock. Disbelief. And moved to step back, but she snatched his hand, holding him in place. "Forget everything else. The betrothal, the promises, the fucking bond. Do. You. Want. Me?"

Something in her gaze caught his eye, and he paused, his jaw flickering. "Yes."

"Then take me."

The mulberry stripes in his eyes flared as Elias appeared over his shoulder, hand clutching the same arm that she held, tight.

Everything in his posture screamed warning. "Don't make promises you can't keep, Kitten."

Warmth pooled below her waist. "I'm not."

"You don't know what you're asking for," Elias said.

She narrowed her eyes, then looked back at Kian, noting the carefully restrained movements.

"Then do it. Whatever it is, I want it."

Elias wrenched her up and spun her, her back pressing into his chest as Kian faced them both. His hardness speared into her spine, and she panted, palming his thighs.

"You made a mistake, Kian, in letting me go from fear. Making promises to that bitch to protect me. If we can't do this the right way, then do it the wrong way."

She could've sworn Elias's erection twitched.

"I'm not noble or kind or worth protecting. If you want me, Kian, for the love of the fucking gods, take me."

Then his hands were on her, clutching her face, his fingers knotting in her hair as his lips slammed against her. Elias released her, and she was up, legs twined around Kian's taut waist as she poured every bit of frustration and pent-up desire into the kiss. Teeth and tongues and moans. She clutched him and didn't come up for air until her head spun. Kian pulled back first, his chest heaving, eyes alight with purple flame. "He needs to die."

Sylvie found herself nodding even as Elias said, "What are you saying, Kian?"

"Rheikar is dark-souled. Even before my abilities manifested, I knew something was wrong with him. His death would do the fae realm good."

Her heart sped up even as Kian's calm tried to slow it down. Plotting a murder was wrong. She knew that. But it didn't ease her desire for it. That was the frightening thing. *Who am I becoming?* Or worse, *who have I always been?*

Kian's thumb trailing down her cheek pulled her from her thoughts, and she swallowed at the look in his eyes. "We'll go, but I can't give you what you're asking for. Not yet."

Her heart plummeted. She didn't even know what he was refusing. "Why?" *And what?*

Elias lifted her from Kian, sitting her on his lap on the bed as Kian took the windowsill, watching them both with interest. His cool lips pressed against her lobe. "You should have a choice," Elias said.

She frowned. "I am choosing."

"I won't do it, Princess," Kian said, but it was clear the refusal pained him.

Elias took over, his hand smacking the top of her thigh. It didn't hurt, but the light sting reminded her of what she was missing out on. "We'll train for the next few days until I'm certain you can protect yourself. With your newly manifesting abilities, it should be easier."

She gritted her teeth. "Fine."

"Fine," Kian agreed.

Elias hummed. "Then it's settled."

* * *

Sylvie filled the next three days with training, eating, sleeping, and pretending that sex and murder weren't constantly on her mind. Not necessarily in that order.

By the third day, she kicked Elias's heavy bag so hard it flew right off the ropes suspending it.

Hand over her mouth, she stared wide-eyed at the spilling sand and rags. "Whoops."

She scooped some of the sand back into the sack and tied the top off, dragging it and leaning it against a tree.

"I'll get Elias to carry you out of here later," she whispered, smiling when the leaves rustled back. She occasionally thought about merging with the tree again, but her nerves got the better of her.

Without control or guidance, it wasn't worth the risk. Elias had told her to keep it a secret, but maybe she could ask Kian about it. Even the thought filled her with giddiness.

"Hey," Kerensa called, jolting Sylvie from her thoughts as she leapt across the stream with something tucked under her arm.

"Hi."

"I have the thing you asked for."

"Huh? Oh." When she'd discreetly asked Kerensa what consummating a bond entailed, the purple-eyed fae had stared open-mouthed, her fangs on complete display as her face twisted in a scowl. She'd spun on her heel and disappeared with a light scoff of disgust lingering in her wake.

"Chapter eight explains the universal marking process," Kerensa said tightly, shoving the book into Sylvie's hands. "Don't damage the tome. It's older than me."

She left Sylvie staring after her, a smile slowly creeping across her face.

"Thanks," she whispered, certain she wouldn't hear it.

With pressed lips and barely restrained excitement, she flicked open the tome and flipped to chapter eight. Detailed illustrations littered the page with incredible anatomical accuracy, from the biting to the fucking to the weird linking that formed during climax. Sylvie burned hotter than when she read erotic fantasy. This wasn't fantasy, it was so—

She closed the book and laid it on top of the felled heavy bag, returning to her training. Not marching to Elias and Kian and prostrating at their feet with the plea to mark her took everything in her. She ran sprints along the tree line until the sky turned hues of pink and blue, and when she spied the book again, she did another three laps. The lust wouldn't ebb. *Fuck me.* As night fell, she plopped herself on a soft bed of grass near the stream's edge, staring at the eclipsing moons while tuning into the sound of crackles and breaking sticks coming from the direction of the castle. If she stayed still, whatever it was might not find her. Or perhaps her recent training might have to come into play.

The worry was pointless though, as Kian and Elias's low voices broke into the clearing.

"I know you're here, Kitten. I can hear you breathing." Elias's low chuckle made a grin spread across her face.

"Come find me," she whispered, knowing only he would hear.

He muttered something low, and Kian laughed. "She's excited," he said.

Damn straight. After that book?

She took a deep breath as quietly as possible and held it, screwing her eyes shut.

"Hold your breath all you want. I can smell your arousal."

She almost burst out laughing but pressed her lips harder to stop the air from escaping. More swishing grass sounded around her left and right sides, and her heart raced. They were circling her.

Staring up at the fading slivers of the moons, dark eyes appeared in her vision. She squealed, flipping onto her belly, trying to crawl away, but two sets of hands grabbed her thighs and dragged her back, flipping her expertly.

"Gotcha," Elias purred with a grin.

Kian's eyes flashed with desire as she stared up at them, panting and chuckling softly. "Come back to the palace," he said.

"No," Sylvie murmured, sitting herself up between them. "Why won't you mark me? I know you want to." It was an assumption, but based on their simultaneous clenching jaws, it was a safe one to make.

"Do you know what that entails?" Elias asked, trailing his fingers down her shoulder. Kian wandered away, and she followed his path as Elias continued to trace a pattern down her torso.

She shuddered under his touch as Kian's breathy laugh rang out in the clearing.

"Some light reading, Princess?" he said, nearing her with the tome in hand.

She fought her grin and failed, biting down on her lower lip. "Kerensa gave it to me."

"Did she now?" he said, shrugging off his jacket and laying it on the grass with the tome inside.

"Mhmm."

Kian dropped to a knee at her side, a smirk on his lips as he tucked her hair behind her ears.

"And what did you learn?"

She barely maintained composure as Elias nipped the muscle along her neck.

"You'll have to refresh my memory."

Kian's white grin lit up the dark and she leaned towards it, the pictures in the tome coming alive in her mind.

"Well, first," he breathed, toying with the zip at her throat, "I would bite you here." He ran a nail along the spot between her neck and collarbone, eliciting a shudder.

"So responsive," Elias said in her other ear. She arched her back at that, the tingles down her spine ending at her toes.

"And then?" she asked, curling her fist into the grass at her sides to stop her wandering hands.

"Then I'll make you forget your own name."

Sylvie laughed; the husky sound rich in her own ears as Kian continued his lesson.

"As you come, you bite me, completing the marking process."

While he explained, Elias took over the play at her throat, pinching the zip that held her in and tugging it down.

He paused halfway, admiring the cleavage her sports bra created as she worked on controlling her breathing.

"When you say bite, you mean until I taste blood?" The thought both turned her stomach and ignited it. When Elias nodded and dipped his head to suck the soft skin of her breast, she gasped.

"How?"

Kian thumbed her low lip, pressing his fingertip into her teeth.

"You're half vampire. I'm sure your sharp canines will help."

She licked his finger before lifting her thumb to her teeth. The canine was slightly pointed, but surely not enough to break the skin. Not without an insane amount of force. Her thoughts withered, though, as Kian pulled her breast free of its confines and pulled the nipple between his teeth.

Oh, this would not end well.

"And then?" The question barely sounded like words as another gasp ripped from her at Kian's light bite on her breast.

Elias sat back and observed with hooded eyes, the colour flickering between red and blue.

"And then," he purred. "It's my turn."

TWENTY-FOUR

Sylvie stood over her Kian and Elias in the grass, chest heaving, her breasts tucked back into her sports bra. "You know, it's not nice to tease."

Kian attempted an apologetic look with mirthful undertones, but Elias's grin was absolutely shit-eating. "Who said I'm nice?" he said.

Her mouth opened in a disbelieving grin, and she shook her head. "Fine. Two can play at the game."

And with as much sex appeal as she could muster, she prowled over Kian's legs until his face lined up with her pussy, then she lowered herself onto his lap, tilting her hips to feel him pressed against her.

With one last smirk at Elias, she closed her fingers around Kian's nape and licked him from the base of his throat to his jaw. He hummed under her tongue, his hands gently gripping her wrists as she nipped his earlobe, her tongue darting out to caress the soft skin before she palmed the front of his shoulders and guided him to the ground.

"Take your shirt off," she moaned, wanting to feel every dip and crest of his muscled body.

His eyes flashed to Elias so quickly that she almost missed it, then he pulled the fabric over his head in one quick motion.

He lay down on his back immediately after, and she let her hands wander along his chest as she slowly altered her position, knees going between his thighs.

It had been a long time since she'd pleasured a man like this—a male—but she crawled backwards anyway, letting her fingers curl around his waistband and pull until he sprang free.

Her lashes fluttered, and the look they shared was utterly criminal as she dragged her tongue from his base to his glistening tip.

"Mmm. Good?"

"Good." His reply was strangled.

She chuckled, circling her tongue around his tip before sucking it between hollowed cheeks. Her hands encircled the parts of him she couldn't swallow and twisted in opposite directions, using her spit as lubrication, and after gagging on his size the first few passes, there was plenty.

She hummed, deep and throaty, as she moved, savouring the way his hips bucked to meet her. His muscles tensed as she passed one hand up the plane of his abs, and she moaned louder. One day, she would lick every inch of his perfect body.

"You are so fucking beautiful," Kian breathed, closing his eyes briefly, as if fighting something. She smiled as much as she could with him in her mouth and gently swirled her fingertip around his nipple before raking her nails down his abs. His eyes shot open, and he froze beneath her.

She pulled back. "I'm sor—" She bit her lip. "Did I hurt you?"

He shook his head, relaxing as she leaned down over him, kissing his tip and reclaiming his length.

Before long, they found rhythm again. He was getting close. She could sense it. His movements grew jerky and sounds louder as she brought him to the edge. That bliss. And stopped, pulling off him with a satisfying pop.

His groan of realisation had her grinning from ear to ear as she wiped her chin with the back of her hand and slapped his thighs.

"You little nymph," Kian said, wincing as his straining cock slapped against his stomach.

She stood with a smirk. "I think you mean tease. But fair is fair. No one is going to be satisfied tonight."

Kian's growing smile and attention slightly over her shoulder were her first clue that something was coming, and she jumped, taking off in a sprint as an icy grip brushed her side. Missed.

She yelped, the giddy laughter getting knocked from her lungs as Elias captured her, flipping them both through the grass in a tangle of limbs.

"Did you really think you were getting away with that, pet?"

"I'll scream," she panted.

Elias hoisted her over his shoulder like she weighed nothing and spanked the back of her thigh. "I can't wait," he said.

She buried her grin in his back before slapping his ass with a hard thwack. He froze then, and her heart raced. *Oh, fuck.*

Elias chuckled. *I'm done for.*

"Go easy," Kian said from behind them, and she actually quivered.

Elias flipped her back on her feet, clasping her bodysuit and tearing it clean off her in two pieces, then the bra, before she could react. She opened her mouth to yell when Elias stuffed it with fabric, pushing her bare chest into her favourite tree. His mouth dipped to her ear and said low, "Tapping out is the safe word for tonight, Kitten."

He didn't give her time to grunt before he slapped her ass. Right side. Three times. By the third, she had to grip the trunk to steady herself.

Then the left side, three more times. She shuddered as his cool hands rubbed the stinging flesh after each blow. *Almost like he cares.* She chuckled, mouth full of what she assumed was her bra, and he snatched it from between her teeth.

"Care to share?" he said, pinching her jaw between his thumb and first two fingers.

She grinned even as he squeezed. "Nothing."

"Good. This is a warm-up." He kissed her shoulder blades, snapping his teeth a hair's breadth from her flesh. "Tell Kian you want him to watch."

Elias nipped her earlobe, wrapping his arm around her waist and tracing his fingers down the leg opening of her panties. He'd have to feel how wet she was.

"Kian?" Sylvie whimpered.

An affirmative noise sounded to her left, and she waved in his direction. "Come closer."

She whined as Elias's digits tugged her panties aside and plunged inside her, curling against her inner walls.

"I want you to watch," she panted as Kian appeared in her vision, a lazy smirk on his face.

"Of course, Princess. It would be my pleasure." He leaned against the nearest tree with crossed arms and eyelids at half-mast.

Elias growled in her ear, thrusting another finger inside as she shivered. "Remember your safe word?"

She nodded.

"Speak the words, Hart."

"Yes."

"Yes, what?"

She writhed as his fingers plunged deeper. "I don't know!"

"Sir, will do. For now."

Her lips quirked up in a smile when another slap bit into her ass. Tears springing to her eyes, she gripped the tree tighter and breathed a soft, "Yes, sir."

"Good. I won't be gentle."

"Good," she whimpered. He kissed her neck, his teeth teasing the skin but not biting, and her back arched as she reached for his dark curls, but he gripped both wrists and pinned them to the tree with the same fingers he'd been fucking her with. "Keep them on the tree."

His dominance sent thrills through her, and she couldn't help herself. "Or what?"

He slapped her ass in response and unbuckled his pants, pulling his belt free in one swift movement. "Are you gonna take it like a good girl?"

She gushed, and her mouth dropped open. "Oh, fuck."

Thwack.

"Yes, sir!" she shouted, arching her back more in the hopes he would change his mind and fuck her right there.

She heard Kian's soft moan from her other side and turned to see him stroking his length, finishing what she started. Naughty fae prince.

Feeling beautiful under their lusting gazes, she flushed, pushing her hips towards Elias. "Please."

"Please, what?" His dark, throaty tone made her even wetter; she was sure he could see her glistening in the moonlight. Again, she shivered from her exposure to the elements and potential wandering eyes.

"Don't be afraid, Princess," Kian murmured, still fucking his hand. "I warded this place myself. No one will interrupt us tonight."

She sighed with relief and a slight twinge of disappointment. Exhibitionism always was one of her favourite porn searches.

Just as she was about to complain about the lack of contact from Elias, a firm pressure kissed her opening.

"Finally," she whispered, squeaking when it disappeared again. Her body tensed as rage drenched her skin, and she dropped her hands from the tree, spinning to face him with a scowl. He immediately wiped it off with a hand to her throat, backing her up against the oak.

"What do you think you're doing?"

"You're taking too long!"

His predatory look and light squeezing on the sides of her neck had her eyes rolling back. A plea died on her lips as he stepped forwards and pressed his thigh between her legs.

"Wait and see what happens if you keep acting like a brat."

Releasing her throat, he hooked his hand beneath her thigh, lifting her leg in the air, and pressed his thumb against her clit.

"Please, Elias." Her skin glistened with sweat as she waited for him to hurry the fuck up. "Please," she begged. "I'm sorry."

The ache between her legs made tears well in her eyes.

"I'm sorry," she whispered when his lips caught hers, hushing her begging and apologies.

His tongue swirled around her mouth, and he tensed before he plunged his fingers inside her again. She moaned in his mouth, rocking her hips as he moved, touching her walls and curling against every ridge. It wasn't enough, though. It wasn't what she really needed. He fucking knew that, too.

When she finally came against his fingers, she sank back against the trunk unsatisfied, her eyes welling in frustration. She almost tapped out, almost sobbed the safe word, but held on as Elias pulled free of her, unbuttoning his shirt as she panted against the tree.

Her breathing slowed as he moved with calm, calculating ease. She almost drooled watching him and fluttered her lashes, enjoying the rippling bark on her bare skin. The familiar sensation of her body merging with nature eclipsed her vision. *Oh, yeah.*

"Sylvie!"

"Princess?"

Elias and Kian's voices shocked her from her reverie, and she staggered forward, away from the trunk.

Just before landing on her hands and knees, two sets of hands cupped her elbows and stood her up carefully.

"What were you doing?" Kian asked, eyeing the tree with narrowed eyes.

She shrugged, her eyes drooping as the high from their play drained from her.

"Leave it," Elias murmured, threading his dress shirt onto her body and scooping her to his chest. "She needs rest. We'll talk about it tomorrow."

"She wouldn't be almost comatose if you didn't go so hard on her," Kian's low grumble made a smile caress Sylvie's lips.

She reached for him with closed eyes and squeezed when his hand clasped hers. "I'm okay, Kian."

A kiss pressed into her hairline and the steady rhythm of Elias's footsteps eased some of the ache their night had left.

Once they arrived at Kian's room, Elias helped her to the bathroom, where she both relieved herself and washed before dressing in a luxurious cotton nightdress.

He carried her everywhere and tended to her as if she were a fragile gem. Very different from the forceful dominance he exuded only a half hour earlier.

"Why are you being so nice to me?" she whispered, stifling a yawn with the back of her hand.

Kian chuckled from the bed as Elias lowered her next to him. "Yes, E. Explain the methods to your madness."

Elias's freshly bathed body slid in on her other side before he tucked the blankets around himself. "Just because you refuse to learn about the nuances of human sexual experiences does not make my methods mad. If anything," he continued, flicking Kian's arm, "you are what humans call vanilla. And this is what they call aftercare."

Sylvie smiled, nestling under his arm while scooting her backside into Kian. "Is that so? Lucky I like both."

Kian palmed her stinging rump, and she inhaled sharply. "Fucking hell, Elias. She's bruised."

She hissed again as he whispered a few words of gibberish. The pain faded to a light graze, and she reached for it with her fingers.

"Careful. It's just pain relief. You're still marked."

She prodded one cheek and sighed, sinking back into the bed. Not the marked she was hoping for.

The silence between them brought a soothing lull to her mind. The thoughts quieted and her breathing deepened as sleep tried to wrestle her into its embrace.

"What are we?" she asked suddenly.

Elias appeared over her instantly, and she giggled in his face. "What?"

"I know you did not just say that."

Kian added, rather choked, "Did you just tune out our voices for the last few weeks?"

Elias was almost nose to nose with her as she replied weakly, "No. I just … are we … are we exclusive. Where do I stand?"

At his flash of disbelief, she buried her face in her hands. "Forget it."

The soft vibration of laughter from all angles set her body aflame, and she groaned.

"Don't hide, Princess," Kian chided, stroking a finger along her side, drawing a giggle and full-body twitch. When she didn't uncover her face, he retraced her ribs.

"Look at us, or I'll tickle you." His finger wiggled into her side, and she quickly jerked her hands down and scrunched her nose at them.

"What?"

"In human terms," Elias started, kissing her furrowed brow, "yes. We're exclusive."

She bit the inside of her cheeks to stop from grinning, but her cheeks won the battle and accepted a dozen more kisses from Elias. Never enough. It would never be enough. She was a fool to think she could go without this kind of adoration ever again. A fucking fool. Her head lolled to the side, eyes meeting Kian's. They flickered lilac in the dark.

"Does your fiancée know that?" she asked.

Kian hummed. A knowing look speared from him. "She will soon enough."

TWENTY-FIVE

"Get in the fucking carriage, Lazuli."

Kerensa spat the words as if they tasted like acid. The object of her hatred gathered her skirts and tearfully climbed into the ornate wooden carriage as glittering obsidian horses whinnied and huffed. Well, not quite horses, but Sylvie had nothing else to compare them to. Their legs were a little too thick and their teeth a little too sharp to be regular horses.

Kerensa climbed in behind Lazuli and Kian after that. Sylvie scowled from her position in Elias's arms a dozen feet away when the door shut with a click.

"I don't trust her."

"We'll be right behind them, Kitten," Elias said into her ear, gesturing to the identical carriage at their side. "He can handle himself."

Sylvie wasn't so sure.

"You ready?"

She leaned on her heels, savouring the hard thump of her back on his unyielding chest as she replied, "If it means we all leave this place without more interference or another rogue female trying to bury her claws in one of us, then hell yes."

Elias dragged his fingers up the velvet sleeves of her dress and kissed the side of her head before lifting her effortlessly into the carriage, his vice grip around her waist. Her home for the next week was spacious and had enough room for her to stretch out and sleep, but not quite enough space to stand at full height. She fisted her flowing skirts and slumped down against the opposite wall. A week in a carriage drawn by sparkling monster horses wasn't exactly her idea of fun, but it meant they had seven days to plan the murder of a fae that the queen of Evergreen feared. They hadn't dared discuss it after Kian's initial idea. The walls had ears after all.

Kerensa wasn't in on the plan either. She'd likely call it suicide, but with her, Kian and Elias, Sylvie kind of liked their odds. She wouldn't fuck with them. But it probably wouldn't be three to one. He'd have guards, followers, spies …

"What are you thinking about?"

She groaned in Elias's direction and his arm wrapped around her waist, pulling her to his side across the plush velvet seats.

"Tell me."

"I'm stupid for thinking this would be easy."

He exhaled into her hair. "Already losing faith?" In him? Never. The thought made her lip quiver. So easy. It would be so easy for him to break her. One betrayal could kill her.

"Fates, Sylvie. Would you relax? You're making my fangs hurt."

"What?"

"Do you trust me?" She cast him a withering look but nodded.

"Then trust that Rheikar will be dealt with, Kitten and— you're bleeding."

Her fingers shook where her index had dug so deeply into her thumb cuticle it sliced her to the first crease of her finger.

He snatched her hand and pried those anxious fingers apart before lifting her thumb to his lips.

"Wait," she said. Her breath hitched as his tongue flattened against her, tasting from nail tip to knuckle. His reddening iris constricted as the fresh blood stained his tongue and he pulled back abruptly, pulling her onto his lap in a straddle and burying his nose in her neck. His inhale had her back arching against him. *Do it.*

The sharp kiss of a fang made her shudder, but he replaced it with his hands on either side of her throat as if that could be the barrier between him and his next, very willing, meal.

"What does it taste like?" She breathed against his lips, still slightly stained with her.

He exhaled long, shaky, his nose bumping into hers. "Life."

The carriage set off with a jolt, and their caressing noses collided hard enough to make her eyes water. "Fuck."

The faintest voice, brimming with humour, reached her ears, and she searched for it, finding the smirking face through the thin rectangular display window facing the horses. Kian mouthed "whoops," and she flushed as if caught cheating and slipped off Elias's lap with a thump to the seat beside him.

"Sorry," she mouthed back. His eyes flashed at the apology, and he shook his head.

"Insufferable."

Kian mouthed it, but Elias was the one to voice the lip read before tugging the privacy curtain down with a wink.

"Why can't he ride with us again?"

"Appearances. We don't want anyone from Stone Court running ahead to inform the lord that his daughter's intended is riding in a carriage with another female, now do we?"

She groaned but leaned into him and breathed in his scent. Just like Kian's emotional influence powers, Elias's presence also relaxed her—until he decided she needed punishment or pleasure.

She hadn't felt the urge to be bratty, though, so he had little reason to "tame" her. She wasn't sure if the fact annoyed him, or if he liked that she was being submissive.

He added, "Plus, Kerensa has been dropping hints you have broken his heart and chosen me."

What? That hit a little too close to what nearly happened. Guilt muddied her thoughts as she said, "If that were the case, then why are we going with them?"

"To show face and prove the lie we've planted. Katarina told Rheikar about you, and to prove you won't be a problem he asked to meet you."

She clicked her tongue. "Kill me, more like."

"He won't."

"And you know that, how?"

"Katarina was thorough with her questions. He only wants to meet you."

She clicked her tongue and threw her head against the floral headrest. "Could have told me this sooner."

"I only organised this last night while you slept. Katarina is on board." She what? The one who was forcing this union in the first place wanted Rheikar dead? Actually, it wasn't shocking. Why was she feeling shocked?

"You trust her?" Sylvie eventually said.

"No, never, but I trust she loves her son. Despite her recent actions saying otherwise."

They sat in silence for a time, the only noise a steady clopping of giant hooves on soil. "I think I'm annoyed."

Elias's exhale sounded dangerously close to a laugh. "Why?"

"You came up with this plan without me, and now I'm basically bait, aren't I?"

Bait could work though. It was a good plan, she just wanted to be in on it a bit fucking sooner.

He gripped her chin and planted a kiss on the tip of her nose. The scrunch from her frown softened as he said, "I'm sorry. I should have told you first."

She sensed no deceit. Only sincerity. Her heart thundered and she nodded, gnawing on the inside of her cheek.

"Kian is okay? With the new plan?" They'd have to pretend it was over and it would need to feel real. Her annoyance flared. They'd only just healed a fraction of the rift between them.

Elias's jaw hardened, his voice dropping as if afraid of being overheard. "We'll find time for you to be together. I don't like the idea of him being trapped in there with her for a week either."

"Do you know anything about her?"

Elias shook his head, but his eyes narrowed. "Besides the dark influence I sensed on the night of the party, no. She hides it well, whatever she can do."

"What *did* she say to you that night?"

His jaw hardened a fraction. "That we had similar tastes, and that if I were interested, she had her own wing in the palace."

"She propositioned you? At her own fucking engagement?" The rage burned so quickly, dog-piling on her previous annoyance, that Sylvie had no time to shove it down. She stood, head smacking the roof, then sat back down, hands over the lump already forming with a groan of pain.

"Are you truly surprised?" He guided her back to his side, interest in his tone.

No. She wasn't. And that only infuriated her more. At this rate, Lazuli could die along with her father. It was irrational and jealous, but the audacity of the fae. She could understand Kian. They'd been betrothed forever. It made sense she would stake some kind of claim over him. But Elias?

"Breathe."

She inhaled sharply and dropped her face into her palms, elbows on her knees. What would Elias think? But when she finally unpeeled her fingers from her face and glanced at him, he was breathing shallow, his dark curls falling into his eyes. She could just brush them—

"Sylvie."

"What?"

"We won't survive a week in here if you can't keep your claiming in check."

"What?"

He sat back and closed his eyes, the gorgeous curls still against his forehead. She brushed them away this time, gasping when he clasped her wrist, his ring-adorned fingers tense.

When did he get those? There was one with a giant ruby she couldn't stop staring at. So beautiful.

"You're killing me," he said.

"Huh?"

"I only have so much restraint with you, and you're testing the very limits."

He released her wrist, and she lowered it to her lap, thumbing where his rings left little indents.

"Okay. I'll stop, I guess."

Restraint. She shuddered. After clearing her throat and subtly tugging her collar away from her throat, she said, "You'll hear if she tries anything, right?"

"Yes, but Kerensa is in there too. She will keep him safe."

Breathing a sigh of relief, she slowly nestled against his side, trying not to test him, and he draped his arm over her body. *Success.*

She drifted in and out of sleep until her carriage window drenched her in darkness.

"We're setting up camp now. Wake up."

"Where are we?"

Elias gave her a look. "How should I know?"

She laughed and regained awareness of her location before sighing. "I never get used to this place. Is it weird that I'm almost missing work?"

A dark chuckle wrapped around her body, and she pressed her mouth into the owner's throat, enjoying the vibrations against her lips. When he stiffened though, she pulled back and opened the carriage door, leaping out onto rough grasses. "Let's go." Maybe she was being bratty after all.

She blinked as the light of the moons illuminated the space in monotonous tones of greyscale.

Short trees framed one side of their position while their carriages blocked the road leaving one side open to endless darkness. The horses were gone, their deep, gritty huffs echoing from inside the sparse trees. What *did* they eat? After the squeal of a small creature reached her ears, she pulled a face. Question answered.

Kerensa tended to a fire in the middle of the clearing while Kian placed stones around it, which Lazuli collected from the roadside.

Immediately Sylvie felt useless, but when Kian looked up at her and winked, she relaxed instantly.

She inclined her head, keeping her gaze even, and approached the fire, crouching to warm her hands by it.

"Is there anything I can do to help?"

Kerensa rolled her eyes in Sylvie's peripheral, and she leaned over to stare at her.

"What? Something to say?" Sylvie quipped with a raised brow. She wasn't being overly flirtatious, Kerensa was just being snotty.

The fae flashed her sharpened teeth and placed another thick log on the fire. "You're going to make it harder if you keep flaunting your bond in front of Lazuli's face."

Her voice stayed just low enough for Sylvie and Kian to hear, but Lazuli's sniffling from the path made her think she heard it.

Shit. Sylvie cast a shroud of indifference around her as she stood and swiped imaginary dirt from her gown. "Lady Lazuli."

"Evening." Lazuli nodded lightly before handing another stone to Kian, completing the circle. When he smiled up at her, Sylvie had to dig her nails into her palm. *Not jealous.* Kian soothed her emotions quickly as Elias approached, kissing the top of her head.

"I-I need to go to the bathroom," Lazuli whispered to Kerensa, who pulled a face and looked half ready to force her to hold it when Sylvie cleared her throat.

She didn't want to be alone with the witch, but she needed to piss, too.

"I'll go with you." Sylvie stood, gesturing towards the dark tree line.

Kian bolted upright and snatched Sylvie back, startling her. "Kian, let go."

She unpeeled his trembling fingers from her shoulders and frowned at him. What just happened? He was going to fuck up the plan. Elias pulled her into his arms, stroking the spot Kian had grabbed.

"You can't go in there," Kian said. "It isn't safe." He gazed over Lazuli and Sylvie, but from his weird, frenzied energy, she was certain he was only worried about her. But Lazuli couldn't be that dangerous. She was a lady who got others to do her dirty work. She'd be fine. Probably. For good measure, she stated, "Elias will keep an ear out for us. We just need to pee, alright? Won't be long."

With that, Sylvie gathered her skirts and wandered towards the trees, listening for the ghostly walk of Lazuli at her side. She swore she heard a whisper and turned to Lazuli in the darkness, her eyes still adjusting.

"Did you say something?"

"No."

They crossed into a dark thicket, the moonlight hardly breaching the foliage above. A sinking pool of dread formed in Sylvie's belly, and she reached for a nearby tree for support.

Immediately her anxiety lessened, and her vision improved as the energy lines from tree to soil to rooted life flashed behind her eyes.

Snatching her hand away, the golden lines disappeared, and she clasped her hands behind her back.

"Is something wrong?" Lazuli asked, stepping over a felled log.

Sylvie shook her head and followed until they found a suitable flat spot. She gathered her skirts and emptied her bladder as Lazuli waited with her back turned.

After covering her business in the dirt, Lazuli did the same a few feet away and sighed.

Sensing a conversation or confrontation, Sylvie reached out for another tree, hoping the strange vision she saw wasn't a fluke.

It wasn't.

The golden beams illuminated the space perfectly, and relief filled her as she watched the micro expressions dart across Lazuli's face.

The fae paused, mouth opening and closing, before her words broke the silence. Words Sylvie never thought she'd hear again.

"Have you ever been abused, Miss Hart?"

TWENTY-SIX

The first thought that crossed Sylvie's mind was: *How the fuck does Lazuli know my name?* The second was: *Yes.* "Why?"

A hammer thumped down on her chest as she waited for Lazuli's response.

Abuse. Not a topic she wanted to speak on. Not at all.

"It's quite a common experience in Erus, I have heard, but here it's more of an oddity."

The surrounding life and tiny flittering humanoid creatures scuttled out of Sylvie's sights as if terrified of the fae lady's words.

"It's a sign of demonic characteristics."

Sylvie let out a soft shudder. *Right.* "Okay."

Lazuli sat on the felled log they had crossed and picked at a patch of dry moss. "My father won't change his mind, even if you're fated. He expects Queen Katarina's debt to be paid."

Picking up her skirts again, Sylvie walked over and sat on the log, planting her palm straight on the bark to regain her magical night vision. To her surprise, it still worked, even though the tree was dead. "I know," she said.

"He wants me on the throne," Lazuli said, either ignoring her or not hearing. "And I ... I need to stay in the Evergreen Court. I can't go back."

Sylvie turned to face her and breathed slowly to calm her racing heart. "Why? Why can't you go back and rule your own home? Why do you need Kian?"

The pause that stretched between them grew heavy. "He hurts me."

Fighting the gasp and swallowing, Sylvie's foot started tapping on the soil. *Who does?* Please be lying. The familiar script poured past her lips before she could stop it. "You don't have to tell me if it's too—"

"No. I've kept his secrets long enough." Lazuli sniffed and held her head high. "In my fourteenth year, my mother died in childbirth, and only weeks after, he started visiting my room."

Sylvie knew what was coming; it was as if she were revealing her own story.

"He said it was time for me to fulfil my duties as a female of the house."

"Lazuli—"

"At first, it was just touching. He would make me touch him."

The welded chest behind her mental walls shuddered and rumbled, smoke billowing from the rectangle slat on its lid. *Stop it.* Sylvie's eyes squeezed shut as if the action could save her. *What is happening?*

"Then it turned to other things."

The box rattled as the chain links fell away. Scratching and clinking. Falling into an abyss. Lost. *Please.* She'd had so many changes recently, so many bombshells, it was like her mind couldn't take it anymore. *Don't do this now.*

"I knew it was wrong, but he convinced me."

Another lock slid free and cracked on the ground, her little hybrid monster peering through the new gap. *No.*

"He was so convincing."

The monster stared through yellow eyes, its long finger hovering under the iron latch. *Don't you dare.*

"I met Kian in my sixteenth year. He was so kind to me. It made me realise what a relationship should be like. What intimacy could be like."

Her mental walls imploded and smoked in a pile of smelted metal as the monster grinned from the top of the chest. So many teeth.

"If you had just stayed away," Lazuli continued, "I could have made him happy. I could have made him love me, and he could have kept me safe from *him.*"

It flicked the latch. The lid blew open and slammed as dozens of images and sensations took over.

A hot breath on her face.

A body pinning her down.

Agony mixed with terrible, disgusting flutters of pleasure.

She retched, spilling her limited stomach contents at her feet.

"I could still make him happy." Lazuli's shoulders shook as she finished, and furious tears spilt from Sylvie's eyes.

It was wrong. So, so wrong. The shuddering breathing between them sent puffs of icy smoke into the air. Immeasurable guilt strangled the words in Sylvie's throat, and she stood, pressing a hand to her collar.

"What if he was dead?" Sylvie's shaky voice drew another sniffle from Lazuli. "Your father. What if you could be free of him? Would you stay in the Stone Court?"

Lazuli didn't have time to respond before Elias's booming voice echoed around the space.

"Sylvie, where are you?"

Lazuli reached over and squeezed Sylvie's arm, making her jump. "I cloaked our voices, but it's gone now. You can call, and he'll hear."

What? She was still scrambling with the blown-open box of horror in her skull to process what the fae woman was saying. Even the bite of Lazuli's nails leaving tiny punctures through the sleeve didn't enter her thoughts.

"I'm here!" She swayed, wrestling the monster to the side to latch the chest. It wouldn't go back in. The memories. They wouldn't … not even a second passed before a hard embrace scooped her off her feet, pitching her eyes into complete darkness again.

"Walk," he growled at the female cowering beside them.

"My apologies for the cloaking; we both decided we needed privacy to do our business. Right, Miss Hart?"

Elias carried her in his arms back towards the glow of the fire, his eyes peering down at her.

She made a small affirmative noise in her throat before resting her head against his chest. He must have known she was lying, but he didn't press her.

"Come and eat," he said, low and gruff, placing a soft kiss on Sylvie's head before lowering her onto a large picnic blanket beside the roaring flames.

She didn't eat. She couldn't. Elias's offering of bread and fruits slowly enticed a few fly-sized pixies over, who quickly snatched a grape each and flitted back whence they came. Sylvie stared after them, the afterimage of their perfect faces and tiny razor teeth enough to stifle her thoughts. She sent them in after her monster, but he just swatted them away from his new perch on the smoking, wide-open lid of her chest. Her very own Pandora's box.

It was open now.

And she was fucked.

* * *

Eyes burned holes into Sylvie's body, rousing her from her rest beside the fire.

She blinked against the dying firelight, and a sleeping Lazuli curled beneath a large quilt materialised from the darkness. Behind her sat Kerensa, the violet hue of her eyes reflecting the smothered flames.

Sylvie went to roll away from the heat scorching her face when she bumped into two rigid forms.

One hot, one cold.

With a glance at the shadows blocking her movement, she winced. Kian and Elias sat back-to-back, one with eyes closed, the other open.

"Are you ready to speak with me now?" Elias's voice remained surprisingly soft as he gazed down at her.

She shrugged and sat up, rubbing her eyes. The gritty itch from crying still hadn't faded. Neither had the burn in her throat from vomiting.

Elias pulled her onto his lap and tilted her chin. "What are you hiding?"

"We were just peeing."

His pointed look and sigh said more than words ever could. Her shoulders drooped. This wasn't something she could share. Not without imploding.

Damaged goods.

She dug her nails into her palms to stop the thoughts. The fire crackled and spat as he tossed a log into it with his free hand, jostling her enough that she moved off his lap, sitting instead between his legs with her head resting on her bent knees, arms wrapped tightly about them.

"I can't tell you. Not yet." Her focus on rebuilding her walls around the busted chest was the only thing keeping her grounded. The only thing keeping the other monsters, the ones that she'd trapped for years, at bay.

Elias's eyes hardened for a moment before softening again. "I may not like not knowing everything about you, Kitten, but I trust you'll tell me when you're ready."

Redness kissed Sylvie's face as he stared deeply into her eyes. She hoped he couldn't tell her flush was from guilt, not infatuation.

"But," he continued with a low whisper, "if Lady Lazuli is asking you to keep secrets that will hurt you *or* Kian, I will not take kindly to it."

She inhaled loudly and turned her face, pressing her knees into her forehead.

He grumbled in warning, but she shook her head. "It's not that kind of secret. Don't worry."

Even as she said it, the lie burned her throat. The secret ate away at her, leaving a trail of death wishes in its wake. Pungent, rotting garbage baking in a back alley in Sterling. Familiar. But telling him wouldn't stop it. Only she could stop it. She'd done it before, but it was years ago, after dozens of therapy sessions and repressing, repressing, repressing.

"Shit." Bile rose quickly in her throat, and she slapped a hand over her mouth, catching some of the warm acid as she darted to the nearest bush.

As quietly as possible, she spat and coughed as her burning stomach lining poured from her lips. Elias appeared behind her instantly, scooping her hair away from her face and placing a firm hand on her back.

When she finished, he offered her a small cup of water, and Kian appeared at her other side with a soft frown.

"Are you alright?" They were supposed to be pretending nothing was between them, but he couldn't help himself. She loved him for it, even if that love could have saved Lazuli. They were supposed to make it seem like she had a chance. Maybe she did. Maybe she should. *No.*

Rheikar was abusing her, but that didn't dismiss all the harm she had done. Kian was a shell when Sylvie had returned from Erus with Elias. A husk.

But if they failed, and Rheikar lived? She couldn't leave Lazuli to that fate. *Fuck!*

Another wave of nausea swept through her, and she retched again.

She turned from both men, waving a hand behind her hunched form. Gods, her abdomen fucking ached. "I'm fine. Don't worry about me."

They left her to her pain, even as waves of Kian's peace washed over and soothed her. It didn't touch the memories, though. Could he see them? Or sense them rather.

He wouldn't want you if he knew.

Oh gods. She did what she knew best and drew a wall between them. A barrier against his probing—his knowing.

He couldn't know. But the only way to stop him was to pull away. For real.

The fire roared to life as she returned to it, the kindling screaming and snapping from the heat. It was her. The kindling. Struggling under the ministrations of the raging heat. If she didn't smother it, the secret would eat her up. It would.

* * *

Sylvie ignored Kian for two days, finding excuses to return to the carriage and refusing to come out at each camp. His presence against her fragile walls slowly ebbed, and her heart ached. The distance only made things worse. But her pain seemed a fitting punishment.

Sylvie lay curled in a ball in the carriage as the group packed up to leave on the fourth morning. She had tried to help, but Elias shooed her away, claiming she was only prolonging their efforts.

The door opened behind her, and a low tongue click drew her gaze.

"What the fuck are you doing, Hart?" Kerensa's low voice hissed.

Sylvie just sighed and stared at the back of the carriage seat.

"Elias told me your plan, but this feels pretty fucking real."

"I'm not doing anything, Kerensa. Just leave me alone."

"He's not himself, and I'd rather we are all at our strongest when we face Rheikar."

Sylvie scoffed. *Strongest.* So much for that.

"What did Lazuli say to you in the forest? Did she threaten you? Because I'll happily kill her and her extorting father."

"No." She rubbed her face in frustration. "She didn't. Just leave it. She's been through enough."

Kerensa offered an expression of scornful reproach and searched Sylvie's face as if it would give her the answers. It wouldn't.

"Whatever sob story she told you, don't be so quick to believe it. I thought you were smarter than that."

Disgust crossed Kerensa's face as Sylvie folded her arms and scowled. "Shut up. You don't know what you're talking about."

She could never dismiss someone's accusations like her foster mother did. To remain neutral in abuse meant taking the oppressor's side by default. She'd never fucking do that, and besides, fae couldn't lie. It had to be true.

Kerensa growled and dragged her from her thoughts. "I know she is wrong for Kian, and as much as I hate it right now, you are right for him. I've never seen him as content as when he is with you, and I'll be damned if I let you give that up for her."

Frustration seized Sylvie's aching limbs. "It's not up to you," she hissed back. *It's not that simple.*

"So, you are rejecting him," Kerensa said, her violet eyes hardening. "She better be worth it, because once he realises this charade is no longer for show, it will destroy him." Kerensa backed out and slammed the carriage door, the force rattling Sylvie's teeth. If that's what she thought, then fine.

It was better than the truth anyway.

TWENTY-SEVEN

Death followed Sylvie. Ever since she was a little girl, it clung to her clothes like smoke and grime smothering her light floral musk.

Sterling wasn't a haven. It was a cesspit of the depraved. The greedy. The sick and starved. She had spent so much of her life in isolation. In a corner, under a bed, in the closet with her nose in a book. Anywhere to escape.

Good. Stay there. No one wants to see you, anyway.

"Hey, kid, you okay?"

Her first friend, or perhaps a guardian angel, sent at the right time to save her from herself.

Stop screaming before I give you something to scream about.

His shaggy golden hair fell in his eyes as he sat on the floor, back resting against her metal cot. "You hungry?"

A jam sandwich on a paper plate slid her way across the pockmarked vinyl floors. It stunk too. Unwashed since the first unwanted child was dropped on the family's doorstep.

You rabid beast, stop squirming.

"Here. It was mine, but you look like you need it more than me."

With a sniffle, a tiny, pale hand snatched the sandwich and shoved it into a gap-toothed mouth, careful not to jostle the red bruising on her cheek or the cut on her bottom lip. She healed quickly. Only physically, though. The rest lingered.

You're damaged goods now.

"Hey," the boy said. "You wanna know a special trick?" He was a good few years older. What magic could he know? She stared through red-rimmed eyes.

"I know how to make a money box in my head where I put everything that hurts me. Every memory is like a silver mark, right? And if I don't want it anymore, I just drop it in the box, and it's gone. It can't hurt me anymore. It can't hurt you either."

She blinked. And chewed. And blinked.

Her raspy voice shocked them both. "What's a money box?"

The money box evolved into an orewood chest that she wrapped in iron chains, welded with fire and gold and enclosed in metal walls taller than Ambrose Enterprises' towers. It was everything.

She was sitting at the dinner table one night when a hand brushed her thigh and she readied the memory mark when the boy stood, took the silver from her little fingers, and walked away, the shadow of a monster in his wake. A mark for his money box instead.

He left a few weeks after that. Ran away, they said.

She rued the fact that his name escaped her mind. The money box worked well in some ways, swallowing memories until not a trace remained. It must have taken his name. His eyes. The first seven years of her life. The little girl with so much violent, all-encompassing rage stuck in a hell of concrete, steel, and glass.

Death.

"Wake up."

She inhaled as her eyes jerked open, the carriage rattling to a stop under her feet. She clocked hushed voices, the horses wandering off for feed, a feminine laugh—a little too happy—and a breaking of sticks.

How many days had it been?

Surely, they only had a day or two left to go. She desperately needed to bathe. The grime of their trip and her cloying thoughts was making her skin itch.

A leisurely wending stream had followed their path for the last day, and she'd observed its delights when she grew tired of the back of her eyelids. It was dark out, but the gentle lapping trickles still sounded above the night noises. She'd still not got used to the differences of Ilfaem. Creatures here sang in lilting keens, with perfect pitch and beautiful melodies. Others without voices chirruped and hummed as if joining in, making an ethereal choir. She could listen to it forever. It was nothing like the dull thrum of cars that never ebbed in Sterling, backfiring as loud as gunshots with sound systems that blasted tunes through sirens zip-tied on their front bumpers.

With a yawn, she shuffled across the seat and pushed the door open, wincing as it slammed against the carriage wall. Silky brown dirt cushioned her fall, the plume clinging to her hem like a foul smell. She patted it down and stretched. The crackle of her joints mirrored the sticks dying on the growing fire that Kerensa tended. Elias and Kian spoke by the horses, absently stroking their coats that merged so well with the darkness that without the glowing embers of the firelight, they'd be invisible. Lazuli was there too. Head resting on the horse closest to Kian, her posture relaxed and open. Inviting.

When Kian reached over and brushed her hair over her shoulder, Sylvie's stomach twisted in knots. *It's not real. Not real.*

It sure fucking felt real. She swallowed and turned, pacing past the fire to the babbling stream. The night songs were louder here, as if the creatures were perched on the drooping cattails and sang into the water.

It was almost beautiful enough to distract her mind.

Almost.

She stripped off her dress and undergarments, leaving only her underwear and camisole on before wading into the tepid water. It rushed around her ankles playfully and warmed her calves as she ducked to scoop water into her hands and pour it over herself. She peered back to camp and met Kerensa's eyes, sharing a nod. It was safe. She avoided Elias and Kian though, despite their gazes settling heavily on her body, the cream camisole and loose shorts completely see-through. The stream wove down a slight hill and widened into a pond, and she followed it, treading lightly as the water rose to her thighs. She never learnt to swim and wasn't about to play damsel. It was far enough.

"Sylvie."

A chill swept over her shoulder as hands slid around her waist, the long fingers slipping beneath her camisole and brushing her belly as she continued scooping the water.

"I'm bathing."

"I see that."

She untangled from the cool touch and bobbed under the water until it encircled her neck, facing Elias.

"I'm fine here." *Please go.*

His eyes flashed. "When I asked you to show some restraint, I didn't mean this."

She ducked under the water to avoid responding, her chest squeezing as a sob shook her. This was so fucked. If Lazuli had said nothing, she could've gone on pretending and planning. Now she was back in that house. Under that bed. But this time, the boy never came.

He never—

Elias hitched her up by the armpits and stared down at her, brows furrowing. "What is happening?"

She shook her head, mute.

"Sylvie."

And that was enough. Her eyes filled with tears, and she couldn't muffle the sobs any longer. He pulled her into his chest and carried her farther into the water, to the opposite bank. He held her and rocked as she poured her heart out, her muffled cries scaring away the night sounds until nothing remained. Just the tears. Just the pain. Just her. Just him.

She could sense Kian on the fringes, probing, questioning, but she turned away. It pained her as his footsteps faded, his despair remaining to join her own. It wasn't pretend anymore. They both knew it.

"Sweetheart." Elias lifted her chin and met her eyes. Only questions there.

Her voice wobbled, broke. "I—I can't tell you. It's not my place."

Sudden flashes of a buried memory resurfaced—a drooping face, gibberish words, and begging. She clenched her fists, shoving them into her stomach to hide the blood as her nails sliced her palms open. He caught her wrists and squeezed the crease, forcing her hands open. "Sylvie." She pressed her lips together. He couldn't know. It was her secret. It was never supposed to come out. *Never.*

No one wants a broken plaything. It wasn't her voice anymore.

He searched her face, swiping the tears away with his thumb.

"This isn't about her, is it? Or even Kian."

"Don't," she begged. "Please."

He kissed each bleeding palm and smoothed them against his bare chest. "I can't help you if you don't tell me."

There is no helping me.

But he wouldn't let her go, even as she leaned away, panic rising in her throat. He would leave. He would. If he knew. If he—

He kissed her. Her cheek, so tenderly her movements halted, breath still shallow and quick. Passed her cheek, his lips brushed the shell of her ear, his fingers brushing the hair behind it at the same moment he said, "Nothing you say tonight will stop me from loving you."

Her heart stopped. Dead.

"Do you understand me?"

He pulled back and stroked her cheek again. She couldn't nod. He hadn't heard it yet. But there was something about him, about his earnestness as he held her gaze. *This is a mistake.*

She found herself saying, "Rheikar. He's abusive."

Elias urged her on with a soft nod.

"Sexually."

Damaged goods.

She shuddered, suppressing the images of a bearded face with white hairs growing along the cheek like a broken crescent moon. *Stop fighting me, bitch.*

251

"Something happened to you, didn't it?" Elias asked, voice thick and gritty.

A ripple of pain and terror sent shock waves through her body, and she pulled away from him, her head shaking violently. "N-no, I never said that …"

"Sylvie." His glowing red eyes followed her as she shrank in his arms. A child again. She was just a child. "Who hurt you?"

She shook as more sobs wracked her body.

Bloodshot eyes and cigarette-stained fingertips pawing at her long flannel pyjamas.

"It-it doesn't matter anymore—"

Elias's grip on her tightened a fraction as anger pulsed through them both. "Of course it matters! Tell me a name, and I'll—"

"It doesn't matter anymore," Sylvie said, interrupting him before revealing the terrible truth.

Or maybe it was the perfect retribution.

Nobody else saw it that way, though.

"It doesn't matter," she tried again, "because he's dead."

Elias searched her face, loosening his grip on her while still trembling with rage. "How?"

"He … he had a stroke," her voice cracked, and her face contorted in pain. "On top of me."

The night went hollow around them. Not silent; no creature or gentle brush of wind interrupted her. Something sucked all the light out, too. The only focus point she had was her kindred's eyes, the same colour as the blood that dribbled down his chin.

"They said if I'd called for help, the doctors could have saved him, but I … I didn't. I got away from him and watched him suffer for a few hours. Then, when I—I got my pillow, and I ..."

"Shhh ... you don't have to say anymore." Elias held her against him, his rage ebbing as his soft touch calmed her panic. "It's not your fault." His words reverberated around the clearing. Words she'd never heard but always, *always* longed for. It's not your fault.

But other voices swarmed her mind. *It is your fault.*

Murderer!

He stood and started walking with her back to the camp, every muscle tense as he cradled her to him, his cool skin staving off the burn of hers. "He deserved far, far worse, my love. You can't imagine the things I would do to anyone that hurt you. He's lucky he's dead."

Her words were broken. Hollow. An echo of someone else. "He ruined me."

Elias growled. It was the first time his composure slipped in the exchange. She wasn't afraid, though. Something clicked in her as his rage echoed her own. The same rage she had hidden away. She didn't want to hide it anymore.

"Whatever they said to you to make you think that is a *lie.*" His voice trembled in withheld fury. "All of it." He believed that. He really did. "You might not believe me now, but they were wrong. You are not ruined."

Maybe she could believe him one day. *Maybe.*

Tears fell as he pressed his forehead to hers. Nose to nose. They breathed each other in. His whisper flared across her lips. "You are not broken."

She kissed him. Slow. Soft. A press of bloodstained lips to tear-stained ones.

"I meant what I said, Sylvie Hart. I am yours forever."

Maybe it was the right thing to say, or maybe she was just finally ready to hear it, but her money box groaned and cracked. The orewood collapsed in a heap, memories stretching out like wiry kindling. She poised herself above it, kicking the remnants into a stack, and struck a match, letting it fall, flaring, to consume the pile.

The memory of her abuse sat in her hand. A silver mark. She scowled, letting it transform. It stretched and writhed into spindling tinder, doused in gasoline. The monster stared from a darkened corner; its yellow eyes full of fear.

Good.

She held her hand above the licking flames and dropped the memory. No more marks to add to her chest. No, this was fuel. And she was going to use it to burn the Stone Court to the fucking ground.

TWENTY-EIGHT

The winking lights of the Stone Court flickered on the horizon as they pulled over for the last night of camping under the open sky.

Their small fire danced and shimmied under a soft breeze as Sylvie gnawed on a piece of flatbread.

Elias sat behind her, his hand resting on the top of her thigh, while Kian and Lazuli mirrored their pose opposite them.

They were almost at Stone Court. It had to look believable. Lazuli relaxed in Kian's grip, a pleasant smile etched across her fair face, her fingers splayed over one of his legs, the sharp silver nails tickling him through his trousers. He didn't seem soothed by it, though. His neck held a strain that his face didn't show. If she wasn't looking closely, she would've missed the shudder that rippled through him as her fingers raked upward, closer to his groin. Sylvie's stomach roiled, and she averted her gaze.

Kerensa walked the perimeter, occasionally sending irritated glances at everyone before turning her attention back to the darkness.

After a few minutes of silence, Sylvie's eyes drooped. "I think I'm gonna go to bed now," she whispered to Elias, when his hand pulled away from her suddenly.

Then, looking up at him with a frown, wakefulness doused her as his head swivelled in the darkness.

"What is it?" she whispered.

He shook his head and offered his hand, pulling her up. "Stay behind me."

Kerensa stalked over and growled, "Something is out there."

"I hear it," Elias grated back. "Hybrids."

"How do you know?" Sylvie asked.

Sylvie gripped the back of Elias's shirt as he answered. She was not eager to see more of the things that had attacked her in his office. "They're clicking."

Then Sylvie heard it too, the faint clicks woven into the night sounds. The rippling song of the fae realm staggered and resumed over and over as the clicks got closer. *They* were getting closer. She pressed into Elias's back, hands shaking.

Kerensa scanned the space, whispering, "You think they're communicating with each other? How many?"

Kian approached and Elias turned, keeping Sylvie at his back. He hadn't told Kian her secret, agreeing it would trigger his protective nature and make their charade impossible to maintain. He'd even asked Kian not to read her emotions for the rest of their trip.

When she asked Elias what Kian had said in response, the answer only hurt her more.

"Anything," he had said. "I'll do anything she asks of me."

She sensed she was asking far too much.

Kian squinted against the darkness. "I can feel at least five different beings' emotions, but they're out of range to manipulate."

"Why are they here?" Lazuli piped up from behind him, curling her hands around his forearm, the sharp nails dangerously close to the veins in his wrist crease.

"They're hungry," Kian replied before heading to the back of the carriage and grabbing a host of weapons—small, sharp blades, a bow and quiver, and a long, thin sword.

He handed a weapon to Kerensa and Lazuli, but didn't offer one to Sylvie. She scowled and rounded Elias's back. "What am I supposed to do, punch the damn things? Give me a weapon."

Elias went to speak when a loud crack echoed around the basin. A few sparse trees stood nearby, but they were juvenile and barely large enough to hide behind completely. Maybe there were larger ones beyond that, but in the dark she could hardly see.

Echoing clicks and death rattle sounds came from the castle's direction, and Sylvie trembled. Elias gripped her shoulders. "Look at me. I want you to run to those trees and try to do what you did while training."

Kerensa and Lazuli stared between them as if he was crazy, but Sylvie knew exactly what he meant.

"I'll come get you when it's safe," Elias said.

Lazuli gasped and tried to say something, but Kian pulled her away.

Her heart began thundering, the memory of the hybrid in Elias's office rearing its head, but she threw it on the fire to burn. She could do this. Elias's wild eyes and kiss to her brow sent her pulse skyrocketing. "Run, Sylvie."

She didn't pause or question. She turned and sprinted, desperately ignoring the rush of limbs and nails tearing through dirt and brush as the hybrids descended.

"Run!" Elias's shout acted like a gust of wind at her back, pushing her onwards to safety. She didn't look back as Elias's voice cut off with a grunt and slash of steel. He would be fine. Probably. Her feet flew through dirt and grass and life, so fast her treadless slippers flew off and she darted barefoot. With every strike of her heel, the world lit up, her vision filled with the light of nature, the tendrils from being to being illuminating the reciprocal relationship between all things. If she weren't being chased, she would have appreciated its glorious beauty.

Sounds of tearing flesh and growls followed her as she sprinted headlong to asylum. It was a long shot. The only times she'd merged with trees were in states of deep exhaustion and relaxation. Neither of those things gripped her now. She was wired. The clicking and thudding behind her grew closer, and she pushed her legs harder, ignoring the burn of her underused muscles. Wind whipped at her face, stinging her eyes, but it was the gust at her back that had her gasping.

She swivelled her head and screamed. The creature, within striking range, bounded after her with its face-splitting grin.

Another solid figure collided with its side in a hard tackle, and they tumbled across the grass. Kerensa?

Spinning back, she cried out in relief, the first trees only a few yards ahead. She kept running, reaching her hand out to them, and channelled a level of calm she did not feel when the wind whooshed out of her body.

Ragdolled through the air, Sylvie hit the tree's base with a loud thud. She groaned, turning onto her back, trying to suck in air despite the screaming of her empty lungs.

A foot from her face, the smiling monstrosity tilted its head to the side as she tried to scramble backwards. She barely moved a foot, her chest wheezing.

"You smell so delicious," it hissed. "But slightly different from the other crossbreed." It looked back towards the campfire and licked its lips. "She will still make a decent meal, but you, little flower, are a delicacy."

"What are you talking about?" Her voice shook as she pressed her spine into the trunk. She evened her breathing and hoped she could slink inside before the thing noticed.

Its head twisted back to grin at her. Before it could speak, the trunk at her back called to her, its soft bark melding with her skin. The hybrid demon's eyes widened, as did its mouth, as it watched her disappear into the tree.

Her vision distorted until all she could see were the golden veins, roots, and energy pulses of the living beings around her, even the hybrid that fell apart.

As the body split in half, falling left and right, another figure remained in its place. From its body shape, she guessed it was Kerensa and closed her eyes with relief.

The thrumming buzz of nature lulled her to a sleep-like state, and she let her mind drift far away.

* * *

The tracing of large hands down Sylvie's body roused her before the gruff voice penetrated her sleep-addled mind.

"Come out. You're safe."

Her lids fought against the sappy stickiness gluing them shut as an all-encompassing light blinded her. The usual golden trails weaving the plants together seemed pumped full of steroids. Was it daytime? But how could that be?

With a stretch and a groan, Sylvie leaned towards the soft touches against the tree bark and felt the crisp air kiss her face. Then, smiling up at the curly-haired, red-eyed beast, she yawned, stretching her waking limbs. "The demons are gone now?"

Elias's pinched expression made her heart flutter.

"What?" she asked, innocence lacing her tone. *Huh. Innocence.* She thought that part of her was gone.

"Nothing," he sighed, rubbing a hand across his face, stopping to pinch the bridge of his nose. "I thought I lost you in there."

She laughed, shaking her head and looking over her shoulder at the strange tree. Its branches bent towards her like it wished to hold her again in its embrace. She lifted her hands to touch the limbs when Elias lightly tugged her out of reach. Rude.

"It's been hours," Kian commented, stepping out from behind Elias with Lazuli clinging to his arm. Her expression held a subtle fear, her wide eyes and bobbing throat catching Sylvie's attention.

"What's wrong with her?" Her unabashed comment didn't go unnoticed, and Lazuli stiffened as Sylvie blinked up at Elias. He didn't shift his gaze from her face, instead taking her by the arm and pulling her back across the field.

The distance to the camp was much farther than Sylvie had thought. The juvenile trees sprinkled between them and the one she'd made her haven. "Damn. I ran pretty far last night."

Kerensa appeared at her side covered in dark ichor and frowned. "So, you're a dryad."

Sylvie tilted her head to the side, and her brows furrowed. "What?" She recollected the words of the hybrid the night before. "Crossbreed. It said there were two crossbreeds." She looked over at Lazuli's pale face, staring silently at her. "I'm guessing that's you, right?"

Lazuli nodded imperceptively before shuffling closer to Kian, who pressed his lips together and looked ahead.

Kerensa cleared her throat, glancing Lazuli's way with narrowed eyes as she said, "A dryad is a nature spirit fae. They're bound with a single tree, and if the tree dies, the dryad dies." Kerensa pulled her braids into a ponytail and secured them with a knotted strap of fabric. Sylvie watched with wide eyes as she spoke. "Do you have a bound tree?" Kerensa asked.

They reached their trashed camp, and Lazuli darted off to clean up as Kerensa and her Elias stared at her curiously.

Sylvie shook her head, but she didn't know. "Before coming here, I hardly ever touched a tree. Let alone get bound to one." Sterling was vast. A concrete monstrosity that took two hours to escape from by car. She'd never had the money to waste.

Kerensa chewed her inner cheek. "Perhaps your vampire blood has lessened some of your traditional dryad characteristics."

Elias walked away and began packing their gear while Kian's gaze lingered on her a few moments more.

"Lazuli is a dryad crossbreed," he said with a slight rise at the end, as if he were asking her a question. Her chest tightened as he spoke her name, the letters rolling off his tongue as if they belonged in his mouth.

On his lips.

"That's what it said."

"Crossed with what?" he asked, meeting her eyes with a strange, wild glint.

She shrugged and scrunched her face. "I don't know. Why don't you ask her?"

He swallowed and turned away, joining the group to finish packing up.

Sylvie trailed behind them and stared between the pair, watching Lazuli's possessive clasp on his body. She always seemed to touch him, caressing or squeezing in a choking grip.

A strange niggle twisted in her throat as she brushed her fingers across her heart over the fabric of her tattered gown. Fae couldn't lie, but Sylvie could. Because she wasn't full fae. And if Lazuli wasn't full fae …

"We need to go now if we want to reach the court before the townsfolk arrive," Lazuli cooed. "I'm sure we'll all need to bathe and a change of attire before we meet with my father."

Everything about her left a sour taste in Sylvie's mouth, letting a seed of doubt creep in.

Sylvie scampered into the carriage with Elias closely behind as the cogs, spurred onward by the growing flames of rage, started spinning in her mind.

TWENTY-NINE

The water pressure in Lazuli's chambers put Sylvie's apartment to shame. Even Elias's office en suite had nothing on the fiery waterfall washing away everything from her body—from dirt to sin.

Elias and Kian remained in the hall after cleansing themselves in a different suite two halls away. Despite Sylvie's complaints, they wouldn't share a room. Supposedly sleeping under the stars with both Elias and Kian was fine, but the idea of her sharing a room with a male would cause too much of a stir in the palace. Fae of fair to tanned complexion had stared as they arrived behind the colossal stone palace, whispering behind dainty hands and elegant frocks. None were as beautiful as Lazuli, her almost white hair and grey eyes standing out amongst the vibrant reds and greens of her court. Many of the fae had swirling green veins and delicate leaves embellishing their skin, clothes, and hair. Whether inked, stitched, or real, she could hardly tell.

"Who is she?" an auburn-headed fae asked, her violent green-yellow eyes raking along Sylvie, then moving to Elias's hand clasping hers.

"Does she look familiar to you?" another whispered. Sylvie searched for the origin of the statement, but Lazuli had hurried them all along through a side door. Surely, Rheikar was already aware of their arrival, but she had to look presentable. Beautifying the bait.

Now she stood in the stone shower and remained there until her skin turned red, toying with the raised fingernail-sized scar on her bicep. It was new. She never scarred, ever. And not for lack of trying, but somehow, she got a scar. Must've happened in Evergreen. Perhaps when she fell headlong into the gorse after her second day of training. She sighed. It didn't matter. A light tap on the door drew her attention and she climbed out, murmuring, "Coming."

She padded across the cold tiles back into Lazuli's chambers, where she and Kerensa stood waiting.

Unlike Kian's ethereal plant heaven, Lazuli's suite was cold stone, carved and chiselled as if someone had chipped the structure from a massive boulder. Stone Court was a rather fitting name.

"Here, you can wear this," Lazuli said, holding up a soft lilac dress, the flowing fabric reaching mid-calf length.

Sylvie bit her tongue at the thanks wanting to spill out and instead settled for, "It's beautiful." With a slowness that may have read as wariness, Sylvie took the gown and stepped into it. She still had a pair of fresh cotton underwear that she'd put on straight after the shower. No bra, though, and she doubted Lazuli's wardrobe would have any with a big enough cup size. Thankfully though, the dress fit her comfortably.

She stiffened as Lazuli stepped closer to assist with the zipper on the back. "It was my mother's," she said.

Kerensa clicked her tongue, making her presence known, and Lazuli moved away, leaving Sylvie to zip the top third of the dress herself.

She faced Lazuli after with a furrowed brow. "You didn't have to do that."

Surely there were other outfits around she could wear, instead of the dress of her dead mother.

Lazuli just smiled, all cheeks and dimples. "It's fine. I've had it for many years now. It doesn't hold sentiment." Pursing her lips, she turned away and collected a small necklace from her dressing table, clasping it around her own neck.

"Well," Sylvie murmured, running her fingers down the silky fabric. "If you say so."

Kerensa exhaled sharply, clear annoyance in her posture. She had washed first but changed back into her own armour. It was mostly clean. "Move it. We want a private audience, and at this rate, half the town will be in the throne room by the time we arrive."

Lazuli ground her teeth for a moment before straightening, her smile not reaching her eyes as she filed from the room. Sylvie followed behind, relief filling her as Elias, freshly shaven and dressed in a pressed white shirt and black pants, materialised at her side, his hand enclosing hers.

"You look beautiful."

She pressed her lips together, the smile faltering as Kian mimicked Elias's actions with Lazuli, their fingers interlinked tight.

Too tight.

Elias raised her hand and kissed the top of it, keeping his gaze on her. He was a welcome distraction. Always. She smiled that time.

Lazuli and Kian led the group, with Kerensa trailing at the rear, the crisp sound of their steps echoing on the rough mineral.

The cold stone halls spiralled in a dizzying maze into the central throne area. Guarding the entrance and holding the doors, which consisted of two seven-foot marble slabs, were four fae with shaven heads. Their dark eyes and pale skin were dull compared to the fae she saw on their arrival. They didn't look Sylvie's way as the group passed. They hardly moved besides heaving the door wider to let them through. A mighty carved chair perched on a high platform, and sat atop it like a solid carved demon was—

"Father," Lazuli said. "Prince Kian and I are here for our engagement tour."

Lord Rheikar, imposing even while sitting, swept his unblinking, crow-like gaze over the group when his stare stalled on Sylvie. They widened before he blinked, leaned back, and frowned.

"Your name?" he asked, not taking his eyes off her.

She stepped forward, acutely aware of the tightening grip on her hand. "Miss Hart."

The empty room held its breath, and Sylvie wondered a moment if there were others here, spies against the walls like in the Evergreen Court. Her spine tingled with unease as if dozens of yellow eyes were raking down her curves. She fought the urge to cross her arms over her chest.

Rheikar grinned and stood, his beastly height dwarfing her. When he stepped off the dais and stopped in front of her, though, she noticed he was taller than Elias—but only by a hair.

Smoke and mirrors.

Built like an oak, with black veins spiralling up his bare forearms, similar to the root systems Sylvie saw while merging with the trees, Rheikar was a sight to behold. His shaven head held a crown of black leaves twisting around thorny brambles and beneath that was a six-inch gash from his left brow to his nape. The old scar sliced his left ear in two. It had been crudely stitched. Surely, with the magic of the fae, he could have healed it better? Perhaps it had been left as a reminder. But of what? Her thoughts emptied as he smirked down at her.

"So, you are my son-in-law's supposed fated?"

"I am."

"But you have disregarded fate?" he said, glancing at her hand in Elias's.

"I have."

His black eyes flickered, a tension rising over his jaw before Lazuli appeared, placing her hand on his forearm. "Father. It has been a long journey. We should retire to our rooms and join you for dinner."

He straightened as she pulled away, then inclined his head, the darkness in his gaze deepening. Sylvie eyed the faint trail of ruddy gold blood drizzling down Rheikar's forearm and evened her shallow breaths.

"Let's go," Lazuli said, pulling Kian back to the door. Sylvie turned and paused, letting Kerensa walk ahead, and then Elias. She casually slipped her hand from his and patted down her dress as they reached the guards and the marble doors. Elias looked back, but too late, as Sylvie palmed both marble doors and heaved. The guards, as if expecting her actions, shoved with her until the doors slammed shut, cutting off the look of confusion in her party's eyes.

She steeled her breath and lifted her gaze to the guards. "Don't let her back in." Things weren't what they seemed. She needed answers without interruption. Without Lazuli's *touch*.

Rheikar's laughter echoed in the space as she turned, abruptly ceasing when he saw her expression. Or the lack of one. "There hasn't been a fated pairing in many years," Rheikar's said then, voice a shade lower. "And you have two?"

She padded forwards with a slight tilt to her head, keeping her face neutral. Blank. "So the Veltus said."

It was his turn to tilt his head, his brow edging upward. "The Veltus Spect?"

"Yes."

He hummed, a thoughtful look crossing his face as he leaned against the platform where his blackened throne sat, arms crossed.

"Why did you wear this gown?" he asked, his eyes lingering on her chest, then flicking to her face in one sharp movement.

Sylvie crossed her arms, the tiny scar drawing her fingers again. She resisted the urge to circle it. Dig her nails into it. "Lazuli gave it to me."

His lips pursed, as if tasting a foul thing. "Clever little hellion, that one."

"That's rich."

His eyes jumped to hers, then narrowed at her steely gaze. "Oh? And what depravity has she accused of me this time?"

This time? She reined her anger in and squinted up at him as if seeing him for the first time. "What was it last time?"

His grin had the hairs rising on her nape and she barely restrained the shudder that darted down her spine.

"You look just like her."

What? And she thought Kian was cryptic. Rheikar's thoughts seemed to be jumping around like a hyperactive child.

She cast her gaze towards the doors, behind which Lazuli inevitably stood. "No, I don't."

"Not her," Rheikar replied. "Her mother."

An uneasy niggle squirmed in her stomach as she raised her brow. "How is that supposed to work? Lazuli looks nothing like me or you; shouldn't *she* look like her mother?"

Rheikar sneered, his upper lip twitching. The first signs of his composure slipping. *Good. Show me the truth. Monster.* "That demon spawn is not my blood. Her visage resembles the creature who fathered her."

Sylvie's tongue darted out to wet her lips. Dry. Everything was so dry. Her throat snagged as she swallowed.

"My true daughter, the cursed thing, killed my fated. She was banished to Erus after that. A changeling fae. I suppose she didn't die as I suspected she would."

No. Absolutely not. That was ridiculous. *Insane.* She couldn't be related to him.

He was fucked up. She wasn't …

She *wasn't.*

The flames in her mind singed her thoughts, and she hissed softly.

"Come now, child. One drop of blood and we shall see whom you take after more."

It was stupid. A small resemblance, and he was claiming to be her grandfather. He was so utterly wrong, but she drew nearer to his outstretched hand, placing her wrist in it, facing up. She had to know. Maybe it would be useful.

She stiffened as his nail sliced her skin, a tiny red drop staining its tip. He lifted it to his tongue and let it drop onto the flat surface as he pressed his opposite thumb on the beading crimson pearls of the wound.

He exhaled, his eyes closing for a moment before homing in on her face. "Maple. I never thought I'd taste that again."

Before she could pull away, he flipped her hand in his. The wound closed and he brushed his cracked lips against the top of her knuckles.

"Head to your room, granddaughter. I will expect to see you at dinner."

Sylvie shook her head. "Why should I trust you?"

He could claim anything from that drop of blood. But why would he lie? What good would it do him to suggest such a thing if it didn't benefit him somehow? She couldn't think of a single way them being related helped him.

He isn't lying. She didn't have time to wonder why the voice wasn't hers.

"Don't," he said.

She slipped her hand from his, heart thudding as Lazuli's accusation swam in her head. She'd seen abusers and he—he wasn't it.

"Don't make Kian marry her."

His expression faltered for a fraction before hardening again, the black of his eyes giving way to the faintest amber glow.

"My agreement with King Kol was forged in blood and promise. Neither death nor fate can change it. Lazuli or a female in my line must wed the Evergreen Court's prince."

He worded it so cleverly that she almost smiled. Almost.

"What about me?"

A slow smile spread over his lips, the act splitting the larger cracks, which filled with rust. "You are more like Milena than your looks, little one. But you do not align yourself with my court. What do I have to gain with your marriage proposal?"

She sensed the underlining words and nodded, letting her face fall.

"It won't do," he said.

The stone doors cracked open despite the four guards still heaving against it. "I'm fine," she yelled. "Give me a minute."

But Rheikar was done, his posture closing off as he returned to the throne atop his stage. *A performance.* She frowned, even more lost than before.

"Off you go, now."

She regarded him for another moment, before filing to the door, the guards unmoved. But their gazes lingered on her then. Hopeful almost.

"And be wary of your aunt, little one," Rheikar said as the doors screeched open. "That whore has claws."

THIRTY

"That was reckless. And stupid."

Sylvie pressed her hands down on her lilac gown and rolled her eyes. "Kerensa. Not now." She had so much she needed to share, and it wasn't the time or place.

"Fine, I'll reserve comments on how stupid you are until after dinner."

Sylvie fought a smile from behind Kerensa. "Good."

They passed fae in all states of dress, attention fixed to the floor as they flitted by, hands full. Some held overflowing bags of seed and grain, some held animals, while others carried children. Maybe her impressions were wrong. Maybe Rheikar was exactly the fae Lazuli accused him of being.

Sylvie doubled her pace, stepping in time with Kerensa. Her voice rasped, "What is happening?"

She scowled back. "How the fuck should I know? Hurry! Your vampire is pissed, and my brother isn't helping the situation."

They'd been walking for minutes and still hadn't crossed paths with either male. She was shocked and a fraction proud they hadn't been hovering right at the door when she exited. Kerensa was, though, face as stern as the tax collectors in Sterling.

She'd be a great enforcer.

"Why are you worried? They're friends."

The scoff that left Kerensa's lips startled a passing fae, and she clicked her tongue. "Friends that beat the Hel out of each other when needed." She glared sidelong at Sylvie, fatigue sitting in the dark circles under her eyes. "Kian needs it."

Sylvie's previously steady heart began thudding against her ribs. Whatever happened wasn't good. It had to be big to stop Elias from waiting for her outside the door of an accused monster.

Finally, a door opened to dirt outside, the path littered with gravel and browning weeds. She crossed it with a frown, not recognising the view. On the left, a ten-foot hedge garden appeared. Three entry paths lay signposted by carved statues of six-legged beasts with teeth the length of her fingers and cocks the size of her forearm. She shuddered. If the front of the hedge was any sign, it wouldn't be pretty farther in. It was odd how green the maze was, though. The scraggly forested area on the right side opposed its elegance and growth in every way, as if the maze had taken all the soil's nutrients.

Kerensa tugged her towards the hedges, and she slowly made out harsh voices.

"Let go of her, Kian."

"She's mine."

Sylvie spotted the upper body of Kian wrapped protectively around Lazuli while Elias's form remained out of sight. The glimpse of his embrace boiled Sylvie's blood. Not against him, though. Her. Lazuli, whose claws were latched so deeply into Kian's forearms that his shirt was torn and glistening with gold blood. Even as Lazuli said, "Kian. It's okay. I'm with you."

A sickened grunt poured from Sylvie's lips and she dug her heels into the gravel.

Kerensa rounded on her. "What are you doing?"

She shook her head. They could deal with this one without her. Barrelling in and trying to claim Kian wouldn't do any good, because the Kian she knew, the one who would do anything for her, was already gone. Not permanently. She couldn't even wander down that thought process. But Elias, who had fought for him just as much as he had for her, knew it too from the way he shoved Kian back, forcing Lazuli out of his embrace.

She needed to be tactful. "I need a minute."

"You can't wander off around here," Kerensa said, glancing around. "It's not safe."

"I can disappear into a tree at a whim. I'll be fine."

"Hart."

"Kerensa," she bit back. "A minute."

After the bombshell from ten minutes ago, she probably needed more than a minute. Without another word between them, she spun and stormed off, not once glimpsing back at the harsh voices.

The castle stretched beside her, its carved architecture far more rudimentary from the outside. Besides the turrets and holes for windows, it maintained the look of a gargantuan boulder, to its detriment. It held none of the beauty of the Evergreen Court. She rued the fact that her mother came from here. That *she* came from there. It was so cold. So ugly. She soon reached a paved stone path and passed beneath the carved marble arch that framed it. Her feet pattered on the stones, and she let out a begrudging smile. Alright. Not all of it was ugly.

The surrounding space quieted, and she sent a small thanks to the universe, and Kerensa, for giving her the isolation she craved. No creatures sang here, no insects hummed. No wind rustled.

She frowned as the silence grew unnerving. The lack of sound made the hairs on her body rise in the crisp air. Even her footsteps dulled to nothing.

"Hello?" she jumped at the abruptness of her own voice. At least it wasn't her hearing failing.

The wooded area didn't invite her in like the Evergreen Court. In fact, as she crept along the fringes of the forest, her stomach plummeted any time she wove too close to the trees. *Stay back.* She crossed her arms to stave off the chill. *Not safe.* The leaf cover shrouded most of the sunlight and cast the fourth and fifth rows of trees in almost complete darkness. *Danger.*

Sylvie cast her gaze up at the gnarled branches reaching for one another. Like children linking arms to bar her path into the forest, the trees grew darker and more twisted as she wandered further from the hedge garden and castle walls. Another border of trees rose between her and the castle until she was surrounded on both sides.

As far as she could tell, she was alone, but the growing itch across her neck started to illicit images in her mind of spying eyes. Then, just as her goosebumps turned into a total body chill, a decaying stench wafted up her nose. Wrinkling it, she paused her ambling.

"What is that?"

275

At the end of the path, the stones weaved to the left and out of sight. Sylvie peered over her shoulder, expecting to see the castle, and when all that stood behind her were ugly trees, she inhaled sharply.

"Fuck," she whispered, turning and taking a few tentative steps back from where she came. It wasn't her best decision looking for solace in woods bursting with ugly fucking trees. Even the thought of merging with one of them made her stomach roll. Sterling smelled better.

A cold gust blew the foul odour against her back, wrapping her hair around her face and causing her to misstep on a loose stone. Her hands flew out to catch her as she tripped and landed hard on her knees, the roar of tearing fabric almost as loud as her curse.

Pressing her lips together against a string of vulgarity, she sat, swiping her hair out of her eyes to scan Lazuli's mother's gown. Her *grandmother's* gown. A four-inch gash across the front hung open, revealing her knees already starting to purple with bruises.

"Fuck!" She fingered the frayed edges and her face twisted. It was just a gown, and any decent seamstress could probably fix it and make it look good as new, but it fucking sucked. She had the blood of a vampire and a dryad in her, yet she held the clumsiness of a toddler. *Useless.* A frustrated scream bubbled from her chest and tore from her throat as she clenched her hands in a fist. Now she was going to tantrum like one too. *Pathetic.* There was nothing to hit. Nothing to hurt but herself. She slammed her fist into the dirt at her side again and again until her knuckles were bloodied. Her furious shrieks bounced off the trees around her for a few minutes before she peeked at them, sure they would be nearer to her, ready to devour her into their twisted flesh. *Maybe you should let them.*

She scowled. The voices weren't her own, but they stoked her flames. *Get out of my head.* Their pressure lessened as she took in the space again. The world remained still; the trees remained on the edge of the path, and the creatures of the wood remained silent.

They mocked her with their absence. Or perhaps they respected her enough to keep quiet as she let a fraction of her rage free in their home.

Maybe she scared them.

Sometimes she scared herself.

Casting her gaze around the path, a lone crow caught her attention, its black, marbled eyes staring straight at her from where it perched on a low-hanging branch.

So she wasn't alone after all.

Sniffing and staring, she offered a slight bloodied wave to the creature.

It tilted its head and puffed its feathers slightly, revealing hues of lilac and teal under its jet-black outer feathers.

She stood, ignoring the groan of her muscles, and peered again at the crow. It stared back, its beak opening and closing.

"Do you need something?" Sylvie asked, voice raw from screaming. She stepped closer, and the bird's body puffed up at her movement. "Sorry. I didn't mean to startle you."

She sniffed, peering over her shoulder, then back at the bird. It had moved. It now stood in the centre of the path with the same inquisitive tilt to its fluffy head. She hadn't heard it make a sound. "Are you magical?"

Its mouth opened as if to caw, but nothing came out. Sylvie swallowed and walked towards it. Its beak opened again, and it jumped back along the path, matching her steps. It didn't make a single sound.

"This is stupid. I need to get out of here," she said, spinning to walk the way she came. Something about the trees, though, made her pause. Was that the way she came from? After falling, her bearings were way off.

Stubborn tears burned along her waterline as she spun back to the crow. It faced the path away from her, and she sighed. "Fine. I'll follow you. You better not lead me to my death."

The crow hopped along the flat stones, and Sylvie followed, her eyelids drooping with exhaustion from her emotional release. Every step she took following the bird grew more sluggish and sloppy.

Her eyes closed briefly when a rigid, slimy surface smacked against her forehead. The rebounding force sent her flying backwards, landing hard on her tailbone.

Moaning, she leaned her head back against the ground as tears of pain leaked out and trailed towards her ears. Blinking them away, she scrunched her face at the gnarled, twisting monstrosity looming above her. The tree looked more like a swamp monster than a living plant. Black sap dribbled through the squishy, peeling bark, which she imagined was stuck to her head.

From her position, she could see the giant had few leaves and a thick clawing root system above the ground. No other tree breached the perimeter of this central monstrosity. If plants could show fear, the ones giving a wide berth Sylvie's new least favourite tree were the perfect example.

The branches of all the other trees leaned away like the petals of a blooming flower, leaves quivering despite the absence of a breeze. Even the crow wouldn't perch there, instead clawing at the dirt beside her sprawled form.

She rolled away from the bird and stood facing the tree, crossing her arms tightly around herself when a cold, sharp sensation pressed into her back. The bird flitted away in silence.

A warmth tickled her ear, the beginning of a laugh, she inhaled sharply to scream.

THIRTY-ONE

Sylvie spun, swinging, and her fist clipped Kerensa's jaw so hard spit flew onto the decaying soil. Her eyes widened as Kerensa staggered back, working her jaw. She spat a glob of gold at her feet and regarded Sylvie with a raised brow.

"Solid throw, but you're still dead."

She squinted, peering down at herself. Dishevelled sure, dead no.

"I think you're mistaken."

Kerensa dug a knuckle into her own cheek, lifting her other hand with clawed fingers. "If I were a hybrid, you would be."

"Lucky you aren't a hybrid, then."

"Indeed." With a final spit of blood, Kerensa shifted the satchel on her hip and flipped the top, riffling through clinking bottles.

Sylvie leaned in on tiptoes. "What are those?"

"Vials, potions, poisons."

She continued her perusing.

"And?"

She pulled out a vial of effervescent milky liquid in a glass globe, the stopper coated in black wax.

"*And* when the Fates give us an opportunity, why squander it?" She faced the wretched tree at Sylvie's back and thumbed the black wax.

Sylvie glanced over her shoulder. Rheikar's bound tree. Holy shit. She gripped Kerensa's wrist as she strode past and shook her head.

"This is what we came here to do, Hart."

But she had more questions. He might be the last direct descendent of hers still alive. It was likely. By the looks of his tree, though, he wouldn't be for much longer.

"Just wait, alright?"

Kerensa bared her teeth, the grip on the vial constricting. "You're starting to piss me off."

"And what happens when the lord of the Stone Court suddenly drops dead? We don't know where Elias and Kian are, and we still don't have answers about Lazuli."

Kerensa paused, her expression turning from annoyance to curiosity. "And what answers might you be seeking?"

She sensed a presence on the path they'd come from. "Ones best not shared in unknown company."

Kerensa whirled as half a dozen armed guards appeared before them, eyes glazed, and weapons drawn.

"You can't be here."

Kerensa inclined her head as she stepped to Sylvie's side. "Of course. I was just reminding my handmaid that it's best not to wander unaccompanied in unfamiliar courts. Would you be so kind to escort us to our chambers? We share the royal wing."

Sylvie barely withheld her expression of shock at Kerensa's honeyed words. The guards bowed. "My deepest regrets for my harshness, Princess. I did not recognise you. Of course, we would be happy to escort you."

"Wonderful." Kerensa held out her hand, potion nowhere to be seen, which the lead guard took, threading it over his elbow.

With what could have been mistaken for a genuine smile, Kerensa gestured for Sylvie to do the same.

She did. Although begrudgingly; the reek of their body odour was almost as pungent as Rheikar's tree.

Kerensa walked ahead, the swish of her hips leaving little to the imagination with her tight trousers and vest. She dressed more like the guards, but they didn't seem to care. She was still as stunning as a female in a full gown.

By the time they reached their chambers, the sun beamed overhead, and sweat beaded on Sylvie's brow.

"Someone will be sent to summon you for dinner with Lord Rheikar."

Kerensa drew her arm free and nodded, smiling without teeth, before she sashayed into the room with Sylvie trailing after. Sylvie's thankful grin turned more into a grimace, and she tensed when the door slammed at her back.

As their clipped steps faded into silence, Sylvie found a place to sit on a bench beneath the carved window. A pane of foggy glass shielded her from the weather while she looked at the forest from above. From there, Rheikar's tree was barely a speck. She sighed. They'd be lucky to make it there again, now that he knew they had seen it. The guards were probably marching there to tell him right now.

"Anything to say?" Kerensa asked.

She leaned against the stone and regarded the fae. Her severe look had Sylvie balking. Kerensa had never hid her hatred for Rheikar or Lazuli. If she knew Sylvie was one of them, would it change things?

Yes.

They weren't friends, but they weren't enemies either. It wasn't worth fracturing the relationship. Not until she had more answers.

"Rheikar said nothing could interfere with the deal he made with your father. Even death."

Kerensa picked at her teeth with a pinkie. "Doesn't mean we can't kill him."

Sylvie exhaled through her nose and fought the very human urge to laugh. She'd met her match in obtuse arrogance.

"Lazuli is half demon, by the way."

That dropped the air of obnoxiousness, and shock took its place. "What?"

Sylvie crossed her legs and leaned back, satisfied. "You heard me."

"Rheikar said that?"

"Yep."

Kerensa threaded her fingers atop her head, elbows wide. "And you stopped me from killing him?"

"He's not her father."

"Hart—"

"I'm serious."

"And he just told you this?"

That was where the confessions ended. She shrugged. "Said I reminded him of his dead wife. He got sentimental."

She shook her head, processing and disbelieving. "We need to get Kian away from her." That was something they could both agree on. But in this place, it was risky. Home turf of your enemy always was.

"Let's just wait for dinner." They'd learn more about the half demon, half fae holding her fated hostage and uncover the truth about Rheikar's abuse.

Kerensa's lip twitched. "Yes. Let's."

* * *

Hours went by. *Hours.* Sylvie napped, changed, ate some of Kerensa's rations, and grumbled. Once the night was thoroughly upon them, even Kerensa started pacing.

"Why do they eat so fucking late?"

Kerensa tried the door. Locked. "They don't. Seems we've been uninvited."

Kerensa murmured under her breath, and the lock snagged before clunking open. A teeth-rattling alarm bell tolled as Kerensa twisted the doorknob and Sylvie jumped to her feet. "Was that you?"

"No." The obvious tension rippling down Kerensa's spine had words dying in Sylvie's throat. Uninvited? No. Sylvie had intrigued Rheikar. She'd felt it. He wanted to speak with her, so something had to have gone wrong if the plans changed.

"Something's wrong here."

"Obviously," Kerensa said from the door, still not opening it as footsteps thundered by. "Six bells." Kerensa darted about the room, gathering weapons, including a long wooden staff covered in markings, a sword, and a curved knife the size of her forearm.

"What is six bells? What's happening?"

"Demons." Kerensa's statement was punctuated by the shrill screams of fae and rattling clicks.

Sylvie grabbed her arm as she passed. "I want to help."

"Don't be stupid."

"I can defend myself."

Kerensa laughed, the sound not cruel, but it was daggers to her heart no less. "You have probably totalled twelve hours of training in your life and landed one good punch. You'd die out there in the time I take to tie up my boots." She rubbed her jaw again. "Maybe my vest too."

Fair. Fair, but fucking harsh. "Fuck, Kerensa, you really know how to woo a girl."

Kerensa looked at her, a hint of the alluring air from earlier settling into her expression. "Oh no, Hart. You wouldn't stand a chance."

Sylvie picked at her thumb, letting her lip curl. "Fine. At least leave me a weapon, then."

Kerensa held out her knife, which Sylvie took, hand dropping under the weight of it.

"Sharp end in the enemy," Kerensa said. "My brother would never forgive me if you impaled yourself on his knife."

Sylvie regarded the blade, noting the pattern of vines seared into the silver metal. Beautiful. The wooden hilt was carved in the shape of a tree trunk, the branches acting as the cross guard. Kerensa left without a goodbye. The only signal of her absence was the click of the bedroom lock re-engaging.

"Thanks."

She darted back to the window for any sign of Kerensa or her males and found nothing but a maelstrom of guards fighting hybrids and terrified fleeing fae, the same ones who had passed her in the halls. Even seeing Lazuli would be a welcome distraction from the chaos. She would put up a fight. While Sylvie was hiding in her room like a coward.

Kill her.

She jolted upright and dropped Kian's blade on the windowsill, burying her fingers in her hair. "Shut up!" *Get the hell out of my head already!* The foreign presence eased, and her thoughts were her own again. *But for how long?*

The bedroom door latch clicked and swung in as a figure stepped in. She stood, snatching the blade up and tucking it behind her back as they came in to view.

"Lord Rheikar."

"Granddaughter." He leaned against the door to shut it, his body brimming with tension.

She swallowed and inclined her head. "Why are you here?"

His black gaze snagged on her face, her mouth. "I do not know."

The breathing from the both of them was heavy, stress laden in every inhale. This was all wrong. *Don't make a fool out of me.*

"Then maybe you should go. Help your people." She jutted her chin to the window, where screams turned to gargles and death rattles.

"I wish to."

But he stayed, frozen. Restrained.

Her focus narrowed from the blade pressed against the back of her thigh to the rapid rise and fall of Rheikar's chest.

"What is the nature of Lazuli's abilities?" she asked.

Under her feet, the stones quavered, and Rheikar lunged. Faster than she'd expected, pinning her back to the wall, her hand strangling the hilt of the blade even as it sliced into her hamstring. She would not drop it. Even as his head dropped to her neck, inhaling her scent as if it were the finest wine.

"Milena."

"No. I'm not. Let go of me!"

A gap appeared between them, and she jerked as he began pawing at her skirts, lifting them with one hand as the other unbuckled his belt.

"Stop!"

Her fire burned as old memories churned the smoke. A tongue on her throat. Fingers twined in her hair. Pulling. Guiding.

She screamed, jamming the blade between them, pushing through jerkin, skin, and bone. It was so much denser than she imagined. Thick.

Rheikar staggered back, hands gripping the hilt sticking from his chest and pulled, a torrent of rust and black and dirt dousing the stone floors. Dousing Sylvie's feet.

Betrayal seeped from his wound, too. Hurt.

"I'm sorry, I—"

His eyes cleared for a moment before darkening again as humour filled him, escaping with a tainted hiss.

"Sorry? Now you owe me a debt, little one. I own you."

He gestured with the drenched knife at her face, his grin feral, and she pressed her lips together. *Fuck! Oh, I've fucked up big time. When Kian finds out—*

"Lord Rheikar, whatever did I deserve to earn your company for the evening?" Kerensa's lilting voice snapped both of their attention to the door. Coated in black goo, she tilted her head with a saccharine smile.

He bowed his head, the muscles in his back trembling as Sylvie edged along the wall. Outside, screams drew her focus. Where was Elias and Kian? Were they okay?

"I wished to invite you both to dinner, but I fear the opportunity has passed."

Kerensa lowered her staff, dripping in viscous pus, to the ground. "Indeed, it has."

He swept from the room, past Kerensa and into the hall, disappearing as quickly as he came. The only sign he was there was the pile of blood by her feet.

She stared at it. Stared unblinking until her eyes burned. She didn't notice the door shutting or Kerensa's presence until they were nose to nose.

Kindling. It was kindling, not silver marks. They were not memories to keep, but memories to burn.

Yes. Burn.

"What happened?"

"I fucked up," Sylvie said over Kerensa's question.

"You stabbed him."

She sighed, glaring at Kerensa through her lashes. "I apologised."

Kerensa's expression pinched, then slackened. "You did not."

"Is there any way to get out of owing him a debt?" She knew there wasn't, otherwise Kian wouldn't have drilled her so hard on it.

"Yeah. We kill him." Kerensa pulled the white vial from her satchel again, holding it between them in a question. When Sylvie's stomach sank, Kerensa added, "He isn't good, Hart. His people fear him for good reasons. Your vampire found his scent around the portal that led the hybrids here. I watched one cleave a faeling in half and eat her because of him."

Her heart plummeted. How could she have been so wrong about him? One inkling of a family and she lost her wits. Kerensa was right. Rheikar was a dead male walking.

Yes.

"Either you do this, or I will," Kerensa said, a final strike to the anvil.

No!

"No." Sylvie coughed, fighting against the returning foreign voices and taking the vial in steady hands. "I will."

They sat in painful silence for a beat before Kerensa said, "Flora killer. Eats everything it touches."

"I figured." She hadn't, but she didn't need to know the murder method. "When are we doing this?"

The screaming had receded, but no other bells tolled to inform them it was safe. Maybe everyone was already dead.

"No time like the present," Kerensa said.

THIRTY-TWO

"Psst, bird!" Sylvie hissed.

Kerensa and Sylvie slipped through the winding wings of the Stone Court palace and out into the tepid night air. The cloying scent of death lingered on the breeze.

"Here, birdy …" Sylvie tried again, squinting to make out anything in the darkness as she wrapped Kerensa's thick coat about herself.

"Hush. We will find it again on our own."

Sylvie slid her feet over the ruddy stone steps and gave Kerensa a look, the purple of the fae's irises thinning in response. Smiling. Wincing?

"We've been walking for too long," Sylvie said.

"You're moving like a sightless elder. Use your fae sight, dryad."

Fae sight, huh? Not with these trees.

"Kiss my ass. How about that?"

Kerensa's eyes narrowed for a second time, and this time the expression was unmistakable. Withering.

She should be the one offering that look. The trees here were a sick mockery of the ones in the Evergreen Court. The stench of rot curled its dirty finger in her hair and tugged. How many of them had lost their dryad tonight? Did the trees die too?

Questions for another time.

A clicking sounded in the distance and Sylvie's foot snagged on the uneven ground. She swallowed a cry as Kerensa grabbed her shoulders and slapped her other hand on her mouth. *Click. Click.* They stood, Sylvie's back heaving against Kerensa's chest, long enough for the clicking to recede into the distance once more. A shrill scream took its place.

They were killing them. Why would Rheikar do this to his people?

How could he be so cruel?

"Is that your bird?" Kerensa rasped, her heart a solid thud against Sylvie's shoulder blade.

Sylvie squinted, following the end of her finger, and nodded. Dark as the night they concealed themselves behind. Fluffing and preening, head tilting in a semblance of humour. The marbled eyes gleamed in the faint crescent moon's glow. It was the crow alright.

"Hi, again." A small shadow flitted from twig to soil, scratching the dirt in a come hither. "Can you take us to the tree?"

It hopped down the path, but as Sylvie went to follow, Kerensa grabbed her bicep. "That isn't a natural creature."

A shudder knifed down her back. "What's that supposed to mean?"

Kerensa released her, but neither female moved. "It's a dryad familiar. Some ancient dryads have creatures tied to their spirit. It could be Rheikar's spy."

Sylvie followed its shadow as it scratched and pecked the ground, saying out of the side of her mouth, "Why would it lead me to his tree if it was a spy for him?"

Kerensa clicked her tongue. "How should I know?"

The crow flew to the path in front of them and fluffed its feathers, its large head tilting to the side.

Sylvie pressed her lips together and shot a pointed look at Kerensa. "We're out of options, and besides, it looks trustworthy enough to me."

"And that's why I left you in the chamber."

Sylvie huffed but moved.

Following the crow sped up her movements by double, and soon the scent of rot coiled her insides.

"What happened between you and Rheikar?" Kerensa asked, her silent footfalls at Sylvie's side giving her a ghostly essence. It wasn't a question she expected or wanted to entertain.

She just shrugged. "Nothing."

"Did he touch you?"

Bile churned in her gut, and she dug her index fingernail into her thumb. "He thought I was someone else."

Kerensa said nothing. She didn't have to. It wouldn't excuse what he did to her. The path bent and the stench assaulted their senses as they followed it. The bird hopped from path edge to path edge.

"I've had worse."

Kindling. Fuel. Flames.

"I misjudged you, Hart."

Sylvie stopped where pavers shifted to blackened soil and grimaced at Rheikar's tree before her, imposing in its scent.

"I … I really doubt it."

Kerensa touched her shoulder, the contact light. It wasn't the time. Any other time, but not now. She didn't need to feel. To remember.

"When the time comes, I will stand by your claim of my brother against my mother. You *would* make a good queen."

But that wasn't what Sylvie wanted. She wasn't made to lead.

A gentle whoosh of wind on their faces drew their attention before Sylvie could respond, and they peered at the crow, on a branch above them, its feathers sticking out as if it had been electrocuted.

"Damn impatient bird," Kerensa muttered, rounding the tree, clearly not wanting to linger in sentimentality any longer. She sniffed, then spat a glob at the twisted roots. "Demon blight."

Sylvie stepped beside her, pulling the glass vial from her coat pocket and thumbing the wax-coated stopper.

"What is that?"

"It's a condition influenced by demonic affiliation—possession usually. Sometimes it's external. Other instances it's cruelty and violence. The five fae courts demand balance, and when the scales tip too far, there is always a cost. Our choices have consequences, and a promise made is a promise kept."

Sylvie gnawed on the inside of her cheek, lifting the vial into the moon's beams. The white liquid bubbled and swirled, an incandescent sheen catching the light as if dancing.

"Won't I be tipping the scales too far? Who will lead the Stone Court if Rheikar is dead?"

"Not your problem. My mother has much to mend, she can start by appointing a new lord here. One that doesn't invoke evil in our realm."

Our realm.

The one link she had to this place was about to die because of her. Stabbing him in self-defence was one thing, but this? This was cold-blooded, calculated murder. Her voice wobbled as she said, "Let's just do this."

Yes.

Kerensa's warm presence at her side kept her steady as she picked the wax from the stopper. Little by little the glass top appeared and the liquid inside shimmied. She inhaled sharply as a sliver of wax embedded under her thumbnail. Blood rolled in crimson rivulets down her thumb. Fuck. The last of the wax fell to the ground, and she dislodged the sliver with her teeth.

"How does it work?"

"Pour it on the roots. The poison will climb."

She used the crease between her thumb and index finger to pop off the stopper and winced as a drop of blood slid inside the bottle. She stared as the white creatures inside danced around the drop, yet they didn't eat it. It just sat, suspended atop the liquid. "Are you sure this will work?"

"Yes. Just do it already. Fae are dying as we speak."

She clenched the bottle, nodding her head in a jerky affirmation. She could do this. She had to do this.

Do it. Do it now.

Her hands shook as she held it before her, tilting the bottle slightly. The liquid hummed under her hand, eager.

In moments, her grandfather would die. Would it be fast? Painful? Would he know it was her?

Along with her breathing, her hand stalled. Eyes burning, she lifted her gaze to Kerensa and begged silently.

Don't be pathetic. Do it!

"I can't." She lowered the vial. "I can't do it."

Kerensa didn't waver. She took the vial from Sylvie's hands even as the voices in her mind screamed and poured the liquid around the base of the trunk in one smooth arc. Like lightning, it pulsed and climbed until the bottom quadrant was petrified and smoking. It was done. Rheikar would die. She swallowed the flood of saliva in her mouth and pulled air through her lungs. Vomiting was not an option. Not after she failed to follow through. *Failure.*

"I'm sorry—" she choked, slamming her fingers to her lips, but it was too late. The words had already escaped.

Kerensa didn't turn. Her gaze stayed soft. Open. Understanding. It was better when she held disdain. Sylvie was familiar with disdain. This … this was new. Kerensa stilled until the tree groaned and sighed. "Don't be," she said, finally facing Sylvie. "Mercy is not a weakness."

"That's not what the voices are saying." She offered a bland smile, but Kerensa didn't return it. Instead, she pressed her lips together and exhaled, searching Sylvie's eyes. When she didn't find whatever she was looking for, she leaned back.

"We should go."

With a nod, Sylvie took her hand, and they shuffled back towards the path. Her crow had vanished, and she rued the fact she couldn't offer gratitude to the tiny creature for helping them. She wasn't sure how, though. Kian had said offering thanks was off the table, too. So many rules.

The moment the stone monstrosity came into view, terrible, hoarse shrieks pierced the night air. Guttural. Agonising.

Kerensa shoved Sylvie behind her and took up a fighting stance, blocking her view of the world beyond the cursed forest.

"Don't do it, Rheikar. Let your last act be worth remembering," Kerensa said.

"What have you done?" His wet, gurgling words doused any anger inside Sylvie until only guilt remained.

Over Kerensa's shoulder, she made out his staggering gait, broadsword dangling from his grip and a dark pulsing orb in the other. His mouth gnashed strange archaic chants as spittle and blood cascaded from his nose. His eyes.

"You did this?"

An involuntary gasp escaped as Sylvie saw his face. The skin was melting. Cream bone glistened beneath his brow ridge. She could've fainted. Nobody answered him. The horror had rooted her to stillness. Silence.

"No matter," he said. "I shall take comfort in your death."

"Stop, Rheikar. Don't take your people with you. They are innocent."

He paused then, as much as one could with their eye dripping from its socket. The orb in his hand flared and dimmed. Yellow lights winked from inside it and Sylvie squinted. *What is that?*

His arm lifted an inch as if to hand the orb over, but his hand degloved, the fingers slipping off bone with the orb stuck to the flesh.

Kerensa tensed, a hiss passing her teeth as it hit the ground, the glass smashing and liquid inside splattering. The rest of Rheikar followed it, his skin bubbling as the dark liquid pulled down, shaping the ground into an endless void. The yellow lights, Sylvie realised, were eyes. Dozens of them. The sight took away the guilt of her grandfather's dying spasms and replaced it with fear. Icy, wretched fear. Kerensa backed up, one hand guiding Sylvie past the statues with foot-long dicks and into the hedgerows.

"We need to get out of here," Kerensa said, her head peeking around the statue. From Sylvie's vantage, everything was obscured beyond the rigid lines of Kerensa's back.

"The orb?"

"A portal in a bottle. Highly illegal. A fucking nightmare to contain."

Sylvie worked her jaw. "A portal to where?"

Kerensa glanced over her shoulder, winced. "Don't ask questions you already know the answer to."

An earsplitting din cracked through the night, and Sylvie ducked, blocking her ears. She was too exposed. Weaponless.

"Do you have any more of the white stuff?"

Kerensa exhaled sharply, jerking her head from Sylvie's face to her satchel as she rummaged. "What are you planning?"

With a tinkling of glass, she pulled a thin tube with a metal cap free and rolled it between her fingers as Sylvie answered, "I don't know yet." She took the tube from Kerensa and pocketed it in her coat's outer pocket. After seeing what it could do, the farther from her skin, the better. "I'll let you know when I come up with something."

The stones beneath them lurched, and Sylvie kept her footing as hisses and clicks filled the air. Kerensa peered down at her with lips pressed in a straight line, her voice barely audible over the sound of claws raking over rocks. "Now would be a great time to tell me you've got vampiric killing abilities."

Despite the horror of what was to come, Sylvie managed to smile. "You read too many books."

Kerensa exhaled through her nose in something as close to a laugh as Sylvie had heard from her. "Well," she said, "it was occasionally pleasant knowing you."

"Sylvie." The voice brushed against her ears moments before the darkness at her side flickered and warped, leaving Elias and Kian standing there.

Relief coursed through her as Elias's hand brushed her cheek in silent question.

"I'm okay."

"You'll tell me everything later."

She nodded and squeezed his forearm as Kian hovered on the fringes. No Lazuli hanging off his arm, so that was something, but his gaze didn't fix on her. Not at first. Even in the dark, Sylvie made out a veil between them, unfocusing his eyes.

She peered from him to Elias, noting the pain in the latter's expression, and swallowed. "Do you have a plan?"

Kerensa clicked her tongue to her teeth and jerked her head. "Yeah, you two kill them, and I close that portal."

Kian straightened. "Let's get this over with."

Their voices faded under the crunch and slurping from behind the hedge, and Sylvie found her gaze drifting to the sound. She leaned in, prying apart a few branches to see beyond the hedgerows. She wished she hadn't.

Elias pulled her back, but it was too late.

A femur, in halves, the skin dangling around the gnarled fingers that held them. A toothy grin sucking marrow like gravy through a straw.

And yellow eyes a foot away, peering back at her through the branches.

THIRTY-THREE

Elias shoved a fist through the hedge, catching the hybrid's hair, and yanked it into the bush far enough for Kian to behead it in one clean swing. The head landed by Sylvie's feet with a hard thunk, and she recoiled. Finally, Kian looked at her. Really looked. *Welcome back.* A faint brush of his mental touch cascaded down her body and she let it, leaning in as he took her hand and placed a feathery kiss on her knuckles. An undertone of pain shone in his bloodshot gaze.

"Be safe," she said as he rose and moved next to his sister. Kerensa kept a lookout as Elias offered one last chaste kiss on her brow, whispering against her forehead, "Stay hidden."

Before they moved, Sylvie leaned forward, placing a hand on Kerensa's shoulder. She tensed but didn't wrench away.

"What is it?"

"Be careful." At Kerensa's smirk, she added, "And do you have a spare weapon? Rheikar took the other blade."

She faced the palace with a sharp inhale and threw a knife into the ground with the flick of her wrist, one inch from Sylvie's big toe. She barely caught the sound of Elias's growl or Kian's clicking tongue as the switch-knife—*her* switch-knife—gleamed up at her in the moonlight.

The trio drew a collective breath and darted from the hedge cover, disappearing behind it in moments. *Don't die.* Sylvie stared after them for a beat before retrieving her blade. As shiny as the day she left it, strewn in the passenger seat of her car.

It was small, but it would do. She spun the handle in her palm, pointing the blade away from her thumb, and steeled herself. Her one job was to hide. Hiding wasn't that simple when her scent drew hybrids from Hel.

Kian and Elias could hold off the horde for a while, but not forever. She peered down. The black bile and ichor flooded the dirt beneath the dismembered head, and she nodded. It would do. As a cacophony of clicks, shrieks, and weapons tearing through flesh filled the space, she dropped to her knees. She scooped the blood and smeared it on her arms, legs, and neck, the mixture gritty with soil. When that ran out, she lifted the head and squeezed the neck stump, gathering the last dregs in her skirt and painting her face with it. She winced the whole time, disgusted, but there was something poetic about it. Something that stoked the coals in her flames until they warmed her.

When she was thoroughly coated, she peeked through the hedges again, admiring the deadly dance unfolding. For every parry from Kian, Elias counter-struck. The pair moved in synchronicity, as if they had rehearsed the fight for years. Sylvie sensed this wasn't their first battle together.

Kerensa hacked and slashed at any hybrids daring to sniff closer to the hedgerows and moved in a smooth arc towards the void, where more and more monsters crawled through.

Soon they were almost overrun, some hybrids darting into the castle, some straight past Sylvie to the main road where a town must have been connected. Her males movements didn't slow, or appear to tire, but the space for grappling shrank until Elias and Kian stood back-to-back, slashing their weapons in fierce arcs. Finally, Kerensa reached the portal, slugging her own luminescent orb of amber straight down into its centre, smashing it against the clawing bodies. She turned and sprinted in the opposite direction as the dark hole squeezed, popping a hybrid torso from its lower half, and exploded outward, raining disjointed limbs and brain matter across the ground in heavy thunks. The blast threw Sylvie onto her ass, blowing the hedges into a steep lean above her. Hands up, she braced for an impact that came from a different source. Not from being crushed by a ten-foot shrub, but Elias groaning in pain behind them.

"No, no, no …" She crawled to the maze entrance, searching for him, but under the writhing mass of hybrids, he was invisible. Gone.

"E! Where are you?" Kian's shout reverberated in her ears until panic wound around her throat and choked her.

"E!"

Fuck. *Fuck!*

She fiddled with the blade in her hand and dragged it across her palm in one swift movement, pinkie to thumb pad, the blood welling and spurting from her fingers a second before the pain hit.

She let the drops hit the ground, and she stood, screaming, and screaming, and screaming. For Elias, for herself, for the fucking mess they were in. The nearest hybrid's head swivelled and homed in on her form, dripping with their blood and hers, terror for her kindred fuelling her.

"No!" Kian appeared briefly in the maelstrom, eyes half on her, the other searching. Searching. The horror in his gaze matched the feeling in her heart.

Elias didn't appear, but his pained yell reached her before anyone moved. As if he spoke between seconds. Just to her. Always to her.

"Run, Sylvie!"

As she turned, the faint glimmer of an ethereal figure floated past a window on the highest floor of the palace. The image lingered in her mind like a foul smell.

She ran anyway. Ran into the maze, switch-knife in one hand—the uncut one—and the tiny vial of white poison between her blood-slick fingers.

She ignored the grinding of claws over stone and gnashing clicks of pointed canines. She ran. And ran. The hedgerows loomed on either side as she made right turn after right turn until she hit dead space. A space she was about to die in. "Fuck!" She rubbed her dripping palm along the bushes, hissing at the sharp pain shooting up her arm. It wasn't healing like normal. Maybe she'd cut too deep. She tried the other hand, squeezing a branch with a strangling grip. *Could she merge with other things?* The plants' steady rustle and meagre energy seemed to answer her, and she propelled herself back the way she came. Don't stop. *Don't stop.*

All she could do was hope she had done enough to help Elias as the path opened in a funnel shape, the death rattles and clicking of the hybrids quieting. *Did I lose them?*

At the end of the funnel, two paths veered in opposite directions.

Her head swivelled left to right.

Which way?

She peered over her shoulder as a lean, distorted shadow stretched over the path behind her. *No.*

Both paths were identical. The shadow loomed.

She swivelled on her left foot, about to run, when the softest caw called from her right. Gasping, she faced her newest companion, half sobbing at the sight of the jet-black crow preening itself on top of the hedge to the right.

Thank you!

She darted after the bird as it hopped from wall to wall, only flitting to the ground when she burst through the maze and into a garden framed on every angle by ten-foot bushes. In its centre, a wide willow with a mop of feathery leaves swayed silkily in the night air.

In a silent glide, the crow flew and landed at the point where exposed roots met soil and nestled its head into the bark, cawing once before snuggling beside it.

She buried the rising sadness from the scene and rushed towards her safety net. A tree. She could hide. Once she was close, she spun to face the hedge walls. Waiting. Waiting. The wound on her palm stung, but the blood slowed, coagulating as the edges of the cut began scabbing.

In one hand, her blade shook, clasped in strangling digits. In the other, the vial warmed between her sticky fingers.

She tapped into her fae sight for a second and nodded before allowing her vision to return to normal. She had a plan. One that probably wouldn't work, but she was out of options.

On an inhale, she jogged out of range of the willow's root system and knelt in the dirt. She sucked an anticipatory breath between her teeth and cut her palm once more, forming an X.

The blade tip sliced cleanly, barely disturbing the first cut, and she held her shaking hand over one of her footprints. She squeezed her fingers into her palm, biting her lips to stifle the cry from the pain, and shook every drop she could into the divot. Shivering, she lifted the vial, tugged out the stopper, and tipped the contents into her blood. As it had done before, the white, glittering poison danced in her blood, suspended, not eating anything at all. Waiting.

She cradled her bloodied hand and stood, jumping at the sudden pecking at her ankles. Clicks sounded nearby, and she backed up, careful not to step on the crow as it hurried her along. When the hybrid sounds faded, she exhaled sharply in frustration.

"Hey!" The first yell cracked and came out closer to a squeak. She coughed and tried again. "Hey! Over here!"

The pecking sharpened, and she gasped as, in horrific synchronicity, dozens of wiry bodies and face-splitting grins peered over the maze. They blinked slowly in time and tilted their heads to the right. Tilted them far enough that a normal neck would snap. Bile rose in her throat as she regarded them, a prey animal locking eyes with an apex predator.

They didn't move, just watched her, crouching with their frozen looks of delight. Of hunger.

The silence between them broke with the striking of steel and the death cries of their own. She walked backwards until her spine struck the wood. Kian and Elias would be there soon. Like her movements were tied to the creatures, a coiled wire between them, barbed and dipped in venom, they jerked over the wall and towards her at breakneck speeds. "Let me in." She pressed her back into the tree, her feet digging into the soil, but it didn't open to her. She couldn't merge. "Don't do this." Smothering a sob, she dug her nails into the trunk. "Please! Let me in."

Nothing happened. Nothing but the skittering creatures closing the gap between them, a glint in their yellowed eyes.

She'd failed. It was over. Dead.

A few redirected to the pool of blood she made, lapping up the liquid until their violent screams and contorted bodies revealed the poison doing its work. The others shot for the larger prize—the quivering female covered in their blood and her own.

"Please."

The stench of their breaths hit her face first, and her stomach lurched, the thick pang of rotting garbage and sewage burning her eyes. She squeezed them shut and clawed at the trunk with her blood-crusted fingers.

"Please!"

She twisted her face away from the reaching knotted fingers, when as easily as exhaling, Sylvie's body melted into the trunk. A sharp slice nicked her sternum, but she hardly noticed the sting as the willow sheltered her in its embrace.

"Thank you!" Her essence fell deeper into the safety of the tree. Finally. The warmth of the wood lulled her into a dreamlike state, making the screams and voices outside seem no louder than a rustle in the wind.

She'd just have a nap. She deserved that, at least. Her eyes drifted shut, her breathing slowed, and all was right with the world.

* * *

"Milena? My love, are you alright?"

Sylvie blinked at the smiling face of Rheikar, holding back a scream. "You're alive?"

"Of course I'm alive, darling. Come. Let us feast before your labours start."

Rheikar took her hand tenderly and pulled her down a brightly lit corridor, passing many rooms full of bustling people.

"Mother?"

Sylvie spun to see a fair-skinned girl, no older than fourteen, approaching her with a wide smile. "Is it almost time, Mother?"

"Mother?" Sylvie echoed.

"Lazuli, what did I say about startling your mother like that? You'll put her into premature labour."

Lazuli's face fell, and she looked at her feet. "Forgive me, Father."

Sylvie looked over at Rheikar and swallowed. His glance at Lazuli wasn't anything beyond admonishment.

"Leave her alone, Rheikar," she said, pulling Lazuli behind her anyway, causing a flurry of butterflies in her belly. No, not butterflies. She looked down and brought her hands to her swollen belly. Pregnant?

More kicks bruised her ribs, and she grimaced.

"She is strong," Rheikar said with a proud grin, placing his hand over Sylvie's. She refrained from jerking back from his tender touch as reality slowly settled in her mind. This was a dream—a vision.

The scene faded, and Sylvie gripped a bed on all fours, panting and wailing as sharp, needling pressure screwed into her abdomen.

"Lady Milena, don't you think it's best to lie on your back to birth?"

"No!" Sylvie growled, her body shaking from the sudden rush of endorphins.

A hand pressed into her, and she screamed, arching. "Forgive me, Lady Milena, but it is footling."

"Just get it out!"

Again, the scene shifted. Sylvie lay upright, vision fading, a wailing bundle in her arms. The baby's red face nuzzled towards her, but she couldn't move.

"What's happening?"

"Too much blood, Lord."

"It is a cursed child."

A small cleft in the baby's lip pulled the sweet cupid's bow towards the nose. "So beautiful. Coralie." Sylvie's mouth moved, but the voice was not her own.

Her vision dimmed for the last time, her essence melding into an orb of light.

The screams of her fated, her babe, and her grown daughter all drifted away as her familiar scooped her light in its blackened talons, carrying her to the willow for eternal rest.

THIRTY-FOUR

Knock, knock, knock.

Sylvie startled awake with a sharp inhale, uncurling from her slumber and waving at the incessant noise. The light trails within the willow brightened as she blinked through papery lids.

Knock.

"Hush," she said with a groan, shoving her hand towards the outside world. Some bird was probably fucking with her. *Can't I just rest for once?*

A tight grip circled her wrist—the one attached to her mangled palm—and yanked as she cried out. Not a bird. *Shit, shit, shit!*

Hybrid.

She screamed as her body warped through a kaleidoscope of energy, the sight alone migraine-inducing. Pressure slid up her arm to her bicep and she jerked against it. All this work to hide, and now she was about to be eaten anyway. *Fucking pathetic!*

"No!"

"Princess, it's me. It's me!"

It wasn't until she was curled at Kian's feet did her rocketing pulse settle. She dragged in gasping breaths, blinking to clear the sleep. The sun was up. She'd been in the tree for hours. She sunk into the sensation of wakefulness and checked herself over. The wound on her chest was absent, the X cut on her palm had completely scabbed, and tiredness had rid itself from her body. That was new. She couldn't remember the last time she felt refreshed. She glanced sidelong at the willow trunk and bowed her head. The leaves rustled in answer.

Kian said nothing as she stood, smoothing her wild hair from her face. The hybrid blood was still there. Sticky as tar. The willow's cleansing only touched her mind then. She was grateful, but once she found Elias, she was headed straight for a shower.

"Where is he?" Her voice rasped as if unused for weeks. Or damaged from screaming.

"He's safe. He couldn't face another failed attempt."

Sylvie didn't bother deciphering Kian's words. "Take me to him." She started to stride past Kian, but he retook her wrist. She only noticed then he was changed and clean. Not a speck of blood on him. Maybe she'd been gone longer than one night …

"Wait."

She wrenched away before checking herself. "Sorry, I— fuck." Shaking her head and rubbing her thumb along her palm scab, she tried again, "I want to see Elias."

Kian's expression hollowed, his throat bobbing. "I need to talk to you first."

She peered behind him, not really listening. The spot where she had bled was nothing more than rust in the hazel dirt, patches of ash in the shape of disfigured bodies surrounded it as if the poison had eaten away everything but the dead cells layering the hybrids' skin.

She shuddered. It had worked then. She killed them.

"Can't it wait?" This wasn't the place for a heart to heart. The weight of death had already started settling on her shoulders. "We should go help the fae."

"They've left for now. Just-"

"Kian-"

"It's been five days."

Holy fuck.

"All the more reason—"

"Please," Kian said. "Proximity affects the hold."

Sylvie peered at him then, noting the withered stare, the shallow wince that never seemed to leave his face anymore. His posture sagged, the clothes he wore hung off him, and his fingers trembled. Her breathing turned shallow. "What?" she said. It was hardly a breath.

"More than she thinks it does," he said. Every word seemed like a knife twisting into his gut. "Please, Princess. I can't go back there."

Her teeth chattered and she took a step back from his shadow, letting the sun coat her. Nothing would rid the ice that had spread through her from his words though.

"Tell me," she said.

A glassiness filled his widening eyes, and his throat tensed as if choking. "I-I'm—" His voice cracked as a small tear leaked from the corner of his eye.

Sylvie's heart squeezed, as if she were watching her own implosion. Kian fought with something, then dropped to his knees before her, hands clawing at the clothes around his neck. The words wouldn't come. *They couldn't.*

"Sylvie, I'm sorry."

Her lower lip wobbled, and she straightened. It was okay; she understood. "Tell me everything," she said.

A sigh escaped his lips as she freed him, and his tension ebbed as if she had given him the antidote to Lazuli's poison. In one way, she had. He owed her a debt now; one he would pay with his words.

He almost smiled. The ghost of one kissed his lips as he spoke. "At first, she was kind. We were barely more than faelings. I was glad I could help repay my father's life debt to Rheikar. Maybe then he would be proud of me like he was Kerensa. She was the warrior, and I was the empath. Sometimes he said we were born in the wrong bodies." He winced and Sylvie took a seat before him, tucking her knees to her chest and holding them.

"Lazuli said my affinity was powerful. I could do anything— *be* anything with it. I didn't want to be the male my father thought I was." He paused, and the unsaid words hung suspended between them, threatening to drown them both. "At first it was manipulation. You can get away with many things if people feel safe around you. But it hurt people. *I* hurt people, and when I told her I wouldn't do it anymore, that I wouldn't play her games, things changed."

His anguish lapped at her feet and the frigid cold crept up her body, mingling with her fire until it burned blue. Still, it didn't warm her.

"I fled, joined Elias in Sterling, and I stayed away. Only my family can portal through realms after the Division, so I was safe as long as I never went back."

But he went home to save her.

"She was a threat to you. And if I did what she asked—let her use me; she would let you go. I would have done anything to keep you safe. I did." His voice broke, and the stinging along her waterline spilled over. "I knew if Elias was with you, you'd be safe."

Neither of them wiped away the tears as they regarded each other. "I dreamt of you. For years. I thought of you when she—" His swallow said more than his words could have.

There were no words. It was heinous. Sickening. But he wasn't telling her everything. The shutters behind his eyes were still half-drawn.

"What did she do to you, Kian?"

The sudden rigidity of his form as he stood stoked her chills.

She stood, following his movements as he peered towards the maze exit as if planning to run. Just like she had with Elias the night she told him of her past.

"You have to tell me," she said, trying to keep her breathing even as his chest rose and fell in shallow pants.

"She dips her nails in molten iron."

There was a beat, and in that beat, Sylvie's fingers leapt to the raised bump, no bigger than a pea, on her bicep. Iron. Just like her switch-knife—iron-plated. Her hand would scar then, as did the cut she'd made on his wrist. But that cut was far, far bigger now. She eyed it even as it slipped behind his back. Iron nails.

Her vision narrowed to pinpricks; the realisation so visceral it took her breath away. The flinching, the hiding, the ridges when she hugged him.

"Oh gods."

He took a half-step away.

"Your back."

His lips wavered. "No."

"Let me see it."

He flinched as if she had struck him. "I—I can't."

She closed the space between them and clasped his hands, drawing them between them, hoping he couldn't feel her heart beating from her chest. She whispered the words she had deserved once upon a time, "It's not your fault."

His expression pinched, more tears cutting down his cheeks. "You won't want me anymore."

Her heart cleaved in two as the internal voices she had always heard spilled from his lips.

"She ruined me."

Something clicked inside her and she swallowed a sob. It was lies when she was a child, and it was lies now. "No." She palmed his cheek, using her thumb to brush away a fresh tear. "She could never."

Kian closed his eyes briefly, leaning into her touch before stepping back, gripping the hem of his shirt. There was hesitation in his movements. A silent pleading. And fear. Fear Sylvie knew far too well. She ground her feet into the dirt, rooting down to stop her from tearing towards the castle, towards Lazuli as he pulled the shirt over his head in one movement. She didn't move as he balled the fabric in clenched fists, head down. With a bravery she didn't feel, she slowly wound around him, one hand brushing the crease of his elbow to anchor her to him. To stop him bolting, too. When his bare back came into view, she halted, frozen, mouth gaping. *No.*

Shock clinched around her bones. The sight was unbearable. She tasted metal on her tongue.

"Lazuli did this?"

The umber skin, as muscled as his chest, rippled beneath hundreds of dark textured gashes starting from his nape to his lower back. They spanned from an inch to a foot long. Crisscrossed lacerations, some fresh enough to have scabs still flaking from them.

Scores gouged into every inch of him.

Scars upon scars upon scars.

His nod to her question tugged the largest cuts upwards, the faintest sheen of gold blood appearing under the scabs.

She inhaled to speak, bit her lip, and tried again. "When was the first time?"

"Six months into our betrothal."

She refrained from touching, keeping her fingers latched onto his arm. "When was the last time?"

His head stooped. "The night you returned to the Evergreen Court."

The air fizzled as her fire bloomed. It wasn't a few flames anymore; it was an inferno. She'd left him for years with his abuser and let her get between them. Between fate.

Yes.

Sweat pricked along her hairline as her temperature rose, the fire transcending her mind's cages. At any moment she would burst into flames, she was certain. Kian pulled his shirt back on and squeezed the hem a few times, turning to face her.

Before he could sense her emotions, she threw up a wall, one of sadness, distress. It wasn't hard tapping into those emotions and hiding the truth. The rage.

"You are as perfect to me now as you were when I met you," she said, steel in her tone. "I swear it."

His dark eyes searched her face, and she met the gaze with fearless honesty. It was the last time she would tell him the truth in this conversation.

They breathed each other in, and she pushed up on tiptoes to meet her lips with his, the soft skin encapsulating them both in apologies and missed opportunities. One female—one monster—had stood in their way when this—*this*—could have been theirs all along.

He sighed against her as they moved in slow, assured harmony, their lips and tongues gently brushing in silent question. Both gave consent immediately. Sylvie tilted her head and opened her mouth wider to accept him, moaning at his silky caress. His chest pressed into hers, his shaking hand burying in her knotted waves as he stole her breath—her heart.

He was her, and she was him.

As she cupped his cheek and withdrew, a swirling sentiment spread through her chest, cloying her throat. She kissed the column of his neck on her descent to flat feet, thrusting the image of Lazuli's smirking face into the seething blaze. "We need to go back to the others now."

Her voice was low, shaky, but not with fear.

"If I go back—"

"I know," she whispered. "I know it isn't you."

He followed as she crossed the dead to the exit, her fae sight showing the path out through the maze.

"What are you thinking?" he asked. She didn't look at him. If she did, the walls she was reinforcing could fall, and it was too soon to show her hand.

"That I'm ready to go home."

Liar, liar.

Everything was more vivid like this. The sky was brighter, the sound of Kian's breathing was louder. She could smell the faint iron trace from his back, as if with every drag of Lazuli's nails, she'd left a piece in him.

That beast had manipulated him, raped him, and mutilated his flesh. There was no coming back.

No forgiveness.

No peace.

Every step towards the castle solidified her fate, and Sylvie would fulfil it. It was what the voices demanded all along.

Kill her.

THIRTY-FIVE

Be wary of your aunt, little one. That whore has claws.

Sylvie stayed one stride ahead of Kian as they finally passed the maze entrance, stepping over the felled six-legged gargoyles. Sweat trickled down her back. She was ablaze. Elias and Kerensa spoke in hushed tones near the castle, both turning towards them as they neared. Sylvie scanned them both. Unscathed. Perfect. Lazuli stood, still dressed in flowing white finery in the nearest doorway of the stone palace, her lips upturned in a pert smile. Keeping her pace even, Sylvie adjusted her direction to pass Elias, and even at their distance his eyes narrowed. He started closing the gap between them as Lazuli ran towards Kian, her hands—claws—outstretched.

Sylvie followed the motion, letting the inferno inside her explode outward.

Burn, bitch. Elias called her name, but too late. Her arm jutted out, catching Lazuli by the throat. With one violent jerk, Sylvie slammed her to the ground as Lazuli's taloned fingers reached beyond them. Sylvie then snatched her wrists, pinning them under her own knees as she straddled Lazuli's waist and punched her in the jaw.

"Don't. Fucking. Touch. Him."

Hands grappled for Sylvie's shoulders but were wrenched away. She didn't bother to make sense of it. There was no sense anymore. Only pain. Only revenge. She slammed her knuckles, bones screaming against flesh, into Lazuli's face again and again, her skin splitting and healing while Lazuli turned into a swollen mess, silver hair mingling with the gravel and dirt.

It wasn't just for Kian. It was for the little girl in her that Lazuli had exploited, the one that lost her haven when she smashed open her money box of memories. It was for everyone, anyone, who she had controlled. Hurt. Scarred.

"Sylvie!"

Sound fled until the only noise in Sylvie's ears was a ringing. Her throat burned as she grabbed one of Lazuli's arms and wrenched her limp hand into hers, threading their fingers together until they formed a claw.

Do it.

"Sylvie, stop!"

No. Kill her.

A scar for a scar. In one swoop, she dragged their hands over Lazuli's face, and the fae bitch screamed in both agony and realisation. Three wounds carved Lazuli from brow to opposite jawbone, her own nails tearing through her left eye. The pop it made would haunt Sylvie forever. The remaining eye stormed, holding her gaze with an alertness it shouldn't have. Lazuli was already healing, but that wound never would.

"Hart."

Voices finally settled into her brain, and she came back into herself. Her vision expanded and the scent of fresh blood coated everything. Even her tongue. Lazuli was a mess, and a sickening thought settled in. One voiced by the foster family that had loved her when no one else would. *You are no better than the female beneath you.*

She had lowered herself to that.

With a grunt of disgust, she threw Lazuli's hand to the ground and stood on shaking legs. Everything shook—her hands, her breathing, her vision. The reprieve she had received from her time in the willow was long and truly gone.

Exhaustion painted her.

What did I do?

She was half turned when a shuffle by her feet drew her eyes, and the kiss of iron carved her from cheekbone to clavicle. Kerensa was there, staff thrusting into Lazuli's sternum as Sylvie blinked. *What just happened?* Warmth doused her dress between her breasts when the heat bloomed. She palmed the wound and finally faced her males. Elias held a barely restrained look of fury mixed with pride, his arms holding Kian back, while her fae fated stared at the wound on her. He wasn't struggling anymore, and Elias let him go, striding to her and adding pressure to the parts of the wound she couldn't reach.

"Is it bad?"

"It'll heal soon."

Kian appeared at their side; his words broken. "No. It will scar."

But Sylvie took his gaze, gripping his chin between her bloody fingers. "And you will love me anyway."

Something clicked into place between them, and she nodded, turning to the female she had assaulted. Besides the three deep grooves across her face and the milky left eye, the rest of her had healed. Not a bruise or sign of swelling in sight.

Kerensa pinned Lazuli between her staff and the wall, her posture proving she was ready to finish what Sylvie started, but Lazuli just laughed, teeth still stained red. "Kian—"

Elias was there in an instant, hand around her throat, choking the words off before they could take root. "Shut your fucking mouth, demon. You do not speak his name again or I will make my kindred's attack on you look like foreplay."

Sylvie shuddered, leaning into Kian as he wrapped an arm around her, his body as relaxed as she had felt before Lazuli.

"You don't understand," Lazuli choked out, face mottled pink. "My father's promise must be kept, or the throne is mine. Either way, you lose."

Sylvie laughed then, the sound drawing a scowl from the other female.

"What was the phrase again? Lazuli *or* a female in Rheikar's line?" Lazuli caught on before the others, her undamaged eye widening.

"That's not you, though, is it?" Sylvie said, a grin settling on her lips. Lazuli bucked against Elias and Kerensa's staff, but her hands stayed pinned to her side.

"No," Sylvie answered for her. "That would be my mother." She sniffed. "Or me, of course." Kian stiffened, but Elias showed no change. She envied his stoicism. One day she'd have a mask that resolute. Even Kerensa paled.

"Lies. I killed that cursed faeling. I left her in the middle of a freeway."

Desperate words for a desperate fae. Kill her. Sylvie's heart snagged at the mirrored life she shared with her birth mother. Why would she give her up in the same way? She smoothed her expression to cool composure. "Is that why you put me in Milena's dress? Did you suspect me? I mean, how many half dryads are out there running around who are also a dead ringer for Milena?"

"Don't you speak her name!" Lazuli hissed, but Elias shoved her again, baring his fangs until she submitted.

Sylvie rolled her shoulders and peered towards the main road. Where were the carriages? "Let's go."

"Wait," Kian said, taking a confident step towards his abuser. "This betrothal is ended, and any expectations the Stone Court has over the Evergreen Court is settled. A marriage will happen when both parties are ready, and it will never be to you."

Lazuli choked. "The marriage must benefit the Stone Court. Rheikar made that explicitly clear."

Sylvie picked at her cuticle even as Kian continued speaking. Rheikar had said something about her proposal not being enough. *An old male wanting his court to prosper.* The voices weren't her own, but this time she didn't force them away. They eased her nerves instead. It was a problem for another time.

"You are to remain here as a lady of the court for the rest of your days with a new lord of Queen Katarina's choosing. If you step foot outside of the Stone Court's borders, you will be held in contempt and put to death immediately," Kian said.

He then pulled a dagger from his belt and carved a line into his palm before coating his forefinger in it and crossing his heart with the blood.

"Do you understand me?"

Lazuli shook, her eyes locked on Elias, then Sylvie, then Kian, a tight smile on her lips. "Yes."

Kian nodded and turned away, walking towards the main road alone, posture strong despite the tremor in his fingers. Pride swarmed from her and when it reached him, he glanced back at her, offering the slightest smile. Sylvie returned it and faced Elias once more, her hand still clasping her oozing wound.

Kerensa pulled her staff from Lazuli's abdomen and made her way to Sylvie's side. "You did well, Hart."

Her gaze never left Elias. "I appreciate that."

Kerensa chuckled. "Knew you'd learn, eventually." And then she left too, leaving Elias the only one restraining Lazuli. He barely needed to hold her, though. The power in her had fizzled. Maybe her new face had something to do with it.

"I won't be so forgiving," Elias said, looming over Lazuli. "If I ever see you again, I'll make it slow."

Lazuli's milky skin blanched as Elias withdrew. He turned his back on her and met Sylvie, his hand slipping into hers easily. It was over. They were finally going home, and Kian was free. It would take time, but he had plenty of it, and she would be there every step of the way if he let her.

They left the Stone Court, sharing a carriage while Kerensa went alone in the one ahead, and not once did they look back.

Maybe they should have.

* * *

The first ten minutes of the ride to the Evergreen Court had two issues come up. Sylvie still needed a shower, and they were at least a week away from one. She stewed on her filth as Elias sat cross-armed in front of her with a smirk. Kian smiled with half-lidded eyes, the scenery of the window seeming to capture his interest more than her pout and dragged his fingers over her thigh absently. Her sticky, bloodied thigh.

Ugh.

"Now what happens?" she asked with a yawn. Despite the state of her, Kian tugged her legs onto his lap and rubbed the top of her shins. "We'll cancel the elaborate wedding my mother planned and take you home."

Home.

Fuck.

"We can't cancel the wedding."

Elias tilted his head. "More secrets?"

"No, it's something Katarina said. If Kian leaves Ilfaem without being married, the promise will be broken. We can't leave."

Elias changed seats, sitting beside her and guiding her head to his lap as another yawn ripped out.

"Fae bullshit. We'll be fine," Elias said.

Sylvie's brow furrowed as she regarded Elias, and she sighed. There was no harm in being cautious, and besides, why waste a perfectly good party?

"Why can't you just marry me?" The forwardness of her question slammed her in the gut. Tiredness made her blunt. It was also a test to see if he still wanted to marry her. After what she'd done. They still hadn't spoken about her brawl with Lazuli. *Attempted murder, more like.*

"I mean, only if you want to. It doesn't have to be serious— I … I mean, it can—we haven't spent much time together, so you can just marry me so I can date you without this stupid promise over our heads and—"

Elias pressed his thumb to her lips to stop the endless flow of breathless words and chuckled.

"Kian, would you put her out of her misery?"

Kian's expression had shifted from surprise to contentment in less than a second. "You want that? After everything?"

Because of everything.

Silence stretched between them, and her cheeks flushed as Kian's stroking on her shins rose higher, flirting with the rising hem of her skirts.

Elias's fingers swirled across her scalp before plunging into her matted hair and curling into a light fist, the firm tug drawing a groan as he lowered his face to hers.

"Your fated asked you a question, Kitten."

She flitted her gaze back to the fae prince and nodded, a breathy, "Yes," escaping. "I want to."

She tilted her head back until Elias was in her sights again. "And you," she said. "Eventually."

His smirk sent flutters between her thighs. "I'm sure we can have that arranged." He lifted his gaze to Kian. "Do you agree?"

Kian's strokes on her thighs climbed higher until he thumbed her panties.

"I agree. And now that you are our betrothed, I suppose we must keep you pure." There was a darkness still cloaking him, but his eyes crinkled as he smiled. Then winked. "Until our wedding night, of course."

Sylvie's mouth dropped open as Kian slid her legs off his and placed her feet firmly on the ground. When Elias followed suit, sitting her up between them, she gasped.

"You cannot be serious right now. Elias!"

His responding grin and raising brow stabbed a heat straight through her core.

"For your virtue, my lady." With that, he pulled open the door of the moving carriage and disappeared. Kian slipped out too, clambering onto the roof and kicking the door shut behind him.

They'd left her there. Aroused and alone. For her *virtue*.

"What the fuck?"

Kian's head appeared by the window, upside down, with a dopey grin. She scowled at him as he mumbled through the glass, "We'll stop off at the stream shortly for that wash! Rest up, Princess."

His laughter echoed after him, and she couldn't stop her returning smile.

THIRTY-SIX

Queen Katarina stared down her nose from the front steps of the Evergreen Court's palace, a gaggle of well-dressed fae around her, some preening, others braiding the ends of her waist-length hair.

Sylvie stood before her, a male on either side, and Kerensa lagged around the carriages cleaning her weapons. They'd arrived only minutes prior and thankfully the queen hadn't made them wait long before addressing them.

"You succeeded in your intentions then, child."

Rheikar's bubbling corpse and Lazuli's blind eye flashed in her mind as she nodded. "Yes."

The queen glanced at her face, tracing the pink and silver scar running down her cheek with her stare. "Not unscathed."

Sylvie clenched her fists to stop herself from touching it. It had become a soothing act, circling the raised skin above her collarbone, while Elias and Kian maintained their duties of upholding her virtue. *Fuckers.*

"Rheikar is dead."

The fingers twisting around Katarina's braids halted, and some of the fae gasped. "The lord is dead?"

"Who will guard the stone lands now?"

"What of his daughter?"

Katarina raised her hand, and the voices halted. Even breathing quieted.

"He was luring hybrids to the Stone Court. We fended the horde off, but they ate him," Sylvie said.

The fae's skin paled, their mouths twisting in disgust as Sylvie spoke. She would leave out the part about him already being dead when the hybrids consumed his marrow, and his relation to her. And a few other details.

"We barely escaped with our lives." Sylvie fought a smirk as the gazes on her turned from contempt to pity. *Interest.*

"The Stone Court fae are in hiding," Kian added.

Katarina made a sharp click with her tongue against her teeth and the crowd retreated within the palace walls. "And what say you, Daughter?"

Her gaze had cut to Kerensa, who clenched her teeth and forced a thin smile. "She speaks truth."

Katarina's expression tightened a fraction, the air between them turning stale. "You will return to Erus then?"

Kian took a step forward. "Actually, Mother, I intend to wed my fated."

Heat wove around Sylvie's throat, and based on the death glare she was getting, she couldn't be sure it wasn't Katarina trying to kill her with unnamed powers.

"No."

"It is not up for discussion. Just like my betrothal wasn't. We will continue with the wedding as planned. Only my bride will be who the Fates intended. Who I choose."

That time, the redness was her own flush. If she were a weaker female, she would have melted at his feet. She glanced his way, and he winked at her. Maybe she was a weaker female.

"My son, one day you will rule the five courts. Do you truly believe she would make a fit queen? And what of the vampire?"

Katarina was the only fae that never blanched at the sight of Elias; she hardly even seemed to notice he was standing right there. Elias said nothing, but his shoulder brushed Sylvie. A silent, cold comfort.

"He shouldn't be here, anyway. The Division makes it so. Will she spend half her life here with you and the other on Erus? The Evergreen Court needs strong leadership."

To Sylvie's shock, it was Kerensa that spoke up. "She is strong. And unless you plan on dying soon, Mother, I can't see why it would concern you."

"Kerensa—"

"Don't. Are you really so blind to your children's suffering?"

Everyone stilled. They had breached uncharted territory in Kerensa's past. Unhealed wounds. Sylvie shrank away. It was too close to home.

Kerensa sighed, heading up the stairs past her mother's regal pose. "In the event of ascension, I will be her guardian. I will ensure the Evergreen Court is well led." She reached the main doors, then turned back to Sylvie. "Now hurry up, you have a wedding to prepare."

She barged through a swarm of fae who had been congregating at the threshold and were now shrieking at being caught, and Sylvie let Elias and Kian guide her inside, still reeling from the confrontation. Was it decided? It didn't seem decided. Was that how normal families came to an agreement? She rubbed her scar along her neck and winced, staring at her stone-faced males. "What the fuck is a guardian?"

* * *

"Evergreen Court and outer realm travellers, we are delighted with your presence as we unite our beloved Prince Kian and his fated, Miss Sylvia Hart, in marriage."

They had practised the stupid thing twice, and the stout officiant still got her name wrong.

Idiot.

A few gasps ripped through the congregation. Obviously, someone hadn't done their job very well at informing every one of the new circumstances. Perhaps it was intentional. Maybe they wouldn't like her. Maybe they would think she stole Kian from their precious, beautiful Lady Lazuli.

Kian squeezed Sylvie's hand, and her thoughts eased as a soft smile curled his lips.

"Eyes on me, Princess." His whisper was just for them, but it nearly became everyone else's problem as her heart dropped into her crotch. It was not the time to be so sexy, but in his deep indigo attire—regal yet timeless—he most certainly was. She had over a week of salacious thoughts churning in her spank-bank, so it wouldn't take much. His words refocused her internal raging inferno, too, into a containable simmer, yet with the passing of each snooty second, the officiant was threatening to awaken it. He cast his amber gaze across the rows of visitors, all of whom were beautiful and all of whom looked at her with a vein of contempt.

The fae sat under the shade of her ancient tree while she stood barefoot in the long grass. After lots of begging, Kerensa had agreed to help her arrange the clearing as the occasion instead of being cooped up in the throne room.

Leaning cross-armed against the first tree she'd ever merged with, an easy smile playing on his full lips, was the only other familiar face. A gorgeous face. Elias Ambrose. She smiled back before drawing her gaze to the beautiful male before her. Her smile widened at his wink, and the officiant continued.

"Do you, our dearest Prince Kian, take this … female—" *Prick!* "—to be your wife, to honour Ilfaem, the Evergreen Court, its laws, and its royalty? To live together in matrimony, to love her, comfort her, honour and keep her, in sickness and in health, in sorrow and in joy, to have and to hold from this day forward, as long as you both shall live?"

Kian chuckled, squeezing her hand once more, sending a wave of calm about her arm as she shot daggers at the officiant.

"I do," he said.

"And do you, Sylvia Hart—"

"Sylvie," Kian corrected, with a quick side glance to the officiant, who nodded politely, hand to breast, amber eyes flashing like a tiny sun.

"Forgive me, earnestly. Sylvie, do you take Prince Kian to be your husband, to honour Ilfaem, the Evergreen Court, its laws, and its royalty, to live together in matrimony, to love him, comfort him, honour and keep him, in sickness and in health, in sorrow and in joy, to have and to hold, from this day forward, as long as you both shall live?"

She swallowed. *Fuck.* This was real. *So, so real.* Why were there tears in her eyes? *Holy shit.* So many people were staring. Kian touched her cheek, thumb brushing away a traitorous tear. "We don't have to," he said.

But she shook her head at him. They had to, but that was okay. It was more than okay. She didn't realise how much she actually wanted something like this, even if it wasn't in the way she thought. Even if they hadn't even said they loved each other yet. Did she—

"I—uh." She cleared her throat and held Kian's stare. Strong. Assured. Ready.

"I do."

The officiant nodded and gestured for Kerensa to step forward. She obliged, offering small silver boxes to Kian and Sylvie, each containing their rings. It was the one thing they kept secret from each other, and Sylvie finally relaxed into the moment. She'd been looking forwards to this for days.

"Prince Kian and Miss Hart have chosen rings to exchange with each other as a symbol of their unending love. As you place this ring on Miss Hart's finger, please repeat after me. With this ring, I thee wed and pledge you my love, now and forever."

Kian opened his box with a bashful grin and pulled the wedding band free, pinching it carefully between his forefinger and thumb.

Sylvie gasped as he recited the officiant's words and placed the band on her right ring finger. The cool gold metal framed a polished strip of wood circling the entire band. Immediately, a soft zap tickled her finger, and she looked wide-eyed at her almost-husband. "Is that?"

"A small piece of your favourite tree, so no matter where we are, you will always have a part of it with you."

Kian smiled down at her as her eyes filled with tears.

"It's perfect."

Shit, he's good.

The officiant cleared his throat. "Miss Hart, if you will—"

She nodded, shivering, and pulled her creation free. She'd worked on it for hours with the Evergreen Court's outer town's jeweller, who happened to be the husband of the clothing enchantress Elias went "way back" with.

"With this ring, I thee wed and pledge you my love, now and forever."

The pure gold signet had his family crest stamped on the front, intertwined with a tree to represent her. On the inside was an inscription in Ancient High Fae from Kerensa's begrudging translation. *"Forever yours."*

A rush of love travelled up Sylvie's arms, and Kian suppressed his grin. "I love it." His low voice sent flutters through her stomach, and their impending wedding night started stealing her focus.

"By the authority vested in me by the queen of Evergreen and the four outer courts, I now pronounce you husband and wife!"

Before the officiant could proclaim their right to kiss, Kian pulled her towards him and dipped her back elegantly, stealing her breath away while the fae watched on.

Queen Katarina stepped forwards as they pulled apart and placed her hand on each of their shoulders. "Congratulations." It wasn't as hollow a sentiment as Sylvie expected, but there was ice wrapped around it. She turned to Sylvie and swallowed. "Take care of my son."

Sylvie's face slipped into a mask of calm despite her rocketing pulse. It may have come late, the maternal instinct, but it was welcome. She almost envied Kian. How did it feel to be loved in that way? "I will," she said.

With that, the queen spun and raised her hands, the signal spurring the thundering applause of the guests. "And now, before Prince Kian returns to Erus with his bride, we feast and celebrate this fine occasion."

Only a few hours of mingling passed before they flitted away under the cloak of dusk. Everyone was drunk or high on verferum, so their absence seemed to go unnoticed.

Sylvie giggled hysterically, a little drunker than she had been in a while, but not high—well, a little high—from her vantage over Kian's shoulder. Her head bumped rhythmically into his lower back as she hung her arms down, brushing his taut thighs with smooth strokes.

Her train dragged along the floor beside Kian's surefooted marching. One misstep would have them both sprawling.

She hiccupped. "Are you going to take my virtue now?"

Kian slid his hand inside the slit of her dress, his warm, calloused grip grazing the back of her thigh, her ass, the edge of her panties.

"Quiet, Princess. Before I take you right here in the hall."

A rolling pulse started in her stomach and ended between her legs. The fire in her mind had moved. Evolved. It didn't spur her to violence. Instead, the intense urge to burn every piece of clothing barring her from her fated took hold. The tome Kerensa had loaned her flitted across her memories. Would they mark her tonight? Her cunt throbbed again. *They fucking better.*

Elias's dark chuckle wound its way around Sylvie's throat until a moan slipped out.

"She'd like that. Wouldn't you, Kitten?" Elias wasn't an emotion reader like Kian, but he could scent her. And after a week of teasing, her pheromones were overpowering. Even she could recognise them. A soft, flowery scent.

She anchored her grip on Kian's hips and lifted her head. Elias's eyes glowed red in the dim candlelight of the hall and she bit her lower lip, offering her best bedroom eyes. They hadn't failed yet; Elias had the restraint of a saint. "Yes," she said in answer to him. A grin took hold as Kian stiffened and dropped her a few inches, her hold on his hips slipping until her face pressed into his belt.

With a peal of laughter, she tugged at the restraint.

Kian's groan filled her with need as he hoisted her into a bridal carry and pressed her against the palace wall, slamming his lips on hers until her thoughts turned fuzzy. He kissed her like nothing else existed. Like he had waited years for a chance to taste her skin. A whine escaped her when she realised he had.

Don't let her ruin this.

When Kian pulled back in question, she shook her head, dragging him back for more. With her still in his arms, he sidestepped to the right and the wall at her back vanished. She gasped against his lips, eyes snapping open, and squeezed his shoulders. The night air whipped her back, and she peered over her shoulder to see how far the ground was as her ass planted on a flat bench. "Do you trust me?" Kian's low voice recaptured her attention, and she nodded, shivering as the cool breeze toyed with the snarled curls around her nape.

He kissed her again, parting his lips and inviting her in. She obliged, her tongue dancing wildly as if with the right movements they could become one. His hand slid up her thigh again, fingering her lacy garter before detaching his mouth and following his hand under her skirts.

Holy fuck.

She clawed at the window frame as his teeth nipped the fabric, his hands moving around her thighs and holding like a vice. She vaguely noticed Elias leaning against the neighbouring wall, arms crossed and watching her every expression with a honed eye. *Fuck, he's hot.* Hotter than hot. He was fucking smoking, and she had the power to drive him insane without even touching him.

When the white heat of Kian's kiss brushed her inner thigh, she hummed, her nails chipping wood from the window frame. Her underwear came away with little effort and soft kisses instantly replaced the silver lace.

He moved against her, inside her like she was his home.

His tongue flat then firm, outside, then in, circling, then sucking.

This was new. This was ecstasy. This was—

Was—

"Kian!" His touch shifted back to her thigh, and she shook. "No, please. Don't stop!"

A hum, or perhaps a low growl, vibrated against her soft skin before he returned to her.

High. She was so high up.

Her fingers skittered on the frame, wood chunks crunching under her hands. The gravelled path, two stories below, wasn't particularly inviting. Especially not in the dark. Perhaps she'd land on a drunken reveller.

Elias appeared at her side, his huge hand engulfing her back and supporting her weight as the last of her grip failed.

She smiled, wrapping her hands around his bare forearm as Kian coaxed her closer to climax.

In her leg-shaking haze, she reached for Elias's crotch, but his free hand strangled her wrist. "No."

A few profanities escaped as he tucked her hand back into the crook of his elbow and the peak of her high approached rapidly. Her mind quieted, her breathing stopped, and the moan Kian drew set her alight. Elias tensed under her touch as Kian hummed in affirmation against her. The vibrations tipped her over the edge, and finally, she rode the throbbing contractions of bliss. *Bliss!*

"Fuck!"

She shivered as he pulled his warmth away, appearing from beneath her skirts with a half-smile.

One orgasm and I'm stuffed.

"Are we done?" Her breathlessness had both men chuckling softly, and Kian stood wiping his chin and lips, licking her wetness from his fingertips.

"Oh, Princess, we're only just getting started."

THIRTY-SEVEN

Fresh candles warmed Kian's bedchambers, inviting Sylvie in with the soft yellow shade, the vines climbing each bedpost glimmering in the dim light.

"Bit of a fire hazard, don't you think?" She regarded the space from Kian's arms, the walk from the hall having proved too challenging on trembling legs. Elias hummed a soft affirmation and tugged off his tie, tying the cloth strip over the doorknob before closing the door with a faint click. No turning back. He passed her, unbuttoning the top two fastenings on his shirt before perching on the window seat, leaning against the frame with crossed arms. Sylvie smiled his way as Kian lay her atop the bedspread, his knee pressed between her legs and his fingers tracing the dress straps on her shoulders. His brow rose in silent question, and she nodded. She was ready for him, body and soul.

"Take it off," she said, angling her shoulder towards him and letting the milky strap slip down.

His expression turned playful as he tugged the other strap over her shoulder and down, letting her decorated breasts free, the embroidered lace artfully exposing her hard nipples through swirling vines and flowers. Kian dipped his mouth to her, his sigh brushing the crest of her breasts. He placed a kiss at her pulse point, then at the base of her throat, right over her scar, and she bit her lip. This would be a long night.

She leaned back, lifting her hips as he guided the rest of her gown off her body. Every inch of skin exposed captured his stare as if he were uncovering a masterpiece. When her lower half was revealed, bare from their last encounter, the mulberry of his eyes flashed.

"You're beautiful," he said, running his fingers down her sides, the action making her jerk from the tickling sensation before bucking when his thumb found her clit. "So wet for me."

Her breathy laugh forced her against his touch. "Yes."

The night air swept about the room, but the candles didn't even bother with a flicker as it ruffled her hair. Over her shoulder, she smirked at Elias, still demonstrating his insane restraint. She didn't miss the dip of his lashes as he homed in on her breasts, the subtle moonlight dusting them in silver, nor did she miss the tightening of his form as she bit her lip.

When she faced Kian again, she sat and tucked her finger into his belt, pulling him close enough to whisper in the shell of his ear. "Can Elias play too?"

She tugged Kian's belt off, and his cheek quirked against hers.

He pulled back, still wearing his glorious smile, and nodded, lowering to his knees to kiss her inner thighs. She shuddered.

"Elias …" Her singsong voice wobbled as she fluttered her lashes at him over her shoulder.

Crimson flashed, and he leaned in, elbows on knees. "It's your night with Kian." Finality laced his tone.

With a pout, she twisted more until her breast was visible and she cupped it, kneading and tugging. "I know. But you're mine too, right?"

A muscle in his cheek twitched.

"Please, sir."

He stood, tension dripping down his frame. "Sylvie," he warned.

She took her lip between her teeth again and put on her most demure expression. "Please," she said again, but this time with a request he could never refuse. "I want you to take control tonight."

Fangs flashed, and she hid her grin.

"Tell me what to do while Kian fucks me."

He was upon her faster than she could comprehend, his grip on her neck squeezing just enough to draw a soft whine.

"Get on your knees."

She grinned.

Kian's throaty hum of approval had her shivering, and his kisses disappeared. She followed his instructions, sitting on her heels, head bowed. Kian kneaded the curve of her hips, his breath fanning across her nape, when Elias spoke next.

"Lie on your stomach and arch your back."

She took the scenic route, sliding her breasts along the duvet and wiggled her ass in Kian's direction. He palmed it, squeezing, kissing.

All that was missing was biting.

She stilled as Kian pulled his cock free, already painfully hard, and slid it over her, letting the wetness coat him. When he did it again, she could've screamed. She'd waited long enough. "Stop teasi—"

But her words cut off with a gasp as he plunged inside and bottomed out, his hips grinding into her ass.

"Fuck."

Their harsh voices blended, and Sylvie laughed at their identical response. Kian stopped her laugh with a full withdrawal before slamming himself to the hilt and wrapping his arm around her thigh to stimulate her clit. He rocked against her, the pleasure hot and immediate as he hit every erogenous spot at once.

Her fire burned. Pulsed and scorched until her skin dampened. Elias's gaze had her melting. "You take it so well," he said.

The dance of very real flame in the room amplified his shadow until his imposing figure engulfed her. A dominant alpha male. She could have lost herself in his gaze, those irises lit up the colour of blood as candlelight shimmied over his pupils. A bonfire gaze. A pyre of lust and power. Of control.

The caress down her spine and lapping emotions drew her back to Kian and his steady thrusts. His touch, always gentle, always considerate, was a stark juxtaposition to the slapping rhythm against her sex.

His fingers stalled over her bra, pinching the clasp until it snapped apart, freeing her breasts from confinement.

She snatched the lacy fabric and slid it across the bedspread to Elias, turning up her hand in offering as she prostrated herself before him. He took it, slipping the lace into the pocket of his tailored pants before carving a line down her scar with his index finger. "Touch yourself for me, Kitten."

Kian's groans filled the space, spurring her own. Careful not to disturb his perfect tempo, she slid her hand under and upward, circling right over her swollen clit.

They were close. So close.

A thought hit and her head lifted, fingers falling away. The tempo disrupted.

"Did I say stop?"

She shook her head at Elias's narrowed gaze and fingered her throat, right where the claiming would be.

"Mark me."

Kian's rhythm slowed and deepened, caressing every inch of her quivering walls before he pulled out, his cock bobbing against her ass.

She faced Kian. "Please."

Kian didn't speak, didn't pull away. He turned her over and lifted her into his arms, stealing her breath with a kiss. The world spun and jolted as he sat on the bed and Sylvie sat astride him, legs crossing behind his back. Over his shoulder, Elias watched on with a predatory stillness.

She nodded at Kian, more a question than an affirmation, and tilted her chin up, exposing the unscarred side of her neck. His lips reclaimed her mouth first, then toyed with her jaw before settling on the juncture between throat and clavicle. Somewhere between movements she shifted atop him, letting the thick length of him fill her as his teeth grazed her flesh. The bite was light at first, and an unbearable calm muddled her senses as it hardened, and sharpened, and burned. She moaned as he moved in her, the sting of his bite blossoming into something more painful—more desperate. The rolling waves of need in her peaked as he pulled back, a stream of blood down his chin and throat. She didn't think. Couldn't. She licked him from the hollow at the base of his throat to his lips, the groan she pulled from him enough to kick-start the pulses of her innermost walls.

Grinding against him in a frenzy, she clamped her arms around his neck. Her canines ached, feeling a little longer and sharper than normal. She nuzzled into his muscled neck and whispered against his fiery flesh. "Like this?"

The bobbing of his throat captured her feline gaze, and when he nodded and arched his neck like she had done, she opened her mouth, tongue darting out as a warning.

She stroked his cheek, wary of causing him any pain, but his light tickles along her skin and slow breathing eased the fear. He would be okay.

Pressure rose in her belly as the climax neared, the cliff looming as she poised to jump into bliss. Her canines touched him first, then her bottom teeth as she closed her jaw. It took far less pressure than she expected, his skin splitting and his syrupy, honeyed blood filling her mouth. It was easy to swallow. Too easy. Kian's hiss grounded her before the taste consumed every thought and she widened her jaw again, detaching from him. His movements had gone jerky, and she held onto the last thread of reality before the climax she had been waiting a lifetime for stripped her soul bare.

The skin over her heart burned, the pain mingling with pleasure until everything hurt, until everything felt so fucking good.

"What's happening?" Her words were barely coherent, a begging, desperate whine.

Kian's head dropped onto her shoulder, his response disappearing in the uneven rasp of their breaths as the world turned white and exploded, fireworks dancing around their heads, through their souls. The clenching of her walls viced around Kian's cock again and again until she didn't know where she ended and he began.

When they finally pulled back, slipping free of one another, she finally understood what he had whispered into her hair like a sweet nothing.

The mark.

Her mark. Scarlet and emerald swirls interlinked in a swooping pattern above his left nipple, the shape unlike anything she had seen. It was etched into his skin like a scar, and he traced it with wide eyes.

She glanced down at herself, the mark entirely violet and a third of the size of Kian's carved into the skin over the spot where her heart thundered. There was a thread between them now. A bond, one that ran like a string from his heart to hers. Thin and faint, but present.

She finally lifted her hooded gaze to Elias, the male staring at the mark with awe. With sadness.

She tried to reach for him, to invite him to do the same, but she could hardly manage to lift her arm from her sides.

Kian stood with her, and she kissed him, sleep pulling on her consciousness as he lay her down, head on the pillow. "I'll be back soon," he said, brushing his lips over her brow. Her lids fluttered shut, yet her mind wouldn't cease. Rushing water and ruffling echoed in the chamber and soon a warm, damp cloth slid up her body, cleansing the heat of her skin. She couldn't muster a word, even as kisses followed behind the trail of the cloth. When the room pitched into silence again, she curled on her side towards the figure that touched her with a tenderness she didn't believe she deserved.

"Don't get too relaxed," Elias muttered into her hair. "Kian has quite the appetite."

Sylvie's lip quirked. "No more. Tomorrow maybe."

It was a miracle he understood her mumbling, but he did, answering after taking her hand and kissing each of her fingers. "Don't expect me to go this easy on you on our marking night." He claimed her other hand. "You'll have ten orgasms at least."

She reached for him, squeezing the first part of him she could find. From a brief fondling, she assumed she had his shoulder.

"I love you."

Silence trickled by and she'd almost fallen asleep when his tortured voice finally flowed over her. "I love you, Sylvie Hart. More than life itself."

THIRTY-EIGHT

"Don't get all sentimental on me, Hart. I still don't like you very much."

Kerensa stood ramrod straight as Sylvie clasped her in a farewell embrace outside the palace, but her warm umber cheek pressed ever so slightly against Sylvie's scalp.

"Same," Sylvie said, hiding a smile. "I will miss you, though." It wasn't a lie. Finding friends and keeping them was never her strong suit, and now she was forfeiting this budding friendship for a city she could never call home. A shithole.

She almost groaned aloud just thinking about it. But the Evergreen Court wasn't the place for her either. The queen had made that clear enough.

"Just be careful." Kerensa detached herself from Sylvie's vice grip and glanced Kian's way. "Don't come back here."

It was harsh, the conversational tone barely softening the banishment, but Kian smiled as if he didn't need to be told. Hopefully, he didn't have any more secrets or promises that needed to be upheld because Sylvie was done with surprises. She was ready for the quiet life with her males. As quiet as it could be once her colleagues found out that she'd fucked her way to the top. Natalie was going to be insufferable.

"I trust you'll let me know if I'm needed?" Kian said, looping his arm around Sylvie's waist, fingers brushing the swell of her hips.

Kerensa nodded once and turned her attention to the vampire hovering on the fringes. She stuck out her arm and Elias clasped her wrist, the pair holding each other's gaze for a moment before detaching.

"You fight well," Kerensa said in farewell.

"As do you."

Elias returned to Sylvie's side, threading his fingers through hers.

It was all so mundane. She could almost pretend this would be a regular event, visits and goodbyes with her almost-friend. Her sister-in-law.

But it wasn't. It was likely the last time she'd see her in a long while. Far longer for Kerensa. A light red hue tinged the fae's waterline.

Perhaps she was more affected than she let on, too.

Sylvie held her indigo gaze for a long moment before saying, "I'm grateful for everything you have done." She swallowed. *This is worse than some breakups.* "Until next time."

A tiny, almost imperceptible strangled squeak emanated from Kerensa's throat, but before Sylvie could decipher it, the fae nodded, spun on her heel, and disappeared into the palace and out of sight without a backwards glance.

She staggered a step after her, but Kian held her aloft with a gentle touch to her face.

"She's okay. She doesn't like to be vulnerable in front of others."

She kept her gaze on the darkened doorway, her heart aching. "Is that a fae thing?"

A brush of a smile touched her awareness, and she faced Kian. "It's more of a Kerensa thing." His smile broadened. "Now let's go before she comes out here and kicks my ass for revealing her weaknesses."

Her attention snapped to the palace one last time, and she sighed before inclining her head in a bow.

Kian kissed her cheek and rounded her front, looping his free arm over Elias' shoulder.

Her heart sped up. It was happening so fast. "Is this going to fuck me up like last time?"

"I don't think so."

"How reassuring."

He scrunched his nose at her. "You carry my mark and still have some of my blood in your system. That's the closest you can get to my bloodline. You'll survive."

She rolled her eyes and squeezed both men. "Well? Let's get the hell out of here, then."

* * *

As Sylvie's feet planted atop the grey carpet in Elias's office, she sagged between him and Kian, her head heavy on her neck. The dark sky outside drew her gaze almost immediately, as did the lack of lights in the room. It looked like a tomb.

"What day is it?"

Kian held her up as Elias crossed to his computer and tapped the keyboard space bar.

"Two a.m. Thursday."

"Weird." She yawned, despite only waking a few hours earlier. She wanted to blame it all on portalling, but Sterling always made her feel exhausted. Maybe it was the lack of oxygen from all the pollution.

They stood there in silence for a moment, taking in the space before Kian flicked on the light. Still as pristine as ever, with not a speck of dust in sight. Even Elias's throw pillows looked freshly fluffed and chopped.

She turned to the main doors and managed to smile. "Wanna see my room?"

Kian blinked, his gaze a little wide, and she crossed to him, taking his hand.

"Come."

Just before they reached the glass doors of her room, he said, "I never thought I'd be back here."

Sylvie squeezed his hand, tears and fury mingling as she pulled his hand to her lips, kissing the knuckles. "I know."

Without warning, Kian scooped her up in a bridal carry and pulled the door open as she squealed, rage dissipating.

"So, this is your new apartment?" The wryness in his tone further eased the pain in her chest. Damn fae. She was trying to help him feel better, not the other way around.

"Yes."

"Beautiful plant."

She chuckled through her nose as the plant in question came into view. Elias's gift of nature in a city of steel and death.

"It really is."

Tucking her beneath the maroon covers of her comforter, Kian sat and placed a hand over her thigh. She yawned and blinked, draping her arm similarly and said, "You two will be close, right?"

He nodded, kissing her forehead. "We'll be in Elias's office."

So, this was life now. She slept alone in her little room while her kindred and her *husband*—she hadn't got used to that yet—slaved away for Ambrose Enterprises.

She sighed, fingers tapping atop Kian's muscled thigh. "So, what now?"

His white teeth shone in the semi-darkness. "Well. We need a better home, for starters."

She jolted upright, gripping Kian's forearm tighter than she should have. "What? Really?"

She didn't know what she was expecting. Her current room was far better than the apartment she was renting, but a home? That was—

Kian tucked a rogue hair behind her ear. "You can't honestly believe we would all live here?"

She fought a blush. That was exactly what she'd thought. Keep expectations low, never be disappointed.

A shadow covered the threshold of her room as Elias materialised, leaning against the open glass door with infinite sex appeal.

"How about we find three options and you pick the one you like most? Fair?"

She squinted and crossed her arms as if pondering the question. "Can I make a few preliminary requests?"

Elias's lips quirked deliciously as he inclined his head.

"Trees," she said. "Lots of trees."

Kian laughed before morphing it into a cough at her expression. She was serious. If she never saw Sterling again, she would be a lucky female. Happy too.

"I think that can be arranged," Elias said as Kian stood and left the room with one last goodnight kiss.

Elias lingered. She curled onto her side, elbow propping her up with a fist under her chin as he regarded her. The smirk he'd been fighting finally broke free.

"Rest up. You still work for me, remember? Shift starts at eight."

With a devilish wink, he vanished, leaving her reeling. *The nerve.* Her resignation was still handy in her draft emails. Perhaps she would sneak to her office and send it. That would get his undivided attention back on her. They hadn't discussed him marking her yet, but the spot next to Kian's mark buzzed with anticipation. She yawned. It wasn't the right time. *Dammit.* She rolled onto her back. The chequered ceiling stared back at her. The uniformity forced her tired lids to shut, and while sleep pulled at her consciousness, she fantasised about her future home.

It couldn't be modern. The current style of new builds was so flashy and had zero character. She didn't want a single reminder of the life she was leaving behind. It had to be something wooden, with rolling paddocks and animals and wildflowers. Elias's cabin would've been perfect, secluded and rustic, but after the bear shifter found them there, it probably wouldn't be an option.

"Go to sleep!" Elias's voice called through the wall.

"I am!"

"Kian says otherwise."

She rolled her eyes. What emotions could he be reading? Elation, anxiety, or a growing case of imposter syndrome? She rubbed the warm, slightly painful tingling of his mark over her heart.

"Night then," she whispered.

"Goodnight," they both replied.

The morning came quickly, though sleep eluded her many times as gratitude and beliefs of unworthiness battled for the top spot in her racing mind.

She dragged herself from her bed at seven, dressing in one of her new blouses and tailored pants. It was a little tight. *A little tight?* But when she stood before the exterior windows, using the little reflective quality they offered, she stared. The tightness wasn't in the regular places she held weight; it was in her biceps and thighs this time, the sweeping lines of growing musculature peeking out beneath her blouse and pant legs.

"Holy shit."

Training paid off then.

She threw a blazer on and slipped into a pair of ankle-strapped pumps before wandering to Elias's office. Hair mussed, shirt unbuttoned to show half his chest, and sleeves rolled to the elbows, Elias glanced her way. "Morning."

He had to know what he was doing.

A warm pair of arms slipped around her waist, and she leaned into Kian's chest as he kissed her temple. "Morning, Husband."

She could play the game too. What the winner would receive was anyone's guess.

A hardness pressed into her backside, and she wiggled into him, feigning a wobble in her heels.

Kian chuckled. "It's not nice to tease, Princess."

"No, it isn't," Elias agreed. "You start your shift in forty-five minutes."

She peered between them both with mock innocence. "What do you mean? I was just saying good morning to my husband."

Elias's eyes darkened, a dangerous smile carving one side of his face. Sylvie nestled deeper into Kian, but there was no escape. Not that she wanted to.

"Don't think running to Kian will save you. He may not punish your brattiness, but I can assure you, he enjoys it when I do."

She bit her lower lip and tilted her head in silent surrender. "Well … did you find any nice places?"

Elias rolled back in his chair and inclined his head towards the monitor in answer. It was a trap. A good one. But with a coy grin, she uncurled from Kian and wandered over, standing at Elias's side. She was on his lap in a blink, rolling back towards the desk, a mouse in one of his hands and fingers toying with … something else.

"Take a look." His words caressed her lobe with the low vibrations as his touch slid along the seam of her pants. *Take a look?* She could hardly concentrate on the screen. Drawing her mind from the friction along her front, she regarded the three homes. Two were modern and tidy, one looking more like an architectural marvel, but to Elias and Kian's credit, they both had a variety of trees and greenery framing them in manicured rows. They weren't quite what she was looking for, though. They weren't her.

The third property, though, had her breath catching in her throat. A single-story, modernised farmhouse with a wraparound porch and pergola. Vines and flowers curled over the wooden slats and wound down the standing pillars in neat arcs. Brown shutters adorned each window with hanging baskets of herbs attached beneath them in colourful abstractness, absorbing the striking light from the morning sun.

An ancient-looking forest backed the property, and she could've sworn she had died and gone to dryad heaven, but nothing could've prepared her for the garden. *Holy fuck, look at the size of it.*

"Elias?"

His lips pressed into her jaw as she leaned back. She hadn't realised how close she had got to the monitor, the home lulling her in even through photographs.

"Yes," he answered.

It wasn't a question. He picked up the office phone and punched in a number, keeping his other hand busy while he brought the phone to his ear.

Sylvie arched as if to stand up and untangle herself from her deviant boss, but his touch kept her hooked.

"John, it's Ambrose. Yes. We'll take the farmhouse. Price is no issue."

Just then, the price flashed from the corner of the screen and her eyes bugged. Price certainly was a fucking issue. *Holy hell.* Were they buying the whole fucking forest?

She went to protest when Elias's hand jumped to her mouth, curling possessively over her lips as if her words were his alone. Kian smirked and shook his head as her pleading gaze found him reclined on the couch. *No help at all.*

"Call me when it's finalised. Yes. Thank you."

Only after the phone was snuggled back in the receiver did his hand move to cup her chin and tug it in his direction. She wrinkled her nose at him. "That was rude."

"What's rude is interrupting a phone call, Ms. Hart." His lips brushed hers. "Did our last meeting about your work performance not make that clear?"

She swallowed her grin and chewed out, "Fuck you, Mr. Ambrose."

His feline grin did nothing but rile up the giddy butterflies swarming in her guts. "Not yet, pet."

He had her standing in a blink, his hand pressed into her mid-back and guiding her from his room before her feet knew how to move again.

It was only when the red light of the elevators ascending caught her attention did she realise what was happening. Natalie. Great. It was probably his plan all along: get her flustered and needy and leave her hanging for the day. She dug her heels in though, with two floors left for her colleague to ascend, and smiled over at Kian. "Will you come out with me later for lunch?"

His eyes flashed. "Of course. I'll find you some breakfast, too."

"That is very thoughtful, Husband."

'Brat' glowed in neon over her head as the last floor light pinged.

Elias's face dived dangerously close to her head as the elevator prepared to open. "You're playing with fire, Kitten."

The polished metal opened to an unexpecting Natalie, whose eyes widened a fraction at Sylvie gliding towards her, Elias still likely hovering in the doorway.

Over her shoulder, Sylvie mouthed a quick, "I love the burn," before winking at Natalie, then carving a path into her office and shutting the door behind her.

THIRTY-NINE

Breakfast delivery came and went and based on the chitterings of Natalie in the hall, Kian got her something too. *Smooth.*

By mid-morning Sylvie was a few hundred emails deep and the platinum blond bombshell at reception must have used up the last of her resistance. The knock wasn't a surprise, so when Natalie pressed the door open with her sharp acrylics, Sylvie already had a bemused smile, chin atop her fist.

"Can I help you?"

Natalie leaned on one hip, hand holding herself about the waist as she searched Sylvie's face. "You look different."

Sylvie straightened in her chair, checking that the strand of hair she had pulled to cover her scar was still in place. It was. "What do you mean?"

Natalie's eyes narrowed as if trying to place it, but she just shook her head. "I don't know. Just … more."

More? "Not sure that's a compliment."

Natalie's red lips quirked, and she flicked her pony off her pinstripe blazer. "It is." She slid her hands into her pockets, the action posing her like a model. "Where have you been?"

Sylvie smiled lightly, twirling the wedding band on her finger. "Out of town."

Natalie somehow suspended her disbelief and said, "Well, tell me the address, 'cause I need some of whatever the hell that is." She gestured up and down Sylvie's figure, freezing when Elias's voice boomed down the hall.

"Miss Edwards."

"Coming, sir."

Sylvie missed what they spoke of, but Natalie didn't return after that. By ten forty-five, she'd almost deleted every hint of spam.

"Ms. Hart," Elias's voice startled her and reignited some of the warmth from their earlier encounter.

"Yes, sir?"

He smiled. "Kian and I will organise the clearance of your apartment. Is there anything sentimental we need to retrieve?"

So professional. *So sexy.* If Natalie hadn't been eavesdropping from her desk, Sylvie would have slid from her chair and crawled across the floor, calling him master.

His fingers clawed into the doorframe, voice dropping. "Cut it out."

Her voice dropped too, the thrill of his attention setting her alight. "I didn't know you could read minds."

"I can read your expression well enough."

She gnawed the inside of her cheek, sucking a breath in to dissipate a fraction of the sexual energy between them. "To answer your question, no. I have nothing of value."

Elias nodded, but a trace of anger glimmered in his gaze. Then resolve. "We'll remedy that immediately."

She opened her mouth to reply, but he had gone. "You already have."

The whirring ring of the elevator reached her from the hall, and the moment the doors thudded shut, closing her off from Elias, a nervous energy buzzed through to her fingertips. Kian's mark hummed, but he was gone too, his tether to her thinning as the car pulled away towards her downtown apartment.

Did they both really have to go? Being alone both thrilled and terrified her. Kian said the building was warded so she wouldn't get into too much trouble, but still. *No. I'm a powerful female. I'll be fine.*

And she was. The minutes ticked on, and the world kept spinning. Mundane. Boring.

Until the steady chiming of the elevator returned and Sylvie rolled her eyes at the short-lived freedom. Fifteen minutes was all she would get.

A sharp inhalation stilled her.

"Nat?"

"Rowan?"

Rowan. Rowan Hex? *Fuck!* It was Thursday. She eyed the clock on her monitor. Eleven sharp. So much time had passed since she'd emailed, she'd forgotten he even existed.

"You seem surprised." The voice was gritty and deep, the faintest accent lilting the words and forcing the hairs on Sylvie's neck to rise.

"I am. I didn't realise you were scheduled for a meeting."

They spoke as if they were familiar. Friends, even.

"Eleven. I assumed you organised it."

Sylvie held her breath.

"No, that would be Mr. Ambrose's assistant. She's in there. But I think he's out at the moment."

She stood, heart pounding. There was no way to get her phone and call Elias to come back without them seeing her scurrying off down the hall to her room. *Stupid glass offices.*

"Did you want to wait over there? Or we could talk about the next turning."

"Not here," he growled, the sound making Sylvie jump. The low end of his voice held a dual quality, the bass notes almost animal. Primal.

In flashes, distinct memories that once held no connection clicked together.

Natalie's gibberish fly-away sentences, the bear shifter's story at Elias's cabin, and the reason for requesting a meeting. An artefact. For soulmates. Mates.

Rowan Hex was a shifter, and he was turning people.

She needed to warn Elias.

After a deep inhale, she slipped through the doorway heading for Elias's office. A potent scent filled her nose. She froze as the cologne coiled in waves around her. Fire and wood stain.

Kian's mark twinged, and she touched it over her blazer as she turned around, compelled.

The scent's owner already faced her. Pure muscle in a tailored navy suit, tattoos over his clenched hands and peeking out from his collar before disappearing into a full, dark beard. Rowan Hex was ... unexpected. His hair was equally dark and pulled back into a topknot, a few stray strands calculatedly framing his eyes. From their distance, she couldn't determine the colour, but their lightness struck her.

She matched his narrowed gaze, and said without breaking eye contact, "Natalie, please call Mr. Ambrose. He is just in a meeting next door."

It was a fucking bold lie, but it would explain his absence and her poor planning skills.

But Natalie didn't move. When Sylvie flickered her gaze to her, she realised Natalie was watching Rowan Hex, as if waiting for his approval.

"Natalie."

She didn't look her way. *What the fuck?*

"Fine. Mr. Hex, take a seat. I will ring Mr. Ambrose." She turned back to Elias's office when scathing words hit her back.

"You reek of him."

The gruffness had her pausing, as did the overwhelming urge to sniff herself.

"Excuse me?" She faced him once more, the fire within her crackling as his ire stoked the embers.

"You and I are leaving, and Natalie will encourage your *boss* to return the artefact to me so I can end this falsehood."

This was not happening. She would not be a bargaining chip for a fucking piece of junk. "No. You will wait for Elias to return and discuss the artefact with him."

"Elias?" He said the name with such venom it had her retreating a step. "Are you seeing him?"

That had Natalie's attention flickering.

His disgust set another match alight until her skin burned. "That is none of your business."

"It is."

"You need to leave." When he didn't so much as twitch, she shouted, "Get the fuck out of here!"

That had him smirking. "You will walk out of here with me or I will carry you. You get one chance to make a choice."

His eyes flashed gold as she ripped off her heels, holding them in each hand like a weapon. "And you have one chance to leave before I rip your fucking throat out," she hissed.

His laugh, cavernous and godlike, had her flames roaring as he started unbuttoning his suit jacket.

"Natalie, please," Sylvie said. "Call Elias now."

But she only hung her head. The fucking traitor.

So, Sylvie did what she was good at. After throwing one heel with enough force to crack a rib, she spun and darted for Elias's office.

She'd taken half a dozen steps when a vice grip curled around her bicep. She half turned, kicking her heel into his gut, a sharp jolt running up her leg from the impact. He barely grunted. Instead, he grabbed her ankle and pulled until she fell face first into the carpet, dropping her second shoe. Her forearms took the brunt of the force, and she clawed at every passing doorway while he dragged her to the elevator. She wouldn't go dignified; she never had. She'd go down fighting.

Natalie sniffled as Hex punched the elevator call button. "I'm sorry. I need this to work."

Sylvie had no energy to decipher the bullshit. She just kept kicking.

"Don't worry, Natalie. You are already one of us." A micro crinkle bracketed his eyes as he offered her a smile, before flashing that golden look at Sylvie, still thrashing. "You, on the other hand, are two kicks away from being hog-tied."

"Fuck you!" The kick landed on his shin, and she swore she heard a click.

"Don't test me, woman." The elevator doors opened, and he yanked her inside, tossing her into the back corner like a pile of garbage.

"You don't test me!" She spat at him and rose to her knees, throwing a punch straight at his groin. To her fury, he turned so her knuckles glanced off his thigh, hurting her hand instead.

His dark expression, boring holes in her face, spurred a rage in her equal to the moments when she'd straddled a monster. This time she was the one being straddled. Hex grabbed her screaming wrist and twisted it behind her back until she was face down on the floor. Her stomach lurched as they plummeted down the hundred floors, his thighs pinning her arms against her sides.

"Get the fuck off me." She squirmed and screamed until a soft fabric pulled across her lips and went taut behind her head, the muffled curses only increasing when she realised his tie was clamping her mouth shut.

"There." He gripped her throat and tilted her head until his smirk came into view. "Much better."

Hatred scored into her soul.

She hoped just how much she wanted him to die shone behind her eyes. And from the shuddering expression and failing smirk, it did.

Good.

The elevator was taking longer than usual, and when she twisted to look at the level they were on, her heart shattered. He had an override card that would take them straight to the garage. Natalie.

The doors opened to harsh fluorescent tubes and the loud rumble of half a dozen trucks, all with black, tinted-out windows. No one would hear her scream.

She saved her voice, but snatched off the tie the second he pulled her up by the arm and led her to the second to last truck's back door. "Let me go. I will get the fucking artefact for you, alright? Elias will listen to me."

"Keep that name from your mouth, woman."

He half-pushed, half-lifted her into the back seat and took the tie, using it to secure her hands to the passenger seat headrest.

"Please." She hated the way her voice morphed to begging, the pleading quality grating. Even he turned away from it, distaste written over his features.

"You don't even know what this is about."

Her breathing quickened as adrenaline morphed into anxiety. She was going to be taken. Talking wasn't getting her out of this, and neither was fighting. "Tell me then." Stalling would have to do. Elias and Kian would be on their way. They had to be.

"No." He pulled her seat belt on, threading it under her arms and buckling it, his ear close enough to bite off. She jerked towards it, but he was faster, his forearm pressing into her throat and holding her in place.

"Fucking bastard."

"Your sharp words don't affect me, woman."

He grinned and stepped out of reach, flicking a little lever in the door as she twisted and kicked at him, hurling more insults before he shoved her legs back and slammed it shut. When he rounded the vehicle, stopping to talk with someone, she pulled the head rest out and freed her wrists, keeping her movements slow to avoid notice. But once she spotted his keys dangling from the ignition, she bolted into the front seat, hitting the central lock button with a rush of euphoria. This was it. This was her freedom. When she went to put the truck in drive, though, she faltered. It was manual. Her hesitation was her downfall. The glass of the passenger door smashed inward before the door flew outward and Hex ripped the keys away, taking the last of her hope. Sylvie pressed her spine into the door, eyes wide at his dark gaze, the whites of his eyes almost completely gone as he spoke in the dual-toned voice again. "That will cost you, woman." He looked like he was going to eat her. And not in the good way.

"Fuck you." The curse was a ragged whisper.

His head lowered. Predatory. "You will ride with Ace now. If you try to escape again, he will put you in the trunk." She shifted her eyes to the windscreen, where a burly man stood. Not a man, a shifter.

"I will see you when we reach pack borders. Perhaps the time apart with give you a chance to learn how to behave."

"You're kidnapping me, psycho. This is completely justified." When Ace rounded the truck to the door behind her, she tried to leap into the back seat, but Rowan caught her, lifting her over the glass even as she squirmed and punched his head. If the blows hurt, he made no sign, instead carrying her over his shoulder to the next identical truck. Every movement grew sloppy, and she slumped in his grip. She'd get another chance at escape, eventually. It was better she didn't waste all her energy in this parking garage.

"Please, just let me go."

When he finally placed her in the last truck, he paused above her. He stilled, just staring, face phasing through expressions too quickly for her to pick up on any.

"You still don't feel it."

She stayed silent, a bomb of dread going off inside her. It seeped down her nerves, pooling in her trembling limbs.

The tattoos on his neck flexed as he worked the words. "I don't know what the Fates are planning, but I'll find a way to end this."

"End what?" She hated the way she already knew. She would rather die.

He stayed silent briefly, not pulling his gaze from her as he finally said, "Leave us, Ace."

She hadn't heard him approach. The grace of the shifter, despite his size, was astounding. Horrifying.

The words stuck in Hex's throat seemed to pain him, and the longer he withheld them, the more her dread grew until it was a beast of emptiness smothering her raging flames, until there was nothing left but ashes.

The spot where his leg brushed her inner thigh tingled, dread giving way to yearning, and she knew. She *knew*.

It was all wrong. All wrong. This couldn't be, it couldn't—

"Our mate bond," he said.

ACKNOWLEDGEMENT

Tell me why this is the hardest 200 words to write?

Mum, Dad, I did it. I actually freaking did it. Your daughter the writer, who would've thought? Thank you for supporting me through everything and talking me off the ledge when I told you how much editing would cost. I couldn't have done it without you. I love you! Now, put the book down and walk away. There are some secrets we can keep from each other; smut is one of them.

To my partner in crime, Julius, the one who makes sure my fight scenes actually make sense. (Among other things … the set up was too good to waste!) Thank you for letting me shut myself away and write all day while you play video games. Gamer boyfriend and bookish girlfriend really are the perfect combo.

Thank you to my editor, Courtney. Honestly, I can't thank you enough for helping me bring Erus to life and making my book baby dazzle.

And to all my first draft readers from Wattpad and Inkitt … Hi! Thank you for getting me motivated to even attempt indie publishing and getting us this far. I owe so much to you!

I'll see you soon in Book Two!

Ngā mihi nui

Mikayla Everitt

Milton Keynes UK
Ingram Content Group UK Ltd.
UKHW030004260824
447288UK00004B/134